The Right War

John F. Schork

The Right War is a work of fiction. Any resemblance to actual persons, living or dead, business establishments, events or locales are entirely coincidental.

First edition: June 2016

In Remembrance of
Lieutenant James W. Kennedy, United States Navy

1946-2015

A Shipmate and Friend

"The merest soldier is to-day
The poet of his art,
Though he should neither sing nor say
The transports of his heart.
His genius writes in words of steel,
And utters them in thunder,
While we want speech for what we feel,
Who sit at home and wonder.
Yes, those whom England with a cry
Saw dashed into the strife,
Those men of ours who rode to die,
Like men who ride for life;
Whose should, ere well the word was gone,
Into the smoke were hurled,
Who, bound on bound, went charging on
Into another world;"

— From *War Music*
by Louisa and Arabella Shore, 1855

Part One
Turning Point

Sevastopol, 1854

Karkanit Bay

Sea of Azov

CRIMEA

Kalamita Bay

Black Sea

Sevastopol

Balaklava

N

W   E

S

Europe, 1854

"Cannon to right of them,

Cannon to left of them,

Cannon in front of them

Volley'd & thunder'd;

Storm'd at with shot and shell,

Boldly they rode and well,

Into the jaws of Death,

Into the mouth of Hell rode the six hundred."

—From *The Charge of the Light Brigade*
by Alfred, Lord Tennyson, 1854

Chapter One

"The politicians are too stupid and the generals too old."

Lord Richard Warren, the second son of the Duke of Southwick, shaded his eyes against the afternoon sun and surveyed the mass of men, animals and wagons covering the beach at Kalamita Bay. The September weather was warm and he felt grateful for a light breeze on the hill overlooking the massive British landing on the Crimean Peninsula. The sun shimmered off the water of the bay, which was crowded with transports and small boats ferrying to and from the beach. An angry seagull screeched behind him.

"A bloody cock up," he said to himself, feeling a total lack of enthusiasm for events unfolding in front of him. But he was a soldier and he was expected to accept whatever he was ordered to do. And, he had to be somewhere, why not in this dung heap of a country. At least he was in the company of good men.

His horse Gypsy moved nervously.

"Easy, girl, easy," he said and gently patted her neck.

The nightmare voyage aboard a series of overcrowded transports had affected his normally quiet mount and she seemed unusually anxious as they stood watching the frenzied activity on the water's edge. Fresh air, good food, some exercise and she would be right as rain, he told himself.

Six months en route from England, with an interim stop in Bulgaria, the English expeditionary force and their French allies were finally landing in the Russia Crimea. Their stated purpose was to capture the Russian port of Sevastopol as retaliation for Russia incursions into the Balkans and Turkey. However, Lord Warren, captain in the 13th Light Dragoons, felt they were on a fool's errand. Unlike most of his contemporaries, Warren spent a great deal of his time studying his country's foreign policy and its interaction with military doctrine. This ill-conceived expedition had little chance of success in his opinion, which he had shared with his fellow officers of the regiment.

Unfortunately, regimental cavalry officers were expected to concentrate their attention on cards, drinking and chasing a pretty leg. His rejection of that line of behavior had not endeared him to the mess of his first regiment in India, the 45th Lancers. Then, as now, he cared little for what his contemporaries thought of him. Ruggedly handsome, his dark hair framed a square face highlighted by dark brown eyes. Tall for a cavalry officer, his athletic ability was complimented by his riding expertise. To all observers, Richard Warren was an accomplished soldier, gaining seniority that would someday see him in command of his own regiment, despite his rebellious attitude. But doubts had begun to invade his thoughts.

Warren turned as a rider on large Arabian crested the ridge. Coronet James Pickering, sweat gleaming on his face, grinned as he reined his horse to a stop next to Warren.

"Too hot for me, I'll tell you. Can't wait for the weather to turn."

"We'll see how you feel in December, Mr. Pickering. It can get devilishly cold. I expect you might look back at these days with longing."

The junior officer looked surprised. On his first great adventure, only six months on active service, Pickering was the picture of enthusiastic youth. His slender frame and boyish good looks reinforced that perception.

"December? We should have the Russians broken and be on our way home by then. Don't you think, sir?"

"The way this embarkation is being run, we may still be on this bloody beach at Christmas," Warren said dryly. "Now let's be off and try to make some order of this chaos."

As they made their way across the beach, Warren surveyed the confusion and wondered again what in God's name they were doing on this barren beach a thousand miles from England? Politicians and public perception had been overcome with the notion that Russia was becoming a threat to the peace and safety of Europe. It was simply folly, Warren thought. Men would die to satisfy the fools in England.

"Sergeant Scully."

Sergeant Michael Scully turned as his squadron commander rode up.

"Sir!"

"I am most interested in your opinion of today's landing," Warren asked in his most sarcastic and officious voice.

Scully ginned fiercely, "Well, as expected, sir. All the little darlings are ashore, but for the two replacements. That dull-witted quartermaster thought they should be unloaded in the next couple hours, but he has his head so far up his arse he has no fucking idea."

"Sergeant, the British army only assigns its very best to the quartermaster corps, as you most certainly know."

Scully, a tall powerful Irishman, cut his eyes at Warren. The sergeant's sharp features and penetrating blue eyes had intrigued many a lass, just as they had terrified more than one private.

"Aye, sir. The best of English manhood."

Warren laughed, the ongoing national rivalry a subject of many barbed remarks between the two men.

"Any problems?" Warren asked, his voice now reflecting the easy friendship between the two men.

"Private Toney reported a bad gash on his mare's left foreleg. I'll inspect her in short order."

His squadron had lost two horses during the transit, but he felt fortunate, they had fared better than most. Horses and ships simply don't mix. The damned sailors didn't understand them and the horses did not do well in the confined spaces. If England was going to venture forth on foolish expeditions, they should build ships meant specifically for transporting horses. But that would require planning and thought, something the politicians and senior officers apparently were incapable of doing.

"Right. Rally to the colors when you round them all up. I was told we would be on the right side of the assembly area, third regiment in march order."

"Could take several days, sir." Scully grinned again, the give and take resuming, "I suspect some of the lads are already out foraging for wine and women in the best tradition of the cavalry."

"Perhaps they're under the orders of an overbearing Irish sergeant?"

"I've always taught them to be resourceful, sir, and that's a fact."

Warren smiled. "It's that very point that has me concerned, Scully."

He tapped Gypsy's sides and they cantered off.

Scully stopped and looked down the beach--another desolate piece of land far from home where they might die for the Queen. The sergeant had been in the army since the age of sixteen. Sent away from a farm near Drogheda that couldn't feed the large Scully clan, he'd adapted well to the hard life of a cavalry trooper. But recently he wondered what might have happened if he stayed in Ireland? Perhaps a wife, a brood of children and a nice farm would await him. It was hard to say, but at his age, those questions came to a man.

Warren and Pickering walked their horses through the assembly area looking for others from the regiment. The din of shouts, animals protesting and supplies being unloaded, rolled over the beach. A quiet and serene bay had become a place of bedlam.

"Richard!"

Warren turned to see Captain John Oldham trotting toward him on his big white charger, Julius.

The two men had become good friends following Warren's joining the regiment the previous year. A senior captain, Oldham grinned as he reined his horse to a stop.

"You look completely at home, I must say."

"Not much different from India, John. It reminds me of the northwest frontier, actually. No bloody trees there, either."

"So you did this all the time?"

While Oldham was senior, he had never gone on an overseas assignment. He would listen to Warren's tales of India with undisguised fascination.

"Certainly not in my experience," Warren said. "Nothing on this scale and I assure you we never took baggage like that."

In the distance, a group of civilian women, likely soldier's wives, gathered around a commissary wagon. Oddly, their plain dresses looked drab next to the bright uniforms of the regiment.

"Does seem rather out of place, if I may say," Pickering added.

Oldham laughed.

"You may indeed, Mr. Pickering. Now let's find the colonel."

Warren chuckled.

"The veracity of youth."

Pickering's face flushed with embarrassment.

Lieutenant Colonel Charles Edmund Doherty stood with his legs apart surveying the activity around him. Behind him, the regimental colors of the 13th Light Dragoons waved slightly in the light breeze. Doherty knew there could be no one in the world more miserable than he found himself at this very moment. Loose bowels told him that what he hoped was seasickness might in fact be a far more dangerous malady. To this point, both the French and English forces had lost thousands of men to disease. The specter of typhus and cholera hung over both armies.

In normal times, the smell of horses and leather brought out the best in the regimental commander. Now he felt sick to his stomach and it seemed as if the smell of manure was covering him like a blanket.

"Sergeant Major Ryan!"

A short wiry man with a mutton chop beard walked up to Doherty and saluted.

"Sir!"

"Do we have a count, for God's sake?"

"Aye, sir. Eighty troopers and mounts from all squadrons currently mustered and awaiting orders."

Less than half ashore or found, he thought. Christ, this will take all damned day.

"Very well. Do what you can to expedite muster."

"Yes, sir!"

"And try to find some bloody water," he said as he swatted at the flies circling his head.

"Criminy, Harry, now what are we supposed to do?"

Trooper William Ragsdale of the 13th Light Dragoons stood at the water's edge, his trousers and boots soaking wet after wading ashore from a jolly boat. The short transit from the transport *Marie Anne* had been a welcome change after the confined and stinking quarters aboard the ship, located in what were actually cargo holds. Now they found themselves in what only could be described as total chaos.

"We do what we always do, Billy. We wait for the bleeding sergeants to talk to the bleeding officers then we do what they tell us."

"But my boots are soaking wet, and the beach smells like shit."

Harry Smith liked Billy Ragsdale, but the young man from Derbyshire could try a man's patience. However he had to admit the stench of the ship had now been replaced by a foul smell on the beach that reminded him of the tide being out at Gravesend, near his home in Kent. In addition, the clinging sand was thoroughly infested by some type of sand flea, which took flight as men walked through the sand, sending hundreds swirling around each soldier.

"Alright you two, this ain't a fucking day at the beach. Form up over there with the rest of the lads, and be damned quick about it."

Corporal Sullivan moved on down the beach looking for more stragglers from the 13th. It was time to get this bloody show on the road, he thought. And time to get away from these damned insects!

"We can only thank God that the Russians weren't waiting for us," Warren said as the three men approached the regimental assembly area. "Thirty well dug in and defended cannons would be all they needed to drive this mess back into the ocean."

"But the navy has ships. They would protect a landing, surely," Pickering responded.

"You place more trust and confidence in their ability to tell friend from foe than I do, Mr. Pickering. It has been my experience that when the navy begins to shoot their cannon, no one is safe."

"My God, Richard, one would think you were on the other side." John Oldham's voice reflected their constant argument about the viability of their mission and the ability of the senior officer's to carry it out.

"The politicians are too stupid and the generals too old," Warren said, his anger apparent.

"That's why it's up to us, my good man. You know as well as I do, captains of the cavalry will carry the day, as we always have!"

Oldham saw the colonel and turned his horse toward the older man, saluting from the saddle.

"Good morning, colonel."

Doherty moved his arm in some semblance of returning a salute and growled, "Damn near afternoon if my watch is accurate, Captain Oldham. What can you tell me?"

"Captain Goad has about forty troopers coming up from the beach."

"Good. I'd like you and Warren to organize the assembly area. Mr. Pickering, circle the area looking for stray men. God alone knows when the order to march will be given, and we must be ready."

The colonel gritted his teeth as a cramp ran through his bowels. Sweet Jesus, he thought, I'm going to shit my trousers in front of the regiment.

"Bloody dry," Scully observed. "And damned hard on the beasts."

The 13th advanced slowly behind the 11th Light Dragoons. The squadrons of both regiments were in column of three abreast and now five miles south of Kalamita Bay. The warm sun and brisk wind sapped the spirit and energy of the men as the army moved south on the peninsula toward the enemy.

Warren said nothing in response to Scully's remark. It had been five days since the landings had commenced, and the total lack of organization or coordination infuriated him. Men and horses without enough water, no shelter from the elements and minimal food supplied by the commissary corps. What the bloody hell had all of the disgustingly officious staff officers been doing for the last three months?

Pickering rode up from the rear of the column and saluted quickly.

"Prescott and Harding are both sick, barely able to stay in the saddle, sir."

As always, it's the troopers that pay the price for the incompetence of the senior officers, Warren thought, his anger seething.

"Sergeant Scully, go back and see what you can do. Whatever it takes, keep them in the saddle. There are no provisions for the sick on this march and I suspect there won't be anything set up for some time to come if our staff continues to perform at their current level of raging incompetence."

There should be medical wagons with the army, he thought, particularly because of the sickness that had struck the regiments while waiting in Varna, Bulgaria for the last leg of their journey. But the army had failed to bring wagons and the few they were able to commandeer locally were dedicated to ammunition and food. God help the men who were wounded.

"Couldn't have said it better, myself, sir," Scully grinned and saluted, turning his mount toward the rear of the column. He had known Warren for a very long time and he respected the captain's penchant for speaking his mind regardless of what might be considered proper. He'd have made a damned good Irishman, Scully thought. But damned if I'll ever tell him that. Swell his head, it would.

Scully knew the vile smell. The troopers had shit themselves, unable to control their bowels, the liquid diarrhea staining their pants. Both men were riding bent over, their uncovered heads bobbing in rhythm with their horse's slow gait.

"Prescott, hand me your canteen."

Trooper Tom Prescott raised his head, his face white and covered with sweat. With vacant eyes, he handed the cloth-covered canteen to Scully.

Reaching into a bag that was tied to his saddle, Scully pulled out a square glass bottle, which contained a white powder. He poured a small amount into Prescott's canteen, replaced the cork and shook it vigorously then handed it back.

"One mouthful every hour, understand?"

"Yes, Sarge."

He repeated the procedure with Trooper Henry Harding.

"Trooper Smith, keep an eye on these two. And make damned sure they stay in the saddle. Understood?"

"Yes, sergeant," Smith replied as Scully turned his horse toward the front of the column.

As they rode forward, Pickering asked, "What was that, sergeant?"

"An old Irish remedy, sir."

"What would be in the concoction?"

"I can only share that with another Irishman, sir. I would be damned to hell if I told an Englishman the secret of the white powder."

James Pickering understood that while he did outrank Scully, the Irishman was a seasoned veteran who had been

11

with Warren for over ten years and carried "special" privileges. But he respected the sergeant and knew that senior sergeants really did run the army.

"Of course," he said, "We wouldn't want that to happen, sergeant."

Scully liked the young officer. Not like so many of the spoiled gentlemen, Pickering was doing his best to learn to learn how to lead and fight a cavalry squadron. He would do fine, the big Irishman thought, perhaps another Warren in time. But it was going to take the continued attention of the sergeants to teach Pickering, if he was to become a real cavalry officer and not one of those parade ground dandies. But what do you expect when officers can buy their commissions, he thought, where leaders were promoted by purse, not by performance. It was a damned foolish system that only the English would tolerate.

The British column continued south, crossing a small river and finally stopping on the northern side of another river. Scrub bushes dotted the landscape with the odd small tree that had been able to survive the changing weather of the Crimea.

Warren checked the map and saw the river was named "Alma." Not much of a river as rivers go, the thought.

"Over there," Pickering said, his arm pointed across the Alma.

Warren pulled a small spyglass from his sabertache, extending it as he brought it to his eye. Across the river, on the hills above the Alma he could see large numbers of soldiers. Many of them were in the open, their blue and grey uniforms standing out in the waning light. He could also make out trenches, which had been dug on the hillside, telling him the enemy had been in place for some time. Would their artillery already be sighted and ranged to decimate attacking troops? If they were smart, the answer was yes.

"It appears the Russians have decided to make a stand, James."

John Oldham rode up and reined Julius to a stop.

"We're to bivouac here tonight."

"And tomorrow?"

Captain Oldham smiled.

"A battle, of course," he said brightly and he spurred off carrying orders to the rest of the regiment.

"Isn't it exciting?" Pickering asked, his voice barely able to contain his excitement.

Warren knew battle. The rage and brutality was something a man would never forget once he had experienced it. He thought of his own first time as a young coronet in India. It wasn't a battle like the one tomorrow would be, with formations of men and horses moving in tactical response to the enemy. Instead, it was a frightening fight against men using the hills as cover and their horses in lightning strikes against the small British cavalry patrol. His confusion and terror had quickly changed to a desperate wish not to let his men down. He would never forget kneeling behind a rock as rifle shots cracked past him and he saw Scully drop beside him, a grin on his face.

"Sir, the buggers are going to keep us here unless we rush them or run away. Orders, sir?"

It was on that crazy charge toward the tribesman, that he had killed his first man, cutting the tribesman down as almost a reflex action. After that, the rage had taken over until they had triumphed. He knew from that day forward he was a soldier and would always be a soldier.

"Look after the troops, James. If they're going to fight a battle tomorrow, we need them fed and rested."

"Yes, sir."

Warren watched the young officer canter off, full of enthusiasm for what he didn't understand and couldn't imagine. He'll learn, he thought and dismounted.

"What do you think about all this, old girl?' Warren stroked Gypsy's neck and gave her an affectionate pat. Was there a better animal on the earth, he wondered? She would go where he told her, carry him into battle and die if needed. If only the politicians had hearts as pure as Gypsy.

"Were we ever that full of piss and vinegar?"

Warren turned to see Scully.

"I'm sure we were, Michael. But it's been so long I can't recall."

It had been a long time, Scully thought, from when he had first met the young officer and through the years as he watched Warren turn into a hardened veteran. He thought too of Charlotte Truscott, the beautiful young daughter of an East India Company trader who had fallen in love with the young dashing cavalry officer. It had been one of those matches that seemed right from every view, and Warren had fallen for her just as hard. For a year, their romance and courtship had grown despite the demands the army had made on Warren. Then, as had happened so many times, an epidemic of cholera had swept through the towns and villages of the Punjab. When Charlotte succumbed, Scully had seen a light go out in Warren. Since that time, he had never entered into a relationship with any other woman. But that's why Warren was Warren, Scully thought, and so be it. Perhaps someday the light would return.

"This place is the bloody end of the earth," Harry Smith said, and broke off a piece of hard biscuit. He dipped the bread into his metal cup, which held his two-ounce ration of rum.

The four troopers sat around the pathetic little fire, trying to boil water for their coffee.

Able to find only bits and pieces of dried bushes to burn, the water refused to reach the boiling point.

"The sarge said there would be meat tomorrow," Billy Ragsdale added, poking the small fire with a skinny stick.

"Rum and hard tack, that's all I need," Leonard Small added, sticking his finger into the small pot on the fire to test the water.

"Goin' to be a battle tomorrow," Ragsdale said. "The Russians are waitin' across the river."

"That's what we came here for, now isn't it?" asked Trooper David Sandgren.

"Oh, Christ, listen to him, would you," Small laughed. "You probably believed the bleedin' recruiting sergeant too, didn't you?"

"Well, we did come here to fight," Sandgren retorted.

"And likely as not, die," Harry Smith added, his tone morose.

"Piss off."

The other two men said nothing, but continued to watch the small pot refuse to boil.

Doctor Louis Thomassy pushed through the tent flap into an interior lit by several glass-encased lanterns. A tall, distinguished man wearing a white medical coat, he was in his late thirties, his fair features set off by deep blue eyes. As expected, he saw his assistant, Kimberly Scharff, arranging bandages on a large folding table.

"I thought you might be here."

She turned and smiled.

"I couldn't sleep."

He handed his wife one of the cups of tea he carried.

"The sun is just rising," the doctor said, moving over to a campstool and sitting down.

"Will there be a battle today?" she asked.

Louis saw the look in her eyes. Kimberly was a lovely young woman who should be far from the horrors of a battlefield. But she was also a nurse, and it was here she would be needed. He knew she was dreading what could happen when the fighting started.

Louis considered himself a very lucky man. Kimberly was ten years his junior but seemed happy in their marriage. They had met during his advanced medical studies in Vienna. He'd been immediately attracted to her shyness, and Kimberly had blossomed with his attention. Now married for two years, he felt he had found his partner for life. A strange journey for a girl born and raised on a farm in Austria, he thought. Attracted to the big city by her intrigue with medicine, she was now an accomplished nurse waiting on a bluff overlooking the River Alma. Waiting for men to die.

The doctor kept wondering if what he was doing was crazy. He'd joined after being approached in Vienna by a Russian doctor hiring military surgeons for the Czar's army. Not only had Louis concluded his advanced studies at the University of Vienna, he had also spent his first four years as a doctor in the

16

service of the United States Army. As an assistant surgeon he had seen battle and treated wounded soldiers during the Mexican war of 1846-1848. Financially, the Russian offer was very attractive and the idea of spending more time abroad had seemed exciting at the time. However, that had been before the clouds of war had descended over Europe.

I should have never brought her with me, he thought.

"I don't know how it can be avoided," he said. "The British and French are across the river, coming south for the city. The general has decided to make his stand here. If he can stop them at the Alma, Sevastopol will be safe, for now."

General Alexsandr Menshikov led the 35,000 man Russian army that had marched north from Sevastopol to meet the invaders. The general knew the Anglo-French forces outnumbered him. Some of his staff thought the odds were two to one. Menshikov hoped that with prepared defensive positions and the River Alma as a barrier, the Russian forces might hurt the enemy before they could encircle Sevastopol. It was a gamble, but it might be their only chance.

Several of the medical orderlies came into the large tent and opened the flapped entrance. The sun was now rising, revealing the Russian army beginning to move to their positions atop the hills overlooking the river.

Thomassy touched his wife on the arm.

"Come, my dear. It's time to get ready."

Pulling himself, into the saddle, Richard Warren felt oddly at ease. It was a world he knew and he had confidence in the men he commanded. An odd lot, they came from all over England and Ireland. The common thread was their knowledge of horses, most having grown up on farms. The army had taught them how to fight on those horses and they knew their job.

"Top of the morning, Sergeant Scully."

"Aye it 'tis, sir." The sergeant fastened the top button of his tunic and adjusted his sword belt.

"Have the men ready to ride, but stand easy until I check with the colonel."

Warren saw John Oldham coming out of the regimental commander's tent.

"Good morning, Richard."

"John, what's happening?"

"What's happening, my fine friend, is that our colonel has the shits."

"I'll send Scully to his tent. Perhaps he'll let an Irishman help him."

Oldham grinned.

"Right now he's so miserable he'd take help from the Russians."

"Do we have orders?"

Oldham shook his head.

"Assemble in one hour and await orders. The French will lead the attack on the right flank, assisted by their ships. If they can force the river or divert the Russian's attention, then we attack on the left."

"Right. I'll ride back and send Sergeant Scully up. Perhaps he can work his miracle with the colonel."

As the day wore on and the sun climbed overhead to drive the temperatures up, the 13th Light Dragoons waited for orders, as did the remainder of the British cavalry regiments. That there was a heated battle in progress was obvious as the sounds of field artillery, naval guns and rifle fire reverberated down the Alma river valley. Several times Richard Warren rode to his right and up on a grassy hillock. He could see the infantry divisions as they surged forward and back, driving south at the Russians. Smoke hung over the river valley from rifle volleys that preceded the spirited charges by the British infantry. The deeper crash of the horse artillery cannon echoed off the hills, the sound oddly like thunder.

And still there were no orders for the cavalry. The fools, he thought. Why doesn't Lord Raglan send the English cavalry around the left flank to come in behind the enemy? Is he too old or too stupid? His thoughts appeared pointless now, as the army was doing what it does so well, blundering forward.

Her years in nursing had simply not prepared Kimberly for what she had witnessed in the last seven hours as Louis tried to save the lives of Russian soldiers wounded on the Alma Heights. The horrific injuries inflicted by artillery and the new minie ball had taken young men and turned them into pathetic, maimed creatures. It seemed to her that the stream of wounded would never stop. The pain in their voices reached into her heart, most of them only able to grunt or moan, wanting water or their mothers. How would the medical staff care for so many wounded men?

Looking down at a young soldier, she carefully removed a blood-encrusted rag from his lower abdomen. The glistening blue covering of the boy's intestines was sprinkled with dirt and grass. Blood began to flow again, a pool forming on the wooden board supporting him.

"Louis?" she asked, her voice carrying a sense of urgency.

He stepped over and quickly looked at the wound.

"Have the orderlies take him outside. There's nothing we can do."

She looked at the boy's face. Thankfully, he was unaware of what was happening around him. He is dying and doesn't know it, she thought, perhaps that was the best way.

"A hand, please," Louis called to her. "This man's leg needs to come off."

Kimberly turned her back on the young soldier and moved to her husband's side. It was as if their tent had become a corner of hell. The roar of battle outside coupled with the smell and horror around them.

The man was lying naked on a wooden table already caked with blood. Only his right foot remained covered, the boot lying at an impossible angle. No wonder, she thought, why remove a boot when the leg is coming off anyway? She felt her stomach tighten as Louis reached for the mangled leg, a scalpel ready to slice into the man's flesh.

A commotion at the front of the tent caused Kimberly to look up from the gruesome task on the table. Several men in dark blue uniforms were pushing their way across the room, carrying a man under each shoulder.

"Here, we need a doctor," a captain of the general staff, called.

"Put him down over there," Louis said without looking up from his work, a bone saw already scraping through the man's femur. Both husband and wife had become competent in Russian after a year with the army. Now they shifted from English to Russian without thinking.

"Now, man! Can't you see he is bleeding to death," the other man, also a staff officer, barked back at the doctor.

"Kimberly, see to those men, please." The severed leg was grabbed by an assistant and thrown in a bucket next to the doctor with a soft thud.

She walked around the table to where the two staff officers were laying their charge down on a recently vacated stretcher, which was already stained with blood. The wounded man had a crude bandage on his forehead, streaks of blood running down his face.

Leaning down, she carefully removed the bandage, and was shocked by the lack of any significant wound. Peering closer, she saw there was a single cut, likely from a piece of shrapnel, about one inch long that had peeled back the scalp, but had not reached the skull.

"Quickly, he is bleeding," the captain said, the urgency almost comical.

"This is a simple flesh wound, there's nothing the doctor need do. I will clean the wound and apply a fresh bandage."

Kimberly wondered how a major could have made such a commotion over a wound that many men would not have even tended. Perhaps that was the way of staff officers in the Russian Army.

"I demand the doctor examine my wound," the major finally said, his anger evident and he spoke with an American accent.

Rather than argue with him, Kimberly turned to the operating table where Louis was wiping his bloody hands off with a towel.

With a look of disgust at the major, she asked Louis in English, "Doctor, if you would check the major's wound?"

"Is it serious?" He answered, also using English.

21

"No, but he certainly seems to think so," she said and stood aside, seeing the look of fury in the major's eyes.

Louis walked to the stretcher and stopped.

"Major Hart, we meet again."

"God damn it, Thomassy, look at my head. It hurts like the devil."

The doctor bent down and examined the wound.

"A cut, nothing more. We need this space, Hart, someone will tend to you outside," he said and turned away to the next man being laid on the operating table.

Just then an artillery shell exploded close by, the concussion smashing into the tent, and several pieces of shrapnel slashed through the canvas.

The major rolled onto the ground and covered his head.

Louis looked down at Hart and shook his head.

"As I said, major, they can dress your head outside."

Hart looked up from the ground, realizing no one else had taken cover. He got to his knees and stood up, quickly walking out of the tent.

Ten minutes later, Louis decided to go outside to find Hart. The two had met twice before, when Hart was also working for the Russian Army. A West Point graduate, class of 1844, both men had been in Mexico, but had never met until Russia. Louis didn't like the man, but he was an American. The doctor was told that the three officers had ridden south toward Sevastopol.

John Oldham reined to a stop.

"We've got them on the run, by God!"

Warren waited for the explanation.

Oldham remained in the saddle, his hand reaching down to stroke Julius' neck.

"The French have pushed forward on the right. Our infantry finally forced the river and have taken the heights."

Warren realized the sounds of battle had diminished, but he knew that battles don't just end. How would the day play out?

"And orders for the cavalry?"

The senior captain laughed wryly.

"You, my friend, are the only squadron currently under orders. And those direct you to take your squadron and cross the river on the left and try to determine the direction or intent of the Russians."

This was the cavalry that Warren loved, detached from the ponderous formations where the generals and colonels were never able to make a decision.

"Sergeant Scully, be ready to move in five minutes."

Scully, who had been listening to the exchange, made a most correct salute and moved off toward his men who waited in loose order.

Water splashed up as the mounted column moved into the river. As they had come down the slope toward the water it was clear that the Alma River was neither deep nor moving with any speed that would threaten a horse and rider.

Warren had taken his men two miles inland before fording the river, seeing no signs of the Russians on the opposite shore. The troopers were traveling lightly, ready for battle. Each man carried a Victoria carbine with sixty rounds of ammunition and their sabers. Some of the more senior men also carried a Lancer's pistol, but it was still the saber that men counted on for close combat.

After crossing the slowing flowing river, Warren brought the squadron to a stop on the far bank. He turned to Scully.

"Take two men and move forward on the right. See what we're dealing with. I'll take the squadron and move up this gully."

"Johnson, McWhorter, with me," Scully called.

Two men pulled out of the second rank and moved forward.

Scully glanced at the troopers then lightly tapped the rump of his mount, Henry, moving off at a trot.

"Forward by twos, at the walk," Warren called behind him. With a gentle pressure on her side with his knees, Richard Warren and Gypsy led the squadron south. At least they were finally doing something, he thought.

Louis urged the horse pulling their ripon up the steep hill. The small carriage bounced as the ironclad wooden wheels struck rocks scattered across the slope. They had been moving east for almost an hour, trying to distance themselves from what had become a rout of the Russian army. It was clear by late afternoon that the British and French had forced the river. With the emplacement of field artillery the British now had the entire Russian line under direct fire. The lack of experience and discipline took a deadly toll on the Russian infantry. Many of them had only been in uniform a short time and against the continuing assault by the British and French, they had finally lost their will to continue the fight. Once the men began leaving their prepared positions, the exodus became universal. Despite the desperate efforts of the officers, no one was going to stop men who were overcome with fear. The perception of safety to the south in Sevastopol was too great.

The small ripon carried most of Louis' surgical equipment, hastily gathered up in the confusion and two valises. Kimberly held on tightly as they bounced over the top of the hill.

"Whoa," he called to the horse pulling the ripon. The descending slope was much steeper and suddenly he realized they were in danger of overturning. Fighting to keep the horse steady, he felt the left wheel hit something hard, throwing the carriage into the air just as the horse stumbled and slid down the embankment.

"Louis... Louis."

Kimberly leaned over her husband and brushed dirt from his face. The doctor lay on his back, his left arm under his body, the angle telling her that a dislocation or broken bone was the first of what she feared might be more injuries. He'd been thrown over her as the carriage rolled on its right side. The momentum and the horse's weight flipped the ripon over her as she hit the ground, shearing the flimsy traces at the trace hooks and rolling the carriage over him. Now, the horse stood at the bottom of the hill, apparently unharmed, with broken traces and harness draped over it.

She felt his body shudder and he groaned, moving his head from side to side.

His eyes opened and Kimberly put her hand to his face.

"Just lie still," she said, trying to remain calm.

Louis cried out as he began to move, immediately stopping any attempt at getting up.

"Wait. Just wait."

She tried to dig her feet into the slope to gain some purchase and support his weight.

He cried out again, the pain overwhelming him.

Kimberly knew how to care for the injured, but not how to rescue them. Tears came to her eyes and she looked down at the horse, standing as if nothing had happened. They were in trouble and alone.

The reconnaissance by the squadron had revealed that the Russian army had not chosen to move east from Alma, which didn't surprise Richard Warren. Falling back to Sevastopol made sense militarily, where land forts guarding the harbor and access to the sea would be critical for support. But it still made their ride, now ten miles east south east from the battlefield, rather boring. Warren took solace in that at least they were covering ground, not sitting in camp waiting for the next foolish order from headquarters.

He saw Scully crest a low hill and make a direct line for the column.

As he approached, Warren saw the look on his friend's face was not of concern or alarm. But he appeared to have information to pass.

"Find any Cossacks?"

Scully grinned.

"Not a one, but I did see something we might want to investigate."

Kimberly struggled, trying to push Louis up so she could try to ease his arm out from under his body. She kept sliding down the slope before she could leverage his torso in the slightest. Frustration was giving way to panic, what could she do? Louis was in and out of consciousness as the pain ebbed and flowed. He was not going to be able to help her. Then she heard the riders.

The men in the column of cavalry riding up the small valley were wearing blue uniforms with flashes of yellow and gold. Kimberly immediately knew they were not Russian and she was afraid. These men could kill her and Louis. They were totally helpless. She watched as the men halted, the commander issuing orders that sent several scouts riding out into the valley. The tall officer dismounted and with another soldier made their way up the hill.

"We are British. Can you understand?" he asked, stopping several feet below her.

Kimberly nodded, afraid what these men might do.

"I speak English," she said, her answer cautious and slightly wavering.

The German accent took Warren by surprise.

"My husband is injured," she added, her voice more forceful.

Warren knelt down and felt the man's neck for a pulse.

"He's alive, sergeant. Grab the blanket off my saddle and bring five men."

"Aye, sir."

Warren looked at the woman, despite the mud splattered dress and dirt on her face, despite the anxious look on her face, he could see she was a beautiful woman.

"What in God's name are you doing here?" he asked.

She hesitated. This man was a soldier and she detested the military.

"Were you at the battle?" he continued.

Kimberly nodded.

"My husband is an American doctor. I am his nurse."

Scully returned and spread out the blanket with the men at the edges.

"Do what you must, sergeant," Warren said and stood out of the way.

The Irishman quickly deployed the men and they carefully lifted the doctor's head and torso, slowly moving his arm from beneath his body.

A terrible cry of pain from Louis made everyone jump.

"All right, lads. Let's get this blanket under him and then down the hill, and, mind you, be easy with him."

Warren offered his hand to her.

"Madam, may I help you down the hill?"

"Thank you, I will manage," she said.

Scully knelt over the doctor and placed both hands on the injured man's head.

"Is he a doctor?" Kimberly asked.

Warren smiled.

"He has a way with things. Be it horse or man, he seems to be able to heal them."

She turned to look at the officer, not sure what she expected of a British cavalry commander. The Russians had been rough and loud men, both officers and troops. This man was quiet, but at the same time clearly in charge. He carried himself with confidence and that made her feel uneasy. Soldiers kill, and she had already seen the bloody results of the British attack.

"See what can be done with that carriage," he ordered several men who were watching Scully.

The horse, standing by the overturned ripon, appeared calm.

"His shoulder is out of the socket. Shouldn't be too difficult to put things right," Scully said as he stood up. "It's the insides that worry me. Only time will tell."

Kimberly knelt down next to her husband and looked back at Warren.

"What will happen to us?" she asked, her eyes betraying the fear she felt.

"My men will inspect your carriage," Warren said easily. If it can be repaired you'll be on your way. That would assume we have no interruptions."

"What do you mean?" she asked.

"We are one squadron of dragoons. I have no intention of taking on the Russian Army."

"Sergeant Scully, assist Mrs...?"

"My name is Kimberly Scharff, captain. My husband is Doctor Louis Thomassy."

Her look told Warren he was going to get no further explanation.

"Quite so."

"And you, sir?"

"Captain Richard Warren, of Her Majesty's 13th Light Dragoons."

In two hours, Corporal Hinchley, who had worked for a carriage maker in Dorset, completed repairing the ripon. While it would not likely hold up to a long journey, the repairs should last until a permanent repair could be made.

Louis had returned to his senses and it appeared the dislocated shoulder was his only serious injury. A large dose of laudanum chased with a glass of brandy had dulled the pain and

29

relaxed the doctor to the point where Sergeant Scully had been able to ease bone back into the joint. Now the men carefully helped the doctor into the ripon, where several blankets provided a comfortable seat.

"You have our utmost gratitude, sir," Louis said looking down at the British officer, his voice weak but clear.

"Doctor, you and your wife are non-combatants. The rules of war allow me to offer my assistance and I'm glad we were able to do so."

Warren helped the doctor's wife onto the small seat and handed her the reins.

"You'll be able to handle this?"

"We have carriages in Austria, captain. I shall be quite all right."

"You know that our forces will take Sevastopol under siege. There will be much death and suffering, many of it by innocent civilians. I hope you will not be in the city when that happens."

"Thank you, captain, but we go where the army is," the doctor said.

A single rider approached from the west and pulled up next to Warren.

"Large group of cavalry about two miles west, sir, coming this way."

"Doctor, we must be off. Please remember what I said."

He mounted Gypsy and turned her south, taking one last glance at Kimberly and Louis.

"Forward, column of twos."

Kimberly watched the line of riders as they trotted down the long gulley toward the River Alma. The unease she had felt with those men was now replaced by a cold fear of the future.

Chapter Two

"A bit of smoke in the air."

"Three more men listed sick this morning, sir."

Warren looked up from his mess kit to see Scully.

"Likely from eating this swill," he said. Several small pieces of salt beef lay among the watery gravy made from crushed hardtack biscuits. It remained hard to believe the army could provide nothing better than weevil-infested bread and salted meat for the men to eat. He suspected that Lord Raglan was eating a good deal better than the army.

"A good slumgully would surely sit well, like ma used to make in Kilkenny. Potatoes and carrots all tucked in around a nice piece of lamb."

Richard Warren put the tin plate down on the ground and read the small report chit.

"Cholera?"

Scully shook his head.

"Not likely, no watery shits yet."

It had been almost a month since the Battle of Alma. Now deployed around the small port of Balaclava, the British had tried with limited success to secure the right flank of the siege forces surrounding Sevastopol. For Warren and his squadron, the orders had sent them patrolling to the north and east searching for enemy forces attempting to break through to the seaport. The simple fact was that the French and British did not have enough men to adequately lay siege to the city. Now those forces would have to battle a Russian force that had the advantage of size and geography. With the weather turning cold, the ongoing fight for survival was sapping the men of the Allied Expeditionary Force as certainly as shot and shell.

"Can you keep them out of the field hospital?"

Scully nodded.

"It's their only chance to survive I'm thinking. Sweet Jesus, I was by that cesspool two days ago. The poor bastards were lying on boards, not a cot to be seen. The mud was everywhere and the stink was enough to make your hair go straight."

Criminal, Warren thought. It seemed the British army had forgotten how to wage war in the years since Waterloo. No plan for the wounded, no supplies for man or beast. What little arrived in the port of Balaclava couldn't be transported to the army in the field. And the men simply soldiered on. They deserved better.

Scully continued, "I've heard the frogs have real hospital tents with clean bedding and good food."

"You know the French, sergeant. It is all about form."

Scully followed Warren toward the trooper's tents.

"Not a bad thing, if you ask me," he muttered.

"I agree," Warren said over his shoulder without looking back.

"Carbolic soap and hot water, sergeant."

Scully looked at his captain, his face curious.

"Could be a bit difficult to find, sir."

Warren took a small leather purse from his sabertache. He pulled several gold coins from it and handed them to Scully. While he did not stand to inherit his father's vast wealth, Warren was well taken care of financially by the duke and was ready to spend that money on his men.

"Do what is necessary."

The two men stood outside one the of the small canvas tents that had finally reached the regiment. Four men were assigned to each tent, sergeants shared a tent and officers had their own. The cold weather and rain were now constant. Trying to keep the tents dry inside had become an ongoing battle in a miserable setting only soldiers in winter can understand.

"We can't rely on the fools in the commissary department. I want you to set up a system to wash and dry underclothes and socks first, then uniforms, as we can. The damn lice are already with us."

The enemy of all armies in the field, lice infestation spread quickly and with it, typhus. Warren had seen the results in India and did not intend to watch it happen in the Crimea without fighting back.

Sir?"

Warren turned to see a haggard James Pickering, his uniform showing the wear and tear of a month of hard riding and living on the land.

"Mister Pickering?"

"Sir, Captain Oldham has asked if you would join him at the colonel's tent."

"Are you well?"

Pickering hesitated then said, "Yes, sir. Just a bit wobbly, I'm afraid."

Warren looked at the young man, his face very pale.

"I want you to stand down today, and see the sergeant."

He watched Pickering walk away, his gait that of an old tired man. Warren suspected his young charge had finally lost all sense of the romance of war.

"Gentlemen, it appears the Russians have been moving troops south to either reinforce the city or attack our flank." Lieutenant Colonel Charles Doherty slouched in an improvised camp chair, his face ashen white. "Lord Lucan has directed a reconnaissance to the northeast. Captain Oldham, you will command with Captain Warren's squadron in support. You will leave immediately."

Oldham nodded and looked at the colonel, not asking the obvious question.

"Use your discretion, sir. Find the damn Russians. If you're not back in two days I will assume the worst. Understand."

Oldham nodded again.

"Yes, sir."

The two men left the stuffy tent and walked into the brisk wind.

"We'll leave within the hour, Richard. How many men can you muster?"

"Twenty five are almost healthy. I wouldn't want any of the rest on a hard ride and this will be that, I would expect."

"Indeed it will. If there's a Russian force moving into the peninsula, we'll run into their cavalry and I've heard the Cossacks are tough fighters. But I know Lord Cardigan feels we are highly superior in all respects."

Warren remembered the tribesmen he had fought on horseback in India. Hard riders and fearless fighters that the

34

British quickly found they couldn't underestimate. He would not make that mistake with the Russians. He climbed into the saddle and looked down at his friend.

"The horses are underfed and men sick, why wouldn't the generals be confident? And if it hasn't become clear to you at this point, Cardigan is a God damned fool."

With that, Warren nudged Gypsy with his knees, and rode off in search of Sergeant Scully.

Oldham knew his friend was right. The supply situation had only improved slightly and everyone was suffering for it. But the cavalry's job was to carry on and do their best, certainly Warren knew that, but his friend had always had a rebellious streak. In a way, Oldham envied Warren, but knew he would never say such things. It just wasn't done.

The next morning found the two squadrons of the 13th almost twenty miles northeast of Balaclava. The previous day's patrol had revealed nothing save scattered tenant farmers trying to scrape a living from the barren soil of the Crimea. A cold night huddled under thin blankets made the morning tea a welcome relief.

Scully handed a steaming cup to Warren.

"Top of the morning, my lord."

Scully seldom used the title accorded the son of a Duke and Warren realized the Irishman was in a particular good mood.

Squatting down next to his commander, Scully raised his tea.

"To good hunting."

Warren took a sip and with pleasure realized the hot tea was laced with Irish whiskey.

"Sergeant, you do Ireland proud."

The men drank in silence, watching the camp take their quick breakfast and pack up.

Oldham approached and motioned Scully to remain sitting.

"You two look as if you're planning our next move."

"Your thoughts," Warren asked.

"Two arrows have more chance of hitting a target than one. I say we split the squadrons. I'll move due north and you take your men northeast," Oldham said.

Warren nodded.

"I have one man who's ill. The sergeant thinks we should send him back."

Oldham thought for a moment.

"I'll detail Corporal Burnett. He can go back with your man and deliver a report to the colonel."

The first sign of the enemy was a slight trail of dust from the reverse side of the far slope just after mid-day. While Warren had seen it, he also saw the outrider making his way back from that direction.

Trooper Prescott reined to a halt and saluted Warren.

"Cavalry, in column of twos on the far side of that ridge, sir. Must be at least two hundred riders."

"Any infantry or artillery?"

The man nodded.

"Four guns bringing up the rear. They look like our nine pounders; the infantry's behind that. I didn't see the end of the column."

So the Russians were on the move. But how many and where were they moving? Was this the vanguard of a larger force or something else? He had to find out and get the information back to Balaclava. His disgust with the entire campaign immediately forgotten as the enemy approached.

"Sergeant Scully, we shall shadow that column. I want you to take the squadron over into the next valley and move south for one mile. Have Corporal Sullivan select three troopers. I'll move up to the top of the ridge and take a look."

Scully glanced at Warren. He didn't like to leave the captain's side, but with Pickering sick in quarters, it was up to him to lead the squadron. At least the captain would have Liam Sullivan with him. The wiry corporal was as tough a trooper as there was in the brigade and would watch over Warren.

"Aye, sir."

The slope of the valley did offer some cover as the five men moved slowly toward the crest. As they neared the top, Warren signaled with his hand for them to dismount. Surely the Russians will have outriders, he reasoned. Dismounted, the British stood less a chance of being discovered.

Handing Gypsy's reins to Corporal Sullivan, Warren walked the last few feet to the ridge's crest. Below him, he saw the Russians. The cavalry led the column and he immediately recognized these were experienced troops. Their uniforms were dark brown and dark blue, with fur caps on all the riders. The horses were magnificent. They must be the Russian Dons. He'd heard of them but never seen one. They were renowned as strong and reliable, the perfect animal for the brutal Russian terrain.

Behind the cavalry, four artillery field pieces were being towed by eight horse teams. The barrels appeared longer than the British field pieces, but Prescott was right, they looked like nine pounders. Marching in four-man ranks, the line of infantry stretched for a half a mile. Three or four battalions, Warren thought, a force that could do damage to any encampment or fortification outside of the heavy siege lines surrounding the city. But where were they going?

Corporal Sullivan moved up quickly and knelt down next to him.

"Sir, down the ridge," he said pointing north, his voice quiet as if the enemy could hear him.

Two riders, wearing the same uniforms as the cavalry column were slowly riding along the crest one hundred yards away, coming directly toward them.

Looking back downslope, Warren saw their horses were well concealed by several large rocks and bushes. At least the Russian outriders couldn't see them. If Warren tried to retreat with his men back down into the valley they would be seen immediately. If the Russians moved down toward their column they would miss the British altogether, but he knew that was unlikely. They must be dealt with.

"With me, corporal."

The two men carefully moved down to where the other three troopers waited.

"Two Russian riders coming this way. The corporal and I will move up and try to take them by surprise. Harris, Lowell, get your carbines and be ready to shoot them if they discover us. Harding, you stay with the horses. I don't want any shooting if it can be helped. But if it comes to that, we'll dispatch the enemy riders and ride like the hounds of hell are behind us. Understood?"

The men grinned and nodded, Harris and Lowell slid their carbines from the saddle buckets.

"Come on," Warren said to Sullivan.

Carefully returning to their observation point, they saw the Russian riders were now fifty yards away, still moving along the top of the ridge.

"We'll take them right there," Warren said, pointing toward a rock outcropping. "Sabers from the side, right?"

Sullivan nodded and followed him. He knew from experience that the captain was the best swordsman in the regiment, but this would be a simple, brutal and deadly attack.

The two British soldiers heard the Russian riders talking as they approached the outcropping. While Warren couldn't understand what they were saying, the tone was that of two men tired and bored.

Hooves sounded louder on the hard ground, telling the British the moment was near for the attack. Holding sabers at their sides, Warren and Sullivan pressed against the rock ready to spring.

Shying to the left, the first horse sensed the attack before its rider.

Springing forward, Warren drove his saber up and into the first man's side, feeling the blade slide through the coat into flesh.

Fighting his horse, the man cried out in pain, one hand desperately reaching back toward the sword buried in his side.

The Englishman turned the blade slightly and pulled down hard, doing more damage as the sword came out of the man's back. He reached up and dragged the wounded Russian from the saddle, slamming him to the ground. Warren drove the saber into the man's exposed neck. Blood gurgled from the Russian's lips and he went limp.

The second horse, a huge black stallion, rose up on its back legs, the rider fighting to stay in the saddle. Desperately, Sullivan plunged his saber deep into the man's lower back. Wheeling to the right, the horse slammed into Sullivan, who released the saber as he was knocked to the ground. The big stallion stepped on the corporal who rolled away from the flaying hooves. The mortally wounded rider slumped forward in the saddle then rolled left and fell to the ground, the saber protruding grotesquely from his back.

Warren had grabbed the reins of the first man's horse and now lunged to reach the stallion that veered to the right away from him, toward the Russian column.

"Jesus, stop him, man."

Scrambling to his feet, Sullivan put both hands up to steady the stallion and grabbed the reins. The black Don again reared up on its back legs, giving the corporal a start, but Sullivan knew horses and quickly had the animal under control.

"Steady, steady... That's right. Steady there..."

"They're coming in, sergeant."

Michael Scully stepped up on a large boulder and saw five horsemen and two riderless horses moving through the scrub.

"That'll be a tale, I'm sure. Prescott and Brown, help with the horses."

Warren dismounted and handed Gypsy's reins to Brown.

The sergeant saw the dirt and dust on the captain's uniform, his face streaked with sweat. A single drop of blood showed on Warren's neck.

"Bit of a fight I see."

He smiled at his friend.

"I shall be recommending Corporal Sullivan for promotion at the earliest convenience, sergeant."

Warren quickly went over what they had seen and the ambush of the Russian riders.

"This information must get back to the colonel. I don't know what other Russian columns may be between here and Balaclava. I want you to take half the men and get back with the news of this column. Three hundred horse, four guns – nine pounders and three to four battalions of infantry. Mark your map with this position and tell the colonel the Russians are moving southwest. I will shadow them and return tomorrow with updated news."

Scully frowned. "Is it wise to split up?"

"I don't like it either, Michael, but it makes the most sense. Perhaps with news from Oldham, the brass will actually figure out what the enemy's up to. And check on Corporal Sullivan. That black Russian stallion we brought in stepped on him up there. If he's hurt, get it out of him and take him back with you."

"Aye, sir." The captain's use of Scully's first name would have been unheard of only two years ago. But the final year in India and breaking into a new regiment had deepened their respect and friendship.

"You'll be no damn good to him with a likely broken rib or worse, you hard-headed bastard."

Corporal Liam Sullivan stood ready to mount his horse, the pain in his side dull for now.

"I thought corporals were supposed to be tougher than most, that's what you're always telling me," he snapped at Scully. He pulled himself into the saddle and slowly settled himself.

"And sergeants are smarter than corporals, my friend, and you're coming with me.

41

Richard Warren's small group arrived back at the British lines an hour before sunrise on the 25th of October, 1854. The return trip had proved dangerous as the small group of British cavalry saw more signs of Russian troops on the move.

"Damned odd, don't you think, Warren?'

Colonel Doherty had been awakened from his sick bed to hear Richard's account of the encounter with the Russian column and the return journey.

"In what way, sir."

"No strength, man. What general worth his salt would send such a small force toward the enemy's lines?"

"Still more than a patrol or reconnaissance, sir."

"Yes, I suppose so. Well you better report to Lord Cardigan, he can determine what he wants to do with the information."

"One last thing, if I may?"

"Yes?"

"Is there room for one more sergeant on the roll?"

"Why's that?"

Corporal Sullivan is a good soldier and leader. I would like to see him made sergeant."

Doherty thought for a moment.

"We did lose Sergeant Adams to the cholera. But I would move him to A squadron, you'd lose him."

"Hate to lose him, but it's the best for him and the regiment."

"Very well, talk to the sergeant major. Then find Lord Cardigan. Now get out of here and let me try to rest."

Lieutenant General James Brudenell, the 7th Earl of Cardigan commanded the Light Brigade, which consisted of the

4th and 13th Light Dragoons, the 17th Lancers and the 8th and 11th Hussars. A wealthy man in his own right, Brudenell was a politician and aristocrat who had used his money to purchase commissions for himself, and finally to outfit his own regiment. While the rest of the expeditionary force travelled to the Crimea on the ships of the Royal Navy or contracted vessels, Cardigan had sailed on his own yacht, which was now anchored in the small harbor at Balaclava.

"You're in luck, captain."

A coronet in the uniform of the 11th Hussars stood on the small quay holding the reins of a beautiful chestnut stallion. Warren had enquired after Lord Cardigan on arriving at the harbor and been directed to the young officer.

"I am waiting for his lordship. He'll come ashore shortly."

"And you are?"

The man replied, "Sorry, sir. Coronet Harry Grenville, 11th Hussars. At your service."

"Warren of the 13th. Colonel Doherty requested I see Lord Cardigan with possibly important intelligence of the Russians."

Grenville appeared most impressed and the time spent waiting for Cardigan was passed in pleasant conversation.

"Here his lordship comes now," Grenville said, nodding to a small boat, rowed by four sailors approaching the quay.

Sitting in the stern, Lord Cardigan sat erect, his red tunic bright against the greenish brown water of the inlet. Warren had met the man at several functions and didn't care for him.

Allowing for Cardigan to climb up a small set of stairs, he approached and saluted.

"Captain Warren of the 13th, sir."

Cardigan, quickly returned the salute, running his eyes down to Richard's dirty boots and dirty trousers.

"You're looking a bit rough around the edges, sir."

He remembered the man had been pompous the last time they had met.

"Bit of an altercation with the Russians, sir. Colonel Doherty wanted me to convey what we discovered on a patrol to the northeast."

The man's eyes narrowed.

"What patrol is that? I didn't order a patrol."

"I believe the request came from Lord Lucan."

Cardigan's face reddened and he reached for the reins of his horse. As brothers in law, Lords Lucan and Cardigan detested each other.

"Then report to him, sir!"

He mounted his horse and trotted down the quay without a look back.

Warren watched Cardigan until he turned a corner leaving the waterfront. He spat on the ground, mounted Gypsy and looked down at the coronet.

"Apparently he isn't interested, Mr. Grenville. Sorry to have troubled you."

The young officer looked up at Warren, his face flushed.

"Ah yes, sir, I mean no, sir, not at all. Good day, sir."

Lieutenant General George Bingham, the 3ʳᵈ Earl of Lucan, and overall cavalry commander was, at that moment, conducting his normal morning reconnaissance of the British positions with senior members of his staff and several regimental commanders. Seeing a set of signals flags in the distance, the general was curious as to their significance. A discussion then ensued between the senior officers and Lucan's aide de camp, advancing the idea that it might mean the Russians were attacking. The crash of artillery immediately confirmed that the enemy was, in fact, afield.

Richard Warren had heard the opening artillery shots and quickly decided that there was little of import he could pass to Lord Lucan at this point.

Fifteen minutes of pushing Gypsy hard brought him back to camp to find the regiment mounting for battle. He knew this would not be another Alma. The Russians wouldn't be attacking unless they felt they had the advantage. This would be a hard fought battle.

"Bit of smoke in the air," Scully said, almost nonchalantly.

The sergeant had the troop mounted and now saluted Warren.

"Quite correct, sergeant. Are the lads ready?"

Scully nodded.

"Two men still sick in quarters, but I saw young Mister Pickering just now and he appears ready as well."

In ten minutes, the four squadrons had formed and the 13th Light Dragoons moved north with the Light Brigade.

From Sapouńe Heights overlooking the valley, General Fitzroy Somerset, 1st Baron Raglan, in overall command of the British forces, was able to watch the Light Brigade take its place northwest of the Heavy Cavalry Brigade. Made up of six squadrons of dragoons and two of the Scots Grays, the Heavy Calvary was commanded by Major General James Yorke Scarlett.

It was soon evident to the commander in chief that the Russians intended to attack the four defensive positions manned by the Turkish contingent of the allied force.

Lord Raglan watched the Russian infantry and cavalry move forward in several columns into the valley. Was this to be a major attack by the Czar's newly arrived forces? Despite his years of experience as a soldier, he had never been in overall command of a battle, and the enemy's intentions were not at all clear.

The Russians attacked with little delay, throwing themselves at the Turkish positions. Despite support from the Royal Horse Artillery, the Turks soon began to fall back from their positions toward the second line of defense manned primarily by the 93rd Highlanders, supported by the Heavy Brigade, now controlled directly by Lucan.

Two hours into the attack, all four of the Turkish positions had been captured by the Russians, who now launched a massive cavalry attack on the single regiment of British infantry, the only force now left between the Russians and Balaclava itself. In one swift move, General Pavel Liprandi was about to cripple the British ability to maintain their siege on Sevastopol.

Lord Raglan was no stranger to battle, having fought through Spain and Portugal with the Duke of Wellington. An experienced cavalry officer, he had been severely wounded at the Battle of Waterloo, losing his right arm. Now he finally understood the peril to his force. But other than desperately trying to move supporting forces forward, there was little else he could do. From the heights he could see the 93rd Infantry had moved into a thin line in front of their positions. Raglan was surprised and concerned for the regiment. They were not forming defensive squares that many considered mandatory for infantry to defend against cavalry. This could be a very bloody thing.

Raglan raised his brass telescope, surveying the battlefield.

"What are they doing?" he exclaimed.

Several telescopes came up almost simultaneously as the staff officers tried to analyze what was happening on the valley floor.

But by now, there was nothing to say. The Russian cavalry appeared like a lava flow surging toward the British infantrymen who stood shoulder to shoulder, bayonets fixed, ready to absorb the enemy attack. The men overlooking the charge watched transfixed as hundreds of mounted men thundered toward the single regiment, standing their ground with no apparent fear of what was about to happen.

Suddenly a volley crashed out from the Highlanders, the white smoke leaping forward toward the horsemen, who seemed to be little affected.

"My God," the general said, knowing what was about to happen. The battle was going to be lost. But rather than devising a counter move, Raglan simply watched the horror unfolding.

A second volley ripped from the British line into the Russian cavalry who were now fifty yards closer and it was as if the hand of God had slapped across the Russian line. The charge faltered, slowing as men were torn from the saddle and horses brought down with the fusillade of minie balls. The line of red not only held, but a third volley resulted in the Russian cavalry retreating, their attack utterly broken.

"What's happening, John?"

Captain Oldham grinned.

"I may be the acting regimental commander, Richard, but I have no idea."

It was the first time the two men had talked while the Light Brigade waited for orders. In position for over an hour, the men were impatient. Everyone wanted to do something, anything,

47

rather than have to listen to the battle and think of what might come.

"But what a chance, to lead the regiment in battle. Surely a majority for you."

"Does have a nice sound, don't you think, Major Oldham."

"Indeed, it does."

They both turned as Sergeant Major Ryan rode up to them and saluted.

"Sir, Lord Lucan and his entire bloody staff rode off like banshees from hell toward the Heavy Brigade, it seems they're attacking."

At that moment they heard the piercing bugle call in the distance signaling "charge."

Turning to the south, Lord Raglan realized the Heavy Brigade was attacking the disorganized Russian cavalry

"By God, Scarlett's attacking."

Unaware that Lucan had joined the Heavy Brigade, he thought that General Scarlett was acting alone as he watched the British Dragoons crash into the Russians. This might be a different war, but he knew the battle rage was now in full control of his men as they slashed and hacked at the enemy riders. One after another, the regiments of British dragoons hit the Russians, first on the left flank, then the right. The 4th Dragoons surprised the rear of the Russians and the disorganized retreat of the enemy began.

In ten minutes time the momentum of the battle had turned and the commander in chief knew it.

Scully walked up to Warren, who now stood to one side of the line of troopers who remained dismounted and waiting.

"I'm thinking the generals forgot about us."

Warren shook his head.

"That's not likely, but whether they use us or not remains to be seen. How are the lads?"

"Most are nervous, but acting like they aren't. Just like we used to be."

Warren laughed.

"And our favorite coronet?"

Scully frowned.

"I'd prefer he was back in his tent, but he has quite a will that one. Reminds me a bit of you, if you ask me."

How could he order Pickering back to camp and miss another battle? The boy wanted to be a professional soldier and there was only one way to do that, and it wasn't sitting back in camp.

"He'll do fine, he's young and strong."

"Aye, you're right."

"Have him come see me, would you?"

The big sergeant nodded.

"You're feeling well, James?"

"Oh, yes sir. Quite well. Fit for duty."

As skeptical as Warren might be, it was a decision that James must make.

"We might go into action soon. Are you ready to do your duty?"

Warren looked at the young officer, his face paler than normal.

Pickering swallowed.

"I will do my best, sir."

"Remember, they'll look for you to be professional and disciplined. It's the burden we carry as officers. I know you'll handle it well."

Pickering looked toward the men then turned back to face Warren.

"What will it be like, sir?"

He paused. How could he describe what might happen? Men and horses torn apart, screaming and crying, violent deaths and pathetic injuries.

"Not what you think. Expect confusion and noise. It'll be hard to know what's happening around you or even hear orders. What you must do is remember you're in charge of your men and do what you can to lead them to the enemy and defeat him. How you do that is different in every battle. That is what you will learn each time."

"Yes, sir."

"Now go talk with the men. Help get their minds off what might come."

"Thank you," he said, and saluted.

"Now by God, let's do something," Warren said quietly to himself. Enough of this damned waiting.

The frustration of the 13th was not unusual. Throughout the regiments the question of when they would be called into action ran through every man's mind. Knowing the Heavy Brigade had already attacked and hurt the enemy, why didn't the general order the remaining cavalry to attack and finish the job?

That frustration was felt no less by Captain Louis Nolan, an officer of the 15ᵗʰ Hussars, now aide-de-camp to Brigadier-General Richard Airey, Deputy-Quartermaster-General. Nolan, an experienced cavalry officer, who had extensive service in India saw the opportunity that was being lost to the British.

However at the conclusion of the charge by the Heavy Brigade, Lord Raglan simply decided to employ the Light Brigade to prevent a number of cannons, previously abandoned, from being carried off by the Russians. He directed General Airy to compose an order to be delivered to Lord Lucan:

"Lord Raglan wished the cavalry to advance rapidly to the front – follow the enemy and try to prevent the enemy carrying away the guns – Troop Horse Artillery may accompany – French cavalry is on your left. R. Airey, Immediate."

As Captain Nolan spurred off toward the cavalry, Lord Raglan called after him, "Tell Lord Lucan the cavalry is to attack immediately.

Chapter Three

"Insanity. It was insanity."

Across the Light Brigade, the bugle call "to mount" echoed against the low hills. The notes were greeted with a mixture of relief and anxiety. Would they simply be changing locations or was this preparation for attacking the enemy?

John Oldham watched as his squadrons aligned themselves in line abreast, with each squadron commander the prescribed ten paces in front of the troopers. They looked ready for battle, he thought, surveying the men. Many had been sick and certainly the weather was beginning to take a toll, but they were ready to do their duty. He turned to see Lord Cardigan moving to the front of the brigade by himself. To his left, Oldham saw the 17ᵗʰ Lancers, their distinctive ten-foot lances now vertical. He looked over to Warren and nodded.

"Draw swords," Cardigan ordered and across the brigade with the exception of the 17th, blades began to appear along the lines of riders.

From the heights, Lord Raglan watched the precise movement and felt a surge of pride. The finest cavalry in the world, he thought, the finest.

"The brigade will advance," came the call from Cardigan, absent any order by bugle.

Warren moved forward at a walk, matching Oldham, who was guiding on Cardigan.

The well-practiced movement was almost second nature to the experienced troops and the front line of regiments moved forward one hundred yards, at which time the 11th Hussars began to advance. At the same interval the 4th Light Dragoons and the 8th Hussars followed.

"What's happening, sarge?"

Scully kept his eyes front but answered Trooper Prescott who rode beside him.

"We're advancing, Tom, my boy."

"Where?"

"You'll find out when we get there."

Corporal Sullivan grinned.

Having watched events unfolding for over three hours, Warren now understood they were advancing at the enemy, but what was the objective? The battle in the morning had been over the defended redoubts on the heights to his right. Were they to retake those guns? To his left, the Russians in the long valley had gun batteries on the left and at the end of the valley, where the majority of the Russian cavalry had retired after the earlier battle. Watching Cardigan, Warren realized he was increasing to a trot, but also slowly turning down the long valley to the left. Surely they weren't going to attack the main Russian position? To his left he saw a staff officer he recognized as Captain Lewis Nolan, riding hard across the front of the 17th toward Cardigan.

The Russian guns on the left flank opened fire, violent jets of white smoke rolling down the hillside and the crash echoed against the hillsides. The British advance was only two minutes old.

Four explosions in quick order from the enemy battery spooked horses and made men duck involuntarily as shrapnel sliced through the morning air. Poor Nolan had been struck fatally, his horse bolting to the rear. The Russians were firing case shot, the explosions well planned by the enemy gunners.

Lord Cardigan broke into a trot, the first regiments following suit. The brigade now knew where their commander was going.

"Sweet mother of God," Michael Scully's words were lost as more explosions from the Russian artillery began to take a toll on the brigade.

"Maintain formation," James Pickering called loudly as several troopers swerved away from a blast of earth and steel directly in front of the 13th.

Warren felt the heat of the explosion to his right and Gypsy veered left, but came back on line quickly. The smell of acrid smoke now drifting across the brigade as more guns opened up on the British.

Artillery fire from the captured redoubt on the right of the brigade began to explode in the ranks. Dirt, rock and steel flew through the air as shot after shot exploded among the Brigade. By ones and twos, horses were hit, sometimes collapsing with their rider or bolting from the shock and pain. Amid the thunder of the shells, the screams of injured animals were terrible to hear. The Light Brigade was being savaged.

Advancing on the right of the British attack, the 13th was the now taking rifle fire from Russia infantry in the redoubts to their right. The sound of musket balls could be heard over the thunder of hooves as the riflemen began to hit their targets.

Pickering now rode as if in a trance, the dust and smoke coupled with the explosions was like nothing he could have ever imagined. On each side the sweating horses, now at a trot, were like a giant wave surging down the barren valley.

"Steady… Steady," the young officer called, it was the only thing he could think of to say.

Withering artillery crossfire from both sides of the valley continued to rip into the British. Behind the brigade over thirty horses lay dead or wounded, their riders either on the ground or staggering to their feet trying to move back, away from the Russian rifle fire.

Breaking into a canter to match Cardigan, who still rode twenty paces in front of the brigade, Warren saw the Russian guns at the end of the valley, now less than a mile from them. Insanity. This was insanity. The Light Brigade continued their charge directly into the face of the enemy artillery, all the time under fire from both sides of the valley. Belching smoke told him the guns they were charging had begun to fire directly down the valley into the Brigade.

Rapid explosions and the whine of flying metal had turned the precise formation into groups of riders who continued to follow Cardigan deeper into the valley. The main Russian battery fire began to devastate the attackers. Men were torn from the saddle or thrown like dolls through the air as their mounts were hit and collapsed. The full horror of battle was upon them.

Michael Scully knew they were going to die. Yet he spurred Henry on toward the guns. A violent explosion just to his right stunned him for a moment. He involuntarily ducked his head, trying to stay in the saddle and saw Tom Prescott topple sideways off his horse, his right side a mass of blood.

Ahead of the 13th, James Oldham now broke into a gallop, leaning forward in the saddle, his sword leveled forward. They were committed.

Trooper Harry Smith was terrified as men and horses screamed and crashed into the ground next to him. He continued to hold hard with his knees, the gallop actually making it easier to focus on their objective. Dark barricades spanned their front from which flames and smoke belched forth. The world around him had become a nightmare of blood, dirt and screams as shells exploded in the ranks. Smith wanted to turn his horse, ride away from this horror, but he continued to gallop toward the guns. A vicious explosion erupted directly in front of him, throwing jagged metal into the riders. Ducking his head involuntarily, he saw Henry Harding fly backward out of the saddle, a burst of blood exploding from the trooper's chest.

Warren spurred Gypsy, and she understood what to do. Despite the noise and violence, she thundered forward, closing on the Russian guns. He lowered his sword, only two hundred yards to the guns. Behind him he heard men yelling but he couldn't understand what they were saying, only snatches of human emotion in what was becoming a maelstrom of violence and death.

A thundering flash and blast of earth hit the front ranks as they closed to within fifty yards of the guns. The explosion seemed like slow motion to Warren, as he watched Oldham's big white charger roll to the left, both front legs blow off. His friend was already clear of the saddle tumbling toward the hard packed ground.

Scully spurred his horse toward Warren, who now led the first wave, Lord Cardigan nowhere to be seen. He watched as his friend leaped the short bulwark the Russians had erected in front of their cannon. Like a wave crashing against a wall, the British front rank either jumped the short barrier or funneled through the breaks in the wall. They were on the enemy.

Slashing left and right, the 13th attacked the Russian gunners who desperately fought back with whatever they could find. Men were fighting with rammers and short swords, lances and knives. As more cavalrymen surged into the enemy gun batteries, the battle deteriorated into individual struggles, the British attacking with sabers and lances.

Warren wheeled Gypsy right, slashing down at a Russian who had missed him with a poorly aimed bayonet thrust. His saber caught the man across the left side of his face, flaying it open from eye to throat, blood cascading down the man's shirt even as he collapsed.

Reversing back to his left, he saw Trooper Ragsdale being pulled from the saddle by two Russians. The enemy fell on the young Britisher, knives flashing as they stabbed him repeatedly. The din of screams and savage yells filled the air as the frenzy of man-to-man combat took over.

Sergeant Scully saw Warren spurring toward a down man, his saber held ready to strike. He jerked Henry's reins hard to the right and dug his spurs into the horse's side. A Russian with a long naval pike was running toward Warren who had totally focused on the two Russians attacking a down cavalryman.

Warren swung down hard, catching one man on the back of his head, the blow slicing hard into his neck. Blood flowed down the man's gray coat and he fell on top of his comrade who struggled to free himself. The trooper writhed on the ground, his wounds likely fatal.

Henry surged forward and Scully knew his only chance was to crash the horse into Warren's assailant. He would never reach the attacker with a sword thrust.

"Richard!"

Warren turned at the sound of Scully's voice, to see the Russian with the pike just as the Irishman's horse slammed into him, knocking him and the pike to the ground. The two men exchanged glances as they wheeled their horses left and right, sabers at the ready.

Both saw Pickering fighting off three Russians who were attacking with swords and bayonets. The young officer was alone, not a cavalryman within thirty feet. He slashed left and right trying desperately to fend off the men who sensed they had the advantage.

Warren spurred toward Pickering, followed by Scully. The two cavalrymen struck out at enemy soldiers in their way, who were on the defensive and beginning to break. It was then that the Russian cavalry struck.

Pickering realized he was falling from the saddle despite all of his efforts. A stabbing pain in his left arm made him gasp for breath as he fell past his stirrups and hit the ground. Dust and dirt, yells of anger and horses hooves seemed to envelope him as a violent kick in the head sent him into a world of unknowing darkness.

"Cavalry!" Scully yelled, turning Henry to see a large force of mounted Cossacks descending on the gun batteries.

Warren knew they were hopelessly outnumbered, the bulk of the Light Brigade having moved back to the gun revetments and some already retiring back down the valley. He stood in the stirrups to see if there was a path back to the regiment.

Scully reached Pickering and saw he was bleeding from a wound to his arm.

"He's alive!" he yelled.

Turning to make sure he had time to dismount, Scully saw Warren fall from the saddle, Gypsy thrusting forward in confusion. He turned to face the oncoming Russian riders just as a Russian artilleryman broke a wooden rammer over his head, knocking him senseless.

Opening his eyes, Scully winced, the pain in his head massive. Despite the clouds, the brightness made him squint. Turning his head slowly, he saw a man lying next to him wearing the distinctive blue trousers of the 13th. Russian voices told him that the worst had happened.

He rolled over and struggled to his knees. There were Russian troops everywhere, the dead and wounded of both nations covering the ground, flies buzzed everywhere, settling on the dead and wounded. Looking down, Scully realized the blue trousers belonged to Richard Warren.

"Richard," he said.

Then he saw the blood covering Warren's right thigh and pooling under his leg.

"Christ," Scully said and moved to his friend's right side.

A man yelled in Russian behind him, but Scully was focused on the bloody leg. He pulled a scarf from his neck and folded it into a square. The bloody trouser was pierced by a circular bullet hole, blood oozing slowly, forming a puddle in the dirt. Scully placed the scarf over the wound.

Warren stirred, giving a low groan, his face wincing with pain.

Taking a leather strap from his sword belt, the sergeant fastened the bandage in place, prompting another groan from Warren.

He looked up to see a tall Russian cavalryman, obviously an officer, looking down at him from the saddle of a massive black horse. The man surveyed the two British soldiers and issued orders to the men standing around the two captives.

Scully knew they were dead. He was scared but determined not let these men see it. He would show them the kind of men they were fighting. Turning to Warren he saw his friend was still stunned. Perhaps better that way.

Suddenly the men around them moved aside and the Irishman saw a small wagon.

Roughly pulled to his feet, he was shoved to the wagon by several Russians and pushed into the back. Scully saw James Pickering sitting in the front corner his knees up, head down.

The young man looked up as Scully sat down next to him.

"S... Sergeant."

Four Russian soldiers laid Warren in the bed of the wagon and shoved his body forward until only his boots hung out.

Perhaps they were going to be spared, Scully thought, as the wagon, pulled by two tired mares lurched forward. The driver, a very fat man in a filthy gray uniform, looked straight ahead paying no attention to his passengers.

Scully pulled off his coat and put it under Warren's head, trying to make his friend more comfortable. He looked at Pickering who had closed his eyes, his arms folded in front of him.

"Mr. Pickering?"

The young man opened his eyes and nodded.

"Let me take a look."

Fighting the rocking and lurching wagon, Scully carefully examined Pickering's left arm. What he saw was not good and explained why the coronet seemed to be not in the moment. The damage was severe. He could see a fragment of bone protruding from the boy's forearm, with torn flesh grayish pink in the light. The crusted blood covering his hand was dark black with bright red still running down his arm. If they were at a British field surgery, the lower arm would be coming off, no question in the sergeant's mind.

"A nasty one, that is, but I've seen worse. We'll take good care of it, you'll be fine." Lying was easy when there were no other options.

Pickering nodded, the effort to speak too much for him.

Scully found his kerchief and tied it as tight as he could below the boy's elbow to stop the bleeding, which it did in short order.

Sitting back, Scully watched as they made their way off the battlefield. There were dead and wounded men lying around them for the first twenty minutes, likely the result of the attack by the Heavy Brigade. A shot rang out to their left. Was someone putting a horse out of its misery? Or perhaps a man wounded too badly to survive. It really was the most humane thing to do. Certainly the British cavalry had made their mark. The uniforms of the dead were mostly Russian, although the occasional Englishman was easily identified by the brighter uniforms.

The sergeant's mind kept returning to the charge. What was the purpose? Throwing cavalry against emplaced guns, it broke all the rules of war. It just wasn't done.

Hitting a large rut, the wagon lurched hard left and Warren moaned.

"Easy, you dumb bastard!" Scully yelled at the driver, who turned slightly and shrugged.

The fat driver finally stopped just before sunset at an encampment near a small stream. There appeared to be mostly infantry in the camp gathered around small campfires. No tents or shelters were evident. The driver stepped down from the wagon, yelled to the soldiers and began to unhitch his horses.

Three Russians in long gray coats walked over and surveyed the British captives. They seemed to be interested in the enemy soldiers, but displayed no hostility. One man, holding a musket with a long bayonet remained at the wagon, apparently as a guard.

Scully shivered as the sun began to set. It was going to be cold tonight and they had no protection.

One of the soldiers who had come to examine them earlier appeared and tossed several blankets and a canteen into the wagon. He said something in Russian, laughed and walked away.

The sergeant helped Pickering lie down and laid the blanket over him. He turned to Warren and used the second blanket to cover his friend.

"Where?" he heard Warren ask in a weak voice.

Scully grabbed the canteen and helped Warren take a drink.

Laying his head back down on Scully's coat he asked, "What happened?"

"I don't remember much. Woke up next to you, the brigade was gone and there were more Russians than I ever wanted to behold. They put us in this wagon, that's when I saw young Pickering."

"How is he?"

Scully looked at the young man under the blanket, assuming he was asleep.

"Bad wound, left arm."

Warren took a deep breath.

"My leg?"

"I put a bandage on it. Looked like a musket ball about two inches below the family jewels. Bleeding's stopped."

The pain was constant and Warren knew the wound was serious. In enemy hands, his chances of survival would be minimal. He had to face the reality.

"Where are we?"

"My guess is five or six miles north of the battlefield," Scully answered, his voice quiet.

The two men were silent for several minutes.

"You need to escape. If you slip away now, you can make it back to our lines by sunrise."

Scully said nothing.

Across the camp, a voice cried out in apparent anger, perhaps the precursor to a soldier's fight. But nothing came of it.

"And leave you here?"

"Neither Pickering nor I seem to be quite up to a walk in the dark. It's your only chance."

"The only chance you and the youngster have is if I stick with you and take care of those wounds. One can save two. Makes sense to me. Now go to sleep."

Warren knew an argument with Michael Scully would be futile at this point. Come what may, they were together. But then they always had been.

Sunrise brought the fat driver from somewhere across the camp. The man was followed by another soldier, who used his musket as a support for an injured leg. After an exchange of words, their guard walked off, now replaced by the injured infantryman.

While the driver went through the ritual of harnessing the horses, Scully tried to get the guard to understand they needed water and food. He made the motion of drinking and eating until the guard called out to the driver who answered sharply.

"They're not dumb, just lazy," Scully said.

The guard looked tired and irritated, but he did turn and walk back to the camp.

Warren sat with his back to the front wall of the wagon. The pain was constant in his leg and he didn't respond to his sergeant.

Restless all night, Pickering sat in the opposite corner, still cradling his injured arm in his lap.

"What will they do with us?"

"Hopefully feed us, Mr. Pickering. One worry at a time."

Warren smiled to himself. As much as he wanted Scully away from the Russians, he knew having the sergeant with them would make their ordeal easier.

The sustenance provided to the British prisoners consisted of a several pieces of some type of cooked meat, a large piece of bread and a leather skein, which contained foul tasting water.

Scully broke off pieces of bread and handed them to the others. They ate slowly, pausing as the sergeant broke the meat into pieces, adding to their feast.

Tentatively taking a small bite from his piece of meat using his good hand, Pickering chewed slowly, his face remaining impassive.

"Well, I've surely had worse in my time," Scully observed.

Pickering looked up from chewing, his eyes vacant. He nodded and took another small bite.

They took turns drinking from the skein, the odd taste becoming more bearable as they drank.

The guard joined them in the wagon bed, sitting at the open end, his musket lying crosswise. He called to the driver who snapped the reins and the team began to move.

Chapter Four

"Am I going to die?"

It was late in the afternoon when the three prisoners arrived at the outskirts of Sevastopol. Warren felt weak but was able to take in what he had heard was called the "Jewel of the Crimea." What he saw were dirty streets, buildings in need of repair and a dispirited population going about their business quietly. It was as if they had already surrendered to the invaders.

Pulling up to a low building, the guard jumped down and motioned for them to get out. Scully stepped down and turned to Warren.

"Here, give me your arm."

Sliding to the rear of the wagon, he let Scully help him to the ground, the pain in his leg making him wince.

"Shit."

"Come on, Mr. Pickering," Scully said.

His face white, with sweaty sheen, Pickering held his injured arm against his chest and made his way to the rear of the wagon.

Sergeant Scully carefully put his arms around the young man and lifted him to the ground.

"I... I..."

"Just take deep breaths, sir."

Pickering lurched forward and vomited, his body racked by the spasms.

Scully put his arm around the young man's shoulders and helped him stand back up.

Their Russian motioned toward a door on the side of the structure where a single soldier stood guard, his musket slung over his shoulder, bayonet fixed.

Scully put Warren's arm over his shoulder and, acting as a crutch, made his way to the door. Pickering, swaying slightly, followed them as if in a trance.

A quick exchange between the two Russians and the guard pulled open the door and motioned them inside.

The odor of sweat, dirt and dead animals greeted them.

The interior of the building, which must have been a warehouse at one time, had been sub-divided into holding areas using planks and wire. The only light came from several high windows on each end of the structure.

The new guard lowered his musket and motioned with the bayonet toward the back of the building. Walking down what was apparently an alley in the partitions, they saw only two other men, both lying with their backs toward the new prisoners. The Russian opened a door constructed of thin boards nailed on a frame of poles. The soldier said something they didn't understand and indicated they should go into the makeshift cell, which could be more accurately described as a cage. Dirty straw covered the floor, the smell reminding Scully of an improperly maintained horse barn.

Helping both of the officers to sit down with their backs to the wall, Scully returned to the door and saw it wasn't locked in any way. He slowly pushed it open and looked up and down the aisle. No one was visible. It was as if they had been abandoned. Apparently the entire building was considered the jail, the inside simply divided into living areas.

Looking back at his comrades the sergeant saw Warren looking at him.

"We've been in worse places, Michael."

"Indeed we have."

Pickering slumped against the wall next to Warren, his head lolling on his chest, thankfully unaware of his surroundings. Perhaps some rest would help them both, Scully thought. But he knew he was being foolish. Pickering would die if a doctor didn't remove that hand. He knew from his past that a wound like Warren's could easily go bad with death the inevitable result. Normally an optimistic man for an Irishman, Scully knew the future did not look good for them.

He knelt down to check on Warren and felt his forehead. The heat told Scully that his friend was getting worse.

"I've felt better," Warren said.

"On your feet."

Scully opened his eyes and saw several men outside their cage. One man wore plain black working man's clothes while the other three were in uniform.

He got to his feet and said, "They're injured."

The civilian said something to a man who had the look of an officer and certainly had the cleanest uniform in the group.

"And who might you be?"

Scully stared in curiosity at the civilian, who sounded like he had come from the east side of London.

68

"Sergeant Michael Scully of the 13th Light Dragoons. This is Lord Captain Richard Warren and Coronet James Pickering. Who the hell are you?"

"This is Major Hart. He will ask you questions. If you're smart, you'll tell him the truth."

"You never answered me. Who the hell are you?"

The man's eyes narrowed.

"It doesn't matter, just answer the man's questions."

"We need food, water and medical attention for these two officers."

"That will depend on you, Sergeant Scully," Hart said, in perfect English with an American accent.

Hart walked over to Pickering and lifted his face, staring down at the horrible wound.

"Dead man," Hart said to the young man, whose face was glistening with sweat in the poor light.

"And this must be the captain," he continued, eyeing Warren, who followed him with dull, pain filled eyes.

"Not good, certainly not good," Hart said, smiling at the Irishman, as if Warren was a horse ready to put down.

Scully knew they were out of options.

"Ask your questions."

The second time Scully answered "I don't know," one of the major's subordinates knocked him down with a vicious blow to the side of his head. Over the next thirty minutes, between questions, the Russians delivered what Scully would describe as a mighty working over, which left him bloody and bruised. It seemed that whatever he answered was not what Major Hart wanted or expected to hear.

Almost as if on a schedule, Major Hart and his two Russians turned and left Scully on the floor of the cage with the stranger.

Waiting until he heard the outer door open and close, the man turned to Scully.

"They're a nasty bunch, now aren't they?"

"I still don't know who you are," Scully said sitting up and raising a hand to his battered face.

"James William Kennedy, and likely your only friend in this pisshole."

Scully looked at the man, the face was not hostile, but there was no friendliness either.

"Why am I guessing that beating was not for my benefit?" He turned to Warren, realizing the captain had passed out.

"You're smarter than you look," Kennedy replied and grinned slightly.

"How do I get medical attention for these two officers?"

"I have some connections with a doctor from the west, perhaps I could entice him to look at your friends."

Now Scully realized what was happening.

"And what would it cost us for you to perform that valuable service, Mr. Kennedy?"

The man smiled broadly.

"Call me Jim, sergeant, everyone does."

Ignoring the attempt at friendliness, Scully said, "What will it cost?"

Kennedy sat down next to the Irishman.

"You mentioned that your captain was a lord. Might you be a little more specific?"

Scully paused to look at the man, who was grinning at him.

"Second son of the Duke of Southwick."

"You don't say. A wealthy man, the duke?"

"That's well known, a powerful man in the government as well."

Kennedy eyed Scully, his eyes narrowing as he thought.

"Now I'm a business man, Mister Scully. But everything doesn't come down to money, now does it? No, that's something I truly believe. I do you a favor and you do me one in the same."

"What the hell can I do for you?"

"Now that's something we can work out in good time, don't you think? In the meantime, let me see what I can do about having Doctor Thomassy look at your mates."

Suddenly Scully felt better.

"Doctor, Mr. Kennedy is waiting to see you."

Looking up from a medical text, the doctor was not surprised. He hadn't seen Kennedy for almost two weeks and like a bad penny, the man always turned up.

The doctor actually liked Kennedy. Not because he was English and could speak the tongue, although that was a great plus. But Mr. Kennedy could get things which other people could not. The doctor's understanding was that in the ten years the man had been in Sevastopol, he had run a lucrative black market business in everything from jewelry, to sheep to guns.

In the Crimea to escape the long arm of British law, Kennedy had developed a network that included policemen and civil servants. It was rumored that he and the head of the civil police were actually partners. When Louis needed medical supplies, Kennedy was able to provide them.

"Have him come in," he told his assistant as he closed the book and sat back in his chair.

"And what brings you to see me so early in the day, Mr. Kennedy?"

Having removed his floppy hat, Kennedy offered a slight bow of his head.

"Trying to do my best in a hard world."

"I'm sure your efforts will be rewarded in the hereafter. Please sit down."

"Thank you, doctor."

Louis fixed his eyes on Kennedy for a moment then said, "Now let's be direct, shall we. Do you have material I would be interested in purchasing?"

"Indeed, no. This visit is more in the area of human kindness."

Fighting back a chuckle, Louis smiled.

"Now you have my utmost attention. This could be a whole new chapter in your life, I'm thinking."

"Doctor, you jest with me. Surely being a man of business doesn't keep me from caring about my fellow man."

"Of course not, I am sorry for making any insinuation to the contrary. Now what can I do for you to help our fellow man?"

Kennedy said, "I was with Major Hart when he questioned some prisoners recently captured north of here."

"And?"

"Two of the men are badly injured. And they know you."

"What?"

"Three British cavalrymen, a sergeant named Scully, and two officers, one of them is a Captain Warren."

Warren felt a cool cloth on his brow, bringing him out of a restless sleep. He opened his eyes slowly and saw a woman leaning over him.

"We will be moving you very shortly, captain."

He knew her voice but couldn't seem to place it.

She turned away and he heard her say, "He has a fever."

Louis was busy with Pickering, examining the boy's hand under the light of a kerosene lamp.

"Sergeant Scully, there is a medical wagon outside. Please help me move him. We'll come back for the captain."

Louis had encountered little difficulty with the military when requesting that he be allowed to move two English prisoners to Hospital Number Six, where he saw many of his patients. Still officially attached to the army staff, he had not totally understood the reorganization of the forces following the retreat from Alma. However a short visit with the army's chief of staff, General Tamaroff, produced several official passes, which allowed transportation for the two officers and their servant for treatment.

Once Pickering was settled in the wagon, the two men returned to the holding cell. Kimberly knelt next to Warren but moved out of the way as the two men reached down to help him sit up.

"Hello, captain," Louis said. "We meet again. This time it is my chance to help you. All right, sergeant, under each arm and we'll stand him up."

Warren grunted as they helped him to his feet, steadying him for a moment.

"Pickering... How is Pickering?" he asked through clenched teeth.

"A severe injury, captain. But I'm confident he will survive with proper treatment. Now let us help you to the ambulance."

Military Hospital Number Six consisted of two wooden buildings facing Kurchatova Street. Injured soldiers from the two major battles and skirmishes around the defensive works of Sevastopol had combined to stretch the capacity of the city's two civilian hospitals. The army had commandeered a number of buildings to serve as overflow.

Louis entered the ward, which consisted of twenty beds lining the bare whitewashed walls. The Englishmen were in the last two beds on the right side. Scully, still showing the effects of his beating by the Russians, sat in a chair between the two injured officers.

Only two hours since they had arrived at the hospital, Louis was ready to operate on Pickering. After a more thorough exam, he had realized that the only option was amputation. Such a young man, he thought. In his experience, some men were able to get on with their lives after losing a limb. Others died from lack of a will to live a life as a cripple, or they turned to drink and simply took longer to die. How would this young man deal with losing his hand? It made no difference, he thought, if the mangled hand did not come off, Pickering would die.

He motioned to Scully and took the seat next to the bed.

"James," he said, using Pickering's first name, which he had learned from the sergeant.

Pickering opened his eyes and turned his head slightly.

"I wish it wasn't the case, but I have examined your hand and it simply cannot be saved."

The young man closed his eyes for a long moment then turned to the doctor and opened them.

"Am I going to die?"

Louis saw the look in Pickering's eyes. Over the years he had learned that fear came in all shapes and forms. Here was a young man who had likely charged into battle hiding his fear from others, even himself. But now there was no way for him to conceal it. In Mexico, Louis had learned to be honest with his patients and it seemed only right that a man should know the truth.

"Your wound is very serious. However with surgery and proper care I believe you will live."

Pickering looked at the ceiling, the pattern blurring as tears welled up in his eyes. He remembered seeing old soldiers, crippled in the wars, begging on the streets of London. Now that might be him.

Warren had listened to the exchange between the doctor and Pickering. Despite the fever and pain in his leg, the terrible finality made him sick. His thoughts returned to that day and the charge. How many men dead or maimed for life? Killed or wounded by the stupidity of generals who should be back in England sitting by their fireplaces. But the system supported promotion of incompetents and fools, and it was the men in ranks who paid the price. The newspapers would tell absurd tales of valor and the aristocracy would debate military tactics while soldiers lived and died in brutal battles that no one would ever understand.

"I brought you some water, captain."

Warren looked up to see Kimberly holding a cup.

"Thank you."

She helped him take a drink, then put the metal cup on the little table next to the bed.

"I must dress your wound," she said, pulling the blanket down.

He felt self-conscious as she leaned down to carefully examine the wound.

After a minute of careful probing, she placed a pad of cloth over the bullet hole and secured it in place with a long bandage.

He looked at her as she pulled the blanket up to his chest.

"How is it?"

"I am concerned the bullet carried part of your uniform into the wound."

Warren knew what that meant. He had seen minor bullet wounds result in amputations.

Kimberly felt his head.

"Your fever remains. I will bring some cool towels."

He looked at her while she straightened his bedclothes. She wore her hair very different from the women in England, where the bun on the back or top of the head was vogue. Instead, her dark auburn hair framed her face, a large pin fastening a small white nurse's cap. He realized she was a strikingly good-looking woman who seemed out of place in a ward of sick and injured soldiers.

"How long have you been a nurse?"

"Many years, if you are worried about my abilities."

"No, of course not. It's just that you seem so different from what I'm used to."

She looked at him with curiosity and smiled slightly.

"Captain, how, pray tell, do English nurses differ from Austrian nurses?"

Warren winced as a severe pain shot through his gut.

"I'll bring you laudanum."

The pain had taken his breath away and he nodded.

"Can you do anything to save that boy's hand?"

Louis stood in an alcove next to the ward, smoking a cigarette.

He shook his head.

"His future will hold gangrene most likely and death. The best case would be a disfigured claw that was useless for the rest of his life. No, the best course is to remove the damage and let the healing begin."

Kimberly wasn't surprised, but still the loss of a limb was always a horrible thing.

"Captain Warren's fever is no better and the pain is severe. I will dose him with laudanum."

The doctor exhaled. "I'm afraid that is all we can do. Perhaps you should double the dose."

She looked at her husband, understanding what he was saying.

"There is nothing you can do?"

"He's lucky to still be alive. You know that amputation is not an option and trying to open up near that wound would likely kill him even quicker. It was just his bad luck to be shot in the dead zone."

Kimberly knew surgeries in that area were quite rare. The anatomy proved too difficult and the results were almost always fatal. Why couldn't they do more?

Scully wiped Warren's brow, the fever no better. At least he was with him and not locked away in the warehouse. He had been surprised when the Kennedy chap had told him to act like a servant and stick close. It was understood by the Russian guards that the Englishmen's servant would remain within the hospital. If he were found outside, he would be shot.

He watched the doctor walk down the aisle, followed by two men carrying a stretcher.

"Sergeant, we'll be taking Mr. Pickering for surgery. I'll need your assistance."

Scully had been a soldier long enough to have seen field operations and knew what was going to happen. Perhaps he could ease the young lad's trial by being there.

"Of course, doctor."

"I'll be back in one hour," he said, handing Scully a brown bottle and spoon.

"One spoonful every fifteen minutes," Louis said as he walked away.

"Aye, sir."

Scully turned to Pickering, who had his eyes closed.

"Mr. Pickering. I have some medicine for you."

The young man opened his eyes.

"I was listening, sergeant. This will put me out?"

"Maybe not completely out, but it will make it easier. And I'll be with you."

Pickering nodded and took the offered spoonful of liquid.

Scully had walked beside the stretcher on the way to the surgery. Not entirely sure what to expect, he found a room with a large raised table in the center, surrounded by cabinets against the walls. The room was white and freshly painted. Dark green paint covered the wooden floor, which appeared to be surprisingly clean. A smell similar to oil of clove hung in the air.

The two stretcher bearers carefully hoisted the litter up to the table and gingerly put it in place. Then they began securing Pickering's legs and good arm with leather straps.

"Sergeant?" Pickering's words were slurred but understandable.

"Right here."

Scully moved to his side, after the attendants finished their work. Standing on the right side of the table, he looked down at Pickering who was sweating, despite the cool temperature in the surgery.

Louis came into the room, followed by Kimberly. The doctor wore a long apron, tied behind him. His arms were bare, sleeves rolled up to his elbow.

"Did he take all the medicine?" he asked Scully.

"Aye, sir."

"Wasn't sick or vomiting?"

"No, sir, just sweating."

Kimberly carried a tray covered with a cloth over from one of the cabinets and placed it on the table next to her husband.

"For him to bite on," Louis said, handing Scully a piece of thick leather that had apparently been used for that purpose before. "I want you to keep his head steady, understand?"

Scully nodded, his attention drawn to the small instrument the doctor had selected from the tray.

"We will begin," he said. "Sergeant."

Scully responded by placing the leather strap in Pickering's mouth.

"Here, laddie, bite down on this."

The doctor fastened a leather strap above the wound and cinched it tight. He then tightened the larger strap holding Pickering's left arm.

Louis's cuts with the scalpel were swift and direct. Quickly the skin was cut below the strap, blood oozing on the table where Kimberly mopped it up with a small towel. In less than a minute, he set the scalpel down and picked up a small bone saw, which he began using in short rapid strokes.

"There," he said as the damaged hand was severed from Pickering's arm which the doctor then placed in a bucket at his feet.

He quickly began to work on the stump, using thread and a hot iron to stop all sources of blood loss. Finally he used a needle and thread to attach the flap of skin he had created over the end of the wound.

"Done and done," he said, leaning over the young man and saying, "It went very well, James. Let me take that out of your mouth."

Scully watched the boy's body go limp, the tension and pain finally getting the best of him.

"He's lost consciousness," Louis said. "Quite normal, actually. I'm surprised he lasted this long."

"He'll be all right?" Scully asked.

Louis shrugged.

"You never know about these things, but all things being equal he should recover. Now, let's get him back in bed to rest."

What Louis did not tell the sergeant was that one in four men with simple amputations die from post-operative complications.

"How is he?" Warren asked.

"The doctor said it went well. It's in God's hands now. They'll keep him in the surgical ward for observation, but I can see him at any time." Scully replied. He didn't like how Warren looked, his face pale and drenched in sweat. "How do you feel?"

"I've certainly been better, my friend."

Scully knew Warren was going downhill and experience told him it could get bad very quickly.

"If you could get me some herbs, I know I might be able to help him."

Louis saw the concern in the sergeant's eyes.

"What are you thinking?"

"Something to draw out the poison."

Kimberly said, "I'll help you, sergeant. I believe there is something that might help your captain."

Louis shook his head, but said, "It can't hurt, do what you can."

"Elderberry leaves?" Kennedy asked.

"You know what they are?"

"Of course I do, just not sure where to get them around here. The garlic is no problem, the Russians love their garlic. Let me see what I can do."

"This is important, I need them right now."

"Can you pay?"

"I will pay for them," Kimberly said. "How much?"

"One hundred Kopecs, at least."

Kennedy looked at her and nodded.

"I never could say no to a beautiful woman."

She smiled.

"I'll have to remember that," she said and squeezed his hand.

"I'll be back in an hour."

Kimberly worked the pestle hard, smashing and blending the elderberry leaves with gloves of garlic.

"My father taught me this poultice when I was growing up in Austria. I'll make a paste of the elderberry and the garlic. A little honey to bind it, then I'll fill the captain's wound and seal it with honey. Each day we clean the honey off with a mixture of vinegar and water then reapply."

She reached for a small jar of honey, dripping a small amount into the mortar and continuing to mix.

Scully knew the healing properties of many herbs and plants. This combination was new to him, but he trusted Kimberly.

Warren's fever broke two days later.

The next day, Major Hart arrived at the hospital.

The American looked impressive in his Russian uniform. Behind him walked a small man, wearing a plain suit of civilian clothes.

Scully stood up as the men approached the bed.

The major stopped at the foot of Warren's bed and surveyed the surrounding area.

"You should not be here, Englishman. This hospital is for Russian soldiers."

Warren listened to the words, but said nothing. Some way he would kill that man for what he had done to Trooper Smith.

Hart continued, "The doctor may have fooled Tamaroff, but I know what he's about. I will ensure he never crosses me again. And I'll be waiting for you when you return to the stockade, your lordship."

The sarcasm in the man's voice was evident and Warren knew he was dangerous. What the hell is wrong with this man, he wondered. Does he hate all Englishmen or just the upper class?

Hart turned to Pickering's bed.

"Took the hand off, eh? Well, it was a waste of time in any case. You have an appointment with me, Pickering. And if Captain Warren insists on not talking, missing a hand will be the least of your problems." Hart smiled.

The young officer said nothing, but the hate and anger in his eyes told a story of its own.

The major turned back to Warren.

"Looks like the best that England can send at us, just won't measure up."

Hart had seen Warren's type before. Rich, powerful, the people who had kept him down his entire life. Money and power, something Hart craved more than life itself and two things that had always eluded him. He would not leave Russia penniless. There were always profits to be made in war and he would not let this opportunity pass him by.

Kimberly carefully wiped Warren's wound with a pad smelling of vinegar.

All sense of modesty gone, Warren watched the young woman as she reapplied a clean dressing.

"I am very grateful for what you have done, Miss Scharff. Or is it Mrs. Scharff?"

She looked up quickly, her eyes momentarily showing irritation, then she relaxed and went back to the new bandage.

"Once we leave Russia, I will once more become Mrs. Thomassy. I had to use my maiden name because of the Russian authorities. It is silly politics as Louis would say. Please call me Kimberly, which will not change."

"Where did you learn medicine?"

"In Vienna, at a school for nurses. But your poultice was taught to me by my father. On our farm. He used it to save a horse that had been shot by accident."

"A horse?"

"It was a very valuable horse."

"Then I consider myself fortunate indeed."

She frowned at him.

"You are making fun of me," she said, her voice indignant. "You must be feeling better."

Kimberly straightened out the bed sheet.

"Louis and I will never forget how you helped us," she said, now serious.

Warren saw the sincerity in her eyes.

"Now we have helped each other," she said. "And thank goodness Mr. Kennedy was able to find elderberry leaves."

"What?"

"He obtains things for us that no one else can. How he does it I don't know and it's probably better I don't. It is said that he can do anything, for the right price."

Warren opened his eyes as he heard someone approach. Louis stood at the foot of the bed.

"By all reports you are well on the road to recovery, captain."

"I actually feel almost human and it's been some time since I was able to say that."

Louis reached down and felt Warren's forehead, then checked his eyes.

"Let's take a look at your wound."

For the next five minutes, the doctor said nothing as he carefully removed the bandage and examined the wound.

"Your verdict?" Warren finally asked

"Good; very good, in fact. I shall have to apologize to my wife. My experience has been that wounds such as yours invariably result in death. She refused to listen to me. I guess the mindset of battlefield treatment took precedent, never waste time when survival is questionable."

Warren could tell the doctor was not embarrassed by his failure to treat him, but was simply being honest.

"We owe a great deal to both you and your wife, doctor."

"Please call me Louis. And if you had not helped up at Alma, neither one of us would likely have been here to help you."

"Thank you, Louis, and I would ask you to call me Richard."

"Certainly."

"How is Pickering doing? Sergeant Scully told me that he has been withdrawn."

"That's not unusual, I've seen it many times. And he is captive in a foreign city. That's an awful lot for a young man to deal with."

"Is there anything I can do to help?"

"The orderlies will be bringing him back in here today. I think that will help him as much as anything. I would also tell you that your Sergeant Scully has quite the good effect when he's around Mister Pickering."

Suddenly the doctor sat down in the chair next to the bed, his face laced with alarm.

"Are you all right?"

Louis wiped his face, shaking his head slightly.

I... I just lost my balance, it's nothing."

Only now did Warren see the fatigue on Louis's face. He had seen that look before and it was always when men were approaching the breaking point.

"Louis, do you know a major named Hart?"

Louis looked surprised.

"He is rumored to work for the army's intelligence service."

"The bastard shot one of my men."

The doctor did not seem surprised.

"He came to see me also. Apparently he has decided I am disloyal to the Czar and working for the British. I think the man is deranged, but there is nothing I can do. Unfortunately he is very dangerous."

"And you and your wife are trapped here by the allied forces."

Louis nodded.

"I don't know what I'm going to do. I must get her out of Sevastopol."

Warren saw a look of total helplessness on the doctor's face.

Chapter Five

"Am I going to die?"

Returning to the warehouse three weeks later, the three men found the smells just as repellant and more British prisoners in the holding cages.

Pickering moved like an old man, his left arm in a sling, his back bent as if protecting the injured limb. Warren walked with a crutch, but with a strong step, his strength clearly returning.

Assured by Louis that the American would look in on them, they had been escorted by several soldiers back to the makeshift prison. The Russians seemed friendly and carried on a spirited conversation between themselves during the twenty minute journey. But on the prisoner's minds was the uncomfortable reality that they were again at the mercy of Hart.

Warren knew that by now, any actual information he had possessed would be out of date and worthless. Perhaps Hart would realize the same thing. He could only hope so.

The town had seemed little changed to Scully, although were fewer civilians on the streets and more soldiers.

Extra guards were also in evidence at the building when they arrived. All appeared to be young and not battle tested. Recent conscripts, perhaps.

"Here we are, then," Scully said as they were escorted back to their original cage. "Just like we left it."

Warren sniffed and said, "Perhaps more lice, if you ask me."

"Here, Mr. Pickering, let me help you," Scully said, assisting the young man down to sit on the floor, his back against the wall.

Very quiet and withdrawn since his surgery, Pickering would speak when spoken to, but had yet to initiate a conversation. Scully had seen it before. Every man is different and how they recover from a severe wound was always hard to tell. Just give him time, Scully thought.

Next the sergeant took Warren's crutch and lowered his friend to the ground next to Pickering.

Scully knelt in front of the two men.

"You're both now on the mend, we need to think about making our way back to the regiment."

Warren nodded, "My thoughts also, Michael. What say you, James, ready to have a go at getting out of this place?"

"Yes, sir," came the quiet response.

Turning to look at Pickering, Warren sensed a determination coming from him. He squeezed Pickering's good shoulder.

"Good man. Now, we need a plan."

Scully remembered a conversation with Jim Kennedy a week prior. The man had brought them some good black bread with butter. The appearance of bread and butter took the three by surprise. Rationing had been instituted by the military authorities, and shortages were now common in the town.

"Simply have to know who to talk to and what to say." Kennedy had grinned at Scully. "There are always options, my Irish friend and don't you forget it."

Scully turned to his comrades and quietly said, "Kennedy."

Kennedy appeared late in the day, carrying a small package.

"Thought you could do with this," he said.

Scully took the package from him, smelling the same black bread they had enjoyed in the hospital. Looking around, the sergeant motioned Kennedy inside their enclosure.

Pickering remained asleep on the far wall, but Warren rose.

"He brought us something."

Kennedy looked at Warren, his eyes wary.

"Are you feeling better?" he asked.

Warren nodded.

"Much better, Mr. Kennedy."

"Call me Jim. More comfortable that way."

Warren said, "Very well, Jim. What will it take for you to get us out of here?"

Kennedy's face showed mild surprise, but he said nothing.

Continuing, Warren added, "I am prepared to make it very attractive for you."

Saying nothing, Scully moved over to the door and scanned for any listeners.

"The truth is I've learned how to get along with these Russians. But if I were caught trying to help you, they'd shoot me in an instant. Why should I chance that?"

89

Warren sensed that Kennedy had a price, the only question was how high?

"For money, I would assume."

Kennedy's reaction surprised Warren.

"Captain, I'm well off here and my businesses will keep me that way. Risking that makes no sense."

"If you assume the Russians will hold out, perhaps. But war is a very unpredictable thing, Mr. Kennedy. You could be killed in the battle for the city, turned on by the Russians or hung by the British for being a traitor. Are you willing to take those chances?

Kennedy rubbed his bristly.

"Just what are you thinking, captain?"

Warren knew the hook had been sunk.

"According to Doctor Thomassy, you were in quite a bit of trouble with the law in Britain"

Kennedy nodded.

"A run in with the Revenue Service on the south coast about ten years ago. I had spent most of my life at sea, rising to second mate on a large clipper out of Portsmouth. But the owner went bankrupt, so I hooked up with some nasty smugglers near Bournemouth. We had a run in with the Revenue Service and two of their revenue men were killed. I didn't do it, but I was with them. Not wanting a trip to Execution Dock, I sailed south and finally ended up here."

"So you're under sentence of death by an Admiralty court?"

"I never stuck around to be sure."

"What were you smuggling," Warren asked.

Kennedy grinned. "The best French brandy you ever tasted."

"Five hundred pounds to get the three of us out of here. And I will do my best to secure you a pardon."

The look in Kennedy's eyes told Warren he had hit a nerve.

"I won't say yes, but I won't say no either." Kennedy said as he moved to the doorway. "You said a pardon?"

"Mr. Kenn... Jim, my father sits in the House of Lords. The Prime Minister is one of his closest associates. These things are done all the time."

The truth be known, Kennedy had begun to feel the Russians were tiring of his business. He knew the bastards could turn on him in a minute and he had come to like Scully and his companions. This might be the answer to his problem.

"I'll be back later."

"Don't take too long, I'm sure Hart is going to discover we're back here." Warren feared that more than anything else.

"Where in God's name did you get this?" Scully asked as he and Kennedy helped the other two men into the covered back of a horse drawn ambulance. Behind them, the night guards lay in a heap, victims of good liquor, laced with a potent sedative.

"At the hospital, of course. These things are moving around the city and if we get stopped, we're just carrying two wounded men to the ward."

They climbed onto the front seat of the wagon and Kennedy flicked the reins, prompting the swaybacked mare into movement.

"My boat's about a mile away. This time of night most of the sentries are drunk or bedded down with the local whores."

Briefed on the escape plan, neither Warren nor Scully could fault using a boat to leave the city. According to Kennedy, the Russians didn't conduct regular patrols with the few ships that were left in Sevastopol. And his smuggling trade had made *Kestrel* a regular sight in and around the harbor. With the land approaches to the city completely encircled by Russian positions, the chances of slipping through to the British lines were slim. Warren hoped they would encounter one of the British warships patrolling the waters outside the harbor. If not, they could reach the small port of Balaclava, which was twenty miles farther south on the peninsula. Kennedy had seemed confident that once they were past the guns protecting the harbor, their escape was certain. Now they would test his theory.

As the wagon moved slowly toward the waterfront, Scully leaned back into the wagon.

"All right?" he asked Warren.

"Damned cold."

"Kennedy said this wind will help us clear the harbor."

"I hope he's right," Warren replied.

A brisk wind whistled through the standing rigging as Kennedy brought the ambulance to a halt and jumped down to the ground. Across the pier, the fifty-foot sloop, *Kestrel* bumped against the canvas fenders that stood between her hull and the wooden quay. Across the dark harbor, under scudding clouds, the lights of Fort Constantine reflected off the rippled water.

"Let's be quick about it," Kennedy said.

The Englishman called to the boat as he opened the rear flap of the wagon.

"Nick!"

Scully helped Warren down from the wagon.

A figure came across the pier in the darkness.

"Help us get them aboard and get ready to cast off."

The man took Warren by the arm.

"I am Nick, first mate. Hurry."

"Mr. Pickering," Scully said.

Gingerly, Pickering leaned down and put his good hand on the wooden wagon bed. Kennedy and Scully carefully helped him down to the ground.

The three men made their way aboard the sloop.

"Sergeant, I'll need your help up here. Pickering, make your way below. It's not very comfortable, but you'll be out of the wind."

"I can help," Pickering snapped back.

"Still a bit of fight left, eh?" Kennedy laughed. "You'll just be in the way, now do what you're told. Scully, here, take this line. When I tell you, haul away. Nick will help after he casts us off."

The silent man moved quickly to the bow.

"Cast off forward, and raise the jib," Kennedy called as he knelt down and released the after mooring line.

Scully felt the motion as the sloop's bow was pulled off the pier. Behind him, Kennedy spun the wheel hard and called, "Now haul away you bloody Irishman! Haul!"

Squeals from the line moving through the large wooden blocks gave proof that the large mainsail was now rising from the horizontal boom and beginning to catch the wind.

Scully was a strong man, but now he found himself struggling to pull the manila line. His arms ached as he pulled hard, hand over hand.

Then from behind him, Nick picked up the line and with the two of them working hard, the mainsail slowly reached the top of the mainmast.

"Christ," Scully said as the man grabbed the line and made it fast to the bit.

Looking forward he saw the lights moving past the bow. They were on their way.

"Warren? Captain Warren, you say?"

Lieutenant Colonel Charles Doherty looked askance at the young corporal who stood at attention after having reported.

"Yes, sir. Major Fleharty wanted you to know the captain arrived this morning in Balaclava on a fishing boat. Mr. Pickering and Sergeant Scully were also on the boat. They escaped from the Russians."

"A fishing boat? Escaped from the Russians? By God that'll be a story for the mess."

"Sir, is there any message in reply?"

Doherty had intended to ride into the port the next day, but this was a good reason to make the journey today.

"Please tell Captain Warren that I am most pleased he has escaped and will be down to the harbor shortly." Such good news, Doherty thought, and now I'll have to break the bad news of his brother's death. The Lord giveth and the Lord taketh away.

Warren drank the hot coffee, which was liberally laced with brandy.

"I've sent word to your regiment, captain." Fleharty poured himself a cup and sat down opposite Warren at the mess table. "This is quite the news. I'm sure Lord Raglan will want to see you as soon as the news of your return reaches him."

I don't think he would like to hear what I have to say, Warren thought.

"My immediate concern is that Mr. Pickering is seen by the surgeon. There is also the matter of the man who brought us out."

Fleharty worked for the Quartermaster General who controlled the docks and warehouses at Balaclava and also the army's pay.

"What is the issue?"

God damn I hate these officious bastards, Warren thought.

"I told him I would pay him five hundred pounds to get the three of us out of the city."

Fleharty's expression told Warren that the major felt the amount promised was extraordinarily high.

"Captain, that is a great deal of money." Fleharty leaned over his desk as if he was trying to emphasis his point.

Warren felt an urge to slap the man, but instead asked, "Major, have you ever been a prisoner?"

"Why, no, of course not."

The major looked uncomfortable as Warren got up and looked at him across the desk, the anger evident in his eyes.

"Have you ever been wounded?"

"Now what are you implying, sir?"

Putting his hand on the desk and leaning forward, Warren said, "That you can't make that determination... Sir."

Warren stepped on the deck of the *Kestrel* to see Scully sitting on a box, with a bottle and glass in front of him.

"Louis did a tidy job according to the surgeon who examined Mr. Pickering. Would you like a taste?"

"Where is our young coronet?"

"I tried to stop them, but the doctor ordered him into the sick area."

There was no worse place for a man to recover than in the pestilence perpetuated by the army's medical department. If Pickering was to ever see England he must be removed from the brutal care of the surgeons, to say nothing of the medical orderlies, most of which profited from the wounded in one way or another. Despite his relief at being back with his own army, the continuing ineptitude of the people who were supposed to be supporting that army made Warren furious.

Kennedy emerged from the lower cabin, pulling his heavy wool coat tight in against the cold breeze coming off the inlet.

Warren had actually found Kennedy to be a good companion on the trip from Sevastopol. He and his mate, Nick Nicodemis were an odd pairing, but under their care, *Kestrel* was quite the efficient little ship. Nicodemis was a swarthy Greek, who had spent his entire life at sea. His curly black hair and beard make him look like a bloody pirate Warren thought, but his humor kept them all entertained.

"Bloody damned cold around here come winter, I'll tell you that," Kennedy commented, rubbing his hands together. "Makes England look like an island in the South Seas."

"A bit of warmth?" Scully asked, holding up the bottle.

Kennedy smiled.

"For an Irishman, you're a cut above, sergeant."

"I owe you five hundred pounds," Warren said as Kennedy took a metal cup from Scully.

"Aye, I've not forgot the amount."

"I would like to make a further arrangement with you."

"By God, good to see you, Warren!"

Doherty stood next to the cot where Pickering lay, covered with a dirty blanket.

Warren made a semblance of a salute and moved to the edge of the cot.

"I'm glad you're here, colonel. I am taking Mr. Pickering out of here."

Doherty looked confused.

"But, he just got here."

"That may be, but he will recover much more efficiently aboard my boat."

"Your boat?" The colonel asked, clearly confused.

"Indeed, sir. Moored pier side in the harbor. Her name is *Kestrel*. I also must know what happened to my troopers during that bloody charge."

Doherty had desperately hoped that Warren wouldn't want to discuss the charge. There was so little anyone could say.

"Certainly, Richard. I will have the adjutant show you the report." Doherty paused. "I'm afraid we lost many good men that day."

"Colonel, what in God's name happened? Were the generals out of their minds?"

"Now, don't jump to conclusions, sir. There were many issues that day."

Warren watched his colonel, knowing that Doherty was part and parcel of what was wrong with the army. Stupid men who didn't have the backbone to stand up for what was right.

"I feel I must let my father know what happened here. Someone must be held accountable."

"I see..." Doherty said, as if he was trying to understand what Warren had just said. He quickly changed his tone. "Warren, I must talk with you privately, rather bad news, I'm afraid."

Warren still found it difficult to believe that Stephen was dead. The message from his father had said only that a fever had taken his brother. Ten years older than Richard, the two had always been good friends, not bickering siblings. While his friends had always commiserated that Warren would be getting the short shrift from his father's estate, to say nothing of inheriting the title, Richard had never really cared. His brother was suited to the great responsibility of the title and the family wealth. A career in the army truly did suit the younger Warren and he had been content. Now that had all changed.

"I've been looking for you."
Warren looked up to see Scully.
"Hello, Michael."
The Irishman looked down at his friend curiously.
"Something's wrong."
Nodding, Warren told Scully the news.

Modest by most standards, the quarters of the British commanding general were a cut above what the rest of the army endured in their tents. The one story masonry building sat just north of the inlet and was surrounded by tents of the army staff. That Raglan wanted to see Warren had been communicated by one of the several aides and now he waited to be ushered into general's office. A uniform had been retrieved from the regiment's baggage train and after a cold bath and shave, he at least felt presentable. He had replaced the crutch he had been using with a walking cane, which Scully had procured earlier in the day. The pain was less each day but walking was still a task.

"You may go in, sir."
Lord Raglan stood as Warren entered the room, motioning to a chair at the side of the desk.
"Captain, please be comfortable."

Warren considered the general and wondered how a man who looked so unwell and old could possibly run the army. The general's face was drawn and pallid. Pinned to the breast of his plain blue coat, an empty right sleeve.

"Yes, sir."

"First, allow me to offer my congratulations on your remarkable escape from the Russians." Raglan's voice was raspy.

"We were very fortunate, my lord," Warren replied.

"And your wound?"

"Healing, sir."

Raglan nodded and looked out the window.

"That was a difficult day," the general said, still looking away.

Warren had been told of the apparent miscommunication of orders, now hotly contested by all participants, which had sent the brigade into the valley. He had intended to confront the general, knowing he was risking his future in the army, but now he knew it would serve no purpose.

"Lord Raglan, I would like your permission to return to England to convalesce."

The general turned back to Warren.

"You served in India," Raglan replied quickly, seeming to have not heard the question.

"I did, sir."

Raglan paused for a moment, distracted, then said, "My son died in India."

Warren did not reply, not sure where the general was going with the conversation.

"Damned Sikhs, he died on Christmas day in '45."

"India was a damnable place, sir."

"You were there?"

"I was, sir."

Raglan seemed to return to the moment.

"By all means, captain, return to England. We shall do little here until the guns arrive."

"Marseille!"

"Can you make the trip to Marseille?"

Warren stood on the foredeck of *Kestrel* as the cold January wind whipped down the inlet.

"Of course I can," Kennedy replied. "I'll need at least two more crewmen to be safe."

"That won't be a problem, you can teach Scully and I everything we need to know."

"You two are soldiers, I need real sailors. And what happens after we get to France?"

"I'll go overland to a channel port, then to England. You may wait in Marseille to see if my efforts on your behalf are successful or you may simply sail away, with cash in hand."

"How can you get money in Marseille?"

"Bank of England. Once in France it won't be a problem."

Always skeptical, Kennedy believed Warren. It was a long voyage from the Crimea to France. But he had been at sea his entire life and *Kestrel* was a sturdy little ship. Although winter storms in the Mediterranean could be deadly, there were plenty of ports along the way.

"Winter weather means we take our time, anchor if needed."

Warren nodded. "Agreed. How do we get supplies?"

Smiling, Kennedy said, "We sail to Constantinople."

"What does that mean?"

"We're well provisioned for a short trip, and it's no more than four days to Turkey. Once there, we get whatever we need."

Warren found Pickering sitting at the small table, which dominated the narrow cabin amidships. A book sat unopened on the wooden table, the young man staring across the cabin, lost in thought.

"How are you settling in?"

Pickering started, turning on Warren.

"Sir. I, I mean it's quite nice. Sergeant Scully has just gone off to check on the state of the army, as he said."

That's my man, Warren thought, stealing the harbor blind. And well he should.

Sitting down across from Pickering, he sat back against the wooden bulkhead and looked at his charge. That the coronet was still with them defied the odds. Amputations often went bad, even in the best of circumstances. Pickering had lost his hand after a terrible wound in battle and then been captured. But that confirmed for Warren that the young man was a fighter.

"I've decided we all need an ocean voyage."

"Sir?"

"We shall return to England. There we will enjoy the comforts that only a civilized society can provide. Not to mention the benefit of the most modern medical care."

He saw Pickering's eyes glance down, his features sober.

"Whatever you say, sir." He paused then said quietly, "I know my army career is over."

How do I help this boy, he asked himself?

"James, it's only over if you aren't willing to fight for it."

The young officer looked up, his expression one of surprise.

"I can stay in the army?"

Making a bold statement, Warren knew he had to give James some hope.

"Why not? Lord Raglan is missing most of his arm. You just lost your hand. And it wasn't your sword hand in any case." Now Warren was starting to warm to the idea. "I won't tell you it will be easy. But if we go about it the right way, and use some small amount of influence, I think we have a chance."

Pickering listened as Warren described a battle that the captain was going to help him fight, getting an apparatus for his missing left hand, making the case to headquarters and enlisting the Duke's political allies. His spirits leaped from what had become a dark valley of despair about his future.

"You really think so?"

"I do. But we need to get you to England. That will be crucial."

"I told him I needed you to assist myself and Pickering medically during the journey. The colonel couldn't very well object, now could he?"

Scully stood with his legs braced against the rolling of the sloop, which was now under full mainsail, jib and mizzen and tacking north against a northwesterly wind. *Kestrel* had cleared the inlet at first light and now at mid-day, everyone appeared to be settling in well. Two new crewmembers had joined Kennedy and Nicodemis, an Englishman from Cornwall by the name of Engler and Castansos, a Spaniard. Both men had joined from a merchant ship moored at the dock unloading stores for the army.

"Truth be known, I was beginning to tire of the place."

"How is Pickering this morning?"

"Seems well enough," Scully said and staggered slightly as the ship took a steeper roll. "Sweet Jesus, I'm never going to make a sailor."

Warren laughed.

The green of the Turkish landscape appeared on the afternoon of the fourth day. Kennedy had navigated *Kestrel* successfully across the Black Sea, making landfall just north of the Straits of Turkey, which separated Asia from Europe and was their access to the Sea of Mara and thence the Mediterranean. Weather had been moderate with the occasional high winds, but no rain or snow. The only dark cloud had been Pickering. He developed a fever on the second night and remained bedridden in one of the small cabins off the main cabin.

During the voyage from England to the Crimea, the brigade had passed through the Strait on the way to Varna, Bulgaria, but Constantinople had been seen only from ship. Now after an uneventful passage past the medieval forts and minarets of the city, they found themselves in the large bay on the western end of the Strait on the Asian side.

Kennedy had found a small pier that was able to accommodate *Kestrel* and in a short time the ship was securely moored at the eastern end of the waterfront. The variety of ships and boats in the harbor never failed to impress even an experienced sailor like Kennedy. Directly behind them a Dutch barquentine waited to on load its next cargo and return to sea. A French frigate tugged at her anchor, the crew busy in the rigging.

A crossroads in this part of the world, a man could likely find anything he desired in the narrow streets of Constantinople. Kennedy would accompany Warren ashore to begin arranging for supplies while Scully was on a search for medicine.

"How long from here to Marseille?" Warren asked.

The waterfront was busy despite the cool weather. Travelers making their way to or from their vessels seemed in a hurry, baggage following them generally carried by porters or in small carts. Where were they bound, Warren wondered?

Without breaking pace, Kennedy answered, "Need to plan on a month. Could be quicker, but likely not longer. *Kestrel's* a good little ship and I've sailed the Mediterranean many times. For supplies, we'll find Abboud, he can arrange everything."

"You know the man?"

Kennedy laughed.

"You might say we've done business before. He's a trader from Lebanon. I wouldn't trust him with my life, but he'll deliver what we ask for, with no questions."

The three men turned down a street off the main road running parallel to the water.

"And you're sure this fellow can get us medicine?" Scully asked.

"For the right price he'll get you seventy virgins dancing with bells on."

Scully considered that as they weaved their way past the people in the crowded street.

"I'll not be needing any virgins, but good Irish whiskey would set me fine."

The two-story masonry building had no sign on the outside, but an open double door gave the impression it was a place of business. Outside the door a large swarthy man stood like a guard although he carried no visible weapons. He nodded to Kennedy as they stepped through the door. Warren had still not mastered the use of his cane and stumbled slightly at the top of the three stairs.

Inside two large tables sat against the walls, with several wood benches next to them.

A small man with a face like a rat, highlighted by greasy hair in a ponytail entered from the rear room.

"Kennedy, please be welcome," the man said, grinning to show several missing teeth.

"Railah, you poxy bastard, how are you?"

Shaking his head the man raised his hands in despair. "Alive, that is all, Kennedy. Praise Allah."

"These are my friends. We are here to see Abboud."

"Please, sit, sit. I will tell him."

Abboud was an average-sized man in his fifties, well built with a closely shaved head. At one time he must have been physically powerful. Now his face showed the scars of years in the gray world of Constantinople's back streets, his eyes wary as he sat down at the table. Kennedy knew that under the loose fitting robe there would be at least one pistol and a knife that could slice through a man's throat in an instant.

"Jason, my friend. Good to see you," Kennedy said, but didn't rise or offer to shake hands.

Abboud sat back in his chair and opened his arms with his palms upheld.

"I think you have business for me?"

Kennedy shook his head.

"Not this time. My friends and I are sailing west and will need supplies. This is Warren, this is Scully."

Abboud nodded and said, "I am Jason Abboud, welcome to my house. But let us have a drink before we talk business."

Railah reentered the room carry a dark green bottle in one hand, a tray of metal cups in the other hand.

The big man pulled the cork from the bottle and poured into each glass. He then added water from a small pitcher, then handed each man a drink.

"To long life and a fat purse."

They all raised their cups.

Warren smelled the drink as he brought it to his lips. The sweet odor of licorice told him they were drinking Sarak. He'd learned about the sweet liquor in Bulgaria and he actually liked it.

"Now, what can I do for you?"

Kennedy pulled a folded paper from his coat pocket.

"Here is a list of supplies, nothing unusual."

Abboud took the paper, unfolded it and began to read. His lips moved as he went down the page.

"I can arrange for everything on the list. Give me a day and I will let you know the price."

"Jason, we need medicine too."

"That should be no problem."

Scully spoke up, "There are some unusual things I need."

The Turk smiled.

"Scully? Yes, Scully. This is Constantinople. There is nothing that can't be found. It might take more time and more money. Is this a problem?"

"No," Warren said, his voice louder than he intended.

"I understand."

"This is very good," Warren said, trying to sound friendlier.

"Then we will drink Sarak, we will drink wine and you will eat with me."

It was dark as the three men made their way back to *Kestrel*. The streets were less crowded, but still busy. Warren felt slightly uneasy knowing that Pickering was by himself on the boat with only the crewmembers standing watch.

As they came into view of the sloop, a single lantern burned above the small brow that ran from the main deck to the quay. But there was no sign of life. They began to walk faster.

Kennedy was the first man across the brow, Warren having fallen behind the other two as he limped down the road. Scully had already pulled a long sheath knife from under his coat and held it ready.

"Engler, Castansos!" Kennedy called moving up the main deck, port side.

"Aye," a voice answered and Engler emerged into the light, a short sword in his hand.

"All's well?"

"Aye, all's well. The young gentleman is sleeping," Engler replied.

"The Greek?"

"Went ashore for fresh bread."

Two days later, *Kestrel* sailed, fully provisioned with food, water, medicine and an ample supply of Irish whiskey.

Chapter Six

"This will not be a quick victory."

A journey in winter can never be called pleasant, but the fall and winter had left the roads of France relatively dry and their journey to Le Havre proved tedious but uneventful.

Pickering continued to gain his strength. Ministrations by Sergeant Scully made sure that the young man's arm continued to heal although the pain did not diminish as expected. Warren could walk without a cane, although he did have a noticeable limp, which Scully felt would likely never go away.

Contracting for a passage across the channel had taken more time than Warren had expected, but their destination of Harwich was not common and took time to find a ship captain who was willing to sail so far to the northeast.

Landing at Harwich, the men found the rest of the journey pleasant, having located a well-appointed carriage for hire that took them from a small inn near the waterfront to the Duke's country estate.

"When were you last home?" Pickering asked as they reached the end of their journey.

"Not long ago, actually. A month before we left for Bulgaria." But Warren remembered that his father had been angry and distracted by the political events leading up to the Crimean expedition. For some reason, the duke had translated his anger at the government to his son. That, combined with an ongoing disagreement about Warren's military career had made the visit painful and not something he wanted to remember. How would his father be after the death of his brother? With his wife dead for over ten years, Stephen had been the elder Warren's only close family left. The few cousins that lived in the north were black sheep, rarely seen.

Albermarle, the Warren's estate consisted of over four hundred acres lying in the Stour River valley. The main building had been constructed in 1712, making it relatively new by English standards.

Despite the imposing gray facade, Warren always felt happy returning to Albermarle. His memories of a happy childhood and his mother made it a special place for him.

A wide black ribbon hung from the wreath outside the main entrance, a symbol that the house remained in mourning. Warren knew that arriving unannounced was certainly bad form, but it couldn't be helped.

Warren stood at one of the large library windows overlooking the intricate garden behind the large manor house. The biggest surprise was the smell, which he always recalled when he returned to the big house. The mixture of mustiness and roses was unique to Warren even with his travels around the world. Nowhere else had he ever found the same odor, from India to the Crimea.

"I understand you were wounded."

Turning to face his father, Warren was shocked to see how John Warren had aged since they had last seen each other. He had known his father and brother were close, but he never would have expected Stephen's death could have devastated the duke so.

"It could have been much worse. I am nearly recovered."

The Duke of Southwick walked across the room to his son.

"It's good to see you, Richard," he said putting his hand on his son's shoulder. "Sit down and tell me about it."

"First tell me about Stephen."

The duke walked to a richly upholstered chair and sat down slowly.

"It began with a cough, it was nothing terribly bad. But within three days Stephen had taken to his bed with a high fever. Doctor Snowden was with him constantly, but nothing seemed to help. He became delirious, didn't recognize me." The older man shook his head.

"I will miss him," Warren said.

"Now," the duke said, "I will pour us each a brandy and you will tell me of the war in Russia."

Over the next hour Warren related his disgust with the campaign, the ineptitude of the senior officers and the events at the Battle of Balaclava. The duke listened attentively, making the occasional comment, but asked no questions.

"We were extremely fortunate to receive medical care from an American and his wife. Without their assistance I believe I would now lie in a Russian grave. The Englishman we met, who actually orchestrated our escape, was the other stroke of luck."

He paused then continued, "I made a substantial monetary commitment to the man and also told him that you would help him."

"Me?" The duke looked very surprised, his eyes widening momentarily.

"It seems the man may have been under sentence of death ten years ago when he fled England. I told him you would be able to intervene on his behalf."

"That was rather presumptuous wouldn't you say?"

Warren nodded. "Perhaps, but I was there and felt it was necessary if I was to escape the Russians."

"I will look into it."

"I brought Sergeant Michael Scully with me and Coronet James Pickering. The regimental commander was not pleased, but Pickering would have died if I'd left him with those butchers."

"We are hearing dreadful stories of the conditions. I feel there will be a commission or investigation shortly."

His father's political answer angered Warren. "Run by old men who wouldn't know up from down."

"That would include me, I daresay."

"In India, although there was a great deal of pomp and politics, it appeared the men making the decisions understood what they were doing. In the Crimea, it was as if the senior officers were in a world of fantasy. Men died for no reason because of bad decisions and lack of professional planning."

"Well, Aberdeen has resigned. Perhaps Palmerston will right some of the wrongs."

Warren knew the change in prime ministers had taken place, but knew little of the new man.

"It will take a ruthless man to change the course of this war."

"He and I have known each other for a very long time and I have confidence he will do his best."

But Richard Warren had lost faith in Her Majesty's government, regardless of who was leading it.

"You will not eat in the kitchen, sergeant."

Scully had been very quiet since arriving at Albermarle and now as the dinner hour approached, Warren found his friend in the kitchen talking with Mrs. Louis, the head cook. Scully and Pickering had been on their own most of the day, while Warren had been with the duke.

"But I really would be more comfortable in the kitchen."

"Dinner is at six. You will make sure Pickering is there, shaved and brushed off."

Scully could see he was losing the argument.

"I don't want to embarrass you," he said.

"My father is looking forward to meeting you."

Knowing he couldn't win the battle, Scully nodded his acceptance.

"Six o'clock it is."

The three younger men were standing by their chairs when the duke entered.

"Father, may I introduce Coronet James Pickering and Sergeant Michael Scully."

He shook hands with each man, his smile warm.

"You are most welcome, gentlemen. Please do sit down."

As they made their way through potato and leek soup, roast chicken and rice followed by a cheese platter, the conversation became more relaxed as the duke asked Scully and Pickering about their homes and families.

Wine glasses were refilled several times and Warren knew that his father was enjoying the dinner. He looked across the table, Scully being very careful as he reached for another piece of aged cheddar. He knew the decision to return to England was the right one. Only here could he sort out his future.

A full month passed at Albermarle during which the duke had corresponded not only with Lord Palmerston, but also with army headquarters and Doctor Matthew Willoughby. Warren had given his father all of the information he knew of James Kennedy and the event from ten years prior. The prime minister's secretary had been amenable to finding out what Kennedy's exact status was and what, if anything, Palmerston might be able to do. The duke allowed that the prime minister did owe him several favors, which he expected would facilitate an easy resolution of the case. Right or wrong, the ability of the sitting government to affect the outcome of justice in England was well known.

Warren could tell his father had enjoyed the company of his son's friends and in particular he had been taken with James Pickering. Perhaps the loss of Stephen had something to do with it, but the duke had spent many hours discussing every subject from astronomy to architecture with the young man. It was the second week when a journey to London had been mentioned so that James could see Willoughby, a well-respected physician, known for working with war injuries.

The news seemed to raise the spirits of Pickering, who now felt that his future was more promising than he could have ever hoped for.

"Very well done," Doctor Willoughby commented as he finished his examination of James arm. Following a series of directed motions during which Pickering demonstrated how he could move his arm, the doctor had carefully gone over the now healed amputation site. "Much better job of closing than you often see from military surgeons, all slapdash and on to the next."

"We were fortunate, doctor. The surgery was done in a Russian hospital by an American surgeon who trained in Austria."

"Then you were doubly fortunate. I suspect that will make fitting of an appliance much easier."

Over the next fifteen minutes, Willoughby took a number of measurements, methodically recording each one in a notebook.

"Give me one week."

Neither Scully nor Pickering had ever visited London and Warren's last time in the capital had been a number of years ago. Rooms at Claridge House allowed them to see the sights, sample the public houses, restaurants and shop for some badly needed additions to their wardrobes.

Seeing his two friends out of uniform surprised Warren, who had insisted both acquire several suits of quality and style. Both men seemed slightly uncomfortable when they joined him for dinner at Lester's. The establishment was one of Warren's favorites and popular among the well to do of London.

"Might I say that you both impress me mightily? Heaven knows what the women of London might think of two such impressive specimens."

"Bugger off," Scully said as he stretched his neckpiece, trying to achieve a bit of comfort in the unusual outfit.

"Gentlemen, we look the part and this establishment is one of the finest purveyors of beef in the town. Now let us sit back, relax and enjoy our time of leisure."

The waiter approached the table, his face showing a complete lack of emotion.

"Gentlemen, might I bring you a drink?"

"Michael, I think Irish whiskey would be appropriate, do you agree?"

Scully grinned.

"That would be fine, thank you very much."

"James?"

"Superb choice."

Roasted beef loin with baked onions highlighted a superb meal, finished with an apple pudding. As he had on numerous occasions, Scully quietly cut up the larger pieces of meat for James, continuing the conversation as if his actions were completely routine. Several bottles of red wine accompanied the meal and the discussion ranged from the serious to ridiculous. As the table was cleared and glasses of brandy were poured, the three men sat back, in the comfortable quiet of a good meal shared with friends.

"A man could get used to this," Scully opined, taking a sip of his brandy.

Pickering, his injured arm resting in his lap said nothing, but also took a drink.

"But, Michael, I know you would miss the adventurous life of the cavalry."

Scully chuckled.

"Might miss the beasts, but not much more."

"Do you think they will keep me on active service?" Pickering asked, revealing his real concern for the future.

Warren knew from their talks that a career in the army was the only thing Pickering had ever wanted. Coming from a family of modest means it had been a challenge to purchase a commission. Now everything lay at risk.

"Tomorrow we have our appointment at Horseguards. That should at least tell us your chances."

"If they won't keep me on active service, what are my options?"

Warren knew there were none that James would want, from a transfer to a non-combat billet, perhaps with the commissary corps, or a position as a civilian clerk in support of the army.

"Don't worry about that now. Get a good night sleep and let us see what tomorrow will bring."

"Damned back."

Colonel Archibald Morton rose carefully from his chair and walked over to the standing cabinet in his office. An infantryman by trade, the rotund colonel, had been serving for twelve years at the British Army's headquarters, Horseguards, Whitehall. For the last nine years he had been in officer transactions. Now at the end of another tedious day he only wanted to go home and lay down. The pain in his back, which began so many years ago, had been getting progressively worse. Now only a shot of brandy laced with Laudanum could provide temporary relief.

He glanced at the clock. One last appointment and he would be on his way. He returned to his desk to re-read the note from his secretary. A coronet, wounded in the Crimea is requesting to remain on active service. Damned straightforward, he thought. Of course he will remain on active service, unless his injuries would prevent him from normal capabilities. But I must follow official protocol he told himself.

A knock on the door, followed by Carstairs leaning in told him it was time.

"Mr. Pickering to see you, colonel."

"Of course. Send him in."

Debating on whether he should rise to greet a wounded officer from the war, Morton was stopped dead when he say the young man enter. Sweet mother of God, he was missing his entire left hand!

"Coronet James Pickering, 13th Light Dragoons, sir."

The young man looked presentable enough, he thought quickly, but my God.

"Please, Mr. Pickering, do have a seat."

"Thank you, sir."

He watched Pickering sit down, moving his left arm carefully to his lap.

"Your escape was certainly the talk of the town, sir. Particularly after being part of that rather clapped-up attack at Balaclava."

Realizing that Pickering carried no hat, he knew Carstairs had thought this through. Of course, with only one hand, a hat would awkward to manage.

"Now, you are here?"

"Requesting to continue on active service, sir."

"I see," Morton replied although he truly didn't. "That would be active service with the regiment?"

"Exactly, sir."

Wanting another brandy, but knowing he couldn't, the colonel stood up and walked around his desk, leaning back on the front edge.

"I'm afraid that is a problem."

Richard Warren had debated accompanying his friend, but decided it was important for Pickering to feel he was controlling his own future. Working behind the scenes could be as effective and maybe even more so.

"Warren, is that you?"

Looking up, he saw Walter Hutchins, a friend from India.

He stood up from the bench and shook his friend's hand.

"Good to see you, Hutchins. You look well."

Walter Hutchins wore the aiguillette of an aide de camp.

"I've been very fortunate indeed, aide to Hew Ross."

"The artillery Ross?"

"Indeed. He is officially Lieutenant General of the Artillery, but the Commander in Chief defers to him in almost all matters."

"I must say, of the mess in the Crimea, it seemed the artillery was the most prepared. The trouble was the rest of the army, particularly the supporting forces, were a complete disgrace."

Hutchins looked at his friend.

"Come with me."

Sir Hew Dalrymple Ross was a tall, distinguished man in his mid-70's. While Warren continued to think the army leadership was too old, he did recognize that Ross had distinguished himself in battle after battle against Napoleon. His artillery had turned the tide on more than one occasion and he was a confident of the Duke of Wellington. While advanced in years, he certainly seemed to be on point.

Warren described the landings and subsequent battles to the general, who sat attentively, asking a question now and then. His queries were those of a totally professional soldier, well versed in modern warfare.

"I am glad to see that our training and procurement produced an effective force in the field. Unfortunately we underestimated the ability of the Russians to put up an effective defense of the port."

The general's statement surprised Warren, who was not used to senior officers taking responsibility for failure.

"Ah, yes, sir," he said quietly.

Ross cut his eyes at Warren.

"You didn't have to agree so quickly, captain."

Then he smiled slightly.

"Where do we go from here, sir?"

The older man sighed.

"A long and brutal siege, I'm afraid. Raglan is asking for a remarkable number of guns and supporting forces. It appears we shall even build a rail line from Balaclava to the front. This will not be a quick victory."

Richard Warren thought of the men surrounding Sevastopol, the mud, disease and cold. Not a quick victory to the general meant the deaths of more British soldiers. And for no reason, the damned politicians were simply moving pieces of a chess game that would make no difference five years from now. He thought of Louis and Kimberly, trapped in a city under the guns of the British and French with no means of escape. Siege warfare was one of the most brutal aspects of war, deadly to both soldiers and civilians.

"When will you return to your regiment?' the general asked.

"I am not sure, Sir. While my wound is mostly healed, I am with my young coronet who is asking to remain on active service after losing a hand at Balaclava."

"You say he lost a hand?"

"Amputated just above the wrist, nasty bullet wound destroyed most of the hand."

"Damned minie cartridges. We are hearing more of that every day. It will keep the surgeons busy no doubt."

Warren thought of how the art of warfare had become more and more lethal. From canister shot, the new minie ball, even the construction of land torpedoes, which exploded when enemy soldiers approached them.

"Sir, would you be able to help my young officer?"

Ross sat back in his chair.

"I suspect if I can't, I know someone who would likely be sympathetic to his cause."

Warren found Pickering in the lower entry waiting area sitting on one of the benches lining the walls.

"Colonel Morton told me that it simply could not be done," Pickering said as Warren sat down next to him. "He thought there might be some opportunity in the quartermaster service, but couldn't say for sure. I am to check back in a month."

Warren smiled at his crestfallen friend.

"We have an appointment with the Commander in Chief in three days. Just in time for us to see what Doctor Willoughby can do for you."

Chapter Seven

"What do you know of this man?"

Coronet James Pickering, of the 13th Light Dragoons looked quite presentable in his new uniform, just delivered that morning from Stewart and Sons, Mayfair. The military tailors had outfitted Warren since his commissioning and were delighted to produce two dress uniforms, although three days did task even their impressive capabilities.

Now with new uniforms, bright buttons and gleaming braid, the three soldiers waited in the Commander in Chief's anteroom. General Henry Hardinge had held the top position in the army since June of 1854, succeeding the Duke of Wellington. A highly decorated soldier, he had fought at Wellington's side through the Peninsular War and then into France. Most recently he had successfully fought several key battles in India during the tribal wars. He knew warfare, but he also understood men and how to lead them.

"Captain Warren, the general would like to talk with you in private."

Ushered in by a major who did not introduce himself, Warren entered the large office, which overlooked the Horseguards Parade.

When Sir Hew had intimated that the solution to their problem was possible, Warren had tried to quell his excitement. If General Ross had meant the Commander in Chief, the retention of James Pickering would be immensely more likely.

Standing, the general motioned Warren to a chair. Hardinge, seventy years old, still carried himself well, despite the obvious strain his position imposed on him. Sitting down, he returned his empty left sleeve to his lap.

"I am aware of the purpose of your visit, captain. Before we discuss your subordinate I would be interested in your observations from the Crimea."

The tone of the general's request was quiet, yet conveyed a sharp edge. Whether it was frustration or anger, Warren did not know.

"And, Captain Warren, I would request your frankest appraisal of what you saw."

Despite his intent to help James Pickering at all costs, Warren knew now that he had to convey the utter ineptness of the army.

"Sir, I saw an army that was not prepared for service in the field. From embarkation in England through to Balaclava we lacked the correct material, accurate intelligence and any semblance of coordination in command."

Warren saw little reaction from the general, despite what was a complete indictment of the British army's efforts over the last year.

"Go on."

"We sent a foreign expedition with little thought or effort to sustain that expedition on hostile territory. The lack of proper food, equipment and medical care has left an army barely capable of defending itself, let alone capturing Sevastopol."

Hardinge probed with questions as Warren broke down his observations of the transit, the build up in Bulgaria, the landing at Kalamita and the first battle at Alma.

"Now tell me what you saw at Balaclava."

"It appeared to me that the army was surprised by the Russian attack. While I know that word of advancing Russian troops had been sent back to headquarters, no one apparently used the information to prepare the army."

The general rose and walked to the window, staring into the parade ground.

"Tell me of the charge," he asked quietly.

In detail, Warren described the series of events leading up to the fateful order, then his impressions of the actual charge.

"You were cut off from your men?"

"When the Cossack cavalry swept down, the sheer numbers of the enemy overwhelmed those of us who were still within the Russian position." Warren's thoughts returned to that chaos.

"And Lord Cardigan?"

Aware that many accused Cardigan of retreating early, Warren simply said, "I did not see him after the brigade reached the emplacements."

The general continued to stare out the window for a moment then turned to face Warren.

"Tell me of this young man you are representing."

Following a brief background of Pickering's rather humble start in the army, he described his attitude and zeal then the fight at the gun emplacements.

"Very difficult at his age. I lost my hand as a thirty year-old major at Ligny."

Hardinge had suffered a very similar wound and missed the Battle of Waterloo but was promoted colonel by Wellington.

"Yes, sir, I am aware of your injury."

The general continued, "Of course by that time, my active service in the field was as a general, commanding in the field. Lack of a hand had little effect with a pack of aides to assist me. Your man would still be in the thick of things if it came to that."

"I understand that, general. I also understand this army needs young courageous officers who can lead men in battle. James Pickering has shown me he can do exactly that. You will see he has made provisions for his loss and that alone merits a chance to prove himself."

Hardinge's features remained passive, but his eyes showed that Warren's remarks had struck a chord.

As Warren had expected, amidst the expected formality of greeting Pickering, the Commander in Chief could not stop glancing at the prosthetic device the young officer wore on his left hand.

Fashioned by Doctor Willoughby, the appliance consisted of leather pads and straps to attach a steel cap over Pickering's stump. Extending four inches up his arm, the steel shone bright from his uniform sleeve. Extending two inches from the center of the steel cover, a round steel band curved back, attaching to a locking bracket. The design primarily allowed Pickering to attach the reins of a horse although it also allowed him to load a pistol using one side of the appliance as a brace. In what Willoughby thought was a first, the attaching bracket also would support mounting a six-inch fighting knife if needed. An additional feature included a small compartment with room for a short cutting blade and a small pry lever. As the doctor had said, "One never knows when one might need a small advantage."

General Hardinge questioned Pickering for twenty minutes, many of his questions addressing how the coronet would deal with the many problems that the general had faced in the field with only one hand.

"I admire your desire to return to active service, Mr. Pickering. Captain Warren has presented a compelling case on your behalf and it clear to me that you have taken pains to prepare yourself. I will consider the matter carefully and render my decision within the week."

The three friends drank six bottles of what the waiter said was the "best wine in the house" that night at dinner. While a decision had yet to be rendered, Warren felt quite secure that he would be returning to the 13th with Pickering in company. After what they had endured it seemed only right to celebrate, even if slightly early.

"Will we wait in the city or return to your father's?" Scully asked, his words slightly slurred.

"I thought we could take the coach tomorrow," Warren said to Scully, "The city is too crowded and filthy to boot. James, would you like to go home to see your mother?"

A two-day coach ride from London would take Pickering home to Leicester. It would be the first time he had been home in over a year.

"I would prefer to stay with you, sir."

Warren wondered if Pickering wasn't ready for his mother to see what a Russian bullet had done to her only son.

"Of course. I'll let Horseguards know where to contact us. Now, let's see if they have any decent brandy."

Word was waiting at Albermarle that on investigation of the case against one James Kennedy, there was not sufficient evidence available at this time to warrant any further action against the man. The decision of the presiding magistrate had been rendered and recorded at Exeter. It seemed that Kennedy was a respectable subject of the Queen once more.

"How will you contact this Mister Kennedy?" the duke asked after Warren had read the letter.

"I thought we'd travel to Marseille and have him take us back to the Crimea once we hear from Horseguards."

"What do you know of this man?"

"He knows the sea, seems a bit of a rogue, but I trust him. He has delivered everything he promised and if he hadn't intervened for us in Sevastopol, I wouldn't be here now."

"That is certainly something," the Duke said. He poured two glasses of port, handing one to Richard.

"I received word that the master of the *Sonia B* has died. The ship is anchored in Toulon harbor."

Southwick owned a fleet of twelve merchant ships, which provided a highly profitable trading business with both India and the Americas. Warren had seen the *Sonia B* several times and remembered her as one of the faster ships that primarily worked the Atlantic.

"That was Francis Stonemoor," he said, remembering the big Welshman.

"A good man who ran a tight ship. No family that I know of. I will send word to have the second mate bury him in France and assume charge of the ship until I can arrange for a new captain."

Scully knocked on the door of Warren's study and pushed the door open slowly.

"A messenger delivered this just now," he told Warren who sat at a large desk under the window. "It's addressed to Mister Pickering."

Finally, we can get started, Warren thought.

"Go find him and bring him here. I'll get out a bottle of brandy to celebrate."

The two men watched as Pickering stood next to the desk and opened the stiff envelope. The wax seal broke easily as he pulled heavy paper out and unfolded it.

Without taking his eyes from the page, Pickering quietly said, "No. It says no."

He turned to look at Warren, his face showing the shock of knowing his career cavalry officer was over.

"Let me see that.'

In official and proper language, the letter stated that the Commander in Chief regretfully had to disapprove the subject officer's request for reinstatement due to physical limitations. It had been a difficult decision, but the general felt that the demands of active service would impact the ability of Pickering to carry out his normal duties.

"James, I'm sorry. It makes no sense. None at all." Warren found his anger rising as he watched Pickering sit down, his face crestfallen. One more example of the entrenched attitudes than had resulted in thousands of deaths in the Crimea. While not the same thing, it came down to a lack common sense and little interest in a job done well.

"I don't know what to do," Pickering said, looking at his friends.

"Start by having a drink, lad," Scully said, pouring brandy into three glasses on the desk.

"Don't worry. We'll figure it out," Warren said, downing his in one gulp.

"What will you do, Richard?" the duke asked.

"Return to the Crimea, I suppose."

The two men sat in front of a lively fire, waiting for dinner to be announced.

"I understand they are preparing for a massive, sustained bombardment of the city. Perhaps that will force the issue."

"Where did you hear that?" Warren asked, wondering about the source for his father's statement.

"A discussion I had recently with Palmerston. By the middle of April, they will have everything in place, over one hundred and fifty guns with enough ammunition to level the city."

Warren began to put things together in his mind. Lord Raglan had mentioned nothing happening until the guns arrived. And Hew Ross had talked about building a rail line to the front. Wagons can haul food but shot and cannon can be moved much easier on railroads. One hundred and fifty cannons, to say nothing of what the French might provide would make for a massive assault on the city. He had seen the results of the initial bombardment, which had taken place just prior to Balaclava. A small effort compared to what his father had described and that attack had destroyed many buildings. Now it would only be worse. He thought of the doctor and his wife. Trying to save lives, they would be directly in the path of artillery, which would kill the innocent as well as the enemy.

"Shall we have a glass of wine while we wait?" his father asked.

"I need to think, father. Please excuse me and don't delay dinner."

Scully had learned to read early in life, his mother insisting that he spent time at the local Catholic school in Kilkenny. However his life in the army had never allowed him ready access to any libraries. Now he would sit for hours in the Albermarle library happily reading books that he had never known existed.

"Thought I might find you here."

Scully looked up as Warren entered the library, his hair still mussed from the gusty winds outside.

"My goodness, you look the sight. Where were you?"

Warren sat down and flopped back against the cushions.

"Deciding to resign from the army."

Closing the book, Scully looked at his friend.

"I certainly never expected to hear that."

"Before Russia I could have never imagined resigning, the service has been my life. But the army is broken and I'm not in a position to effect any change past a squadron of troopers. I also have to deal with the death of my brother. Now I will inherit everything. My father's businesses are extensive and someone must be in charge. I trust no one to do that but myself."

"My God, you're serious." In the ten years of knowing Warren, Scully had come to know his captain's moods.

"I am totally earnest, I assure you, Michael. And I need your help."

"If I can help, you know I will."

"I know that, old friend, but this is quite a change. If you agree, I will purchase you out of your enlistment. Then we'll inspect every aspect of my father's businesses. I need someone who can talk to me straight. Tell me I'm making a mistake, point out the things I might not see and cover my back."

Taking all of this in made the Irishman's head swim. He had never considered that life held anything for him but perhaps rising to a regimental sergeant major. Now he had chance to completely change his life and destiny. Perhaps this had all been meant to be.

"Alright. I'll do as you ask. But you must give it a week before you resign. If you still feel the same way then, we both go."

"Understood, my friend. And one more thing... we're going back to the Crimea either way."

The next morning, Warren found Pickering at breakfast.

"When you are finished, let's take a walk."

Pickering looked curious and put his napkin beside his plate.

Their route took them behind the large house toward a large field at the edge of the forest.

"I've decided to leave the army, James."

Pickering stopped walking and looked at Warren.

"Leave the army? I don't understand."

"Come on. I need to walk," Warren said and turned toward the field.

James caught up and fell in step.

"I was angry about the incompetence we saw in Russia. That is part of my decision, but it's a combination of things. My father has extensive business interests, which my brother was going to manage. His death has put that responsibility on me. Perhaps the timing was opportune, but I felt what we were doing in Russia was a waste of men and money for no good purpose. I'm done with blindly following the orders of old men."

They reached a gate in the fence and Warren opened it for James.

"So Michael Scully and I are going in a different direction. I thought you might want to be part of that."

"I'm not sure what you mean," Pickering said quickly.

"I need a private secretary to handle all of those many things that private secretaries do."

"I would work for you?"

The look on Pickering's face was quizzical but hopeful.

"Indeed. We would start with the three of us travelling around to visit my father's ventures. After that, we will just have to decide."

"Yes! Yes, sir. I would gladly welcome an opportunity like this."

The look on Pickering's face told Warren that the young man's enthusiasm had returned.

Chapter Eight

"You do know how to swim?"

While spring rains had turned many of the roads of France to mud, the three men made good time back to Marseille, arriving on the 15ᵗʰ of April 1855. Always a bustling seaport, the harbor seemed particularly busy as the men searched out the whereabouts of the sloop *Kestrel.* They spent the better part of the day searching in vain until a man was found who told them they might find the sloop in a small bay at the southern headlands.

Several coins in the hand of a local fisherman resulted in a quick ride to the ship in the man's dory. The sloop looked well maintained, but no one was visible on deck.

"Hello!" Warren called as the local maneuvered the double-ended boat alongside Kestrel. "Is there anyone aboard?"

Kennedy's head appeared from below the cockpit coaming.

"Who's there?" came the question, which Kennedy quickly answered for himself.

"I'll be damned. You did come back."

Reaching down, Kennedy helped the men aboard and then stood to face them.

"Took some time to find you. This is a big harbor," Warren said.

"I like this quiet little bay, out of the way, if you know what I mean. Come below, we'll have a drink."

"Pickering, my God you look better than the last time I saw you."

James Pickering had put on a few pounds and his face had a healthy color.

"Travel suits me, Mr. Kennedy."

"Now, did you drink all the whiskey?" Scully asked.

"I kept one bottle just in case you came back," Kennedy said and motioned the three men below decks.

Over glasses of surprisingly good red wine, they briefly went over their trip back across France. Kennedy told them he had spent most of the time in port, the weather had been bad and he'd only found one job hauling flour to Ligure.

"So you've spent all the money?" Warren asked.

"Not at all, captain, I always make provisions for the future."

Scully picked up a second bottle of wine and poured it around.

"Then let's talk about the future."

Kennedy took a drink and looked at Warren.

"All right."

"I am no longer in the army, nor are any of us."

Raising his eyebrows, Kennedy asked, "You're out of the army?"

"Correct. I'll be assuming control of my father's business concerns. But before we talk about that, I have something for you to read."

Warren handed a leather packet to Kennedy, who put down his glass and opened it.

Finding a single page inside, the sailor unfolded it and read slowly.

"My God, you did it."

"You are free from any and all charges and able to travel back to England with no fear."

Kennedy smiled.

"Thank you."

"Now, I need your help," Warren said.

The tone of Warren's voice set off an uneasy feeling in Kennedy. Was he expected to jump to as repayment for what Warren had done for him? At this moment he only wanted to put to sea, but even that was no longer under his control with the purchase of *Kestrel* by Warren before they left Balaclava. For fleeting moment he toyed with what luck he might have overpowering the visitors and throwing them overboard. But he wouldn't dare tangle with Scully, not if he wanted to see another Christmas.

"How can I help you?" he asked, the question making great sense. How could a vagabond sailor with meager resources ever help the son of a wealthy duke of the realm?

"The French and British armies conducted a bombardment of Sevastopol. By all accounts I have seen, it did immense damage to the city."

Kennedy remembered the old city where he had first met the three Englishmen. He guessed that many of his Russian acquaintances were likely dead now, or suffering from disease or malnutrition. Getting out of there when he did might turn out to be the smartest thing he had ever done.

"And?"

Warren continued.

"I want to return to Sevastopol. Louis and Kimberly must get out of the city."

"You want to what? Are you daft?"

Scully reached over with the wine bottle and topped off Kennedy's glass.

"Just wantin' to see the world, Jim, my boy. We're all going."

Kimberly stepped over a pile of debris at the entrance to Military Hospital Number Six. The bombardment had lasted four long and terrifying days. While much of the enemy ordinance had been directed at the Russian forts defending the city, errant shells had hit the area around the hospital, with one exploding next to Ward One. Two patients had died from the attack and the ward was no longer usable. Daily, the shortages of food and medicine had sapped the strength of the staff and their ability to provide care for the flow of wounded that seemed unending. The destroyed Ward One seemed like the last obscene blow in a brutal fight to care for the wounded.

"Good morning, nurse."

The greeting broke into her thoughts of the last two weeks and she saw one of the medical orderlies.

"Hello, Andre. Have you seen Doctor Thomassy?"

Louis had not returned to their small house the night before. That was not unusual with the demands of surgery each day. She had finally left the hospital when exhaustion told her she needed rest desperately. James had told her he would follow shortly but he had never arrived.

"He's in the office," Andre said.

Louis shared a small office with three other doctors and it was there Kimberly found him, fast asleep on a stuffed mattress

135

that had been commandeered from one of the wards. She knelt down next to the mattress and kissed him lightly. He needed a shave and his hair was longer than he had ever worn it before. The doctor had aged since their arrival in the Crimea. The toll of surgery day after day with meager rations was making him age before her eyes. Their ten year age difference became more obvious every week.

As if his tired body took time to register the kiss, Louis slowly opened his eyes.

"Good morning," Kimberly said, putting her hand on his cheek.

"What time is it?" he asked, blinking the sleep from his eyes.

"Just before seven. When did you lie down?"

The doctor sat up, rubbing his stubbly face.

"Must have been around two. Three badly wounded men were brought in and we had to operate. One man died on the table, the others might survive."

"Let me find you some breakfast," she said.

He kissed her hand.

"Thank you, my dear. I will try to make myself somewhat presentable."

She knew that meant a quick bucket wash and shave, which certainly would help, but not solve the real problem. He needed a long rest, clean clothes and good food, none of which could be found in Sevastopol.

Fair winds and a lack of foul weather had meant a swift transit to Constantinople for *Kestrel*. A fast ship by any measure, the prevailing westerly winds allowed her to average two hundred miles a day, arriving on the morning of the ninth day out of Marseille.

Jim Kennedy had shown his true ability with a ship, on deck constantly ordering the sails trimmed as the winds changed. The small crew seemed to take it all in stride, following Kennedy's orders without hesitation. Only three other vessels came within visual range of the sloop until they closed the Dardanelles. Warren was surprised that he had come to enjoy being at sea, running before the wind and out of touch with the rest of the world. Now they were back.

The route to Abboud's house took them through streets, which were less crowded than their last visit. Warren wondered why the difference? Perhaps the smuggling business had dropped off.

"This is more like it, Kennedy."

Jason Abboud read the list in front of him and smiled.

"Only the very best I see."

The quick departure from France had not allowed them to obtain decent arms for their expedition. Now only four days from an even more dangerous location, Richard Warren intended to be well armed. On the list were Baker rifles and Colt Navy revolvers. While he had no desire for violence, being prepared was the only prudent course of action.

"How long would it take you to get the items on the list?" Warren asked.

"Perhaps one day, more likely two. But have no fear, I can get these."

"And a good supply of ammunition to go with them."

"Of course, but weapons such as these will not come cheap."

"As long as the price is reasonable."

137

Abboud grinned.

"Then let us drink to it," he said, calling for his servant.

"James, let me tell you about Sarak before you learn about it the hard way," Warren said, remembering that Pickering had remained aboard the ship on their last visit.

Kennedy laughed.

"I wish someone had warned me the first time."

Scully downed his drink.

"Can't compare with a good whiskey, but I think I could come to like this. With practice, of course."

He held up his glass for a refill.

Warren and Scully examined the weapons, which arrived late the night before in a covered wagon driven by Abboud's servant Railah.

"Better than the lads in Russia are using, by God," Scully said, raising a Baker rifle to his shoulder

The weapons were clean, well lubricated and appeared to be almost new.

Warren said, "I hope we'll not be in Russia for more than a few hours, but we both know how plans tend to go bloody south sometimes."

Kennedy came down the ladder from topside and saw the men inspecting the weapons. Pickering followed him down the ladder. The young man had spent time with Kennedy during the transit from France and now in port at Constantinople. Their totally different personalities seemed to take to one another, the taciturn officer and the boisterous sailor.

"I don't like the look of the weather," Kennedy said to Warren.

"It's important to get to Sevastopol as soon as possible."

Kennedy shook his head.

"That may be, but you'll be hazarding the ship. And all of us."

The tone in Kennedy's voice had none of the larger than life character he normally assumed. The words were those of an experienced captain concerned for his ship and crew.

"If you tell me that we absolutely cannot make the passage, I will delay our departure. But every day of the siege, the doctor and his wife are at greater danger."

"I didn't say we couldn't make it. I did say it would be hazardous. If you want me to sail this ship to the Crimea, I'll do my best."

Warren thought for a moment, this side of Kennedy unexpected.

"I understand your concern, but I want to take the risk."

Kennedy nodded.

"You do know how to swim?"

Scully looked at Pickering, his eyes widening.

"I'm sure we'll manage. Right, Michael?"

A northwest wind began to build on the second afternoon at sea. By sundown, flecks of white foam raced across the deepening swells. A drop in the glass confirmed what Kennedy had feared, a storm coming down from the north. The ferocity born on land grew dangerous as the storm crossed to the ocean. That brutal front smashed into *Kestrel* at midnight.

Warren struggled on deck, the pitching of the small sloop more violent than he had ever seen or imagined. Black water crashed over the bow, drenching the main deck and sending cascades of water racing back and over the gunwales.

Kennedy and Nicodemis stood hunched over behind the wheel, sheltering from the wind whipped spray. Warren made his way over the wet, pitching deck, holding on to anything that presented itself.

"What's happening?" Warren yelled over the wind.

"Holding her into the wind, we have to ride it out," the captain replied.

Warren felt like a fool. Kennedy had warned him of the storm. But the cavalryman never understood the sheer violence of a fully developed storm at sea. How does a ship this small survive these monstrous waves and screaming wind?

As if Kennedy had been reading Warren's thoughts he yelled, "It should lighten up by daybreak."

"Pickering and Scully are sick as dogs. Is there anything to do for them?"

Kennedy shook his head.

"Not in a storm like this."

Both men had thrown up the contents of their stomachs several hours ago and were continuing to retch small amounts of bile. Warren could not recall anytime that Scully had not had a comment or smart remark to share. Now the Irishman lay on the thin mattress, lost in a miserable world of unending motion.

Kennedy's prediction was remarkably accurate. As the day arrived, the gray horizon now visible, the wind slackened and the waves began to calm. By midmorning the captain decided it was safe to change course back toward Sevastopol.

Pickering emerged on deck, his face pale after an awful night. Warren had told him that fresh air would expedite his recovery and Pickering was ready to do anything to feel better.

"He has arisen from the dead," Kennedy said, grinning at the young man.

"An accurate appraisal, Mr. Kennedy," Pickering said as he sat down on the deck. "I am now quite sure I would never succeed as a sailor."

"We'll alter course shortly and head for Sevastopol," he offered.

Pickering nodded and saw Warren come up the ladder from below. He looked around the horizon before moving aft to join the others.

"Let's get ready, Nick," Kennedy said. "Everyone on deck."

In three minutes the other crewmen appeared on deck and assumed their positions with little ceremony.

"Raise the outer jib," Kennedy called.

The second jib sail was raised quickly and sheeted home, followed by Kennedy shifting the wheel to bring the bow around toward the east.

"Once on course, we'll raise the mainsail. Every man on the ropes will make it go easier," he said to Warren.

"I would be pleased to help," Warren said and moved forward to join the rest of the crew gathered at the mainsail halyard.

Nicodemis released the stays holding the mainsail boom vang amidships. He would adjust the boom's angle once the mainsail had been set and Kennedy decided how close he could run to the wind.

The sloop sliced through the troughs as the bow turned right, water sprayed high over the deck.

"Raise the mainsail," Kennedy called as he spun the wheel to catch the turn.

"Haul away," Engler called, as he took a strain on the manila line.

Warren grabbed the line and began to haul in unison with the other two men, hearing the squeak of the mainsail rings as they moved up the mainmast. The deck canted as the big sail reached the top and Kennedy allowed the bow to pay off slightly. The canvas cracked as the wind snapped it taut.

Nick let out the line and the mainsail boom swung to the right.

"Watch out!" Kennedy yelled, but it was too late as the heavy beam caught Warren in the back. The hull lurched as the wind gusted and Warren, already off balance, fell over the starboard side.

"Nick, get a line," The captain spun the wheel to bring *Kestrel* back into the wind.

"Get the mainsail down, now!"

Engler and Castansos jumped to the cleat, releasing the halyard and grabbing the downhaul.

"Keep your eye on him!" Kennedy called to Nick as watched the mainsail collapse onto the boom.

"Helm's alee!" he called, spinning the wheel to the right.

Nick knew the only chance Warren had was if the captain could bring the sloop around to pick him up. The Turk has spent most of his life at sea and also knew that finding a man overboard in a rough sea depended on keeping him in sight. Standing on the stern, Nick pointed Warren, who was rapidly falling astern.

The sloop wallowed as she moved broadside on to the waves, making it difficult as the first mate moved up the starboard side, his arm still pointing to where he last saw Warren.

Warren knew how to swim, but the shock of cold water, coupled with trying to stay afloat while encased in heavy clothes made his effort increasingly futile. Salt water burned his eyes, the heavy waves washing over his head as he struggled to survive. He pushed hard with both hands, allowing a full gasp of air, then let himself submerge, ripping at the buttons on his coat. Twisting hard, his lungs beginning to burn, he pulled the coat off and kicked to the surface struggling for another breath. Realizing he still wore his brogans, he reached down, undoing the laces and kicking both shoes off. Now he would fight the ocean on more even terms.

Scully came on deck, hearing the excited yells to see the bow swinging rapidly as the jib sails caught the wind.

"Warren's overboard," Pickering called, seeing the sergeant lurch aft.

Kestrel picked up speed as the sails filled. Nicodemis now stood on the bow, pointing directly ahead.

"Engler, get forward and be ready to drop the jib," Kennedy yelled.

Kennedy had seen too many men drown in sight of safety and knew he had to take a chance. He now could see Warren, fifty yards ahead just off the port bow.

"Nick get back here on the helm!" he yelled. "Engler, drop both jib sails!"

Tearing off he coat and shoes, Kennedy grabbed a coiled manila line and secured it to a deck cleat.

"Nick, take the helm. Keep the bow upwind as we approach. I'm going in after him. Once I have him, haul us in."

The Greek nodded.

"Scully, there are sharks around here. Load one of those damned rifles and be ready," Kennedy ordered as he moved to the port side amidships.

By now the sloop was barely making headway and Warren was floating ten yards off the port bow. Kennedy timed his jump and moved as the sloop reached the top of a swell.

Warren began to panic, the cold penetrating his body, the coughing up of seawater making him gasp for breath. Then he felt strong arms around him.

Despite a full glass of Irish whiskey, Warren shivered under two wool blankets. Whether it was shock or cold, he continued to feel the grip of the ocean around him. How stupid he'd been. If not for good timing and a calm sea, he would be dead now, floating face down or sinking into the black depths. Another shiver racked his body.

"Feeling better?" Kennedy asked.

The captain had changed to dry clothes and held a cup of what Warren assumed was more whiskey.

"Damned cold, I'll tell you."

"People forget how frigid the ocean is until they're in it."

"I owe you an apology and my thanks," Warren said, feeling some warmth starting to flow inside from the whiskey.

Kennedy smiled.

"All turned out well. Sometimes that's all we can hope for."

Warren saw another side of the captain that until now had been hidden from him. He was a steady sailor and totally dependable, an opinion he could have never imagined on their first meeting.

"Anchored in Toulon harbor is the *Sonia B*, one of the ships my father owns, she normally works the Atlantic trade."

"What kind of ship?"

"I'm a cavalry man, so I don't know ships. But she's certainly bigger than this one and she needs a captain. Would you consider it?"

Seldom at a loss for words, Kennedy didn't know what to say. He had come to like and respect the Englishman, but was this offer was remarkable.

"Can Nick handle *Kestrel*?" Warren asked.

"Why?"

"She's quite handy. Who knows what need we might have in the future?"

The entire situation suddenly seemed so absurd to Kennedy that he laughed.

"I think the salt water got to your brain," he said.

"I'm serious. Serve three years as captain of the *Sonia B*, and you'll be half owner."

Suddenly Kennedy knew that Warren meant what he was saying and what his answer would be.

Chapter Nine

"Should I kill him?"

Kimberly Scharff stood in the cool wind, waiting for the guard to allow her inside the inner courtyard. Today's visit would be her fifth try to see Louis. The nightmare had started the week prior when three men had come to the hospital and arrested him. All she had been able to find out in the next two days was his location.

Since then she had been unable to see her husband, the sergeant at the Okopna Jail telling her that she would have to come back the next day. When she had tried to enlist the help of their friend, Major Zhukov, he had been told that Louis was being held on suspicion of spying. It was a matter being investigated by the secret police and any interference would be dealt with severely. The head of the hospital was less helpful, telling her that there was simply nothing that could be done.

Today, however, she had not been turned away and now was being led up a flight of stairs to the second floor.

"Here is the Thomassy woman, major."

Kimberly recognized Major Hart, having seen him several times at the hospital when he had come to question James. She knew he was not a man to cross.

"Close the door, sergeant," Hart ordered in Russian.

The major stood up and walked across the room. Kimberly thought his high collar looked foolish with his bandaged head. Obviously he was a vain man.

Hart turned his head slightly as if appraising her, his eyes sharp and piercing.

The blow came like a flash. His flat hand slapped her hard on the face, knocking Kimberly backward into the wall. She stumbled and fell at his feet.

He looked down at her.

"Do you remember me?" he asked quietly in English.

She nodded, afraid to speak.

"I thought you might."

He looked down at her, smiling slightly.

"You husband is working for the British. It seems likely to me that you are also working for them. Certainly a military tribunal would have no problem with my logic."

"It's not true."

"Shut up."

Hart looked down at the woman, her hair disheveled and tears on her cheeks.

It was a nightmare, but she knew there was no awakening from it.

Kennedy's active smuggling business had taught him the shoreline in and around Sevastopol. He now guided the small boat, rowed by Warren and Scully, toward a secluded cove on the western end of the harbor. The sloop had brought them in close to the beach prior to working back off the coast. Nick would bring *Kestrel* in close to the beach early each morning to make a rendezvous if needed.

Pickering knelt in the bow, serving as lookout. Discussing the best way to enter the city, Kennedy had felt that once ashore in the cove, he'd be able to move into the city, avoiding the fixed emplacements, which the army had set up early in the siege. Now they would find out if he was right.

The weather was on their side, the sea being calm for this time of spring. Several lights were visible on the shoreline, and the quarter moon illuminated just enough of the rocks to allow Kennedy to guide the boat precisely to the cove.

"Pull the boat up as high as you can," Kennedy said as they all splashed into the shallow water and began to muscle the boat toward a clump of rocks. Once hidden near the rocks, they inverted the boat and threw handfuls of sand and rocks on top.

"There's a trail that leads toward the harbor," Kennedy said, "Follow me."

Each man carried a Colt pistol, the Baker rifles having been left on the beach. Dark cloaks helped them blend into the darkness and the few people they had seen took no notice of them. Their destination was a stable where one of Kennedy's Russian business partners lived.

"There it is," Kennedy said as they turned a corner on a deserted street. The stable was small with a wooden corral next to it. A light from inside showed through the single window facing the street.

"Wait here," he said. "I'll be back."

Two minutes later they saw him wave, signaling it was clear to proceed.

After so long at sea, the stable stank of manure and wet straw. Kennedy led them to the rear of the building where a small room stood against the wall.

Opening the door, the men went inside, the room occupied simply by a table and single bed. One wall had several wooden pegs with bridles and tack hanging from them.

"This is Pushkin," Kennedy said.

The Russian was short, barrel-chested and totally bald. He nodded to them.

"Sit down," he said in broken English.

Their plan had been simple. Pushkin was to go to the military hospital, make contact with the doctor and make arrangements for their escape.

"It's still early," Warren said. "Can he go to the hospital now?"

Kennedy thought a moment. "It can be done. I'll go with him most of the way, then he will go in the hospital."

"Would you like someone to watch your back?" Scully asked.

"I would," Kennedy answered, "But it's too dangerous."

So it was decided. The three of them would wait for Kennedy and Pushkin. Their best estimate was that they would take ninety minutes. If Louis was working , they would come straight back and possibly arrange the escape for tonight. Everyone knew that was an outside chance but they would try to make it happen.

Warren was pleased with how everything had gone so far. Hopefully their luck would hold.

"Thomassy's been arrested," Kennedy said, sitting down with a grunt. "He's in the Okopna Jail. They picked him up last week, the charges are spying and treason."

Warren listened, his plan now in shambles.

"Apparently that bastard Hart is involved," Kennedy added.

"Should I kill him?" Scully asked.

While Warren knew the remark was flippant, he also knew that Scully would happily kill the Russian. Perhaps it would come to that.

"What about his wife?"

Kennedy shook his head.

"Nothing was said about her, but I know where she lives."

Louis lay awake on the stone floor, a thin blanket providing the only comfort from the cold in the cell. A feeling of despair weighed on him, almost as painful as the bruises on his face suffered during his interrogations. How did this come to be? He had gone over everything he could think of, trying desperately to figure out what led the Russians to believe he was working for the British. It was absurd. He was a physician. He had no interest in politics, only to do his work. The reality that Major Hart, a fellow American, was probably the driving force behind this, made his confusion complete.

The small house on Buzkova Street was dark when Warren, Scully and Kennedy arrived. Pushkin and Pickering were off on their own, trying to contact one of Kennedy's old friends the Englishman thought might help them.

A light appeared in the small window next to the front door after several minutes of quiet knocking by Kennedy. The men heard a bolt slide open and the door opened a fraction.

"Yes?"

"It's Richard Warren, may we come in?"

"Captain Warren? Yes, of course," Kimberly stammered, swinging the door open.

Following her into the sitting room, they stood while she lit two additional candles.

Turning to Warren she said, "I don't understand, captain. Why are you here?"

Warren saw the dark bruise on the side of her face.

"What happened to you?"

"The Russians," she paused then asked again, "Why are you here?"

"Your husband told me he wanted you out of this city. I'm here to make that happen."

Kimberly looked shocked.

"He's been arrested," she said softly, "I can't leave."

Kennedy said, "You can't help your husband. You're probably in danger yourself."

"Let me get you safely away, then we'll try to help the doctor," Warren said quickly, knowing there was likely nothing they would be able to do.

Kimberly asked herself how she could leave Louis. He was alone and even worse, at the mercy of that bastard Hart.

"Why is the British army sending men into Sevastopol?" she asked.

"We're not working with the British."

"I'm sorry," Kimberly said, "I don't understand."

151

"A long story, which I don't have time to relate. Now can you be ready to leave within the hour?"

Scully remained at the front entrance, noting with relief that the street remained deserted.

Kimberly stood her ground, asking, "Can you rescue Louis from the Okopna jail?"

"It's a tough nut," Kennedy offered. "An outer wall with reinforced walls inside around the cells."

"You've been there," Warren asked.

"Several times," he answered. "I had business with one of the senior sergeants."

"Can we get in there?"

Kennedy shook his head. "Not likely, but I'll ask Pushkin."

Pickering stood motionless, waiting for Pushkin, who had entered a single door on the far side of the street. The early morning cold was beginning to work into his bones. An occasional shaft of pain would stab up his left arm making him wince. He had slowly begun to get used to his lost hand. Seldom would he try to reach for anything with the missing hand anymore, a phenomenon that had taken several months to disappear. The device from Doctor Willoughby had proved to be superb, with little discomfort. His dexterity improved every day and the tool possessed a unique utility with the curved band. He was very pleased the lining of the steel cap kept the cold from passing to his arm, which would be a bitch on a night like this.

Pushkin was in search of Anatoly Tolin, a Russian sailor who had crewed for Kennedy for several years and been part of his distribution network across the city. Tolin had a vast network of connections in the underworld of Sevastopol. Pushkin had been honest with Warren saying that he felt Kennedy trusted

Tolin more than was warranted. Kennedy had acknowledged that there are had been several instances in the last few years that made him question if Tolin was running something on the side, but Kennedy never felt the sailor had double-crossed him.

Sleep had been elusive for the doctor. The hard stone floor and frigid temperatures made getting any rest almost impossible. A bowl of soup twice a day with a piece of stale bread at night had provided little if any nourishment. But it was the uncertainty of the future that lay like a stone on his heart. There was no one outside these walls to speak for him and he was truly on his own in a foreign country on the other side of the world from his home. With no diplomatic representation from the United States closer than Moscow, he had little chance of official help.

He heard the bolt slide on his door and squinted as a lamp was thrust into the cell. Two soldiers entered pulled the doctor to his feet, pushing him to the door. The sergeant said something in Russian to the men who turned the prisoner left down the passageway

Standing in front of Hart's desk, Louis watched the major as he read what appeared to be a letter. While his hands were unbound, the two guards remained at his side.

Throwing the paper on his desk, the major looked up.

"I have received authority to conduct a military tribunal to try you for espionage," he said in English. "The outcome is already decided. But for the sake of diplomacy, we will go through all the motions. Then we will hang you, doctor."

Listening to the words should have made him recoil with the terrible reality, but Louis found that he was numb to emotion. Perhaps it would hit him later, but now the pronouncement by Hart seemed simply to be one more act in the play of horrors since his arrival.

"Hart, why are you doing this? What have I done? We're both Americans for God's sake."

The major ignored Thomassy's question. "Perhaps the tribunal will show leniency, it's hard to tell. But if there was information you could provide about who you worked with, it might go better."

"You and I both know I'm not working for the British. I don't know what game you're playing, I'm just a doctor."

"Perhaps I might be able to arrange a positive outcome of the trial," Hart said and smiled at the doctor. "But that would cost a great deal of money, if it could be done."

"Tolin told me there was no easy way in or out of the jail."

Not the answer he was looking for, Warren was at a loss for what to do next. This was not the kind of situation that cavalry training prepared one to undertake.

"So for now we're stuck," he said.

Scully thought for a moment then said, "If the guards are as green as the guards where we were kept, perhaps we could bribe them?

Kennedy shook his head.

"These are jail guards, not conscripts. Not that they might not be ready to take a bribe, but they're not fools."

Pushkin nodded.

Thinking aloud, Kennedy said, "If we could get Hart out of the jail, perhaps we could try and run a scam."

"Like what?" Warren asked.

"Prisoners are always being moved around. We show up with an official order and take him out through the front door."

Warren looked at Kennedy, trying to see if he was serious.

"I can get uniforms and paperwork. It would just take gold."

Scully said, "We don't know when or if Hart would be there"

Kimberly had been listening from her seat by the wall.

"Perhaps I can help," she said, her mind reaching back to just before the Battle of Alma. "I should have thought about this before, General Tamaroff. I met and talked with him the night before the battle. I thought then that he was a decent man and he was the one who Louis went to for permission to take you to hospital."

Warren knew they were desperate. Any plan must happen quickly and allow them to get out of the city. This might very well be the only way.

General Vladimir Tamaroff did indeed remember the wife of the American doctor.

Shown in by the general's senior aide Lieutenant Colonel Azarov, Kimberly knew this might be her only chance to save her husband.

"Madam, it is good to see you," the general said, with a sincere smile on his face. "Please have a seat and tell me what I can do for you."

In a rush of words, she related the events of the last two weeks. The general said nothing, but did look twice at his aide during her description.

"Hart?" the general finally asked of his aide when Kimberly finished her tale.

"Intelligence service, sir."

"General, Louis is a doctor, that's all. He's done his job and nothing more. Ask the hospital. He spends all of his time there, taking care of the wounded."

Tamaroff remembered Louis from Alma and then again when he had asked for permission to treat several British prisoners. That was not incriminating in itself, but damned odd, he told himself.

"But why did he go out of his way to take care of the British prisoners?" Tamaroff asked her.

She told the story of the incident south of the river after the battle.

"Quite a coincidence, I would say," the general observed.

"Sir, I had never seen Major Hart until he arrived in the surgery demanding to be seen. I don't believe he felt that my husband gave him the attention he deserved by rank. But his wound was superficial and we had terribly wounded soldiers to care for."

While the army needed the intelligence service, Tamaroff knew that power was often abused. This Hart needed to be checked on.

"Colonel, I want you to look into his immediately and report your findings to me. Mrs. Thomassy, I will do my best to determine what is happening and if there is reason to hold your husband."

Kimberly felt a great surge of hope. Perhaps the nightmare might finally end.

"Colonel who?" Hart asked the sergeant, trying to place the name.

"Azarov, sir."

"Very well. Send him in."

The major rose behind his desk, his curiosity piqued.

Lieutenant Colonel Leonid Azarov wore the uniform of a Colonel of Hussars. The aiguillette he wore on his right shoulder indicated he was an aide to a general officer. Suddenly Hart felt uneasy.

"Please have a seat, colonel. How may I help you?"

"Are you holding an American doctor by the name of Thomassy?"

The grim expression on Azarov's face told Hart that the question had already been asked and the colonel knew the answer.

"Ah, yes, sir. He is suspected of working for the British."

The stammer was noticed by Azarov, who waited a moment then asked, "What proof do you have?"

Without thinking, the major said quickly, "Several informants, sir."

"Let me see the written records of their statements and their names, please."

Realizing he had been trapped, Hart moved behind his desk trying desperately to think of what he could say.

"That might take some time, sir. With the bombardments, our records are in great disarray. But I assure you I will send for them immediately."

"I will see the doctor now, major."

Feeling he might have deflected the colonel, he said, "Sir, I must ask on whose authority you make this order. This is a security matter."

"I am here on orders from General Tamaroff, major. Is there a problem?"

"No… No, sir."

"Good. Now get the doctor in here."

The bruises on the doctor's face were still livid from his last interrogation. The dirty clothes he wore were rank from his own filth and a raking cough made it hard for him to breath. The dull stare made it clear the mistreatment had been thorough.

While he did not have the full picture, Leonid Azarov did not like what he had heard or seen. Something was going on and he was going to find out what it was.

"Major, I am taking custody of this man. He will be taken to the Military District Headquarters. I expect you to report by tomorrow with the written evidence and the informants. I will question them. Do you understand?"

Chapter Ten

"This is a small boat to cross a big ocean."

A steady wind from the northwest drove *Kestrel* steadily west. At the wheel, Kennedy enjoyed the fresh air. He reflected on the stuffy week they had spent in hiding with Pushkin in the stable. But it had been safe and ultimately the best course they could have taken.

The doctor had been released only the day before and a late night transfer had brought him and his wife aboard the sloop with the rest of the Englishmen. Louis had fought to stay in Sevastopol, but finally his wife had persuaded him that the future held no promise for them in Russia. That was certainly true for Kennedy and every mile between them and Sevastopol made his spirits rise.

"Fine weather."

Warren moved back to the wheel, his steps careful as the deck kept up a steady rolling motion.

"How are our passengers?"

"Both are still asleep."

The two small cabins had been allocated to the doctor, who still had a fever, and to his wife for her privacy. Blankets now lay about the cabin as the rest of the crew tried to get their rest.

Warren looked forward and saw that Scully was sitting on a folded tarp staring out to sea.

"What's your plan?" Kennedy asked.

"Captain, I count on your counsel on all things dealing with the ocean. I will also talk with the doctor and his wife. They must have their say, but we must certainly get to Toulon."

"No problem with weather. A stop for supplies would be warranted, but Toulon is fine with this old sailor."

"The *Sonia B* does need her new master."

Kennedy grinned, "Aye, that she does."

Warren moved forward to sit next to his old friend.

Scully looked up as if torn from thought.

"Good morning, my lord."

"To hell with you, Scully."

The Irishman laughed.

"Did you ever think we would be where we are?" Warren asked.

"No, but it surely is better than the trenches around that bloody city."

Warren thought of the men that would die in the days to come. Should he feel guilty about leaving the army and his responsibility?

"I've been thinking," Scully said, his eyes still on the horizon.

"Something that always gives me cause for concern."

"I would prefer to call you 'Dick.' I suspect no one has ever called you that and I would like to be the only one that does."

"Dick? My God, no one ever has called me that. But if truth be known, it has a ring to it."

Scully grinned. "So where to next?"

"I was just talking about that with our good captain. We were thinking Toulon. After that, maybe the Americas."

"Cross the Atlantic?"

"Many Irishmen have done it before you, Michael Scully."

"Do they have Irish whiskey over there?"

"If not, we'll be certain to take a good supply."

"This is a small boat to cross a big ocean."

"I thought we would make our crossing on the *Sonia B*. In the luxury we both have earned."

Scully decided that the future looked very interesting indeed.

"Have you checked on the doctor?"

"Aye, he was sleeping, but I don't like his look."

Warren knew his friend had a unique ability about these things.

"Can you do anything for him?"

"I need some herbs. When do we get to Constantinople?"

"Kennedy said in two days."

"I hope it's soon enough. If I'm right, I've seen this before. We called it Irish Fever."

Warren looked at him.

"So many died," Scully said quietly. "It's an ugly thing to be sure."

Warren went below deck as Kimberly was coming out of her small cabin.

"Good morning. How are you?" he asked.

161

"Fortunate that I've never had a problem with the motion of the sea."

Pickering asked, "Can I get you some something to eat?"

"Mr. Pickering," she replied, "It appears you have adapted well to the sea."

"Well enough, ma'am. We have bread, cheese and beer or wine."

Kimberly laughed.

"I would have expected nothing less from a boat full of men. Would tea be out of the question?"

Pickering looked surprised.

"No, actually we have a small stove."

"I am from Austria, Mr. Pickering. Beer would be fine with my cheese and bread."

He smiled.

"Might I request you call me James?"

"It would be my pleasure, James. And, I am not old enough to be called ma'am. Kimberly, please."

"Michael has been watching your husband," Warren said. "He's concerned the fever has not broken."

Kimberly's eyes told Warren that she also was worried. To have saved Louis from a Russian jail only to have illness take him would be the ultimate irony.

"I have no medicine with me," she said.

"Michael feels that he'll be able to find something in Constantinople." He saw her question before she asked it.

"Good winds will put us there in two days."

She rose and walked carefully to the second cabin door. Taking a deep breath she opened the latch.

A small alcohol lamp provided light for the little alcove. The single bunk lay against the hull, angling outward toward the stern.

Closing the door she moved to her husband's side. He was laying on his back, sweat beaded on his face, his breathing shallow.

"Louis?"

At first he showed no reaction, then as if with an afterthought he slowly opened his eyes.

She took his hand.

"I'm here," she said feeling the heat coming from his skin.

He closed his eyes as he squeezed her hand ever so slightly.

For the next two days, the captain or first mate manned the wheel, coaching the best possible speed from the sloop. Scully or Kimberly sat at Louis's bedside continually as the pain and fever continued unabated. Delirious most of the time, the doctor fought as they kept spooning water and beef broth down his throat. A little diluted whiskey and vinegar also became part of the ongoing ritual and Scully said that he felt the doctor responded most favorably to the spirits. But the fever did not break and the doctor remained unaware of the world around him.

Warren stood on the main deck, his back against the mast. Ahead, the sea was calm, a few wisps of clouds high above the sloop made it seem like summer, not spring. He was deep in thought, going over the series of events of the last day. Anchoring in their familiar location off Constantinople, they had gone ashore quickly in search of the trader Abboud, only to find that cholera had begun to appear in the port. Abboud had left the city for his own safety and no one knew when he would return.

Warren knew that bringing Louis ashore would be foolish, and so would exposing the crew to the often fatal disease. Kennedy had offered another option. Get underway immediately, cross the Sea of Marmara, transit the Bosporus and cross to the Greek mainland. Their goal was the village of Kalamata. Located at the top of the Messenian Gulf, it was sheltered well from the spring storms, the home village of Nick and where they would find Doctor Keriacas. Kennedy had been to Kalamata, knew the doctor and thought it was Louis's best chance. A quick trip to the local market had resulted in a number of herbs, which Scully packed away for the voyage.

"Having second thoughts?"

Warren turned to see Scully.

"Are you?"

The Irishman sat down on a pile of tarps next to the bulkhead.

"Dick, we've both seen cholera. Irish fever is bad enough, we didn't need any more problems."

"Has he responded to your new medicine?"

Scully shook his head.

"Takes time," he said.

"What did you give him?"

"An old remedy from a midwife in Derrycannan. Uses Yarrow and Black Elderberry, a potion is made from boiling them together."

The two men watched the waves across the seascape, the expanse seeming to run on forever.

"How's she holding up?" Warren asked.

The question struck a note with Scully. How was the doctor's wife dealing with watching her husband die and not being able to do anything about it?

"All right, I suppose. Not much else to do, really."

"The captain told me we'd reach Kalamata early tomorrow morning. I hope the doctor can last until then."

"Why?"

Warren said, "They think this Greek doctor can do something for him."

Shaking his head, Scully got up to go aft.

"Nothing else can be done by this world, my friend. It's in God's hands now."

Under shortened sail, the sloop closed the coast as the sun began to rise. A thin mist hid the land, but Jim Kennedy knew they were close to the coast. The bottom in this part of the gulf was sandy and deep, no problem for *Kestrel* to continue closing the small town of Kalamata.

Nick stood in the bow, his eyes scanning for anything familiar to mark their way. The young Greek was excited to be coming back to his village. He had only been back twice in the last two years and he knew there would be changes.

The two other deck hands waited amidships, ready to make any alterations to the sails during the final approach to anchoring.

"Louis?"

Kimberly thought she had seen his eyes open slightly or was she seeing things? The hours in the small cabin, spelled only by Michael, had taken a toll on her, but not on her spirit. She

165

knew that her husband would survive and she would not think otherwise.

Slowly the doctor's eyes opened and this time remained open.

Reaching for the bedside, she leaned over him.

"Louis?"

Feeling his cheek she realized the fever had broken. He would live.

When Warren thought back about the two weeks they had spent in the little village of Kalamata, he couldn't point to any single thing that made their stay wonderful. Perhaps it had been the mild weather, or the hospitality of the people or even the remarkably good food, but the stress of the last six months seemed to fade into the background.

The doctor had continued to regain his strength, now comfortable in a small house only a short distance from the beach. Treatment from the renowned Doctor Keriacas had proved unnecessary. After a brief examination, he assured Kimberly and Michael that their patient would indeed recover.

Pickering, Kennedy and Nick spent much of their time either fishing in the bay using one of the local longboats or making small repairs to the sloop. James Pickering found that he enjoyed the fresh air and being on the water, a new experience for a boy from Leicester. For his part, Kennedy took the young man under his wing, teaching him about the sloop's rigging, its sails and how they worked at sea.

Warren knocked on the door of the house where Louis and Kimberly were staying. Kimberly opened it, a bright smile on her face.

"Richard, please come in."

"I don't want to intrude, but if the doctor is up to it, I would talk with him."

She said, "I think he would enjoy that."

Louis's face still showed the effects of his illness, slightly sunken cheeks and dark circles under his eyes. But his smile on seeing Warren told the story of a man enjoying being alive.

"You are looking much better, Louis. Your nurse must know her job."

"Richard, please sit down. I almost feel like my old self, ready to get on with things."

Kimberly said, "I will leave you two. I'm going for a short walk."

Louis watched her go then turned to Warren.

"I'm a lucky man."

"Louis, have you decided what you will do now?"

The doctor hesitated then said, "It's something that I find is now occupying most of my thoughts. But I haven't come up with any answers."

"We're at your disposal to take you wherever you would like to go."

"And that, my friend, is the question. Where will we go? Back to Austria to Kimberly's home, somewhere in Europe or back to the United States. I simply don't know."

Warren could see his friend was grasping for an answer that was going to be difficult to find.

"But ultimately I think I would like to return home. Kimberly has heard all of my tales of Virginia and I would like her to see it."

"That is your home?"

Thomassy nodded.

167

"A small town just south of Richmond, on the James River."

"Do you know of Greenville, North Carolina?"

"It's about one hundred miles south of Hopewell."

Warren's father owned a large tobacco plantation in Greensville. What better place to begin their journey?

Ten days later the sloop entered the harbor of Toulon on the south coast of France. The harbor was small compared to Marseille and most of the larger ships were anchored in the eastern side of the bay.

Kennedy, while paying attention to the task at hand, couldn't keep from scanning the anchorage, wondering which of the dozen or so larger ships was the *Sonia B.*? Like a damned groom before a wedding he thought, but he couldn't help himself. Anchoring five hundred yards offshore, by the time the crew finished securing the sails and lines, two small boats had already put out towards them. Bum boats, found in every port in the world, ready to service any ship that dropped anchor.

Kennedy looked down at a dory approaching the side.

"Traversier?" one of the men rowing the boat asked, looking for a fare.

"*Sonia B.*?" Kennedy asked, hoping they might know the ship.

The older man nodded.

Richard Warren walked up behind him.

Kennedy grinned at Warren. "Would you like to go see your ship?"

"I believe you are to be the captain, Mr. Kennedy. That makes her your ship also."

The dory cleared the side of a large but neglected Indiaman and the two men pulled toward a ship anchored north of the main anchorage. Kennedy shielded his eyes from the glare of the sun and strained to see what type of rig the *Sonia B.* might have.

"My God, she's a Blackwaller," Kennedy said, stunned as ship's outline became clear.

"What?" Scully asked as they all looked at the sleek hull which now glistened black across the water.

"It appears the *Sonia B.* has gotten Mr. Kennedy's attention," Warren said.

Kennedy watched as they closed the ship. The *Sonia B.* was indeed a unique vessel. Constructed at the Blackwall Yard on the Thames, she was part of a class of ships that looked very much like a Royal Navy frigate, not a wallowing merchantman. To Kennedy, she was the prettiest ship he had ever seen.

"Ahoy, on the *Sonia B.*"

The lead oarsman had tied the dory's painter to the heavy line that ran down the ship's side from forward.

A face appeared in the entry port.

"What's your business?" the bearded man asked.

"The new captain's coming aboard," Warren called up as he climbed the rope and wood ladder that ran down the side.

It was almost one month later that the *Sonia B* dropped anchor off Kalamata.

"Anchor secured. Appears to be holding, captain."

"Thank you, Mr. Shaw. Please put the jollyboat in the water. Mr. Warren will want to go ashore straight away."

The ship's second mate, Leonard Shaw, touched the edge of his cap and moved forward to find the ship's boatswain.

169

Below deck in the large captain's cabin, Warren poured two cups of coffee from the silver pot, setting one in front of Scully.

"The captain told me he would put a boat in the water in short order. I'll go ashore to collect the doctor."

"It will be good to stretch my legs a bit more than those strolls on deck."

Warren looked out the rear cabin windows, seeing the village of Kalamata where several small boats had pushed off the beach and were heading for the ship. Or they might be going out to *Kestrel,* he thought, which was now under command of Nick Nicodemis, carrying four new crewmen from Kalamata. The two ships had made the transit from Toulon in good time, with the small sloop always in sight of the big frigate.

Kennedy stood on the ship's quarterdeck watching the jollyboat approaching. The previous captain had put a good crew together and it was obvious that they took pride in their jobs. He had found the *Sonia B.* to be in very good condition, well maintained and manned by men who knew their jobs. The ship's officers and senior mates had turned out to be a well-trained crew at sea. It was remarkable to him that a year ago, he had been fighting to survive as a smuggler, now he was master of a truly beautiful ship with the ocean spread before him. Richard Warren had treated him with respect in front of the crew and friendship when they were alone. For the first time in his memory, James Kennedy thought of the future with a note of hope.

Chapter Eleven

"Have you ever seen how your slaves live?"

The humidity reminded Warren of India, to say nothing of the flying insects that had been their constant companions since being rowed ashore from the *Sonia B*. But it did feel good to be on a horse again after so many days at sea. The three men moved west slowly, conserving their energy and their horses. With an early start, Warren expected to reach their destination by sunset.

The ship had originally made landfall at the mouth of the York River, anchoring in Hampton Roads in the heat of late August after an uneventful Atlantic crossing.

During the trip, Louis had continued to gain his strength back and by their arrival he was eager to return to Hopewell. Kimberly seemed anxious to see her new home and they departed after Warren promised to visit.

Following two days of replenishing food and water, the *Sonia B*. put back to sea headed south along the coast. One day later, Captain Kennedy entered Pamlico Sound through one of the numerous channels leading into the large body of water, then continued west. A local sailor hired in Hampton Roads, who was familiar with the Sound, helped Kennedy work his way toward the Pungo River. Judicious use of a shot line, brought the ship to the mouth of the river, and the *Sonia B.* now lay at anchor twenty miles east.

They'd been able to purchase three horses from the local village and get directions to Greenville, which lay twenty five miles west.

"So they grow tobacco here?" Scully asked, breaking the silence of the last twenty minutes.

"Very good tobacco, I've been told. That was one of the main reasons my father purchased Belvoir. He loves his pipe and developed a liking for North Carolina leaves."

"How large is Belvoir?" Pickering asked.

"Just about six thousand acres. But that encompasses the entire property. I don't know the acreage of the fields themselves."

The men rode on, the only sound now the occasional bird calling from the thicket.

Scully laughed.

"Six thousand acres. More than a wee farm I'd say."

Warren smiled.

A lone rider going the opposite direction told them that they were actually on the edge of the Belvoir plantation. The flat terrain was broken by stands of trees heavy with the leaves of summer. The man had told them to head northwest to find the "big house."

They began to pass by fields, the acreage thick with tobacco, rows of low-lying plants seeming to continue on forever into the fading light. The day was now hot and Warren again thought of India, but the smell of the land was different. The forest and fields seemed vibrant and alive.

A dirt road wound around the copse of trees and they came upon a large field, with workers spread across it.

"Up ahead," Scully said looking farther up the road.

Wagons stood parked on the path and they could see men dumping tobacco leaves into them. Behind the last wagon, a heavyset man on horseback, smoking a cigar, watched the workers. The man turned as they rode slowly past the first wagon. He wore a sloppy, sweat-stained hat and his scraggly beard did little to cover his multiple chins. A black patch covered his left eye, held in place with a leather thong tied around his head.

"This is private property," the man said.

"Is this Belvoir?" Warren asked as they pulled their horses to a stop.

The man nodded.

"Yup."

"And you are?" Warren continued.

"I'm the field boss."

Scully had seen this type before in Ireland: an ugly man with a little authority, reveling in his own importance. In Scully's experience, they were dangerous to those who couldn't defend themselves.

James Pickering sensed the tone from Warren and interjected, "What exactly are those people doing?"

The man said, "First picking."

"I see. So there will be additional harvesting?" Pickering asked.

A black man dumped a bag of leaves into the wagon bed next to the riders.

"Get your lazy black ass to work, Henry. And put your back into it, you ain't pulling your share."

The man, slightly stooped, his hair almost totally gray, simply turned away, his head down.

"The worthless bastards," the man said and took a large puff on his cigar.

"I am looking for a Mr. Whiteside," Warren said.

At that, the man looked over, his expression curious.

"He's at the big house," some of the rudeness gone from his voice.

"And that would be where, my good man?" Scully said, his voice just short of nasty.

The fat man looked at Scully as if he was gathering his thoughts. Then he said, "Two miles. Up this road, then go left at the fork."

Warren spurred his horse without another word to the overseer and they trotted up the road.

"I had heard that the Americans in the south pride themselves on hospitality," Pickering said. "Perhaps I misunderstood."

"That oaf had the manners of an Englishman," Scully said, grinning at Warren.

"Why I tolerate you is a mystery to me, Michael."

Two rows of single-story cabins sat on either side of the road, a mile after they had taken the left fork of the path. A few older women sat on the small porches watching a group of small children playing in the dirt street running between the two rows of crude wooden cabins.

Dismounting, Warren led the other three up to the first cabin where an elderly man sat on a three-legged stool.

"Excuse me, we're looking for the main house at Belvoir. My name is Warren."

The man, bald but for a few strand of white hair, got slowly to his feet, the effort clearly hard for him.

"Yes, sir. The main house is no more than half a mile up the road."

"What is this place?" Scully asked.

"This here's the slave quarters for Belvoir, sir," the man answered, a note of surprise in his voice.

Richard Warren said nothing, but felt anger. Slavery was a barbaric practice that England had aggressively fought to destroy around the world after abolishing the practice across the Empire in 1807. But here in their former colonies, slavery continued.

"What's your name?" he asked the old man.

"Tolly, sir."

"Tolly what?"

"Well everyone just calls me, Tolly."

"Don't you have a second name?" Scully asked.

"Well, I'm the only Tolly, and I've lived here most o' my whole life, so never had need of another name."

An impressive two-story residence lay at the end of the road, which Tolly had indicated. The brick building was highlighted by white window frames and porch railings, which ran the length of the front of the house. Several lanterns lit the yard and two smaller lanterns stood on each side of the double door entrance.

"So who lives here?" Pickering asked as they each tied the reins of their horse to the horse posts lining the right side of the drive.

"The manager is a man named Whiteside. He's been here for at least fifteen years as I understand."

Warren banged the doorknocker and waited.

The door opened to reveal a black servant holding a lamp.

"We're looking for Mr. Whiteside."

"Please come in, sir."

Five minutes later a slender young woman wearing a plain brown dress entered the large parlor. The men stood up and she said, "I am Emily Whiteside. My husband is gravely ill and I'm afraid he can't see anyone."

Warren saw the exhaustion on her face and offered his hand.

"Mrs. Whiteside, My name is Warren, Richard Warren. And my associates, Michael Scully and James Pickering."

She sat down in the nearest chair, her face showing confusion then resignation.

"Mr. Warren, you are Richard Warren?"

"Yes, ma'am."

"Hiram told me he'd received a letter from the owner, but with his sickness I'd forgotten."

They all sat and Warren asked, "Mrs. Whiteside, you said your husband was gravely ill?"

She nodded.

"I sent for the doctor."

"What's wrong, if I might ask?"

"He collapsed this morning, I'm afraid it's his heart," she said, tears in her eyes.

"Mr. Scully has some experience in healing, might he be able to help?"

Mrs. Whiteside stood.

176

"I would be most grateful, Mr. Warren," she said, but her tone did not carry any gratitude. "Please follow me."

"Michael, see what you can do," Warren told his friend. "Let us know what you need."

They heard a loud knocking at the front door. Mrs. Whiteside and Michael Scully stood aside as her servant opened the door.

A very young man in a brown coat and trousers removed his hat.

"I'm sorry to be so late, Mrs. Whiteside. A difficult birth delayed me. Where is your husband?"

"Doctor Hanson, Hiram is upstairs in bed. This is Mr. Scully, he has offered his assistance."

"Thank you, sir."

Scully followed the doctor up a set of winding stairs.

The servant introduced himself as Phillip and asked Warren and Pickering if he might bring them something to refresh themselves. He looked surprised when he found out they would be staying at the house and left to prepare rooms.

Hanson and Scully found Hiram Whiteside in the main second floor bedroom, lying on a large poster bed, several flickering candles illuminating the room. The smell of sweat was strong in the confined air.

The doctor removed a tube from his leather satchel and moved to the side of the bed.

Scully had seen the listening device used before and watched the doctor place the small instrument on the man's chest, the other end of the tube already in Hanson's ear.

"Can I do anything, doctor?" The Irishman asked.

Hanson stood up, taking the instrument from his ear.

"I am sorry, Mrs. Whiteside, your husband is gone."

It was very crisp the next morning as Warren walked down the road toward the slave quarters. He had left word with Phillip that he desired an early call, wanting to see what went on at Belvoir. The death of Hiram Whiteside, both tragic and unexpected, had created an immediate problem for the management of the plantation. His father had trusted Whiteside and with the slow communication across the Atlantic it was crucial to have a trusted manager to oversee the large operation. Now he had to understand what happened here and then find someone who could take over the management.

Approaching the cabins, he could see people already in the street as the sun began to show beyond the far trees. To his surprise, he saw Doctor Hanson talking with an older woman at the entrance to the first cabin. The three visitors had shared a drink with the young doctor, who had stayed overnight rather than making the night ride back to Greenville. Warren liked Hanson, who seemed very mature and professional despite looking so young.

The doctor's opinion was that Hiram Whiteside's heart had finally failed after several years of poor health. He had expressed his frustration at the small amount that physicians could actually do if the heart was involved. But he had said that was the way of the world and he would do his best to learn more about the heart.

"Good morning, doctor."

Hanson turned and smiled.

"Mr. Warren, you are about early."

"I might say the same for you, sir."

"It's the only chance I have to see people before they leave for the fields."

Warren looked down the street and noted that men, women and children were already walking south toward the fields.

"When do they start?"

Hanson laughed.

"Very simple, Mr. Warren. They start when the sun comes up and work until it goes down. If there's a good moon, they'll work after sunset. And they do it seven days a week."

Warren could detect an underlying anger or frustration from the doctor, who turned back to the woman. "Lily, you come see me if it gets any worse, yes?"

"Thank you, sir. Thank you," the woman said and went back into the dark interior of the cabin.

"Have you ever seen how your slaves live?"

The term "your slaves" struck Warren like a blow.

"They are not my slaves, doctor. I abhor the institution. This is first time I've seen this plantation and I am trying to understand what goes on here."

Hanson paused for a moment, looking truly surprised, then said, "Very well. Let me show you."

Over the next thirty minutes, the two men moved through the cabins. Warren was shocked at what he saw and the similarity to conditions in the Crimea struck him. Hanson told him of typhus, cholera, and the other diseases that were common among the slaves. He explained that one in four children didn't survive the first year and most slaves died in their forties.

"But that is the way of the world," Hanson had finally said. "You can't change it and I can't, either. So I will continue to do what I can to help these people, but what I can do isn't much."

Warren looked back at the cabins, all of them ramshackle and needing repair. Again his anger rose, he knew the profits that came from this property, why did Whiteside allow this to go on?

"Thank you, doctor. I'll be frank with you. I don't like what I see here and intend to remedy it."

Hanson smiled and said, "I will look forward to that, Mr. Warren. Now, I must be on my way to Greenville. I still have to earn a living and my book of patients is quite thin."

"And why is that, doctor"

"Youth. I'm only two years out of school. Most people want an old, experienced doctor to care for them. Not that I blame them, but I am a good doctor."

"Perhaps I can ride with you for a time."

"I would like that, Mr. Warren. My horse is at the house, shall we walk back?"

Warren returned to Belvoir at midday. He had ridden with Doctor Hanson for almost two hours discussing everything from the slaves at Belvoir to growing tobacco. The young physician seemed quite knowledgeable on the subject and told Warren his family owned tobacco acreage near Raleigh. An argument with his father, who wanted him to help run the business, had resulted in an education in medicine and total estrangement. Hanson felt his family was waiting for him to fail in medicine and come crawling back to Raleigh. The young man had no intention of failing.

He found Scully and Pickering in the dining room.

"Have you seen Mrs. Whiteside?"

"She's been in and out all morning," Scully noted, pulling a piece of bread off a loaf. "They certainly do know how to put a meal on the table, but I haven't sensed any real hospitality. It's as if we are invaders."

"This pork is truly something, Richard. Do sit down and have some."

It did smell wonderful, he thought as he sat down and poured water from a pitcher, wondering about what Scully had said.

"They told me you had gone riding," Scully said. "I assumed you were out surveying the place?"

"Actually, no. I rode with the doctor on his way back to Greenville. There was a great deal I did get to see, but that wasn't my purpose. In fact, I have a job for you two."

Roger unsaddled his old mare, and made sure she had water and feed before he walked to the house, which was a far cry from the large house where he grew up in Raleigh. The two-room cabin provided enough shelter and comfort for Hanson, but he had learned to be happy with very little. So many of his patients paid for his services in barter, he didn't see how he would ever be able to put any money into the local bank. Now shut out of his inheritance, the prospect of a penurious future had begun to enter his thoughts more and more.

He laid a fire in the fireplace, his source of heat and cooking, knowing that his dinner would consist of boiled cornmeal and coffee. His thoughts strayed to the big houses and large practices of the other doctors in the area. What he needed was for some of those old coots to die. Immediately regretting his un-Christian thoughts, he remembered that he went into

181

medicine because it would allow him to help people, not make money. But a little money would surely make life a little easier.

Late in the afternoon, Warren found Emily Whiteside in the parlor, sitting in chair by the window.

"I am sorry to interrupt, Mrs. Whiteside."

She looked up, her face showing that her mind had been far from this room.

"Please come in, Mr. Warren. I've just been gathering my thoughts."

He sat in the opposite chair and said, "If there is anything I can do, please let me know."

Emily shook her head slightly. Despite the strain on her face, she was an attractive woman, her brown hair accentuating deep green eyes.

"I would like to bury Hiram here at Belvoir, he did love this place." She paused then said as if an afterthought, "Even if it killed him?"

"I beg your pardon, ma'am?"

She turned slightly to look him directly in the eye and said, "The doctor may have said it was his heart, but he worked himself to death."

Warren was surprised at the anger in her voice.

"I am sorry," he said, still confused.

"But it was the demands from London that drove him into the ground."

"I would again tell you I am sorry, but I am unaware of this. I only recently began to inspect my father's business interests. And I must presume those demands came from his agents, my father would never immerse himself in those type of details."

Her eyes showed momentary hesitation before she continued, "Perhaps that is even worse."

"I will offer my apologies along with my condolences. That is all I can do." He hesitated then said, "What are your plans?"

"I'm afraid I haven't given it much thought, this has all happened so suddenly." Her tone was softer and she looked out the window, thinking of her time at Belvoir. "This has been my home for the last seven years."

The faraway look on her face touched Warren. He told himself to overlook what she had said. Emotion had prompted him to say many things over the years he later wished to retract. At least give her the same consideration.

"Tell me about it if you would."

Over the next thirty minutes, Emily told how she had met Hiram Whiteside at a nearby plantation and despite the difference in their ages had fallen in love. Both of them came from a long lineage of tobacco farmers and together they had worked to manage the affairs of Belvoir.

"And you, Mr. Warren? What finally brings you across the ocean?"

He explained how the death of his brother had thrust him into the role of succession.

"I spent ten years in the army, but made the decision to leave the service. Now I'm visiting my father's businesses to learn all I can about them."

"What do you know of tobacco farming?"

He smiled.

"Only what Doctor Hanson told me during our ride this morning. I'm afraid my knowledge of working the earth is primarily how to build redoubts."

"Redoubt?"

"A type of fortification. We used them in India and Russia."

"You've been to India?"

He nodded. For the first time since their meeting he saw a spark in her eyes.

"I always wanted to travel, but it never happened."

"Perhaps now you'll be able to?"

"My family is not wealthy, Mr. Warren. Neither was Hiram's. I need to find a means to support myself. Teaching was always something that I felt I would enjoy, perhaps I might find something in Greenville?"

Warren knew what it was like to wonder about one's future.

Over the next two days, Emily rode the length and width of Belvoir with Richard Warren at her side. Her manner remained reserved as she explained the process of farming tobacco and then demonstrated the reality in the fields.

Warren found her coldness irritating, but realized that she did indeed know how to plant, cultivate, harvest, cure and market tobacco. He found it curious, Hiram Whiteside was the manager, but as she explained the work of Belvoir it was clear that she had been very involved in every aspect of the plantation. How different from what he was used to in England. Women simply did not run large estates, it wasn't something that anyone would even consider. While there was a common heritage between the two countries, the evolution required to prosper in this new land had taken the American women down a much different path. He found it very interesting and oddly pleasing. For the briefest of moments his thoughts brushed over Charlotte.

He always fought to keep the pain at arm's length, but it struck him that she would have enjoyed taking part in a man's world. But it would never be.

On the morning of the third day, a small group of local farmers and business associates of Hiram laid him to rest in the small cemetery near the main building. It appeared to Warren that Hiram Whiteside was well thought of in the community and would be missed. Emily retired upstairs after the reception and Warren decided to stretch his legs.

His walk took him toward the slave quarters, which were fully occupied, the workday taken off in respect of Mr. Whiteside. Despite the warmth, the afternoon was pleasant and many of the men and women were out in front of their cabins, the children running up and down the street, playing happily. Warren approached the first cabin and the adults rose from the bench and stopped talking.

"My name is Warren. I'm looking for Tolly."

A tall man in his late twenties said, "His cabin is the last one on this side, sir."

Warren noticed their clothes were in many cases torn and frayed, although they did appear to be clean. This was a strange world he thought.

He found Tolly sitting outside of the on a stool, watching the activities in the street.

"Please don't get up," he said, watching the man start to rise. "You are Tolly, right?"

The old slave smiled and nodded.

"Yes, sir, you remembered."

Warren sat on the top step of three that led into the cabin.

"Mr. Whitehead was buried this morning."

Tolly nodded, "Yes, sir. He was a good man."

"Tolly, my name is Warren."

"Yes, sir, I remember."

"I'm new to this country and I need to understand some things about it."

The man said nothing, his face showed wariness.

"How long have you been at Belvoir?"

Tolly thought for a moment then said, "Almost forty years, Mr. Warren. The old owner bought me from the farm where I was born and raised up. Guess I was ten or twelve, 'cause I been working the fields for some time when they took me away."

"You were sold away from your family?" Warren asked, knowing what the answer would likely be.

"Yes, sir."

Unbearably cruel, Warren thought. The rich and powerful always dominate the poor and uneducated. He realized, that as abhorrent as Tolly's story might be, what was happening in the workhouses of England weren't a great deal better. The thought filled him with anger and frustration.

"Do you still work?"

Now there was real fear in the old man's eyes.

"I'm sick sometimes, but I try, sir. Mr. Slocum gets angry, but I just can't make it to the fields some days."

"And who is Mr. Slocum?"

"Mr. Slocum's the field boss, sir. He's in charge of working the fields."

"What does he look like?"

Tolly frowned then said, "Well, nothing special. He's a fat man, that's for sure, and he only gots one eye."

"Thank you, Tolly. Enjoy the rest of your day."

Warren walked back toward the house, his anger simmering.

The sun was just setting when Warren heard horses outside in the drive. He was pouring a glass of bourbon whiskey from a tray on the table, thinking of the last week's events.

Scully walked into the room and tossed his coat on the long settee.

"Can I pour you a drink?" Warren asked.

"Indeed you can, Dick, my boy."

Warren grinned to himself, no else would ever call him Dick. But from his friend, it sounded good.

The two sat down and Scully reported the results of their two-day journey. They had visited farms in the area then gone into Greenville. Discrete inquires had revealed that Doctor Hanson was, in fact, exactly what he appeared to be. A young doctor with little money, an enthusiastic love of medicine and a reputation for being an upstanding man. When some of the locals were asked why he wasn't their doctor it took them by surprise. They would never think of leaving their long time physician, perhaps when their doctor retired they would seek out the young doctor.

Pickering had come in half way through Scully's description of what they had found and nodded his agreement as he also poured himself a drink.

"Not two shillings in his purse, but a good outlook on the world," Pickering offered. "The kind of man you would like in the mess with you," he added, falling back to his military days.

"Gentlemen, we have a problem here. This plantation needs someone to run it and I don't like what is happening here."

187

"Don't like what?" Scully asked as he got up to refresh his glass.

"This operation has my family's name on it. I don't condone slavery and I won't be part of it."

"I don't much care for it, either," Scully said, turning back to Warren. "But what can you do about it?"

"That's what we have to figure out."

"Good morning, Mrs. Whiteside."

Emily turned and acknowledged Warren. She looked years younger than at the funeral. It was if the pain and exhaustion had been washed away.

"Please, join me," she said.

He sat at the table as Phillip appeared from the pantry with a pot of coffee.

Warren took a sip of coffee and looked at her.

"You look rested."

She nodded.

"I know it will take time."

"You mentioned teaching," he continued. "I would like to discuss another option."

Emily put her cup back on the saucer, her manner wary.

"Another option?"

"Would you consider remaining at Belvoir?"

"I don't understand," she said.

"Belvoir needs someone to run the operation. I think you would be quite well suited to the task."

Surprise showed in her expression.

"A woman running a tobacco plantation? That would certainly get the attention of the local owners."

"You have the knowledge, know the people and I sensed you have an attachment to Belvoir."

She nodded.

"I do."

"But I will insist that some things change around here."

Now she looked cautious, would the answer to her quandary be destroyed by this man's conditions?

"What would you see changed?"

"Mr. Slocum would be dismissed. I will not have a man like him abusing the workers."

"I don't care for the man, but he knows tobacco farming."

"There are surely other men who know how to work the fields, but don't treat the workers like they are animals. Such as Roger Hanson."

"Doctor Hanson? Why would he stop being a doctor?"

"He wouldn't have to stop practicing medicine."

"I'm confused."

"He is, by all accounts, a good doctor and a decent man. But he's not able to support himself."

"What are you thinking?" Her voice was starting to lose its coldness.

"Build him a clinic here at Belvoir. Let him care for the workers and anyone else who is willing to travel here. But he would also be paid for his assistance in farming the tobacco."

"You keep calling our people workers, does the word slave bother you?

"That is the other change. I am opposed to the practice and cannot be part of it."

Emily stood up and walked to the window, her hands held rigidly at her side.

"And your proposal, Mr. Warren."

"To free them. Allow them to work and live here for a fair wage."

She stood at the window for a long minute, then turned to face him.

"I would like to discuss the particulars, but truth be known I am not a supporter of the institution. There are many things to consider, but I believe I can do the job for you."

"Then it's done. I'll have Mr. Pickering draw up papers to make it official."

Emily paused then said, "This will certainly raise some eyebrows around Greenville." Her tone indicated that she might be having second thoughts.

"Will that be a problem for you?" he asked.

She said, "You're the owner, Mr. Warren. The problem will be seen as one of your making."

Warren smiled. "I have some history of making problems, so this is simply in keeping with my outrageous character."

And so the slaves were freed at Belvoir and the doctor came to live at the big house.

Chapter Twelve

"Lawyers — wouldn't give you a pound of beaver shit for 'em"

By the return of the *Sonia B.* late the next spring, the radical changes at Belvoir had become a source of extreme irritation to the other large landowners in the coastal counties. The idea that a woman was making the decisions over a large plantation flew in the face of the accepted role of southern women. However, the change in the status of the workers was beyond what any true southern tobacco farmer was willing to accept. It was known that only two former slaves had chosen to leave Belvoir, the remainder were now working the land for wages and ownership of their cabins. A school had begun for the children, taught by Emily Whiteside and the clinic provided care for anyone who needed it. Belvoir had become a social deviation that disrupted the established natural order of the tobacco-producing world.

Warren found himself enjoying the weather as the coach approached Belvoir. The passage from Portsmouth had been plagued by two heavy storms that had driven the frigate well south into the Atlantic. The rain and wind combined to make the voyage a trial for both men and ship. But after a port call in San Juan to repair storm damage, Kennedy brought the *Sonia B.* north to Hampton Roads, arriving at the end of May. Kennedy and Warren had agreed that the ship would return to Virginia in mid-July after investigating the possibility of establishing a permanent business office in one of the major ports on the eastern seaboard.

"A man could get used to this," Scully said, watching the awakening countryside move by the coach window.

"But Michael, this is not Ireland."

"I understand they can't even grow potatoes here," James Pickering said, grinning at his friend.

"They surely could, but I'm thinking they don't have the patience," Scully replied.

Warren laughed. "Tobacco is much more profitable, if not quite as tasty."

The hired coach pulled to a stop in front of the front door of the main house. A surprised, but always proper, Phillip came down the front steps to greet them.

"Welcome back, gentlemen."

Warren nodded and said, "All is well with Belvoir, I trust?" He knew his question would surprise Phillip, but he wondered how the older man would respond.

"Indeed it is, Mr. Warren, indeed it is." His voice sounded sincere and optimistic

"Is Mrs. Whiteside at home?"

"No, sir. She's down at the village."

Scully asked, "What village is that?"

"Why Belvoir Village, Mr. Scully. With the school and hospital, it seems to everyone that the quarters have become a village, and they wanted it to have a name."

192

The Englishmen looked at each other, the message clear in their eyes.

Emily had always felt she would be a good teacher. Her marriage to Hiram led her down a different road, but now she found that her time at the small school was the highlight of her day. The children of Belvoir had blossomed into a part of her life that she never would have imagined. With instruction in the basics of reading, writing and sums, the natural enthusiasm of life and learning had turned the two-dozen youngsters into a lively and happy group.

Cecil was one of the sharpest of the group and she had begun to spend time with him after class to help him with more advanced reading. As much as she enjoyed watching the young boy learn, she wondered where it might lead. He was now free, but what did that really mean today in the south?

She looked up from the page when the door opened quietly to reveal Richard Warren. Cecil was reading aloud and hadn't noticed the Englishman.

Warren put his finger to his lips and slowly closed the door, standing quietly as the young man finished a laborious paragraph.

"Very good, Cecil."

"Thank you, ma'am."

"Why don't you run on home? I'm sure your momma is waiting with supper."

Cecil stood up and noticed Warren.

"Hello, Cecil," he said.

"This is Mr. Warren, Cecil. I believe he just arrived from England."

The boy frowned slightly then smiled, having remembered where England was on the world map the class had been learning.

"I gotta go," he said and was out the door.

Emily stood up and smoothed the front of her dress.

"We expected you to arrive last month," she said, picking up the book and walking to the large desk at the rear of the room.

Warren said, "The Atlantic refused to cooperate. We had to take a much more circuitous route than normal." He reached down and picked up the book.

"The Eclectic Second Reader for Young Children with Pictures."

"An American teacher named McGuffey wrote them. They are very useful for teaching reading and vocabulary."

He flipped through the pages and then placed the book on the desk.

"And have you found that you enjoy teaching?"

She paused. She was surprised that he remembered what she had said when they first met.

"I do," she said.

"More than managing Belvoir?" he asked, his voice friendly.

Emily laughed and Warren realized it was the first time he had ever heard her laugh.

"I am most happy with the arrangements, Mr. Warren," she said, seeing that he also had a sense of humor, something that she had never considered.

Following a tour of the Belvoir Clinic, Warren and Scully had ridden the fields with Mrs. Whiteside. The repairs from the winter weather were the first points of inspection, then a tour of the fields to examine the young plants, just beginning to grow with the spring warmth.

"Once they've been planted from the seed beds, it becomes a constant battle to nurture the young plants. As they mature, we'll groom them to produce the best leaves possible."

They dismounted and she showed them the young plants and what the workers would be looking for as the season progressed. The morning was still fresh, not a hint of humidity and the three of them stood at the edge of the field enjoying the beauty of Belvoir.

Pickering cantered down the road and they turned as he reined the young mare to a halt.

"There are two men at the house asking to see you, Richard. They weren't exactly friendly, but I ascertained their names were Bloodsworth and Haney."

The two men were sitting in the parlor when Warren arrived back at the house. Bloodsworth was a tall, heavyset man with thinning hair. His companion seemed half of his size, curly black hair and a thick mustache making their difference in appearance almost comical.

Both men stood as Warren and the others entered the room.

"My name is Richard Warren, I understand you are looking for me."

Bloodsworth extended his hand and said, "Lawrence Bloodsworth, pleased to meet you. This is my associate Stephen Haney. I own Rose Springs, I'm sure you have heard of it."

"These are my associates, Mr. Scully and Mr. Pickering. You know Mrs. Whiteside."

They nodded, acknowledging Scully and Pickering, but not offering their hands. Neither man acknowledged Emily directly.

"Please be seated, gentlemen."

"Now what may I do for you?"

Bloodsworth cleared his throat, and said, "I believe it would be more appropriate if Mrs. Whiteside were to retire. What I have to say might offend."

Warren caught himself and maintained a civil demeanor.

"Certainly there could be nothing that gentlemen might discuss which would offend a lady, would you not agree, Mr. Bloodsworth?"

Haney shifted in his chair, his uneasiness clear, but he remained silent.

"Perhaps in England, sir. Not in North Carolina."

His anger seething, Warren smiled at Bloodsworth.

"I forgot, sir, America is still very much a wilderness in many ways."

Bloodsworth's face reddened and he said, "Very well, Warren, it's about this school and clinic that you've started at Belvoir. Your attitude toward your slaves is creating a problem across the coastal counties."

His voice turned to ice and Warren said slowly, "I own no slaves, sir. The workers at Belvoir are free men and women. And if Mrs. Whiteside and I think a school and clinic are beneficial, then that is simply the way it will be. If that is a problem for you, sir, I would suggest that is something you'll have to deal with."

Both visitors stood up abruptly, aware that any discussion had ended.

"You and the rest of the British royalty seem to have forgotten that we whipped you mightily and we don't give a damn what you think. You have not heard the last of this."

Both men walked out of the parlor, picking up their hats from the side table.

"More of that American hospitality," Pickering said.

"Is this the first you've heard of this?" Warren asked Emily.

"There was some talk, but I knew that would happen. Nothing like this."

"But no one has done anything overt?"

She shook her head and said, "Perhaps Doctor Hanson has a better feel for things. He sees more of the county than I do."

Warren had waited while Hanson finished up with one of the pregnant women.

"Richard, it is so good to see you. I wasn't sure when you would arrive."

The two men shook hands and Hanson motioned to a wooden chair while he sat down on a three legged stool.

"Bit of stormy weather, but that is the Atlantic."

Hanson smiled. "Someday you must take me across the ocean with you. I've stood at the shore and wondered what it's like out there."

"It would be my pleasure, I assure you." Warren paused then said, "What do you know of a man named Bloodsworth?"

The look on the doctor's face told Warren that Hanson did indeed know the man.

"I know him," he replied.

"Tell me about him."

"He owns a large plantation, Rose Springs. He's a bit of a bully if you ask me. Tends to push people around to get his way."

"He struck me as a pompous asshole," Warren said.

Laughing, Hanson said, "So you have met him."

"He and a man named Haney just left after a rather unpleasant encounter."

"What happened?"

"They called to tell us that the school was creating a problem in the county."

The doctor said, "I have heard that some of the land owners were less than pleased with our efforts, but I've only been approached by one man, the old field boss."

"Slocum?"

"Yes, sir. In all his drunken splendor. He saw me on the Greenville road and proceeded to tell me that I'd better hope that the new clinic and school didn't burn to the ground."

Warren's anger flared. He knew that emotions about slavery were inflamed, but now he realized that action was needed.

"What did Mr. Bloodsworth mean by British royalty?"

Warren turned to see Emily standing in the doorway to the pallor.

"I don't understand."

She walked to him, her eyes looking for answers.

"Hiram told me your father was a wealthy Englishman. That was obvious, but it was all I ever knew. Now I find out that you are more than that."

"I...." he began.

"Michael and Thomas could not hold up when I began asking questions."

He sighed.

"What difference does it make? I'm Richard Warren, that's all."

What Emily could not bear to say is that his future title meant that his time in America was only a brief interlude in the life of a wealthy, titled gentleman. And, she hated to admit to herself, Richard Warren would never look on her as anything other than an employee.

"I'm, sorry," she said, turning away. "I simply put more into what was happening here than I should have."

Now Warren was confused.

"I'm afraid I don't understand."

She turned back, her eyes wet.

"It doesn't matter."

Damn, he thought, what is she talking about?

"Emily, you're making too much of this, truly."

As she wiped her tears he suddenly knew what she meant.

"I'll be up early in the morning, perhaps you would like to see the area we that could be cleared to open up more land to production," she said, her voice now formal.

As she turned to leave the room, he took her hand.

"Please, stay for a moment."

Her hand was tense, as if she was ready to pull it away from his.

Warren slowly put his other hand up to the side of her face, pausing to look in her eyes and then very slowly and gently kissed her on the lips.

She raised her hand to his cheek and gently returned the kiss.

"You look like the cat that ate the canary, my friend."

Scully carried a mug of coffee as he walked across the porch to where Warren stood looking down the driveway the next morning.

Warren turned and smiled.

"Emily and I had a talk last night, after she had dragged my lineage out of you two."

"She's a mighty persuasive woman, as you well know, Dick my boy."

"Don't I."

"And what did you two decide?"

Warren said, "Actually, I kissed her."

"Bully for you. About time, if you ask me. And I assume the lady was pleased with your attentions?"

"I believe she was."

"Now what?" Scully asked, his tone humorous.

"We need to decide how to protect her and this plantation when we leave."

Scully put his cup down on the banister.

"Do you want me to stay here?"

"Michael, I've come to rely on you and Thomas every day, I need both of you with me. But I can't leave her or the doctor here without taking some precautions. Men like Bloodsworth and Haney are the worst type of scum and I wouldn't put anything past the bastards."

The Irishman thought for a minute.

"I say we talk with young Hanson, he knows the area and might have an idea."

Two hours later, the two men and the doctor were in the saddle, riding to the eastern most boundary of Belvoir. Their destination was the small house of Frank Sanderson, a man that the doctor felt might help solve Warren's problem. Hanson had only said that Sanderson, a trapper and hunter was well known in the coastal counties as someone who was better left alone. The doctor told them he met Sanderson when the man arrived at his old house, asking the doctor to ride back to the cabin, where his wife Ruth lay ill.

"She was quite ill, with the fever, but the Lord was on my side and she recovered. Mr. Sanderson paid my bill in venison, but also told me he was indebted to me. Around here, that means a great deal."

Frank Sanderson reminded Warren of Scully. Tall and powerful, but with a manner about him that told you he knew how to use his brain. He greeted the doctor almost formally, and Hanson introduced the rest by name.

They were invited to join him at an outdoor fire pit that was surrounded by several log benches.

"Come spring, I don't much favor spending any more time in the cabin, 'specially after a long winter."

A crackling blaze took the chill off the light wind that blew in from the east.

"What might I do for y'all? Sanderson asked.

Warren explained who he was and that he was looking for some advice.

Sanderson was surprised.

"And what the hell could I tell someone like you, Mr. Warren?"

"How to deal with a problem, Mr. Sanderson."

"I told Mr. Warren that you had spent your life in the counties and would be a good man to talk with," Hanson said.

Sanderson considered that for a moment.

"I do know these parts," he said, "If I can help, I will."

"Do you know a Mr. Bloodsworth?" Warren asked.

"I do."

"Mr. Bloodsworth and a Mr. Haney came by Belvoir and threatened us because of what we are doing with the workers."

"Haney, he's Bloodsworth's man. Don't care for either of them, bottom scum if you ask me."

Hanson added, "I didn't mention it but Haney is Bloodsworth's lawyer."

Sanderson spat on the fire and said, "Lawyers are shit. If you ask me they're the cause of most of the troubles in this world. Wouldn't give you a pound of beaver shit for any of 'em."

"Would this Bloodsworth do anything to Belvoir?" Warren asked.

Shaking his head the trapper said, "Not him, personally, but I wouldn't put it past the bastard to hire someone."

"What would you do if you we in my place, Mr. Sanderson? I must protect Belvoir when I'm away."

"Hell, that's easy," he said, taking a long appraising look at Warren.

It was just past noon the next day when Warren rode up to the large house at Rose Springs accompanied by Scully and Pickering.

Shown through the house, they found Mr. Bloodsworth on the rear veranda, finishing his midday meal. Standing, he dropped the napkin on the table.

"I did not expect to see you again, Mr. Warren." His manner just short of rude.

"Mr. Bloodsworth, in England, when a man threatens another man, he does it at his peril. I am calling you out, sir. Your choice of weapons, pistols or blade, I don't care. My second, Mr. Scully, will make the appropriate arrangements if you would identify who will serve as your second."

Warren turned and walked out

"Might you know who your second will be, or should I return tomorrow?" Scully asked.

"I... I... This simply isn't done!" Bloodsworth blustered. "I will call the authorities, I will call my lawyer," he fumed.

"Backing out on an affair of honor? That's something an honorable man would not do, sir. But make no mistake, Richard Warren is not a man to cross and you have done just that."

When Pickering and Scully returned the following day, a letter of apology was waiting for them to take to Warren, along with a request to meet.

It was at that meeting that Mr. Bloodsworth, after retracting his threat, was informed that Mr. Frank Sanderson had been employed by Belvoir for security purposes.

Part Two
Distant Trumpets

The Battle of Bull Run, Virginia — July 21st, 1861

"No tongue can tell, no mind conceive, no pen portray the horrible sights I witnessed this morning."

-Captain John Taggert
9th Pennsylvania Reserves
September 17, 1862

Chapter Thirteen

"Eight twelve pounders and two cannonades"

Michael Scully had learned to truly love coffee in the army. Even four years later he still preferred it to the tea that every Englishman seemed to savor. Pouring a full cup, he moved to the window and surveyed the busy waterfront. He could see small boats moving to and from the ships anchored out, ferrying people and supplies about the Portsmouth waterfront. The weather was mild for September, which was known for its unpredictability. The *Sonia B.* was at anchor where the crew was replenishing her and making routine repairs. Three weeks had passed since the frigate had dropped anchor after a swift passage from Charleston, South Carolina. Richard Warren had been on his second trip inspecting the families' properties in America. This trip the ship had carried a full load of tobacco back from the plantation at Belvoir.

Scully had actually come to enjoy their time at sea and the truth be known, he had found their travels wonderfully different from those in the army. In the military, travel was something that was generally uncomfortable and frequently dangerous. But the voyages of the *Sonia B.* had been a pleasure. The ship had travelled to America twice, visiting New York, Boston, Philadelphia and Norfolk as Warren took in the wonders of the modern world of manufacturing and commerce. It had been remarkable to see men motivated by an urge to build and prosper, so very different from the military mentality.

Several properties in the Caribbean had taken the ship to the blue waters and sunny skies of the islands, which seemed a world away from the cold and rain of England. Last summer they had sailed north to Ireland, Scotland and finally Norway. While Richard had insisted their stop at Dublin was needed for minor repairs, and it had given them a chance to visits Scully's family in Drogheda.

It had been a good four years, but something seemed to be unsettling to the Irishman and he couldn't figure it out. He should be a happy man. He had worked hard with Richard and the businesses were doing very well by any measure. Personally he was now financially set for life with large accounts in several banks and a farm near the large house at Albermarle. But he would not dwell on it, he told himself. There was work to do. Kennedy was coming ashore for dinner and Scully wanted nothing left hanging in the office.

Richard Warren watched the bustle of the London streets as the coach made its way across town to the Army Navy Club on Saint James Square. London, he alternately loved and hated the city. The clubs and theaters were the best on earth, but the city was not much different from Constantinople when it came to cleanliness. He had been looking forward to spending time with his father on his return to Albermarle, however a letter had been waiting for him requesting that he call on Sir Hugh Nicholson at his earliest convenience. His father's reaction to the news prompted Warren to ask if the Duke knew the reason for the letter.

"The Foreign Office believes you might be of some service. I think you should listen to what Nicholson has to say."

The look in his father's eyes told Warren that this was not a casual comment.

Warren had met Sir Hugh several times, but only socially. Known for his behind the scenes activities, Nicholson did not serve in any official capacity as far as Warren knew. What could the man possibly want?

Shown to a small waiting room, Warren made himself comfortable, picking up a copy of the Times from a side table.

Five minutes later a door on the far side of the room opened.

"Please do come in."

Nicholson was in his mid-fifties, dressed immaculately and remarkably trim and fit for his age.

Nicholson showed Warren to a comfortable settee and sat down across from him.

"Thank you for coming. I know you have recently been travelling and just returned home."

How the devil did he know that? Warren wondered.

"My father encouraged me to hear what you have to say."

Nicholson looked at him, understanding that Warren was not an enthusiastic visitor.

"Your father has always understood the complexity of dealing with other countries."

"Indeed he has, but that certainly begs the question, why I am here?"

The older man got up and moved to a cabinet, returning with a bottle of brandy and two glasses. Without asking Warren, he poured each a drink and sat down.

"You have just returned from America."

Warren nodded.

"Then you are aware of the tension between the northern states and the south?"

"I would call it more than tension, Sir Hugh. There is a deep level of animosity between the two sides."

Nicholson nodded.

"We have followed developments with interest, but see no clear course for the future."

Warren said, "I don't think the Americans themselves know where this will go. The desire for the rights of the individual states over their national government is an emotional issue."

"As is slavery."

Warren took a sip of brandy.

"A quite emotional issue, Sir Hugh."

"Can you help me understand what is happening?"

This man seems sincere, Warren thought. But there must be more to it.

"I will. But tell me why you are so interested in what is happening on the other side of the Atlantic?"

"Before I tell you that, tell me why you left the army?" Nicholson's voice had taken on a hard tone, telling Warren that the real reason for his visit was about to be made clear.

About to relate the story of having to assume his brother's duties, Warren decided that he would be frank with the man and let things go where they might.

"I was fed up with the utter incompetence of the military and political leaders of this country. Foolish wars, poorly planned and executed, resulting in the loss of thousands of young soldiers and accomplishing nothing." Warren's voice displayed the anger he still felt from the Crimea.

Nicholson finished his brandy and refilled the glass.

"You are right, of course. The government of this country and the military are very slow to change. The Russian war, unfortunately, reflected that. So I would ask you, is there a better way?"

The question was something that Warren had considered after what he had seen in the Crimea.

"We must have professionalism, both in the military and the government. Promotion or position by privilege is absurd. Does the navy allow officers to purchase command of its ships? Of course not, but fools like Cardigan, who have no business leading our troops can gain command by the pocketbook. Whatever party is in power may prosecute a policy that is created by amateurs. It is an insane way to govern an empire and I suspect it will eventually result in loss of that empire."

"You certainly are direct. I'll give you that."

"I'm sure I have offended you in some way. If that is so, I apologize," Warren said, realizing the vehemence he had used.

Nicholson smiled and poured more brandy into his guest's glass.

"To the contrary, it is refreshing to hear. Perhaps I can convince you that there are many who feel the same way, both in the army and at Whitehall."

Sir Hugh could tell by the surprise on Warren's face that he had not expected to hear that comment from someone in the establishment.

"Perhaps," Warren said.

"They do a wonderful roasted goose here. Would you join me for an early supper?"

Alone in a private dining room, the two men continued their conversation, which Warren found more and more interesting.

"You might know Richard Lyons, our ambassador to the American government?"

"I'm afraid not."

"A very astute man, certainly. He's done a fine job so far, dealt with that abominable pig's ear debacle. He feels that the American union is very much in jeopardy. A break up of the states, likely north from south. As those things go, it is unlikely to happen without bloodshed, perhaps even protracting fighting."

Warren knew the level of anger and emotion he had seen on the last trip, there was little doubt that bloodshed was possible, even probable.

"The result of a government breakup opens many doors for England and also presents some grave dangers."

Warren asked, "How so?"

"What effect would it have on Canada? Would it precipitate an invasion by the northern states? Would it allow us to bring any of the southern states into our sphere officially? Trade of course would be a key point, the effects on tariffs and flow of key materials would be at stake."

"The Americans would not be the first country to break apart."

Nicholson finished cutting a piece of goose, taking a healthy bite.

"But if they did, we would want to have some say in the direction of events. Surely we must decide where our most advantageous liaison might lie."

"That stands to reason, certainly," Warren replied.

Taking a drink of wine to wash his goose down, Nicholson sat back in his chair.

"And would you be willing to help this government take and hold the advantage over what might happen?

Warren put down his fork.

"What are you asking, Sir?"

"For your help in a very sensitive issue."

"I wouldn't know where to begin. I'm a businessman and former soldier. I know nothing of politics."

Nicholson placed his napkin beside his plate.

"You know the world and you know war, sir. That knowledge could prove extremely beneficial to this country. If you would consent to provide your assistance, I have already laid the groundwork for you."

He had been set up, Warren thought. But his father had been a party to it and he trusted his father.

"What would you have me do?"

"Return to America, to the south and find out what is happening, from the inside, if you will. As a property owner, you should fit in quite well. Of course, you must use your own judgment on how to proceed, but providing information back to the Foreign Office will be of the greatest benefit."

He immediately thought of seeing Emily. Their relationship had changed so much during the last visit that he kept finding himself wondering when he might bring her to England. Warren forced his thoughts back to the present. What was this man's end game?

"Is there an outcome that England would prefer?"

Sir Hugh shrugged.

"No war and uninterrupted commerce would be preferable. But if there is to be a war, a victory by the south would go a long way toward checking the power of the United States."

Richard Warren had always harbored a keen interest in foreign policy, but this was much more than reading the Times and discussing events over a drink. The issues that Sir Hugh had been discussing were very complicated and perhaps more than a former captain of cavalry was capable of dealing with.

"I have no formal training or actual experience in what you are asking me to do. That raises questions in my mind as to what service I could provide."

Nicholson said, "Don't underestimate yourself. My experience has taught me that men with experience always trump men with academic credentials and sores on their bottoms from sitting at a desk."

Warren thought for a moment and said "Then I will do what you ask."

"Thank you, Richard, if I may call you that. And I assure you that my gratitude will be most sincere."

Nicholson went through the ritual of lighting a cigar after Warren declined.

"We have a man who will serve as your contact, as it were. He was born in England but travelled to America as a young boy. His family retains extensive holdings in Kent. You will know him by the name Rutland. I will be your primary point of contact and you will be briefed on the procedures you should utilize."

The men talked for another two hours framing Warren's mission and discussing what options the future might hold.

"Good morning, gentlemen,"

Pickering and Scully looked up as Warren entered the office.

Pickering had adjusted very well to the loss of his hand and embraced the prosthetic device with enthusiasm. Constant practice now allowed him to do any task without assistance, although Scully would still occasionally cut his meat if they had been drinking wine all night. His desire to overcome any sense of inferiority had resulted in hours of practice with every type of sword aboard the *Sonia B* during the long transits. The result was ability with a sword that few men with two hands could achieve.

"You're back early. Anything wrong at Albermarle?" Scully asked.

"I've been in London, actually," Warren said, removing his topcoat and hat, hanging them on a coat rack.

The two looked at him, the question waiting for Warren to answer.

"I met with a gentleman from the Foreign Office. Not what I would have expected, but I have agreed to provide them with some small assistance."

Scully poured a cup of coffee and set it in front of his friend.

"And what 'small assistance' would that be?"

Pickering walked over and sat on the edge of the desk.

"We shall return to America. Once there, we'll set up a more permanent base of operations, I'm thinking somewhere around Norfolk"

"Norfolk?" Pickering asked.

"We have an investment to examine, the Virginia and Tennessee Railroad, which my father invested in seven years ago. I also think we might see what opportunity there is for a permanent office for our ships, like the one in New York."

Pickering and Scully said nothing, their silence signaling doubt.

"At least that's the story the three of us will tell the rest of the world."

Scully asked, "The real reason?"

"I've been asked to investigate what is happening in the south as events move forward."

"Investigate? What exactly does that mean?" Pickering asked, his voice showing surprise.

"The crown has their official representative to the government of the United States. He is Richard Lyon, the ambassador in Washington. But the Foreign Office wants to establish an informal link with any government that might be formed if the southern states break from the north. It would be imprudent to name someone in an official capacity. Doing that would essentially recognize the legitimacy of any rebellion. If the north prevails, our relationship would be damaged. This allows our government to play both sides while they decide who to truly back."

"Why did you pick Norfolk?" Scully asked.

"I have a natural excuse to be there and the Tidewater area of Virginia is directly between the northern capital and the heart of the south. That should allow us to gain a better understanding of events as they play out. The upcoming election for the American president will certainly be a key piece of the puzzle."

"What do we tell Kennedy?" Pickering asked.

Warren had come to respect his fellow Englishman, but for now, he would not tell him the true nature of their voyage. But he did have to talk with the captain as the times were going to be very different.

The four men sat around the table, enjoying a glass of brandy after a delicious dinner of beef and fish.

"How soon do you see a need to put to sea?"

Warren knew it was now time to talk about his intentions for the ship.

"How go the repairs?"

Kennedy nodded, "Better than I'd hoped. The replacement cordage was available and most of the work is finished. I was going to let half the crew take two days ashore, then swap them out."

The *Sonia B.* was not the typical merchantman and certainly not like a Royal Navy warship, where often the crews were never allowed to go ashore, the captains being afraid of desertion. Kennedy paid his men a good wage and was a fair captain. Most of the men had spent time in other ships and knew they were lucky. Warren knew it, too.

"Good. I think there may be more time for some time ashore for the men."

Kennedy looked at Warren.

"We need to have some work done and I wanted to discuss it with you."

Pickering and Scully drank their brandy and waited to see Kennedy's reaction.

"What exactly do you think needs to be done? There are several spars that could be replaced, but it's not critical."

"I talked with the Foreign Office during my time in London. They feel that the Atlantic is going to possibly be a very different place in the future."

"How do you mean different?" Kennedy asked.

"More dangerous. It's possible this American problem could spill out to include France, Spain and Britain."

"Never really thought about it," Kennedy said, "But I suppose it could."

"I believe we need to arm the *Sonia B.* for protection."

"What kind of arms?"

"Eight twelve pound cannons and two carronades."

"Jesus, man! You want her to be a warship? And how did you come up with those requirements? You just can't throw that kind of weight on a ship like the B without serious modifications."

"I talked with a very knowledgeable officer at the Admiralty. He was confident the dockyard here could do the work, which would include additional ballast and deck support. There are also weapons available which could be mounted as soon as the preparations are complete."

Kennedy looked stunned.

"Sounds to me like you want your own privateer."

"Jim, it's nothing like that. I just want to make sure that we can move freely if a war develops in the Americas."

"Jesus. We'd have to add crew, build a magazine, and find a gunner. There's much to this."

"Pinky, I didn't think anything could every surprise you," Scully said, laughing.

He grinned back.

"And carronades, you say?"

Warren nodded.

"By God, she'll truly be a frigate now." Kennedy smiled and took a long drink.

Two days later, the magnitude of the upgrade to Sonia B. has begun to hit home. Arrangements to bring the ship into a dry dock and visits by naval architects had gone smoothly with their estimate of a completion date by mid-December. A survey of the town revealed a large number of former gunners from the Royal Navy ashore after being paid off. One of the architects recommended one of those men as a possible ship's gunner.

"None better when it comes to knowing his guns. Damned good shot to boot."

In short order, the former ship's gunner in *Euripides*, Mr. Samuel Hogg, was signed on the roster of Sonia B. as "Senior Gunner's Mate." Hogg stood over six feet and was built like a rock. Scully thought he would be a tough opponent in a fight, but he liked the man. Odd for a soldier to like a sailor, but they were about the same age and seemed to be cut from the same cloth.

"So tell me about these, guns," Scully asked after a week of procuring some of the many pieces of equipment that a ship needs to operate large weapons.

"Best cannon ever made," Hogg said. "The twelve pounder long gun will fire a twelve pound ball dead accurate at a mile."

"How about gun crews?"

Hogg blew his nose with a large handkerchief, wiping it several times before returning it to his back pocket. "I'll need real gunners as gun captains. One other experienced man and the rest can come from the crew. I talked with Captain Kennedy and we want seven experienced gun captains, four to man the guns on one side, a standby and then two on the carronades."

"What's this carronade?"

221

The old sailor smiled.

"One hell of a weapon, I'll tell you. Fires a charge made up of round shot about the size of your hand. Sixty small balls packed in a tin cylinder that shreds on firing."

"Canister shot."

"Exactly, but the balls are much bigger. They'll rip open the sides of most ships if you can get close enough."

Scully wondered what Warren had in mind.

"Best be getting back at it," Hogg said and moved to the door.

The door opened and Pickering said, "Look who I've found."

Scully stared with astonishment at Liam Sullivan, dressed in the clothes of a farmer.

"Liam, my God man, where'd you come from?" Scully shook his friend's hand, patting him on the back at the same time.

The lanky Sullivan grinned as Hogg stepped out, closing the door behind him.

"My time was done. Always said I'd go home."

"Sit down, sit down."

Scully filled a cup from the coffee pot and put in on the table in front of Sullivan.

"Home? You mean Ireland?"

"Aye, that's what I was thinking. I've some money saved up and thought I'd try my hand at farming."

"I was there last year, times are tough, Liam."

Sullivan stared at his coffee and said, "I was done with the army. Thought it was time to do what I wanted, not what the army wanted."

"But farming? Damned hard way to make a living and what do you know about farming."

"I can learn and I'll work hard." But it was clear that Sullivan did not feel truly confident in his future endeavor.

Pickering said, "Why not come work with us?"

"With you?" Sullivan asked.

Scully thought for a moment.

"Tell you what. If you want to work a farm, fine enough. You can go to my place and be the caretaker. But you were one of the best fighters I ever saw and we think there may be some fighting to be done."

"Your place? Fighting?"

They explained what they had been doing the last four years, including the acquisition of Scully's farm at Albermarle.

"So what would I be doing? And it would be all right with the captain?"

"Just like in the army, getting jobs done. And Dick Warren would be damned glad to have you join up. And you'll make a damn sight more money than you ever made working for the King."

Sullivan smiled, the relief obvious on his face.

"I'm your man."

Chapter Fourteen

"Where do your sympathies lie?"

Louis Thomassy adjusted his scarf, the November wind cold as the sun began to set. He rode alone down Valley Street making his way back into Richmond proper, the cold wind coming off Shockoe Creek across the rail line for the Central. He'd spent most of the day at the Jeppson farm, supervising the arrival of Timothy Lawton Jeppson, the third son of Edward Jeppson. Mother and son were both resting well after their ordeal and Louis was now anxious to complete his journey and warm himself in front of his own hearth.

His medical practice was thriving and he'd been able to purchase a comfortable house on Marshall Street only two blocks from Bellevue Hospital. Kimberly had adjusted well to a new continent and culture, still assisting in his surgery when needed. But tonight his thoughts were on larger matters. Only one week ago the election of Abraham Lincoln had sent a shudder through the south. From Montgomery to Charleston the anger had burst across the land. Rumors of secret meetings and the stockpiling of arms were common. In his own quiet neighborhood men were actually talking about the dissolution of the Union. How had this come to be? Was the issue of slavery and the right of each state to chart its own course sufficient to tear apart what the Revolution had built? And to what end? Would states become independent again? Would the southern states band together as some were suggesting? Could anything happen without terrible upheaval and civil discord? What an unsettling future he saw ahead for his country, his state and his family. A sudden gust of wind blew leaves across the street and he spurred his horse into a cantor. He wanted to be home.

Hart looked down at the mess of a man lying draped across the wide bed. The room smelled of stale smoke and whiskey.

"America's finest," he said reaching down to shake the man.

"Wake up, Greely, you have business."

A low moan was the only response from the bed and Hart knew where this had to go.

He picked up the washbasin, still dirty from the previous night and threw it on the Honorable Greely Harkins, member of Congress from the state of New York.

"My God," Harkins said, rolling over on his back, covering his eyes against the light from the window, "Son of a country bitch, that's cold."

"God is likely the only one who feels sorry for you this morning, now get out of bed and get dressed."

"Go to hell, Brett."

"You have an appointment with Madison in a little over one hour. I don't need to remind you that your future may very well depend on how well you kiss his ass. Now get up."

Hart watched his friend sit up and look around.

"I need my pants."

Throwing pieces of clothing across the room, Hart said nothing as Harkins struggled into his clothes. Although the two men had been classmates at West Point, Hart did not really care for Harkins. But the former officer of the Czar had no money on his return from Europe and Harkins had needed someone to take care of problems for him.

Career politicians must make decisions on how they will promote their careers and Harkins had long ago decided that he would happily do whatever was required to add to his personal fame and riches. In the state politics of New York and the national capital of 1856, a corrupt politician was able to make quite a handsome living, but the arena was rough. Harkins was a devious and intelligent man, but he was not someone who could operate easily in the dark parlors and back alleys that crooked politicians inhabited. That was where his classmate entered the picture. Harkins had always known Hart was an imposing and brutal man who intimidated people easily. What better compliment to Harkins' slippery but quiet manner.

"I have a rig outside, let's go."

"Will you leave a small token for Clarissa? She was truly exceptional last evening."

Senator Horace Madison, former Democrat, lately Free-Stater, now a Republican had led a long and profitable career in service to his state and country. Certainly that was what he wanted the rank and file working man to believe. The truth was that the state of New York embodied the corrupt body politic of the nation. There seldom was an opportunity for profit that the good senator did not actively pursue during his years as a member of the House and now the Senate. A portly man, he indulged his integrity as much as his vices in the daily pursuit of what he like to call "the blessed American way of life."

"Good gracious, Greely, you look positively atrocious. You must have worked very late last night." Madison did not stop slicing a piece of meat when Harkins entered the private dining room at the Willard Hotel on 14ᵗʰ Street.

"A bit of the ague, I believe." Taking the offer to sit as Madison took a large bite of steak and chewed with relish.

"Ague, my ass. Can you at least get some coffee down?"

Harkins nodded.

"Thank you, senator."

Madison turned to several soft-boiled eggs in a serving dish.

"Damned, nothing better than a good egg with my biscuit," he said, pushing half a soft roll into his mouth to follow a mouthful of runny eggs."

Harkins sipped his coffee carefully, not sure what his stomach might do.

"You're a lucky man, Greely."

"Senator?"

"Because you are going to be re-elected to the Congress by the good people of New York."

"I do hope that is the case, sir."

Contempt flashed briefly in the fat man's eyes.

"You will be elected because I have made that decision."

The younger man put his cup down and sat back.

"Greely, you may be a bit under the weather, but you and I both know there are those who are in control and those who are not."

Harkins nodded.

"And you like what comes with being in control, am I right?"

"Well, yes, sir."

The senator threw his cloth napkin over the now empty plate and pulled out a large cigar.

"There will be a war, Greely. It is the only way this miserable situation will ever be resolved. The election of Lincoln has assured that will happen, I'm just not sure of the timetable."

The enormity of what the senator was saying now Harkins like a blow. He had enjoyed the give and take of everyday Washington D.C. and he was pretty good at playing the political game, but a war was a notion even he found horrifying.

"I've known the men of the south for thirty years. While there are some true gentlemen, they are by and large a foolish and stubborn lot. They will never reconcile their position on slavery and it will come to bloodshed."

Madison puffed his cigar then stood up and moved to the window.

"Now those of us who enjoy controlling our destiny can look at this as a problem or an opportunity. I choose to do the later."

The older man turned to stare hard at Harkins.

"A war will allow our party to secure its rightful place of control in both Albany and this squalid little city. It will also allow pursuit of great profits if done correctly. That is where you come in."

Warren walked forward on the main deck, his boat cloak pulled tight against the February wind. He saw Sullivan standing on the starboard side, looking at the coast of Virginia in the early morning light. The passage from England had been uneventful, only one bad storm and that lasted only two days.

"Having second thoughts, Liam?"

Sullivan turned.

"Good morning, sir. No second thoughts. Just came up to see the land. It seems like a long time since we left Portsmouth."

Warren had been pleased when he learned his former corporal would be joining them. He didn't know what the future might hold, but he was certain a man of Sullivan's experience and toughness would come in handy.

"The captain tells me we'll anchor this afternoon in Hampton Roads."

"Michael showed me a chart last night. He said we might be going inland."

"Richmond, perhaps; or even south to Belvoir. We'll decide once we get ashore."

Warren wondered what they would find, and what he would be able to do for Nicholson.

"Well done, captain."

Kennedy looked up from his chart table to see Warren in the doorway.

"Good holding ground," he said, pointing to the chart. "How long do you want us here?"

Warren sat down on the small bench against the bulkhead.

"Take time to provision, give the men some time ashore. I'd like you to explore the coast from here to Charleston. Let's plan on meeting a month from now at Belvoir."

Kennedy nodded.

"I like that anchorage and the hospitality of Belvoir is always welcome. I'll even be able to relax going ashore with Mr.

229

Smith aboard. The man's a Godsend, truly. Knows the sea and sailors."

It had been a welcome chain of events when Kennedy had become the master of *Sonia B*. The quality of the crew had been a result of the previous captain and Smith. Someday he wanted Leonard Smith in command of one of Warren's ships.

"Tell your lads about the trouble ashore. Although it's an American problem, I'm sure others will be pulled into it and I'd prefer it not be our sailors."

Once ashore, it was evident to Richard that the atmosphere in the state of Virginia was in an even greater turmoil than he expected. He discovered that during their passage, seven states had voted to secede from the Union. A meeting was now underway in Montgomery, Alabama to form a new country. The talk around the city strongly supported secession by Virginia as well. The reality of civil war appeared to have been accepted by both the landed gentry and the man in the street. In discussions with several co-investors in the railroad, Warren was told that the southern states, once united, could defeat the northern states. Not surprising to the Englishman, none of the men had ever actually been to war. If it came to that, Warren knew they would be quite surprised. Amateurs always were.

The mood was ugly as the four men boarded the Tennessee Central Railroad south for Wilson where they would hire a coach for the twenty-five mile trip to Belvoir. Dressed warmly in long wool coats, each of them carried a Colt Navy pistol. Travel had become dangerous as emotions rose in the territory and Warren was taking no chances.

As he watched the barren trees going by the coach, Warren found his thoughts returning to Emily and the last visit to

Belvoir. The remarkable change in their relationship, which had occurred in such a very short period of time, still surprised him. For the second time in his life, the idea of marriage was conceivable to Warren.

Emily had taken over running the plantation, and with the help of Doctor Hanson the tobacco crop had been a record harvest. The Belvoir Clinic had become quite the talk of the area, as had Warren, giving each of the slaves their freedom. While not received well by the majority of the people in the area, the act had been seen as the eccentricity of 'that damned Englishman.'

Warren had enlisted the assistance of Tolly, who had taken 'Washington' as his surname, in hiring the Belvoir workers back to do the same jobs they had done for only subsistence in the past. Initially the men and women had been wary of what seemed like a crazy move by Warren. But when they had seen the pay scales along with the clinic and school, their caution had turned to an infectious enthusiasm. That spirit had been a prime reason for the outstanding harvest of last year.

In a complete break with tradition, Warren, along with Emily and the doctor, had decreed that no one should be working in the fields until they were at least fourteen. Children were either going to attend the school or learn a trade of their own. All in all it had been a remarkable transition.

And his thoughts kept returning specifically to the last evening they had spent at Belvoir before sailing for England. He and Emily had dined alone, Scully having taken his two friends to Greenville to see a traveling review.

After dinner, they had gone for a walk, the early evening already pleasantly cool for June.

"Do you like being at sea?" she had asked, their course wandering in no particular direction.

Warren laughed.

"When I can be on the *Sonia B.* with a crew I know and trust, I do enjoy breaking from the land."

"So there were other times that the sea did not appeal?"

He remembered the storms on the way to Russia and the misery of the waterlogged transport. No he did not love the sea without question. He knew better.

"My first voyage to India took almost three months. As a very junior officer, my accommodations were, to be generous, adequate for the purpose, but nothing I would ever want to repeat. The lack of water and need to eat salted meat made life tedious at best. On the *Sonia B.* we are able to provision her well and allow every man some level of comfort."

"I would love to see what it's like," Emily said, "It seems so exciting."

He took her hand and she turned to him.

"Someday you shall."

She reached up gently, put her hand under his chin, and kissed him.

"I'm afraid I have fallen in love, dear man. But I wouldn't have it any other way."

Richard felt an overwhelming tenderness toward her, leaning forward and kissing her forehead.

"And I do love you," he whispered, the truth comfortable within him. "I truly do."

Watching the countryside pass by the window of the coach, Liam Sullivan sat in companionable silence as the other three men discussed Belvoir, current politics and several of the long-term business projects that were being investigated by Pickering. It had been difficult for the former sergeant to totally relax, despite the welcoming attitude of all three men. He remembered talking with Warren the day after being asked to join the group. He had been alone in the office late in the afternoon when Warren had returned from a meeting with the dockyard.

"There you are. It's good to see you and I couldn't be more pleased that you chose to throw in your lot with us."

"Sir, I don't know what to say. I don't know why you would want an ordinary soldier like me, but I will do my best for you."

"Liam, you're a good soldier and a better man. We're lucky to have you with us."

He knew that Warren meant what he said and for the first time in his life, Liam Sullivan was truly proud of himself.

"Pretty country, isn't it?"

Sullivan's thoughts were broken by the question from Michael Scully.

"Aye, reminds me of Kent."

"They have some of the best horses I've ever seen. You'll get a chance to see them at Belvoir."

"I think I'd like that."

Philip greeted the men, standing on the porch as if he knew they were arriving.

"Welcome back, sir."

"Hello, Phillip. Is all well?"

"Quite well, Mr. Warren. Doctor Hanson is at the clinic and Mrs. Whitehead rode down to check on the drying barn's roof."

The largest building on the property, the drying barn stood almost a mile south of the main house in large clearing that also served as a place to park the plantation's wagons when not in use. The location had been selected to maximize the wind that flowed up the long valley east of Belvoir. Once the harvested tobacco leaves were hung in the barn, panels were opened and adjusted to dry the leaves at the best rate to capture their flavor. A well-constructed and efficient drying barn was one of the keys to success in the business. Maintenance of the barn was something that was taken most seriously.

Warren turned to his companions.

"Why don't you get settled? I'll saddle Alexander and ride down to the barn."

Scully spoke up.

"Liam, before we do that, I'm going to show you some beautiful animals. And, truth be known, I want to see Lady."

Over their time at Belvoir, both men had acquired several horses, but Alexander and Lady were the men's favorites. Alexander, a large Arabian stallion, reminded Warren of Gypsy, smart as a whip and powerful. Scully had taken to Lady, a five year-old mare who had won his heart one morning on their first visit. He had been walking along a fenced paddock area and the young mare had cautiously approached him, curious about the new visitor. Following a lengthy conversation between the two of them, the bond had been sealed.

Two ladders lay against the barn's side. A wagon with a toolbox in the bed was parked next to the barn. Two men were working on one of the large metal hinges that allowed the wood panel to open away from the side to allow air to flow into the barn. Emily Whitehead stood next to the wagon watching the progress. She turned as Warren rode up, her face brightening as she saw him.

"Richard!"

He dismounted and took her hand.

"You look wonderful," he said, and lightly kissed her cheek.

She was wearing a very plain dress with a wool coat, a knitted bonnet covering her hair.

"And you lie quite well, Mr. Warren."

He looked up at the men as they tightened the last bolts on the hinge.

"The work never stops, does it?"

"Not if you want to be ready for next season. There is money to be made as you well know."

"That's all you Americans think about. Money," he laughed.

Her face turned sober.

"I wish that were true, Richard. Now it seems war is the only thing on people's minds. It's a world gone mad."

A gust of wind came down the valley and with it a bite of cold.

"Let me take you back to a warm fire, madam. We have things to discuss. Unfortunately, my visit will be short. I have to travel to Montgomery."

Emily looked surprised.

"Alabama? Why in the world would you go there?"

As they approached the main house, Warren saw a lone rider coming up the long drive. Riding a magnificent horse, the man rode very erect in the saddle, clearly at home on horseback. He reined to a stop as they also reached the front porch. The three riders all dismounted and the man stepped over to Warren.

"Good afternoon, sir. My name is Cable, David Cable."

Warren took the offered hand and said, "Richard Warren, and this is Emily Whitehead."

"Please come inside, gentlemen," Emily said, leading the way up to the porch where Phillip had already appeared.

Emily showed the men to the sitting room and said, "Mr. Cable, may I offer you a drink?"

Cable looked taken aback, but smiled and said, "Yes, ma'am. Whatever is convenient?"

Warren motioned the man to a chair and sat down on the sofa.

Emily entered, followed by Phillip who carried two glasses on a small tray.

"I thought you gentlemen would enjoy a brandy to take the chill off."

Both men stood and took their drinks.

"I'll leave you to talk."

They each took a drink and Warren said, "What can I do for you, Mr. Cable?"

"I am part of a group of men that believe the state's future lies as part of the new Confederacy. We're beginning to mobilize for what we all know will be a war with the north."

"I'm certainly aware of the current situation, Mr. Cable. What is it that you want with me?"

"If I may be direct, sir. Where do your sympathies lie?"

Warren was surprised by the question. But he liked the man and knew many people were being asked the same question across the entire country.

"While I'm an Englishman, my family has several investments in both North Carolina and Virginia."

Cable stood up and walked behind the chair, resting his hands on the top.

"I am convinced it will come to war, Mr. Warren. I hope I'm wrong, but suspect I will be proved right. The south is at a disadvantage, but war fever has many people convinced that the south would triumph in a conflict."

"And you?" Warren asked.

"Until a month ago, sir, I was a major in the cavalry of the United States. I think I understand war as much as the next professional. The south has only one chance. And that is to fight a defensive war long enough to bring the north to the bargaining table. We don't have the industry to fight an offensive war. There's also the matter of manpower. The north has a large advantage in population and this could likely be a bloody affair."

"I would then ask why you would take the side that you think will lose?"

"Because I am from North Carolina, sir. I know that a war, if lost, will bring a scourge upon this land and I dread the possibility. I will fight and hope the south can produce a stalemate. That is the only hope for North Carolina. I think you might agree that your investments, certainly this plantation, are very much at risk."

"Mr. Cable, you raise many questions. Perhaps you would stay for supper?"

Cable asked, "You haven't answered my question, Mr. Warren."

"No, Mr. Cable I haven't. But I would like you to stay for a meal with us."

"Then I thank you for the hospitality, sir and would be most pleased to take supper with you."

"Might we intrude?" Michael Scully asked from the entryway.

Warren's three compatriots entered and introductions were made.

"I've asked Mr. Cable to have supper with us, he has some very interesting things for us to consider."

They had all just sat down to dinner, with Emily at the head of the table. When Roger Hanson returned from the clinic, there was a warm reunion and introduction of Liam.

"Roger, Liam has joined our group following an extended period of service to the Queen."

"A pleasure to meet you," Hanson said.

Warren continued, "And this is Mr. David Cable. He is here to discuss several issues that might be pertinent to all of us."

When they all sat down and began the meal, Cable asked, "Mr. Sullivan, you were in service to the Queen?"

Sullivan looked at Warren, not sure what to say.

"I should have been more specific. Until recently, Liam was a sergeant of cavalry in Her Majesty's 13th Light Dragoons."

Cable smiled, "A cavalry man, indeed. It is a pleasure to meet you, sir."

Liam now looked even more confused.

Continuing, Cable said, "Until recently I was also in the cavalry."

Scully poured another glass of wine and said, "I should have recognized a fellow horse lover. I saw your horse when we rode in, a truly beautiful beast."

"Thank you, Mr. Scully. She is a true joy."

Warren's thoughts flashed back to Gypsy. When they returned to Balaclava, he discovered the mare had never returned from the charge. He never knew if she had been killed or simply captured by the Russians in the chaos after the battle. It was something he would always regret, not knowing what happened to her.

"You were a professional soldier, sir?" Pickering asked.

Nodding, Cable said, "West Point, class of '44."

He looked around the table and said, "And I sense that it is not just Mr. Sullivan and myself that fit into that category."

"We all served in the 13th, Mr. Cable. But that was a long time ago."

Cable thought for a moment.

"The 13th Light Dragoons. They were one of the six regiments in the charge at Balaclava." He remembered Pickering's missing hand. "Were you in the charge?"

"We all were. A misunderstood order which sent a lot of good men to their deaths for no good reason. Not the brightest moment for the British military."

The talk shifted away from the past and Warren was able to get Cable to expand on his previous comments about the current crisis. By the end of the meal, Warren not only felt he understood the situation, but he decided that it was a unique opportunity.

Later in the sitting room, the two men were again alone.

"I should be going to bed, I'm afraid," Warren said. "We leave tomorrow for Montgomery."

Cable nodded slightly and said, "That is a coincidence, I'm also going to Montgomery, perhaps we might travel together."

Warren thought for a moment, it was an interesting coincidence.

"By the way, Mr. Warren, I never did give you my full name."

"And that would be?" Warren asked, thinking that Cable's comment was odd.

"Cable, Colonel David Rutland Cable."

So much for coincidences, Warren realized and said, "Perhaps a walk would be in order?"

The long driveway served Warren's purpose and he led Cable away from the big house.

"I should have guessed that your appearance was not happenstance, colonel."

Cable walked on silently.

"But I am curious," Warren continued, "Exactly where do your loyalties lie?"

"Do you mean, am I loyal to the south or just playing the part for the Foreign Office?"

Warren answered, "Precisely."

Stopping, Cable turned and looked at Warren.

"What difference would that make to you, as long as I can assist you in your mission?"

"My task would be easier if I knew how you felt," Warren said.

"I can tell you, but why would you believe me?" Cable responded, his voice taking on an edge.

"Leave that up to me, colonel."

Almost as if making a formal statement, Cable paused then said, "My ultimate loyalty is to my home state and thus the Confederacy. But I will serve the foreign office until there is a conflict of interest, because I am convinced that the south and Great Britain can be allies."

Warren considered the man and what he had said. Was there enough there for him to trust Cable? For the time being, yes, he decided.

"That is enough for me."

Chapter Fifteen

"We are all working for the same purpose."

Warren stood in the hallway with Cable, both men silent as they waited to be shown into the large parlor.

"This way, gentlemen."

While not large by British manor house standards, the receiving area in the Davis residence was spacious and well appointed.

"Mr. Davis will be with you shortly," said a young man in civilian clothes. The assistant carried himself like a man with military training. Not surprising, Warren thought. As the United States Secretary of War, Jefferson Davis likely came to know many young military officers who could have joined him when he left Washington D.C.

Cable and Warren remained standing, taking in the pictures on the wall and impressive fireplace and mantel. In one corner, under two tall windows, a grand piano stood, with cut glass candle holders positioned to provide illumination to the sheets of music open on the rack.

"Good evening, gentlemen."

Both men turned to see the Provisional President of the Confederates States of America. Davis was a tall man and carried himself with an imposing bearing.

"Colonel Cable, it is a pleasure to see you, as always."

"Sir, may I present Mr. Richard Warren."

Davis fixed his eyes on Warren's before extending his hand.

"I am pleased to meet you, Mr. Warren."

"Mr. President, thank you for receiving me."

Motioning to a long sofa, Davis sat down in one of the high back chairs across the low, circular coffee table.

Warren knew that the president was in his early 50's, but his face showed the strain of his office and Davis appeared older.

"You come to our country at a tumultuous time, Mr. Warren. The inauguration of Mr. Lincoln seems to have added fire to what was already a spreading inferno. The Congress has authorized the formation of a volunteer army. I'm afraid that the current animosity will result in war across this land and for that I am truly sorry."

"War is a terrible thing, sir."

Davis smiled wryly.

"And we three in this room have known war. Did Colonel Cable tell you that he served in my regiment during the Mexican War?"

"No, sir, he didn't mention it."

Warren looked at Cable, who looked uncomfortable.

"You were with Her Majesty's forces in both India and Russia, I understand?"

"Yes, sir. Two very different conflicts."

"Quite so," Davis replied. "As a young officer I took part in our action against Black Hawk, a most unconventional enemy. In Mexico, the war was much more like the textbooks had described it at West Point."

"The resemblance to what I saw in India and Russia sounds very similar."

Davis asked, "You were a dragoon, I've been told."

Warren nodded.

Smiling, Davis went on, "I was in the initial cadre of the First Regiment of Dragoons, and quite a group we had." His eyes seemed to be looking back at those days as a young cavalry officer. He returned to the present.

"Mr. Warren, I'll be honest with you. If we are to prevail in this dispute, much like the original colonies, we will need outside assistance. Great Britain is currently the South's largest trading partner and has the industrial capacity to provide the type and quantity of arms we will need. I do understand the very difficult position of Her Majesty's government, but I must try to forge those bonds. I am going to appoint three commissioners to your government as an initial step toward formal recognition."

Warren found himself listening with great interest, not only knowing that this was history unfolding, but he liked the tone, demeanor and carriage of Davis. The task in front of this man was enormous and he seemed very well suited to the challenge.

"Mr. President, I'm not a diplomat or a politician, but I might be able to provide some valuable input to my government in support of your cause."

Davis sat back, looking interested, and said "Please go on."

Warren had given this a great deal of thought and now he laid out his assessment.

"Sir, if this does come to war, I know there will be great interest by all of the European nations. Much like we saw in Russia, military observers are likely to descend on both sides to evaluate equipment, tactics and who the likely victor may be."

Davis nodded. He understood war and how it was conducted.

"I'm sure my country will have military men on both sides."

"That is reasonable to expect," Davis said.

"But I know the reports would return to Horseguards, our military headquarters in London, and not to the Foreign Office. I fear that the military and the civilians barely tolerate each other and sharing of information is limited at best."

"What would you suggest, Mr. Warren?"

"Allow me to take the field with your forces. My information would flow directly to the Foreign Office."

"That might be a double-edged sword, sir."

Warren replied, "It would be, Mr. President. But hear me out. I'm a landowner in North Carolina and I have railroad investments that cross several southern states. While I am officially neutral, I have a great interest in either preserving the peace or a victory by the south that protects my property."

"Your honesty is appreciated."

"I would also be able to keep you informed about what is actually happening in the field."

A look of surprise came over the President's face.

Warren pressed ahead.

"In Russia, I saw how the failure of information from the battlefront crippled the forces trying to fight the battle. Senior officers play politics and the soldiers pay the price. I can't imagine the army of the South would be any different. I have no purpose other than to see exactly what is happening in the field. I think you would benefit from an independent observer. Certainly any recognition by Her Majesty's government must be based on a true and honest appraisal of events."

Davis stood up and walked to the window. He remained looking out at the garden for a long minute. Turning to face them, he said, "You make an interesting point, Mr. Warren. Let me consider what you've said. Perhaps your schedule would allow you to return tomorrow afternoon?"

Both men stood, understanding the meeting was over. Warren tried to read any indication of Davis' reaction.

"Certainly, sir."

The next afternoon, Cable and Warren arrived at the President's residence at precisely 6:00 pm, the hour an aide to Davis had specified. They were shown in and awaited the president. During the time since the initial meeting, Cable had professed ignorance as to what Davis might likely do in response to Warren's offer.

"He's an intelligent and thoughtful man, but I learned many years ago not to try and guess what he might do. That is what made him a good regimental commander. He often looks at a problem with a viewpoint many men can't grasp. But never doubt he is a driven man who will do whatever it takes for the South to succeed."

Warren wished Scully were with him now. The Irishman had always been able to help him see every side of an argument. Strange, he thought, a man with no education other than the rough life of a soldier had the wisdom that one seldom found in the "educated" gentry of England. But he knew he felt better with his friends watching over the plantation, not to mention Emily.

Davis walked into the room and greeted the men.

"Mr. Warren, I have given your offer a great deal of consideration. Your perception of the world of politics and its influence on the military is unfortunately accurate. I observed much of what you discussed in Mexico. For that reason, I feel your assistance in observing what is happening on the war front would be invaluable. But I also think you would face obstacles as an unknown Englishman whose presence would likely be questioned."

"Yes, sir, but I will have to deal with it."

The President continued, "Or accept a commission in our provisional army that supports your presence anywhere the army might be located."

The surprise on Cable and Warren's faces brought a smile to Davis's.

"There is logic in my proposal, Mr. Warren. It protects you from overzealous patriots who will see a spy behind every tree and it will allow you to utilize official channels to communicate with me."

Warren, once past the initial surprise of the offer, realized that Davis had given him exactly what he wanted, the ability to look very closely at the forces of the South and evaluate whether or not they could possibly triumph over the North.

"Your military background certainly supports a commission," Cable added.

"I find myself agreeing with you, Mr. President, although it was the farthest thing from my mind."

"So you would consent?"

Thoughts went through his mind, what was he not thinking about? Did this truly make sense for his mission? It was a remarkable offer and he knew that it made sense to at least see where it would lead.

"Yes, sir, I would."

From Warren to Nicholson: Jefferson Davis is a most impressive leader, but I sense the new government's organization is haphazard at best. It appears that the primary loyalty of the southern citizens it to their own state. I suspect it will be difficult for them to mobilize an effective military force in a timely manner. The question on many minds is how soon will the Federal government be ready to attack?

The faint odor of urine greeted Louis Thomassy's nose as Benjamin Therrell lowered wool pants to reveal dirty, knee-length drawers.

"Bend over the table and drop those drawers," the doctor directed.

Therrell untied the drawstring and let the dirty garment fall to the floor around his boots.

Louis bent down slightly to examine a large boil the size of a walnut.

"My goodness that must be painful."

The doctor gently pushed the side of the boil, eliciting a howl of agony from Therrell.

"How long has it been like that?"

The man gulped, caught his breath and said, "Only bad since the day before."

Straightening the sheet, which Therrell had shoved almost onto the floor, Louis said, "Get up on the table."

247

The doctor moved to the washbasin and washed his hands with a mixture of soap and vinegar. While in Vienna he had come to know a Hungarian physician by the name of Ignaz Semmelweis, who had convinced him that cleanliness was critical to the practice of medicine. Since that time he had always used some form of cleaner on his instruments, hands and the patients themselves if possible.

He soaked a folded bandage in vinegar and carefully cleaned the reddened area surrounding the boil. Taking a scalpel from the tray next to the table he told Therrell, "This will hurt. Are you ready?"

"Go ahead."

The doctor slid the scalpel into the boil slightly below the inflamed heard, immediately Therrell yelled and gush of bloody pus released from the boil.

"Hold still," the doctor ordered, wiping the mess up with the vinegar soaked bandage. He packed the incision with a small piece of tree moss to allow the boil to drain. "Now just lay there while I put a bandage on it."

"Doc, you gonna join up?"

"I haven't thought about it," Louis said, knowing it was a total lie.

"There's a war comin' and I want to do my part. 'Sides, the damned Yankees are a bunch of titty-suckin' babies and we'll thrash 'em."

The doctor applied Lugol's solution liberally on the wound and surrounding area.

"Shitfire, that hurts, doc!"

"It's supposed to hurt, that way we know it's working."

"Damnation ..."

Louis adjusted the cotton pad.

"Hold still while I put some plaster tape over this. Now take it easy and if the bandage comes off, you have your wife put another plaster on it. Understood?"

"Can I get up now?"

"Yes."

Therrell gingerly slid down until his feet touched the floor then bent down and lifted his drawers in place, tying the cord. He pulled up his pants, slipping the suspenders over each shoulder.

"Feels better, I guess," he said, taking a short step.

"Just take it easy for a few days."

Therrell nodded.

"There's a war comin', doc, better decide what you're gonna do."

Louis watched the door close, knowing that Mr. Benjamin Therrell was committed to war and fighting for the South. Louis had seen enough war to last him the rest of his days, but as a loyal Virginian, he couldn't abandon his home. He could only hope it didn't come to war.

"It's an early planting this year, second week of April."

Scully turned from watching the morning's activity in the fields.

"What exactly are they doing? It looks like total confusion."

Emily laughed.

"No, Michael. It's just how tobacco is grown. They're transplanting seedlings from the seedbeds to the main fields. The warm weather has moved our schedule up from most years, but early plantings normally produce bigger crops."

The two had become friends during Warren's absence. Scully had kept close to Belvoir while his two compatriots had surveyed the surrounding counties to get a feel for the terrain.

"I never did take to tobacco, though most soldiers do like their pipes."

"How about Richard?" she asked.

He turned to smile at her.

"In India I did see him with a cigar on occasion, but that's been a long time."

"I enjoyed his stories about India, so exciting compared to growing tobacco in North Carolina."

"Murderous heat and terrible odors are what I remember. Nothing very exciting."

She laughed again.

"Michael, where's your romantic soul?"

"Don't worry, ma'am. I'm an Irishman. We live for romance."

"I don't think we're talking about the same type of romance, Mr. Scully."

This one is a rare lady, Michael told himself, and he could only hope that Warren was going to do something about it.

Two days later, word of the bombardment of Fort Sumter arrived at Belvoir. The next day, Warren returned.

"I was in Charleston," Warren said.

"You saw the attack?" Emily asked.

He nodded.

"Not much by the standards of Sevastopol, but the bombardment did force the federal troops to surrender."

"So it is war?" she asked.

"I'm afraid it is. President Lincoln has called for 75,000 volunteers. From Montgomery to Charleston, we saw militia companies turning out."

"You were still with Mr. Cable?"

"I was with him, but it's Colonel Cable."

"Colonel? He seemed like such a quiet man."

He hesitated then said, "I have more news, of a more personal nature."

Emily sat quietly, expecting him to tell her that he was leaving for England.

"I've accepted a commission in the Confederate Army."

"Would you repeat that?"

"It is now Lieutenant Colonel Warren, at your service, madam."

A look of shock and surprise came over her as if she was struggling to comprehend what he had said.

"You are going to fight for the south? How can you do that, you're an Englishman?"

"Most armies of the world are made up of different nationalities, it's not unusual."

Emily rose and walked across the room, sitting down next to him on the sofa.

"I don't know what to say," she said, sounding truly shocked.

"More important, we need to talk about what might happen if things go wrong."

Warren saw the troubled look in her eyes and wished she didn't have to go through this.

From Warren to Nicholson: I witnessed the opening shots in what is now a war between the northern states and the southern confederacy. My impression is that the southern forces are enthusiastic, but amateurs in every sense of the word. I question how effective this new army will be when battles must be won.

Cable was tired. Leaving Warren in Raleigh, he had continued on to Richmond to deliver dispatches from Jefferson Davis to the Commander of Virginia's growing militia forces, Robert E. Lee. Cable had known Lee during the Mexican War and was pleased the Virginian had been given the leadership of the forces that likely would battle the federals first. Lee had been a well-respected member of the engineers and served in key staff positions during the final push in Mexico. Now he had the imposing task of coordinating the fielding of a new army while hostilities were already underway. The questions of supply, communication and command structure were only beginning to be addressed. If the federals attacked across the Potomac and struck south, the outcome would likely be very unfavorable for the south. Somehow, using the experienced military leadership of former U.S. Army officers, now fighting for the south, the line must be held.

Events were racing ahead, Cable thought, and his only hope was that the federals would not push south until the Virginian forces could organize. It was long journey from independent companies spread across the counties to a field army able to conduct an organized battle.

The two men had not seen each other in almost two years and Cable was surprised how much Lee had aged in such a short time. His jet-black hair was now heavily gray, as was the beard, which Cable had never seen Lee wear. Lee wore a gray uniform that appeared to be newly manufactured, a light gray coat with gold buttons and three stars on the collar.

"Cable, it is good to see you. Please make yourself comfortable."

"From President Davis," Cable said, handing a leather folio to Lee.

"Thank you. What news from Montgomery?"

Cable replied, "The concern in Alabama is what will happen with Virginia."

Lee nodded. "It's a difficult issue," he said.

The state was very much divided over the issues of states' rights and slavery. In the west, loyalty to the union seemed predominant. In the east, including Richmond, the sentiment leaned toward rebellion. Virginia was a wealthy state located front and center on what was becoming the initial battle line between the North and the South.

Continuing, Lee said, "But we must prepare our defense. Tom Jackson is bringing together the Shenandoah companies to form a brigade. As we build up that department, I will ask Joe Johnston to take command."

Cable knew Johnston and had heard of Jackson, who he believed was an artillery officer

"President Davis has directed me to visit the Shenandoah."

Lee was not surprised, he knew that Jefferson Davis was a man who preferred to be involved rather than trust others.

"We're all working toward the same purpose. I hope you will lend your help and expertise to Jackson.

"I will keep you fully informed, of course."

"Thank you, colonel, I would be most grateful."

Brett Hart adjusted his new hat and considered himself in a full-length mirror. His new uniforms had been delivered that morning from Findlay's, where he had paid extra for a rush order. Now, seven days after receiving confirmation of his appointment as the second in command of the 69th New York Regiment, he was ready to report.

The regiment, comprised primarily of Irishmen from the city of New York, had actually been established in 1849, the result of the emigration of a large number of Irishmen to the United States following the failed Rebellion of 1848. Now there were many regiments mobilizing for the upcoming conflict and Hart had seen his chance. The political power of Horace Madison had been all that was required to secure him an assignment. Now, for the first time in nearly five years, he was returning to the world he understood. The Irish Regiments were zealously protective of their heritage and Hart was fortunate to have come from the O'Hart lineage, well known by the transplanted Irishmen of New York. His military experience had made it an easy move for Madison and Hart expected to be well received when he arrived at their camp just outside of Washington D.C.

But Hart really didn't give a damn about a bunch of rough-necked Irishmen from New York. He knew this war would be short and grabbing glory early on would be a ticket to wealth afterward. Watching that fool Harkins, he knew he could run for Congress, get elected and work the system as well as anyone. Perhaps he'd go directly into business to take advantage of the chaos that always follows conflict. Yes, Hart would not only survive this war, he would profit by it immensely.

Warren was torn. As he prepared to leave for Virginia, he wanted Scully to remain at Belvoir to oversee the protection of the plantation. Not surprisingly, Scully intended to accompany Warren, who knew it was a battle the Irishman would win.

"I decided that you would likely choose to stay with me."

"As we've seen over the last fifteen years," Scully said, "You need someone to watch your back. That's my job and I'm not leaving it to someone else."

"Even Sullivan?"

"I'd trust Liam to do the job, but not as well as me."

Warren handed him a folded piece of paper.

"What's this?"

"It's an appointment in the Confederates States Army."

Scully smiled as he read.

"I'll be damned. A sergeant major at last."

"You were insufferable as a sergeant, I can't imagine what you'll be like now."

"Don't you worry, colonel, I'll be the very model of what a sergeant major should be."

"Then Sergeant Major Scully, we are off for Virginia."

Standing beside the saddled horses, Emily looked at Warren and said, "I'm still not sure I understand all of this, but I know that you wouldn't go if you weren't needed."

Warren had told her some of what he was about, but the ultimate reason for his journey to the war was still known only to his compatriots.

"I go knowing you're in good hands with James and Liam. They'll make sure no harm comes to you. Trust them, they know what they're doing."

She nodded, aware of the cache of weapons and powder that had been accumulated over the last month.

He continued, "Hanson will assist you in every way. I have great confidence in the young man."

Scully mounted his horse, steadying her as she stepped to the side.

"We best be going, colonel."

She looked at him, her eyes misting slightly.

"I never thought I could love another, but you have proved me wrong," she said quietly. "Please take care of yourself."

He leaned down and kissed her.

"My love will be with you, always."

He pulled himself into the saddle and taking the reins, turned Alexander down the driveway. For the first time in his life, he realized he would have someone waiting for him. For all of his years in uniform, after losing Charlotte, that had never been the case. Now he found it oddly discomforting.

On the raised porch, Pickering and Sullivan watched their two friends ride down the road, wanting to be with them, but understanding their responsibility to Warren.

Chapter Sixteen

"And you, sir, are a liar"

Warren and Scully arrived in Richmond on the morning of June 2, 1861, having boarded the train at Goldsboro. Alexander and Lady had been loaded in a boxcar for the trip north, which took almost six hours. The quiet of Belvoir was in stark contrast to the crowded and busy streets of Richmond. Uniforms were in evidence throughout the city and the atmosphere was electric.

Their purpose for stopping in Richmond was two-fold. They needed to procure uniforms and equipment before arriving in the field and a visit to Louis and Kimberly was long overdue. Securing lodgings at the Spotswood Hotel, they asked directions to Marshall's Clothing Emporium where they were able to order two sets of uniforms for each of them. The clerk had been reluctant to take their order with the huge demand the store was experiencing, but full payment in gold coins guaranteed the uniforms would be ready in two days.

"This must be the house," Warren said, checking a piece of paper against the street numbers painted on a small placard attached to the wooden railing.

Following instructions from the clerk at Marshall's, they had walked ten blocks to the Thomassy house. Now they climbed the steep steps up to the small porch. A black wrought iron knocker was centered on the front door and Scully rapped hard three times.

The door opened in less than a minute to reveal Kimberly in a long blue dress with an apron tied around her waist.

"Can you provide two poor travelers with a cool drink on this hot summer day?" Warren asked, smiling at her.

She put her hand to her mouth in surprise on realizing who they were.

"Richard, Michael, what...please come in, please," she said opening the door fully.

Kimberly ushered the men into a small sitting room off the entryway.

"Please sit down and I'll bring you some cool tea."

Warren looked around the tidy room. One framed print of a bridge over a stream hung on the wall opposite the window, which was framed with white lace curtains. A world away from the Alma River, he thought.

She returned and poured tea for each of them.

"Why are you in Richmond?" she asked. "Checking on your businesses?"

"Actually, no," he replied. "Michael and I are on our way to Winchester, in the Shenandoah Valley.

A quizzical look came over her.

"Isn't the Confederate Army in Winchester?"

Warren nodded.

"Part of it."

"But why would you go there? People are saying there will be a battle soon."

Hesitating, Scully cleared his throat, looking quite uncomfortable.

"Kimberly, Michael and I are on our way to join the army."

Her confusion grew.

"Why would you join the Confederate Army? You're English."

"And Irish," Scully said quietly.

"The reasons are too complicated to explain easily, and that was not why we called. We simply wanted to see you and Louis before events overcome everyone."

"He's at the hospital, Bellevue. You must have seen it on your way here."

Warren asked, "When do you expect him?"

Smiling slightly, she said, "A doctor's time is never his own. But he should be home shortly."

Almost as if it had been planned, the front door opened.

"Kimberly?"

Louis stopped as he saw there was company in the sitting room. He began to put his bag on the table before he recognized the two men.

"My God, it is you two. I thought my eyes were tricking me."

The men exchanged handshakes while Kimberly left the room.

"How long has it been? Four years?" Louis asked.

Warren nodded.

"We've been remiss in not visiting sooner, but we never seemed to travel near Richmond until now."

"You must be on your way north. This is not the place to be right now," Louis said, shaking his head.

Warren smiled.

"As members of the armed forces of the Confederacy, we're heading north, but not across the Potomac."

The shock was evident in Louis's tone.

"You two are fighting for the south? Why, in heaven's name would you do that?"

"I have property in the south and business investments, I'm simply protecting them."

"And you, sir, are a liar," the doctor answered.

"It is that obvious?" Warren asked.

"I think I came to know you well enough on the trip home. I don't believe that you're willing to go to war over possessions. You know what war is."

"Louis, I'm assisting Mr. Davis and the British government to arrive at whatever relationship that might be advantageous to both. That is something I would not wish repeated."

Kimberly entered, a decanter of whiskey on a small tray with three glasses.

"I think this might be appropriate," she said, sitting the tray on a table in front of her husband.

For the next thirty minutes, the men caught up on the last four years and then discussed recent events in Virginia. Kimberly sat quietly listening to her husband and her friends.

"The state is very much divided," Louis said. "West of the mountains most people are loyal to the north while this side is solidly with the south."

Warren agreed, "I saw the same thing in India. And even though they were of the same race, the hatred I saw between tribes was more savage than anything between European countries."

"Perhaps the closeness breeds a special type of animosity," Louis said, "I certainly never saw anything like this in Mexico or the Crimea."

"As an Irishman, I can tell you we hate no people more than the English. Although there are a few decent ones," Scully said, grinning at Warren.

Louis laughed.

Scully's tone changed and he asked, "And what will you do, doctor?"

He shook his head.

"I wish I knew. I don't ever want to see another battle. I'm sure there will be a need for physicians here in Richmond, but I fear the city will become another Sevastopol. But rather than being surrounded by the British and French, our own countrymen will bombard us into submission. It appears I have dragged my dear wife into her second war."

Warren knew his friend was right. The north would cross the Potomac and drive south toward Richmond, then on to Norfolk, driving a dagger into the south. Militarily, it was the best chance for the Federal government to end the rebellion quickly.

"Louis, I'd like you to consider something. Pickering is at my property in North Carolina. He's charged with protecting the property and a woman I've become quite fond of. There's another man with him and they are very experienced. Plans are in place for securing the property and there is swift access to the sea from there if necessary. James Kennedy is in those waters with the *Sonia B.* Kimberly would be much safer there until these issues are resolved."

Louis thought for a moment then nodded.

"It appears you have come to my rescue once again, Richard."

Hart looked down from his saddle at the milling crowd before him on the temporary drill field. Any resemblance to a trained and disciplined military unit was painfully absent from the sweating, confused recruits in front of him. The angry and profane orders from the platoon sergeants seemed to have little effect on what the men were doing. It was another blazing hot day, the dust raised by marching men covered everything with a thin film and coated the already parched throats of the new recruits.

Hart had never liked the capital, which seemed to him to have been built in a stinky backwater of the slow-moving Potomac. The city was too hot and humid during half of the year followed by frigid winds, which whipped down the same damned river in winter. Now with thousands of new soldiers in and around the city, the stench from sewage and attack of insects was incessant. Hell, he thought, march this rabble south if only to escape the ongoing putrefaction of the summer.

Hart turned as Colonel Michael Corcoran, the Commanding Officer of the 69th New York rode up on a chestnut mare. The relationship between the two men had been professional, but certainly not cordial. On reporting, Corcoran had made it clear that he accepted Hart because of his experience in combat, but had great reservations about his being Irish in name only.

"How are the drills going?" Corcoran asked.

Shaking his head, Hart said, "They might have been effective in the city, colonel, but I have great reservations about

262

their ability to deploy from the line of march to attack formation."

Corcoran said nothing for a moment, watching the chaos on the drill field.

"I've been called to headquarters. My suspicion is that the days of drill are over for us, I believe orders to march will be conveyed to the regiments today."

"These men are marginally ready for a straight-forward attack, but God help us if McDowell tries to be too fancy, they aren't ready for it, nor are any of the other regiments I've watched."

Knowing his deputy was likely correct, Corcoran did not want to publicly question the competence of the high command. Besides, he told himself, my boys are Irishmen and they know how to fight, they'll measure up.

The trip from Richmond to Winchester took Warren and Scully two days, using rail transport to Warrenton then riding the rest of the way. Now in uniform, the two men appeared to be part of the forces now mobilizing and making their way to the expected battlefront. To the northeast, General Pierre Beauregard was in command of the forces taking up defensive positions to thwart a push south by the federal troops now massing in Washington D.C. Beauregard, who had titular command of the forces bombarding Fort Sumter, had become the South's first military hero and had gained the support of the public. Unfortunately, he had not impressed the new President of the Confederacy, who possessed a great deal of military experience himself. Davis had much more confidence in General Joe Johnston, the only former general officer from the United States

263

Army to switch allegiance, who now commanded Confederate forces in the Shenandoah Valley.

The journey had been pleasant, the weather good and Warren always loved being on the move. But they were shocked back into the real world when they came upon the bodies of two black men hanging from a large oak tree by the side of the road. The two had been hanging there for some time based on the damage done to both their faces by the birds. Each man's hands and feet were bound tight with wire and their necks stretched hideously. Each man wore a sign, notifying the world the man was a slave who had tried to escape to the north. Warren's anger and opposition to slavery was something he had tried to keep to himself, knowing the attitude of most southerners. But he was afraid this might only be the beginning. How would he be able to hide his real feelings?

Both he and Scully had seen the bodies of criminals hanging in England, but this was different. These two men had tried to reach freedom.

"I don't much care for that, Richard."

Warren shook his head in agreement as they rode on.

They found the headquarters of the 1st Virginia Brigade located in a small cluster of tents three miles south of Harper's Ferry, on the northern bank of the Shenandoah River. Challenged only once, they had ridden through several bivouac areas noting the rather haphazard pattern to the tents, which were anything but uniform. It struck Warren that these truly were amateur soldiers, not the disciplined regiments he had known in the east. What would happen when they first faced the brutality of battle?

"We're looking for Colonel Cable," Scully said as they stopped their horses in front of what looked like a combination of a duty desk and guard post. Two soldiers stood next to two wooden crates piled one on the other to form a platform. They wore brown shirts, tucked into blue pants, no insignia of any type, but both were armed with long rifles.

Scully's accent apparently surprised the two men who walked up to Warren, their rifles held casually in front of them.

"Who are you?" one man asked.

The difference in demeanor struck Warren. Never would a British sentry have conducted himself in such a cavalier manner.

"Lieutenant Colonel Warren."

The man looked hard at the two of them. Something must have registered with the man, who saluted and said, "I can show you the way... Sir."

They found David Cable in a large tent, which was also the billet for several other officers judging by the equipment and bedrolls. Cable wore only his breeches and a white shirt, open at the collar. Despite being in the shade of a tree, the tent was stifling and sweat glistened on his face and neck.

"I've been expecting you," he said, offering his hand to Warren, then Scully.

"Welcome to the Army of the Shenandoah," he said, offering them small wooden barrels that had been repurposed as stools.

"And how big is the army?"

"We have nine regiments of infantry, four companies of artillery and about 300 cavalry. More troops are expected to arrive shortly and we'll have a cavalry formation within two weeks."

Warren asked, "What news of the federal troops?"

Cable took them to a map, which lay on a wooden crate. The area depicted included the Potomac River and Shenandoah

Valley, extending to the border of northern Virginia. He moved his finger across the paper.

"Word was received this morning that several thousand Federal troops are approaching Romney, here. General Johnston has directed two of the Virginia regiments to move on the enemy. They may be the advance elements of McDowell's army starting their move south. The plan is to march the army to Winchester to be ready to defend the valley south and the rail line."

The three men spent the next hour going over order of battle, dispositions and the planned tactics, which Cable felt Joe Johnston had arrived upon.

"If our sources of intelligence are correct, the Federals will outnumber us both on this side of the mountains and certainly in northern Virginia. With our shortage of supplies and fully trained troops, the general decided that defending Harpers Ferry was playing into the enemy's hands. Once south of the river, our boys know the land and we plan to travel light, mostly because we don't have supply trains holding us down."

Warren remembered the ponderous movement of the army in the Crimea, where the combined force was only able to move at a snail's pace and barely able to sustain itself.

"If we can get each man 60 cartridges, a pound of flour and a bag of coffee, we can move faster than a wild turkey in a thicket."

The idea struck Warren that the southern leaders thought of their infantry much like the Europeans thought of their cavalry. Move fast and defeat the enemy by maneuver, not brute force. Perhaps these ragtag troops might surprise the northern army after all.

"By the way, I want to introduce you to our cavalry commander, Colonel Stuart. I think you'll like him. He knows his business and is one of the best natural leaders I've ever met."

The three men found Lieutenant Colonel J.E.B. Stuart kneeling down in front of a beautiful black Arabian, inspecting the animal's left foreleg. He ran his hand down each side, then stood up and stroked the mare's neck.

"Just fine, just fine," he said, moving to pull himself into the saddle.

"Colonel Stuart, a moment please."

Stuart turned to face them. A big man, his ruddy complexion was evident above a remarkably luxuriant, full-length beard. Blue eyes narrowed slightly, then Stuart said, "This must be our British visitor."

"Colonel Stuart, this is Lieutenant Colonel Warren and Sergeant Major Scully."

Stuart removed his glove and extended his hand.

"Welcome to Winchester, Colonel."

As Stuart turned to Scully, the Irishman came to attention and saluted formally as if on a British parade ground.

"Sir."

Stuart returned the salute.

"Sergeant Major."

Several men on horseback approached, reining to a halt ten yards away.

"You have caught me on my way out to reconnoiter the Federal forces to the west. Perhaps you would care to ride along, colonel, we could get acquainted."

Twenty minutes later, the small group had left any evidence of Confederate positions behind and was making its way west through the rolling, lightly forested terrain.

"Colonel Cable told me a little of your background, sir. British cavalry, stationed in India then part of the Crimean expedition."

"That's right, colonel."

"Shall we dispense with formality, I go by "Jeb", a derivative of my initials."

"Very well, Jeb, my given name is Richard."

"Now that's behind us, Cable said you were in the charge at Balaclava?"

"I was."

"The reports said that mistakes were made."

Warren liked the man. Although Stuart was younger than Warren, the Virginian carried himself with a sense of purpose and authority.

"That is a gross understatement. The mistakes were unforgivable. The result was cavalry charging emplaced artillery. The age of Napoleon is over and unfortunately too many European generals don't realize that."

Stuart turned to look at Warren.

"Is that why you left the army?"

Warren nodded.

"For the most part."

They rode on through the quiet countryside, with several outriders moving on their flanks.

"Cable tells me that you are part of the aristocracy," Stuart said, breaking the silence.

"That is true, sir, but I am here as a lieutenant colonel, nothing more."

Stuart chuckled.

"Which begs the question. Why are you here?"

The man's directness appealed to Warren and he answered truthfully, "There are several reasons. I feel I may be able to help Britain if recognizing the Confederacy is eventually considered. I also own property in North Carolina and think defending one's property is prudent. And I am a soldier."

"We are both cursed with that malady I'm afraid, Richard. It's all I've ever done, but then it's all I've ever wanted to do."

For the next two hours the scouting party moved west, encountering the occasional deer, but none of the Federal troops reported on the western side of the valley. It became very clear to Warren and Scully that these men knew horses and how to travel across country. Their uniforms were just as diverse as the troops he had seen in camp and if he wasn't mistaken, Stuart himself wore U.S. Army trousers tucked into his tall cavalry boots.

An outrider moved back to the main group and reined to a stop next to the commander.

"Federal troops 'bout a mile ahead, colonel. Looked to be a company, maybe two. They're settin' up camp. Saw tents goin' up."

"So Patterson is trying to outflank us. Thank you, Butler. Fetch Jenkins back from up left and fall in with the group."

"Colonel Warren, are you here as an observer or a participant?" Stuart asked.

The tone of the Virginian's voice had an edge to it and he looked directly at Warren.

"Your orders, Colonel Stuart?" Warren answered.

Stuart grinned and said, "I'll take half the men and work to the right. You do the same on the left. I would prefer not to let

269

the enemy know of our presence, but if a fight is needed, do not hesitate."

"Sergeant Major Scully, detail six men and follow me," Stuart said. He turned to a lean man to his right. "Sergeant Hawkins, please assist Colonel Warren."

Scully looked quickly at Warren who nodded.

"Aye, sir."

The sergeant walked his horse next to the Englishman. A tall man, Hawkins stood well over six feet tall, but was thin as a rail. A slouchy gray hat sat on his head as casually as he sat astride a chestnut quarter horse. While many men now sported full beards, Hawkins's face was shaved, although the dark stubble denoted a man who could have grown a beard as impressive as Stuart's.

"Yes, sir," Hawkins said, "Your orders?"

Warren saw the sergeant carried two Colt revolvers and a very long knife in a leather sheath; clearly a man who liked to fight in close.

"Follow me, sergeant."

Moving single file, Stuart led his small group forward through the quiet forest. It took only twenty minutes for them to see and hear the Federal troops setting up their camp. Scully moved up next to Stuart.

"Looks to be a cavalry patrol, sergeant major. They must have come a long way to be making camp this early."

"That makes me think the enemy general is getting ready to move south," Scully replied quietly.

"My thoughts exactly," Stuart said without taking his eyes from the enemy troops less than 300 yards in front of them.

"I've seen enough, let's pull back and see what your colonel found."

One hour later, Stuart sat on a fallen tree in the copse of trees agreed upon as their rendezvous point. He turned on hearing the approach of Warren's column.

The Englishman was leading the troopers, with one very surprising addition riding behind him.

Warren saluted and dismounted.

"What have we here, sir?"

"Private Joshua Parker of the 2nd United States Cavalry."

Stuart turned so the young private couldn't see his face and winked at Warren.

"Sergeant Major Scully," Stuart called.

Scully jogged over from the where the horses were tethered.

"Sir."

"We have a prisoner, sergeant major. I intend to question him immediately."

Scully was watching the colonel, and was surprised to see him wink.

"Yes, sir, of course."

"Would you prepare the ropes and line up the horses?"

Instantly Scully knew what was happening.

"Aye, sir. Might I recommend using four horses, this one looks a bit stronger than the rest."

Stuart fought to suppress a grin.

"Good idea, sergeant major. See to it."

Private Parker appeared to be no older than twenty, a big farm boy, Warren guessed, who ended up in the cavalry because he could ride.

Stuart turned to the private.

"Soldier, I'm going to question you. I've found that prisoners are much more inclined to talk when they're suspended between horses, pulling their arms and legs in different directions. If you answer my questions quickly, you may only suffer dislocations of your joints. Any delay answering my questions will likely result in the loss of an arm or a leg, which will most certainly spell your demise and in a most painful manner. So let's be about it, men, get him down."

A terrified Parker, pulled from the saddle, kept his mouth shut until Scully fasted a length of rope to his right wrist. At that point, the private decided that he would tell the rebels whatever they wanted to know.

"That soldier will have quite a tale to tell someday," Warren chuckled as they rode east on their return journey.

Stuart said. "I believe General Patterson is planning to send his troops south in the very near future. That is good to know, but we also think Patterson enjoys numerical superiority over us and it will be a difficult fight."

When the patrol reached camp, Warren and Scully found themselves alone as the rest of the patrol took care of their horses and made arrangements to send the prisoner back to headquarters.

"You played your part very well today, Michael."

Scully laughed. "Stuart is quite the character."

Warren's tone changed.

"I feel a battle coming, my friend. Are you still comfortable with what we're doing?"

"Aye, I am. Truth be told, I like being back in uniform, even if it is a strange one at that."

Richard Warren understood what his friend was saying.

Later that night, Stuart was walking past the picket line where he saw Sergeant Israel Hawkins pulling the saddle and blanket from his horse.

Stuart had known Hawkins since arriving in the Shenandoah. The Virginian was a superb horseman and seemed to have the respect of the troopers assigned to him. He was a man of few words but wasn't reluctant to tell anyone what he thought. Stuart had been curious about the quiet man and found out that Hawkins had spent the last fifteen years traveling through Virginia, Maryland and North Carolina trading horses. It was rumored he had killed a man in a bar fight in Hagerstown, but charges were never preferred. There was little doubt in Stuart's mind that Israel Hawkins was the type of soldier that would allow the South to prevail.

"Evenin' sergeant."

"Colonel."

"Well done today, taking that Yank prisoner."

Hawkins mumbled something which sounded like, "Yes, sir."

"How did it go with the new officer?"

"He talks strange," Hawkins said.

Stuart laughed. "I suspect he feels the same way about us, sergeant."

"He knows what he's doin', though."

Coming from Israel Hawkins, that was high praise indeed and Stuart smiled.

"Good night, sergeant."

Pickering stared out the window at the driveway not believing his eyes. It couldn't be.

Louis pulled the carriage to a stop and set the brake.

"What a lovely place," he said stepping down and turning to assist Kimberly.

"Doctor, Kimberly!"

They both turned and saw Pickering running down the steps toward them.

For the first time since leaving Richmond, Kimberly felt good about her decision not to fight Louis about remaining in the city. She didn't totally understand the country or the conflict and if Louis thought it would be safer at Belvoir, so be it.

"Thomas, it's good to see you!"

The two men shook hands and Thomas turned to Kimberly.

"How is my favorite nurse in the world?"

She laughed.

"Always the charmer, Thomas, but it is wonderful to see you again."

Emily Whitehead came out of the door and down the steps.

"Emily, this is Doctor and Mrs. Thomassy. They are old friends of Richard, Michael and myself."

Louis removed his hat and offered his hand.

"Mrs. Whitehead, it is a true pleasure to meet you. Although I am afraid we've taken you by surprise."

"You are most welcome, in any case. Please come in. Phillip will take care of your rig and bring in the baggage."

Twenty minutes later, now joined by Liam Sullivan, Doctor Thomassy told them of Richard's offer.

"I think it is a very wise course of action, doctor. Richard and I talked about the possibilities in these uncertain times. You

274

will find that Thomas and Liam have prepared us for all eventualities. And Mrs. Thomassy, you are most welcome."

"Thank you, and please, call me Kimberly."

"And I am Emily. We'll be quite a team, I'm sure of it."

"Doctor, what are your plans?" Thomas asked.

"I'll head back tomorrow. The coming battles will test the medical establishment and I must do my part."

Emily saw the look in Kimberly's eyes, not knowing that the young nurse had seen the horror of modern battlefields.

For two weeks after Warren's arrival, the 1st Virginia Cavalry conducted constant scouting patrols across the Shenandoah Valley south of the Potomac. Stuart was right about the Federals moving south, and on the 2nd of July, a force of over 8,000 enemy troops, led by Major General Robert Patterson, crossed the Potomac at Williamsport, Maryland and headed south into the Shenandoah. Johnston had anticipated the Union general's move and ordered Colonel Jackson with his brigade to march north to support Stuart's cavalry, which was harassing the Federal drive. Aware that the Federal forces outnumbered Jackson, Johnston had directed the Virginian to fall back in an orderly manner while still attacking the advancing enemy. The battle was joined at a small creek known as Hoke's Run. Jackson commanded four regiments of Virginia infantry and a four-gun battery of artillery, the 1st Rockbridge Artillery.

Confederate intelligence operatives in Washington D.C. continued to confirm that Irwin McDowell's Army of the Potomac was preparing to march south in the very near future. Estimates varied, but it most observers felt the Federals would field at least 40,000 troops or more. General Beauregard's army in Northern Virginia now numbered 20,000. The first clash could well decide the future of the south if the Federal could defeat Beauregard and drive south. General Johnston knew he must be able to support Beauregard, but fifty miles separated the two armies and in the Shenandoah and the Federal were advancing on Johnston. The issue was now beyond critical.

Sporadic rifle fire echoed across the terrain as Warren and Scully, now accepted as members of Stuart's staff, climbed into the saddle. In appearance, the two looked no different than the rest of the 1st Virginia Cavalry. While some of the officers had chosen to carry rifles, Warren and Scully each carried two Colt Navy pistols and a light saber.

Over two hundred riders were in the saddle as Stuart rode forward taking the lead of the column. Without bugle calls, the troopers followed their colonel north toward the enemy.

Warren rode easily as the sound of firing increased. Two Confederate riders appeared from the woods and rode directly to Stuart who held up his hand to halt the Virginians. These men were part of the scouting force that Stuart had kept active in the valley for the last two weeks. Now they brought word of exactly what the enemy forces were doing.

According to the scouts, the Federals were advancing in column down the pike toward Martinsburg. Some cavalry had been observed, but seemed to be holding close to the main column. The firing sounded like initial skirmishing with volley fire still to come. Now it was up to Jackson to press his attack and then fall back in good order.

Stuart knew his cavalry would be critical in protecting Jackson's flanks. With fewer men, the Confederate brigade was vulnerable to flanking movements, particularly by Union cavalry. He also knew that he must fight fire with fire.

Splitting his force in half, Stuart directed Warren to take a column to the left and determine the location of Jackson's left flank. He would do the same on the right.

"Don't let the Federals get behind Jackson," Stuart called as the two columns broke apart. "Sergeant Major, you're with me," he said to Scully and spurred north.

"Sergeant Hawkins, send two scouts on the left, we'll follow that ravine as far as we can," Warren ordered.

In one motion, the lanky sergeant ordered two men forward and replied, "Yassir."

Warren pulled Alexander's head left and tapped the big stallion's side.

The wooded terrain presented a challenge to the riders, now forced to move in single file. Warren knew full well that a line of infantry or cavalry is most vulnerable when approaching an enemy that might be deployed in line abreast or behind fortifications, but sometimes there was no choice.

Artillery fire echoed down the ravine, but in the wooded area, Warren was unable to decide if it came from the enemy or Jackson. The column broke out of the thickest part of the woods to see trees on the left with Confederate infantry firing across an open field. Warren knew he had found Jackson's troops. But where were the farthest left positions?

Reining to a halt with Sergeant Hawkins next to him, Warren called, "Who commands here?" Behind Warren, his two captains ordered the remainder of the column to halt. To Warren the two junior officers looked like teenaged boys, but both seemed to carry themselves well. Hiram Dooley was from Richmond, while Robert Tyler came from Northern Virginia.

An infantry major came out of the woods, paying little attention to the snap of bullets in the tree branches. As usual, new troops were shooting high. That would change.

"I'm Major Henry of the 33rd Virginia, and you are?"

"Warren, with Stuart. Looking for Jackson's left flank."

"You have found it, sir. No one left of the 33rd but Federals."

Warren looked about the immediate area, but most of the men were concealed in the trees.

"Are you holding?" Warren asked.

"For now, but they will advance soon. After that we shall see."

Artillery fire increased off to Warren's right, perhaps the Union troops were moving forward.

"Captain Tyler, Captain Dooley."

The two officers joined Warren and Hawkins.

"If the enemy can get behind these men, they can gain the advantage. A smart commander would be doing just that. Our job is to stop them. We will advance to the left. We must count on surprise and audacity today, gentlemen. My intent is to close with the enemy unless we see artillery. If we encounter cavalry, then it will be up to us to hit them swiftly and break up their formation."

Warren looked into the young men's eyes. They looked anxious but ready.

"Who's senior?" he asked.

They looked at each other.

"I am, sir," Tyler replied.

"Then if I fall, you will command. Rejoin Colonel Stuart when you are sure the Federals are no longer a threat. Understood?"

The young man nodded.

"Gentlemen, we will advance."

India kept returning to Warren's thoughts. This was the type of cavalry fighting he had seen on the northwest frontier and it was the way he liked it.

"Ready, sergeant?"

Hawkins grinned. It appeared this damned foreigner really did know what the hell he was doing.

"Damned straight, colonel."

Warren was glad he had Hawkins with him. The sergeant had a second sense about him, as if he had been born to this.

The column moved forward at the trot, the sound of equipment jangling, the only noise in the wood. Alexander seemed to sense the moment, the big horse gliding effortlessly through the forest.

Warren saw a flash of color on the far side of a small ravine about one quarter of a mile to their left. He raised his hand to stop the column and then moved slowed forward using a stand of bushes for cover.

Coming out of the far woods, Union riders were moving down toward the bottom of the ravine, now clearly in column.

Returning to his men, he pulled the Colt from its holster and held it above his head.

"Forward at the charge!" he yelled and spurred Alexander, bursting from the tree line.

Warren knew that Stuart had trained his men to hold their fire until close enough to inflict damage. A pistol shot at fifty yards from a moving horse had little chance of hitting its target. Now would the fury of the charge wipe out that training?

Years of training now drove Warren toward the head of the Union column. Kill the leader and the battle is almost won.

Closing to fifty yards, he could distinguish an officer leading the column, gesturing with his free hand, trying to mount a defense. Behind him he heard his men screaming their war cry as they closed on the Union troops who had begun to deploy in line abreast, but it was too late.

Sporadic fire came from the Federals, the smoke of the discharging pistols hanging in front of the blue clad soldiers, two of which tumbled from their saddles, hit by Confederate fire. Some of the Federal troopers were losing control of their mounts, trying to guide them forward to face their attackers.

Warren tensed his legs, stabilizing himself in the saddle, aiming at the Union officer, now only twenty paces away and squeezed the trigger. The man jerked back out of the saddle, crashing to the ground. The attacking line now collided with the Union troops, pistol shots ringing out as the men maneuvered their horses to fight man to man. Pistols were the weapons of the day and Warren methodically fired his Colt until it was empty. The Federal troopers were beginning to fall back, everyone lost in the acrid smoke of pistol fire.

Turning Alexander hard around to clear behind him, Warren saw Hawkins fire his pistol at point blank range into a Federal, a mass of blood erupting from the man's back. Looking around, Warren saw no additional enemy troops in evidence, deciding this was the entire unit. Several Federals broke away from the fight and galloped up the ravine into the tree line. Some of the men now threw down their weapons and raised their arms to show surrender. Suddenly it was over.

"Throw down your arms! NOW!" Sergeant Hawkins yelled and immediately the stunned union troopers did as ordered.

As the frenzy of the charge and killing abated, the cruel reality was heard across the ravine. Wounded men cried to their comrades for assistance. One man, fatally wounded struggled to stand, his last effort on this earth failed as he collapsed into the mud.

A most terrible sound came from a butternut mare laying on her side crying and kicking as she struggled to live, blood soaking her coat from three bullet wounds. Hawkins dismounted next to the wounded horse and knelt down. He put his hand on her neck to settle her down. Dropping his head as what he was about to do crushed him, he pulled out his revolver and put it against her head.

"Sleep, girl."

The final shot of the brief skirmish echoed across the ravine.

Warren watched his sergeant stand up and holster his weapon.

"Sergeant Hawkins, sound recall and take control of the prisoners. Well done to all."

The lean Virginian turned to Warren and nodded.

"Yas, sir." But Hawkins was reflecting on the foreigner. The son of a bitch had led the charge, he thought. No panty-waisted gee-gawker like so many of the officers.

Warren looked across the ravine at the ragtag troopers, now taking weapons from the Federals. These men are fighters, he thought. Not military perfection like Dragoons on the parade ground at Piershill, but by God, they are cavalrymen.

Warren's detachment found the rest of the Virginia cavalry six miles east of their skirmish site as the sun was setting. After the initial battle with the Federals, no further effort had been made by Patterson's troops to force the Confederates left flank.

As the sounds of battle died, Warren knew the next phase of Johnston's strategy was about to take place.

Major General Robert Patterson, who commanded the Union forces in the Shenandoah Valley, was 69 years old. He had last seen war as a Major General of volunteers in the Mexican War. Prior to that, he had served as a volunteer in the War of 1812. Now, when it was within his power to bring Johnston to battle, possibly destroying the only force that could provide the manpower to support Beauregard, he failed to act. The Confederate forces remaining in the valley were able to convince Patterson that Johnston remained at Winchester. The Union general was to discover that he had underestimated his opponent.

Chapter Seventeen

"Don't run, boys. We are here."

Warren remembered the plodding trek from Kalamita Bay, south to the Alma River, the lack of urgency and the resultant slow advance of the British forces toward the Russians. Now after twelve hours in the saddle, with only a two-hour rest break, the Virginia Cavalry was completing the journey from the Shenandoah to join the forces of Brigadier General P.G.T. Beauregard. Tired and sore as he was, Warren was proud of these hard men of the south and their embodiment of the cavalry spirit. The 1st Virginia Cavalry was joining Johnston's infantry, which was making the forty-mile trip by way of the Manassas Gap Railroad. The forces of Beauregard, once outnumbered by McDowell's army, were now more evenly matched.

Halted at the edge of a large field, the men waited as Stuart rode to headquarters for orders.

"How is she?" Warren asked when he saw Scully kneeling in front of Lady, inspecting her right leg.

Scully looked up and grinned.

"She's grand. In much better shape than this old Irishman."

He stood up and stretched his back.

"Every bone in my body hurts," he said.

Warren laughed. "You're getting to be an old man. Perhaps we should keep you in the back to rest up."

Scully's response was cut short by Cable's greeting.

"I found you. Good," he said, dismounting and offering his hand.

"Are you in charge of this chaos?" Warren asked, smiling at Cable.

"Not I, sir. I'm just an observer, like you and the sergeant major."

The tone of Cable's comments told Warren that the events back in the Shenandoah Valley had come to his attention. Rather than try and deflect Cable's apparent ire, he decided to face it directly.

"Colonel Stuart asked for my assistance and I felt it was my duty to oblige him."

"Richard, it would have been most difficult to tell President Davis that his observer in the field had been killed leading a company of cavalry."

Warren realized that Cable wasn't truly angry, but more frustrated. Likely because he'd been ordered to General Beauregard's headquarters and missed the Shenandoah fighting.

"David, I saw what these troops are capable of doing. There was no better way to determine that than going into action with them. And I will tell Davis that he has some of the best cavalry troops I've ever seen. To not use them aggressively would be a crime."

"What about our Stuart?"

"He's good, damned good. The best blend of common sense and aggressiveness. If he'd been in Russia, we would have ridden circles around the Czar's army."

"Today, we're only concerned about Irwin McDowell, my friend."

"Do you know the situation?"

Cable nodded.

"Early this morning, the Federals tried to turn our left flank at Sudley's Ford on the Bull Run."

"Bull Run?" Scully asked.

"We sometimes call a small creek a run," he said. "While Evans was holding that advance, they pushed forward on our right, toward Henry Hill, about a mile forward on the right. Jackson has been ordered up to reinforce the line. I don't know what orders the cavalry will have. All I know is that the battle is very confused. We still don't know where the main Federal thrust will be."

Behind them, they heard the sound of a horse approaching. Turning, they saw Stuart, who reigned to a stop and waved his hat toward his officers, drawing them to him.

"Jackson's been ordered forward to hold the position on Henry Hill. Hampton is holding the right, but it's up to Jack to stop the Federals. He's ordered the cavalry to hold his left flank. We shall move forward on Sudley's road and be ready to attack. Gentlemen, to your troops and follow me."

With the discussion with Cable now moot, Warren pulled himself into the saddle and followed Stuart. Scully mounted Lady, slapped his reins on her flank and rode to catch Warren, as almost two hundred riders moved out, following their colonel.

Cable looked back toward Beauregard's headquarters, pulled his revolver to check the percussion caps and pulled himself into the saddle. Enough of this damned staff work, he thought. There are Yankees that need killing.

Thomas Jackson had always been his own man. Devout, disciplined and convinced in the righteousness of the southern cause. Now he stood as the only real obstacle to the Federal's final thrust that would split the southern forces and capture the Manassas railroad junction. If the Confederate forces were turned, there were no other southern units between the Union troops and Richmond. Jackson knew that and decided that here his brigade would stand.

Hart watched with frustration and resignation as the Union infantry moved forward. The 69th New York was part of Colonel William Tecumseh Sherman's brigade, under the overall command of Brigadier General Daniel Tyler. Hart had met both of the men and had decided that Tyler was too damned old to be commanding anything and Sherman was a West Point horse's ass.

The Union troops had been marching since before sun up and now as the noon hour approached, the heat, humidity and their lack of training was showing all too clearly. He thought back to Russia. Pull a few of these cretins aside and shoot them in front of their regiments and we would see some response to orders. Crossing the small creek, which ran across their line of advance, he looked up the hill and could see only a few enemy soldiers. Perhaps as bad as these shits may be, the other side is worse, he thought and moved his horse through the shallow creek.

The sounds of volley musket fire and artillery rounds could be heard to the north as the southern riders approached the road that led to Sudley's Ford. After sending our several scouts, Stuart

286

motioned to Warren and the two rode forward, moving down a gulley with trees on both sides.

"The Federals tried to turn our flank once already today," Stuart said and they rode further down the gulley. "I saw the map and frankly, it was a smart move. Thank God we were able to slow them down. The only question now is whether they'll continue the attack or retire to prepare for another day of battle."

In Warren's mind, that would make the most sense. The day was hot and now the worst heat of the day was almost upon them. Why not regroup units, resupply ammunition and be ready to attack at first light?

"Both armies are new to battle," he said. "That might be the smartest thing, but I don't think we can count on anyone to do the smart thing today."

Stuart reined in his horse.

"There," he said pointing at gray-clad men coming toward them. "They're breaking and running."

The biggest fear of any battlefield commander was that his men would panic and run. Now it appeared the southerners were fleeing from the Federals.

Stuart raised his hat and called, "Don't run, boys. We are here." But his words had no effect on the mass of soldiers moving toward them.

Sweet mother of God, Warren thought, that's a Union flag.

"Stuart, those are Federals!"

The cavalry commander realized his mistake and spurred his horse back toward his own troops.

The southern cavalry had known that the Federals were on the attack, but it was still remarkable to Warren how quickly Stuart was able to initiate an attack. The Virginians were in the saddle and charging toward the Federal troops in less than two minutes.

Years of training took over as Richard Warren pulled his saber free of its scabbard and spurred Alexander forward. Following him, a group of thirty riders, with Sergeant Hawkins in the front were pulling revolvers and yelling a blood-curdling cry of attack.

Scully found himself on the far side of Hawkins's group and turned Lady toward Warren, using the spurs as he seldom did. She responded and he followed his friend only thirty yards behind as the Confederate riders broke into a full gallop.

The Federals at first seemed oblivious of the approaching riders, but as if a switch had been turned, several of the men turned and raised their muskets. But the full gallop of the Virginians carried them into the Union infantry before any real defense could be mounted. The long-known truth that infantry cannot stand up to cavalry unless in a defensive box was born out again. The first horsemen crashed into the front ranks of the infantry and began to fire on the stunned soldiers. Smoke from the revolvers drifted over the broken ranks of the infantry as men fell wounded or broke and ran from the onslaught.

Warren saw a soldier raising his musket at him and knew he couldn't reach the man in time to prevent the shot. Lunging forward, hoping to spoil the man's aim, he felt the blast of the musket and swung down with a killing saber cut. The man stumbled back, dropping his weapon as a huge wound opened up across his neck and chest. Warren swung once again and the man pitched forward on the ground, blood gushing from his neck.

The savage screams of attacking men were blending in with the terrified cries of the men being shot and stabbed by the riders. Scully also had his saber out, slashing down at the union soldiers and driving Lady forward into their ranks. Dust and smoke swirled around the men as the southern riders pushed into the union ranks.

To the right, Warren saw two artillery pieces, the crews frozen as they watched the infantry being savaged by Stuart's troops. He was now in the rage of battle, attacking anyone in his way. He turned to see a Union sergeant standing wide eyed as the ranks began to pull back from the attacking horsemen. Urging Alexander forward, he slashed down and caught the sergeant across the back, feeling the blade slice through uniform and flesh. The man screamed and fell forward as another rider fired his pistol into the man's face.

As the troopers emptied their revolvers, more sabers came into action and that seemed to finally break the Federal's spirit. The broken ranks began to fall back, seeking the apparent safety of the far bank of the small stream. Union officers and sergeants tried to rally the panicked troops, but a collective fear had now taken over.

Hart watched with disgust as the regiment became an unorganized mob no longer bearing any resemblance to trained infantrymen. He knew they would break. No better than gutter scum, what should the fools in command expect? He pulled his horse to a stop, as the rear ranks of infantry began to retreat. The rebel cavalry was pushing forward less than fifty yards in front of him and he knew the chances of rallying these amateurs were slim, but he had to try.

He drew his sword and ordered the fleeing men to turn around and face the enemy. But his efforts were in vain, the men acting as if he wasn't there. Looking forward he saw that most of the officers must have fallen in the southern attack and so it was

289

now every man for himself. His plan to cover himself with the laurels of victory today was not falling into place.

Scully forced Lady forward, trying to reach Warren. He was only ten yards away, but several Union troops were fending off saber blows with their bayonets. The clash of steel had now replaced the crack of revolvers on the field. Stumbling over their fallen comrades, the soldiers began to thrust at the riders with their bayonets. To Scully's left, he saw a soldier drive his bayonet into the side of a chestnut bay, the horse veering hard to one side, throwing her rider to the ground. In a moment, two bayonets had been driven into the unlucky southerner. Scully leaned forward and slashed down at one of the attackers, opening a massive wound in the man's shoulder.

Recoiling as a bayonet glanced off his right boot, Scully slashed down again, the fatigue of wielding a sword in the oppressive heat starting to catch up with him. He was tired, but knew that finding that extra reserve was what kept men alive in battle. Turning to find another target, he saw a lone Federal officer moving slowly west, seemingly uninvolved in the battle. The man was in profile and memories flooded back to Scully. He didn't know how, but that bastard Hart was here. He spurred Lady forward.

Surrounded by the smoke and noise, Warren looked north and saw a Union officer separated from his troops, almost as if he had withdrawn from the battle. He turned back to the fight, then realized he knew the man. He spurred Alexander toward the figure, who was gesturing toward the retreating troops. That man is going to die, his mind screamed at him.

Hart sheathed his sword, the effort at rallying the retreating soldiers was futile. Perhaps now was the time to

290

discreetly fall back to direct regrouping the men and await orders.

Warren was less than 100 yards from Hart when he saw Scully only fifty yards from the enemy officer. His friend was leaning forward in the saddle, his saber extended in perfect 13th Dragoon form. A single broken line of Union infantry stood between Scully and Hart, but they seemed oblivious of the charging rider.

Happy that his day of fighting was over, Hart turned his mount toward the stream. On his left, a single rider was charging with sword raised. What the hell, he thought? The he saw the man was wearing Confederate gray and coming directly for him. Hart turned his horse back to face the charge and pulled his revolver, which he had not used since loading it earlier. He raised the weapon and calmly fired.

Warren watched Michael spin out of the saddle and crash into the short grass. It happened so quickly that he continued on his own charge as his friend rolled across the ground toward the line of soldiers.

Spurring his horse, Hart turned him hard and headed back across the small stream. Enough of this, he thought, I've done all that is required to finish the day with my own self-respect in order.

Breaking into a canter, Hart headed north toward the main road just as a fused shell exploded to his right, throwing him face down into the mud.

Warren saw the Union soldiers advancing with bayonets toward Scully, who lay face down in the mud. Without thinking, he pulled Alexander hard right and toward the enemy troops who were moving at Michael with bayonets lowered. Sliding his saber into the saddle sheath, he pulled the Colt, cocking the hammer and leveling it at a man only five yards from his friend. Firing a pistol from a moving horse is an art that most cavalrymen never practiced. The lack of more than one shot with a muzzle-loading pistol made it a waste of time. But with the advent of six shot revolvers, Warren had developed an ability to fire accurately. Now his first shot dropped the enemy soldier and he pressed forward, firing at each of the Union men, hitting three. The attack seemed to stun the men who moved back from Michael.

Warren holstered his pistol and drew his saber as he moved past Scully and drove into the Federals, slashing left and right at them. The ferocity of Warren's attack, despite the disparity of numbers, broke the spirit of the soldiers and they turned, jogging down the hill away from the crazed cavalry rider.

Looking around quickly, Warren realized that he and Scully were in between both armies, but he didn't plan on being here for long. He jumped down, holding his reins with one hand, and knelt down. Scully lay face down and Warren gently pulled him over onto his back. Blood soaked the upper part of his tunic, flowing from the bullet hole evident above Scully's right breast. The Irishman's face was deathly white and his eyes were only partially open.

"Michael!" Warren yelled, hoping for some response, fearing that his friend might be dead. He felt the neck for a pulse and could find nothing. The terrible truth was beginning to dawn on him.

Then Scully mouthed some response and moved his left arm up from the ground.

"You bastard," Warren yelled with relief. He knew he must get his friend over Alexander's back if he had any chance of getting back to their own men. Soon the Federals would regroup and musket shots would follow.

He heard noise from behind and turned to see three riders led by Sergeant Hawkins rein to a stop.

"Is he dead?" Hawkins asked as if he was inquiring about the time of day.

"No, damn you. Help me get him up on my horse."

"Jacob, go retrieve the Irishman's horse," Hawkins ordered one of his men as he and Warren lifted Scully off the blood-soaked ground.

Chapter Eighteen

"Spoken like a true cavalryman..."

Lack of an official position in the Confederate forces allowed Warren a liberty that would have been unthinkable in the regiment. To take a wounded man for care was simply something that an officer of the 13th Light Dragoons did not do, particularly if the wounded man was from the ranks.

Hawkins had helped them get to the Confederate lines after crudely bandaging Scully's wound. While the two men worked on Scully, several other men, whom Warren recognized as Hawkins's mates, watched the battlefield for any signs of the enemy. The men carried themselves with the same easiness of Hawkins. Older than many of the men in Stuart's command, Warren guessed they had all known each other before the war.

Having gone only a mile, the men dismounted and the sergeant helped Warren lash Scully's legs in the stirrups.

"This'll hold him in the saddle for now," Hawkins said, running a rope from Lady's saddle horn around Scully's back then securing it to the horn.

One of Hawkins's men rode up and pointed south.

"Those boys said there's s'posed to be an aid station 'bout a mile down there."

Hawkins checked his knots, then said, "Thurgood, you get back to the company and tell 'em we be takin' the English fella to the get some help. You boys go with him. I'll be along shortly."

"That isn't necessary, Sergeant Hawkins."

The tall man looked at Warren and shook his head.

"Middle of a battle, you two wandering around behind the lines, talking funny like that? Some son of a bitch'll shoot you. Hell, I would."

"Thank you, sergeant."

The directions turned out to be accurate and in less than twenty minutes, the men rode up to a makeshift camp with several wagons parked under a large stand of trees. Men lay in rows, some on blankets, and others directly on the ground. The smell hit Warren like a blow from the past. Wounded men all smelled the same, urine, feces, blood, sweat, dirt and gunpowder combined to produce a smell that was like no other. And, as always, that smell was accompanied by moans of pain and cries of terror. For an instant Warren rebelled at taking Michael into this hell, but there was no other choice.

Hawkins and Warren untied Scully's restraints and gently moved him out of the saddle, laying him on the ground.

"I'll go find a litter," Hawkins said, and strode off without waiting for an acknowledgment.

The Irishman's eyes opened and he looked up at Warren.

"Bloody hell," he said through gritted teeth.

"Lie still, Michael, lie still."

Scully grimaced with pain, his face covered with sweat."

"Did you see that bastard?"

Warren nodded then turned as Hawkins returned, followed by a man wearing a white coat, streaked with blood.

"My God," Louis Thomassy said, kneeling down next to Scully.

For the next thirty minutes, Richard Warren remained next to his friend as Thomassy worked on the Irishman. Removed to a makeshift operating table under a tree, Scully was in and out of consciousness as the doctor, assisted by one other man, probed the wound.

Warren made himself watch as Thomassy cut the crude bandage off and removed what remained of Scully's shirt. The flow of blood had slowed, Warren thought, grasping at anything that might be positive.

Thomassy used a number of instruments that he pulled from his bag, the other man mostly wiping away any excess blood. Warren had seen many wounds, but the mystery of medical ministrations always escaped him. He always found himself simply waiting for the results of the physician's efforts. He knew that Michael could be in no better hands, but would that be enough?

Stepping away from the litter, Thomassy wiped his face and exhaled. He looked at Warren and said, "I don't know, Richard. I tried to repair what I could, but the damage was extensive. Luckily the ball exited Michael's back."

"Luckily?"

"If it had glanced off a bone, it might have gone in any direction, doing who knows what damage."

Warren didn't want to ask the question, but could not stop himself.

"Will he live?"

The doctor shook his head.

"I don't know. It could go either way. Michael's a healthy man and stubborn to boot. Sometimes that makes the difference."

Warren remembered Russia. The only reason that he had survived was because Scully stood by him. Now he found himself in the same position.

Cable rode up as Warren was preparing to head back to find Stuart. The doctor had assured him that there was nothing for him to do for Scully and Warren knew he should report back to Stuart. Louis would keep a close watch on Michael.

"President Davis is here. He's in conference with Beauregard and Johnston, but told me that he wanted to talk with you when he was finished."

"Where is he?"

"He'll return to the railroad junction for the return trip to Richmond. I would try headquarters first and the rail line as a last resort."

In a fluid battle, finding a particular unit or individual can be very difficult. But Warren was able to find and rejoin the Virginian cavalry as the tide of the battle was beginning to clearly turn to the South's favor. The Union attack had finally lost all momentum, the heat, terrain and Confederate defense combined to stop the last regimental attack. And then something that no one would have ever expected prior to the battle happened. The Union infantry broke and ran. It's hard to say what is the final thread that breaks and drives men, who only a minute before were advancing under a disciplined attack, to turn and run. But that is what happened in the late afternoon. The Army of Northeastern Virginia turned and ran. Panic took over and individual survival took priority over everything for thousands of men who only that morning were certain of their ability to crush the Confederate army.

The sky was showing the first signs of evening as Jeb Stuart realized the pursuit of the Union troops was at an end. Tired men, worn out horses, low stocks of ammunition and the promise of darkness all contributed to his order to retire southeast toward Johnston's headquarters behind Henry Hill.

Warren understood the quiet among the troopers. Now that the frenzy of battle had concluded, each man had time to reflect on the sights he had seen that day. For most every man, a set piece battle was only something they might have heard about. Now they knew the fear and elation of bringing one's enemy to battle. But more was bothering those exhausted men as the sun began to set over Bull Run. Today's battle had been a brutal back and forth, which clearly showed that neither side was the ultimate master of war. It was now that they all began to understand that this conflict was not going to be ended in any short time. And it made their odds of surviving that much worse.

"I was told the sergeant major fell during the charge."

Warren nodded to Stuart, who had ridden up aside him.

"He's at the aid station. The wound was bad."

"I will pray for him, colonel," Stuart said, "Sometimes that is all we can do."

Warren had never been particularly religious, but he knew that Stuart was devoted to his church and God as much as he was to the southern cause. He found that it was something that made him appreciate the Virginian even more.

"President Davis is in the area and has asked that I see him. All seems quiet now and I will try to find him before he returns to Richmond."

Warren met with the President privately in a tent at the headquarters of Brigadier General Beauregard. Davis seemed both excited and frustrated. He related that neither Beauregard nor Johnston thought that pursuing the Union army was prudent, but upon pressing he was told by Johnston that he would move on the right flank to discern the enemy's disposition.

"And what did you learn from this day, colonel?" Davis asked.

"It was clear to me that the South has good commanders, sir. There is also no doubt that your troops are committed to victory and have a high level of courage," Warren started.

"But you intimate that there are problems," Davis interjected.

"There are problems in every army, as you well know, Mr. President. But it was also obvious that both armies were inexperienced and still not sure of what to do."

"As expected, surely."

"My point, sir, is that what I saw of the Union forces were well equipped and until the very end they were as brave as our men."

Davis cleared his throat.

"Colonel, I am not one of those amateurs who believes that one southern boy can whip five Yankees. Remember I have seen them all fight against the savages and again in Mexico."

Warren saw the President was getting angry. Perhaps that was what he needed.

"What I am saying, sir, is that the inherent strength of the North makes it crucial that the South find the very best leaders and then fight a war that uses southern strengths, such as knowledge of the area and swift movement of troops."

Davis looked at him and smiled slightly.

"Spoken like a true cavalryman, Colonel Warren. I will take your advice to heart. Now I am afraid I must return to my train."

"Sir, will there be wounded transported on that train?"

Davis said, "I would assume so. In fact if there aren't, I will want to know why. But your question has more to it."

"My sergeant major was grievously wounded. Getting him to Richmond might make the difference in whether he lives or dies."

"Louis, I know I'm being selfish, but do this for both of us."

"There are still so many wounded to attend, Richard. How can I leave them?" The doctor looked at Warren, the conflict written on his face. "What am I saying?" He said after thinking about it for a moment. "Of course I'll go with Michael." His tone reflected his realization that but for Warren and Scully, he likely would be dead on the other side of the world.

"Thank you, Louis. I will travel with you."

The train was scheduled to depart at nine o'clock and there would just be time to get Scully to the rail junction by wagon. A quick meeting with Cable allowed Warren to pass on his authorization from Davis to make the trip to Richmond. Cable assured him that he would convey that clearance to Stuart as soon as he could.

Warren had always been ambivalent about railways. Certainly they were good investments and once the cost of building the line was complete, the profits were considerable. And he had to admit that they were much more comfortable than a coach or wagon. But now he saw their value as he never had before. Not only had Johnston been able to move his men quickly to the battlefield, they arrived fresh and ready to fight, not worn out from a forced march. He wondered how the long march from Washington D.C. had impacted the Union troops, particularly in the oppressive heat. But even more, as he sat next to Michael's litter he came to see rail transport as a means of saving lives. The speed of conveyance to rear area hospitals was remarkable, thirty to forty miles an hour. In addition, as Louis had discovered the stability of the train, he realized he would be able to tend to the wounded as the trip progressed. Warren could envision trains totally dedicated to moving wounded in the future.

Despite the initial confusion on arrival in Richmond, they were able to have Michael in bed in Bellevue Hospital by 2 a.m. He'd remained in and out of consciousness during the trip, but became more lucid by the time they reached the hospital.

"Where?" Scully asked, his voice raspy.

"Bellevue Hospital in Richmond," Warren answered. "We came by rail," he added, "luxury travel, indeed."

Scully's mouth moved in a slight smile.

"Louis is here to take care of you."

The smile turned to a grimace, the pain obvious.

"How bad?" he rasped.

"You'll live, he assured me of that," Warren said, his voice steady. "In any case, I've gotten quite used to having you around and so your purpose must now be to recover as quickly as possible. Now rest. We'll talk in the morning."

What Warren did not say was that Louis did not know if the Irishman would regain the use of his right arm. But as he watched his friend close his eyes and drift off to sleep, he knew it had to work out. It had once before and now that favorable outcome would serve a critical purpose.

The staff of the Bellevue Hospital found themselves overwhelmed by the casualties arriving from Manassas over the next several days. Wounded from the battle were distributed across the city's hospitals bringing home the terrible reality that the Confederate Army was simply not equipped to deal with the effects of a modern battle. The confusion and overcrowding reminded Warren of the Crimea. Why did the care of wounded always come as a second thought to generals and politicians?

Louis moved Scully to his own house on the morning of the second day, fully aware that the overcrowded conditions at Bellevue would replicate the horrors of Sevastopol.

The doctor also arranged for a woman to nurse the wounded sergeant following Louis's very explicit directions, which included remarkable attention to cleanliness.

An odor of vinegar and soap permeated the guest bedroom where Scully lay on a bed fitted with a large board under the mattress. Sunlight streamed through the partially open window, the smell of summer flowers just perceptible.

"You look better, Michael. Truly you do," Warren said as he entered the room.

Scully smiled slightly, the pain showing in his face.

"I had some porridge," he said slowly, the positive results obvious.

"Are you being nice to Mrs. Todd?"

The big man glared at Warren.

"Ah yes, I forgot, you are still the ladies' man, are you not?"

"She's taking quite good care of me. That's well enough."

Warren could tell that his friend's words were slightly slurred, the effects of the laudanum, according to the doctor.

302

"When will Michael be able to travel to Belvoir?" Warren asked.

Louis had just finished changing Scully's bandage and they now stood in the hallway.

"Perhaps a week if he continues to get better and doesn't develop a fever."

"And his arm?"

The doctor shook his head.

"No way to tell, but it doesn't look good. The muscles and tendons have been cruelly damaged."

Warren sighed, the terrible truth of battle. Not the flags and bands, but the individual soldier, laying in pain, maimed for life in many cases, the refuse of the conflict. Not something the politicians and generals bothered themselves with. Perhaps you couldn't be a great general and still worry about the pain and death. And politicians only cared about themselves.

"In any case, I know very well that he would benefit from being at Belvoir. Doctor Hanson is there, as is Kimberly."

"Let's hope we can consider a move. And if so, I'll leave it up to you to arrange the most comfortable transport possible."

"Agreed. Now, if Michael's out of immediate danger, I should get back to Manassas."

Louis nodded slightly.

"He's stable for now, no indication of suppuration at this point, which I consider a positive sign."

"God willing, Louis, God willing. Warren paused, "I've become quite used to having him around."

"That I well know, Richard," Louis said smiling.

Warren continued, "By the way, I'm expecting James Pickering to arrive shortly from Belvoir. He'll go north with me as soon as I can confirm his commission. Once we leave, you should be able to wire me via Colonel David Cable at army headquarters."

"When we get Michael to Belvoir," Louis said, "I intend to return to the army."

Smiling, Warren said, "I think I might have a job for you if you do."

Chapter Nineteen

"They'll ride like hell and they're damned good shots"

Warren, accompanied by newly commissioned Captain James Pickering, found Stuart's headquarters after a two-hour ride from the Manassas railhead. Several rows of tents stood in a field just next to a thick stand of trees. Warren could see the lines of tethered horses, several campfires and a number of armed pickets. The southern army was learning the ways of war.

They found Stuart in his tent.

"Good to have you back, colonel."

Stuart had several maps spread on a table in front of him.

"Sir, may I present Captain Pickering. He was with me in Russia."

Stuart looked at Pickering curiously. His eyes strayed to the hook on Pickering's left hand, but he quickly offered his hand.

"Welcome to the 1st Virginia Cavalry, sir. Let me brief you on what we know of the enemy's disposition."

Over the next twenty minutes, Warren found out that following the final effort by Johnston, which had accomplished little, the army had spent the time since the battle recovering from the fight. Scavenging weapons and cannon from the battlefield had proven very successful and replacement companies had joined the order of battle, helping to replace the men lost at Manassas. Patrolling by both sides had resulted in several small skirmishes, but nothing of note. Both armies seemed to be taking a long breath, not sure exactly what to do next.

"How fairs the sergeant major?" Stuart asked, the tactical briefing concluded.

"I believe he's out of immediate danger."

"That is good news, indeed it is. Now, Captain Pickering, if you would excuse us, I need a walk to clear my head. Colonel, would you walk with me?"

In ten minutes, they were clear of the encampment and making their way across a grassy field toward what appeared to be a small stream.

"Richard, what I have seen in the last three months has changed my view of war as we know it."

"Really?"

"The advances in science and technology are almost too hard to take in. Rapid communication with wireless, moving troops with railroads, longer range weapons, it's a new age of warfare."

Warren said, "When it comes to killing each other, mankind has always used ingenuity to be more effective."

Stuart stopped and turned to him.

"I think that what we have seen so far is just a start. Who knows where it will go?"

"I don't disagree."

The southerner stepped off again and continued.

"We must have the best intelligence of our enemy if we are to try and deal with these advances. Because, as much as it pains me, I know the north will lead in innovation, which is just the way of things."

"I expect you're right."

"And that is why I would like to discuss an idea with you."

The Honorable Greely Harkins detested the smell of Seminary Hospital. Putrefaction, sweat and feces all combined to put a man off his feed, but he had regularly journeyed to Georgetown to visit his friend, Brett Hart. Found by a retreating unit late in the afternoon at Bull Run, Hart had been returned to the capital to have his wounds treated and for recuperation. Two shell fragments had torn up his back and left him painfully immobile, but he was expected to be up and around within the month.

"Hello, Brett. How are you today?"

Hart lay with two pillows holding his torso steady, his gaze vertical from the pillow.

"Much the same as yesterday, but on the whole I think I actually feel a little better."

Harkins looked down and had the same reaction as before, his friend looked like hell. Normally clean shaven, a scraggily beard covered Hart's face, now shiny with oil and perspiration. Hidden from the sun for over two weeks, his skin now had an unhealthy white pallor. Certainly not the dandy about town he was only a month ago. But you had to stand by your friends, particularly in times like these, even when they smelled like a rotting carcass.

"Senator Madison was asking about your health only yesterday. I assured him that your recovery was progressing well and you were looking forward to returning to your regiment."

"Go to hell," Hart said, his eyes still fixed on the ceiling.

Harkins pulled up a chair and sat down next to the head of Hart's bed.

"Perhaps you might be more interested in a position on the General Staff?" He asked quietly.

Hart began to add to his original comment, but paused.

"What do you mean?"

"Rumors are circulating around town that George McClellan is going to replace McDowell. The senator is very well acquainted with this new general and feels that having someone on his staff would be prudent."

Hart knew that Madison was one of the most corrupt politicians in the city. Surely this was part of a scheme to profit from inside knowledge. But Hart also had no illusions as to his what his future might hold. The conflict was not going to be short affair and if the horrors of Bull Run were to continue to occur, many more men would die. And Lieutenant Colonel Brett Hart, late of the 69ᵗʰ New York, had no intention of being one of them. Lying on his back, looking up at the off-white ceiling, Hart knew he wanted no part of field service. The odds increase against a field grade officer surviving this war. But on a staff, he would have the power of the general and a reasonable chance to avoid direct fire of the enemy.

"The senator is a very intelligent man."

Harkins said, "I thought you might see it that way."

Sergeant Israel Hawkins appeared almost as an apparition by the campfire where Warren and Pickering sat drinking coffee after dinner.

"Hello, colonel," he said, his greeting conveying that it was all he needed to say.

"Sergeant Hawkins," Warren nodded and stood. Pickering put his metal coffee cup down and rose.

"Colonel Stuart said I should talk with you, didn't say what about."

"This is Captain Pickering, he's been with me for a very long time."

"Pleased to meet you," Hawkins said.

"Sergeant," Pickering said, offering his hand.

Warren looked around, noting they were a distance away from any other soldiers.

After the three of them sat down, Warren poured coffee for all and began to go over Stuart's idea.

The sergeant listened without comment for twenty minutes until Warren had finished.

"So Jeb wants to make a small outfit that can go snooping behind the lines and let him know what's happening."

"That's the idea, sergeant. I know the colonel would prefer to do it himself, but he's being given more responsibilities for troops and won't have the time for such activities. The general has also told him that the south can't afford to have their best cavalry commander captured."

Hawkins spit into the fire.

"Makes sense to me. And so my men and you and your captain here are gonna go snooping for him."

"Are you willing?"

309

Smiling, Hawkins said, "Hell yes. I don't much like them damned big battles, much rather be slippin' around where I've got some cover."

"Do you know the country?"

"Me and my men ran horses from Pennsylvania down's far as Charleston. Course most of the time was in Virginia and Maryland."

"How many men do you command, sergeant?" Pickering asked.

"All together 'bout a dozen. They'll ride like hell and they're damned good shots. Men you can count on."

"Then that's settled, sergeant."

Two days later, Warren and his new band departed Manassas as the sun was setting, moving north. Their ride took them through part of the battlefield and even in the darkness, evidence of the struggle remained. Following Hawkins directions, the group of fifteen men rode through the night, finally making camp in dense woods northwest of Centreville. Their first destination was the occupied area surrounding Fairfax Court House. While they were to gather any information on Union troops they encountered, the reason for their first stop was to contact a young woman.

Stuart had explained that this young lady, whose brother served in Stuart's command, had been providing information she overheard from the Federal troops billeted in the area. A handsome woman, she apparently was also a bit flirtatious and took advantage of every man's penchant for bragging.

A rendezvous had been arranged in her last communication with her brother and Warren had been ordered to be at the bridge where Walney Road crossed over Flat Lick

Stream. She would be riding a chestnut mare and wearing a red ribbon around her neck. If at all possible, she would cross the bridge at high noon.

Warren knew they were now close to the Federals, although in this area there were no defined borders and only the occasional patrol by cavalry detachments. Still, the Englishman was sensitive to the accepted rules of war and each of the men could be recognized as a Confederate soldier despite the assortment of different hats, coats and britches.

Two hours of reconnaissance convinced Warren that he could meet the lady and still have several routes of escape if surprised by Union troops. Hawkins had shown them a ravine where most of the men would remain, out of sight, while Warren and the sergeant went to the bridge. Pickering would remain behind with the men. One single lookout would be stationed halfway between the ravine and the bridge to bring word if anything should go amiss.

A blessed breeze down the Flat Lick kept the temperature bearable and fortunately the mosquitoes had not made an appearance.

"Quiet day," Warren commented from the secluded spot overlooking the bridge.

"Never saw lotta folks on this road. Don't know why."

"So you spent time in this area?"

"Lord, yes. Some of the best horseflesh in the country comes from these parts. Fetch a nice price up north, not so much down south. Too many southerners think only their horses are any good."

Warren smiled. It sounded very much like parts of England.

The horse with a female rider came into view just after noon. She was sitting sidesaddle and the rhythmic gate of the mare made the woman's hat bob fore and aft. She guided her mount to the side of the road under a large tree when she saw the two uniformed riders.

"Let's go, sergeant."

The two men covered the distance to the woman in less than a minute, reining to a stop, the dust rising from the sun-baked road.

"My name is Warren," he said, removing his hat. "This is Sergeant Hawkins."

Dark brown eyes showed caution or perhaps fear from the young woman that Warren estimated to be in her early twenties.

She looked around as if expecting more soldiers.

"Perhaps I should have said, 'We are from Beauty'."

"Thank you, colonel," she said with a smile, "My name is Charlotte Tyler."

His mind flashed to another Charlotte in another time, the memory still painful.

Stuart's nickname had been used as a recognition signal and now the young lady looked very relieved.

"I was told you would have a letter for us," he said, immediately, putting thoughts of Charlotte Truscott out of his mind.

Nodding, she reached into her short riding coat and pulled out a brown envelope, handing it to Warren.

"I don't know if this information is important, but it is the least I can do."

Warren saw the earnestness in her face and felt that he had seen something very special, a belief in a cause that she was ready to risk everything for. Bravery made her look much wiser than her years.

"Be assured, every bit of information is useful. We will ensure this is delivered to Beauty."

"You are not from the south, if I were to guess, sir. Have I misjudged?"

"Not at all. My loyalties are driven by motives other than my birthplace."

She smiled and said, "This terrible time has turned everything upside down. I don't know what the future may hold, but it will certainly be different from the past."

"You are very perceptive, Miss Tyler. I only know that this struggle is just beginning."

"And so many men have already perished at Bull Run," she said, the sorrow evident in her voice.

"Soldiers die, Miss Tyler. It's not good or bad, but simply the way of things." He saw the startled look in her eyes and for a moment was sorry for his remark. But it was the truth, he thought and she was old enough to recognize it.

"Colonel, we best be moving on," Hawkins said, looking up and down the road.

"Good day, Miss."

"And to you, Colonel Warren."

Charlotte Tyler was shocked at what Warren had said. She thought about her brother said a silent prayer for him.

"Miss Tyler?" Warren asked, curiosity getting the best of him.

She turned.

"Would your brother be Robert Tyler, of the 1st?"

"Do you know him?" she asked in response.

Warren nodded, "I do, miss. A fine young man."

Chapter Twenty

"Shoot the horses..."

Louis departed Belvoir three weeks after Warren's meeting with Miss Tyler. He left knowing that Michael Scully was not only in good hands medically, but that he was well on the road to recovery. The question remained as to the use of his arm, but he knew that was something that would not be resolved for a very long time.

"Fried eggs, bacon and grits, Michael. And I expect you to eat everything. You need your strength." Emily helped Scully sit up and carefully put the tray on his lap. He did look better after only two days at Belvoir. But from what Louis had told her of the crowded military hospitals in Richmond, it was not surprising that a clean bed with close attendance by a professional nurse could make such a difference.

Watching Kimberly change the bandage, Emily saw the expertise the young woman possessed. Kimberly's instructions for taking care of Michael were in many ways even more strict that Louis' basic guidelines. But whatever was needed, Emily

.

would make sure that her favorite Irishman received the very best of care.

"I am hungry, and truth be known, I've come to like grits."

"A good sign. Now I'll go down and get some coffee. And when you are done, Kimberly will bathe you and shave off that beard. For goodness sakes, Michael, you're a handsome man and I just won't see you in a beard."

Scully began to protest, but then realized it not only would do no good, but it felt truly wonderful to be taken care of like this. It was the first time in his life that anything like this had ever happened to him, and except for the pain of his wound, he was going to try and enjoy it. And he was sure that he could convince his ladies that a medicinal dose of Irish whiskey would be key to keeping his spirits up during the recovery.

Over the next several months, Charlotte Tyler provided a great deal of information to Stuart. She passed letters to Warren on the first occasion and Pickering on the second.

"Miss Tyler, my name is Pickering. James Pickering. Colonel Warren was unable to make the rendezvous and I am here in his stead."

Sergeant Hawkins nodded from the saddle.

"Miss."

Charlotte Tyler watched Pickering, who looked like a veteran, but acted as nervous as a young colt.

"Sir, do I detect that you are also not from the south?

Pickering felt like the tongue-tied adolescent around this woman.

"England, actually, miss. I've been with the colonel for a number of years."

Charlotte's eyes glanced down, noticing the prosthetic on his left hand, her face momentarily registering her surprise.

Hawkins broke up the awkward moment.

"Captain, we best be getting the letter and let the lady go on her way. There's likely Union patrols out this time of day."

She reached into her jacket and withdrew the envelope.

"Please take care of this, I think this is critical information for Beauty."

"Trust me, miss, I will put it in his hand myself."

"I hope I will see you again, Mr. Pickering."

He smiled, raised his cap and turned his horse to follow Sergeant Hawkins.

Charlotte watched the two men ride into the wood on the far side of the road. She realized that she was quite taken with the young officer and that shocked her. Pulling her horse's head around, she spurred him in the direction of home.

Over the next month, Warren and his troop covered the entire war front, stretching from Yorktown west to Parkersburg. Sergeant Hawkins's knowledge of the terrain not only made their intelligence gathering more effective, but on multiple occasions prevented clashes with Union patrols. It became clear to Warren that sentiments were indeed pro-Union west of the mountains of Virginia, in stark contrast to the eastern portion of the state. He also noted that with the exception of a sparse railroad network, the entire area was made up of small farms clustered around the random village. Certainly he did not see anything that would support a sustained war effort by the Confederates.

It was also very apparent to Warren that the mindset among the leaders in the Confederate Army was how to defend against the inevitable onslaught by the Federals. The approach by itself told him that the South knew the war was not theirs to win, but the Federals's to lose. Could they fight off the stronger Union forces long enough to force a stalemate? If what he had seen of the southern resources so far was prevalent throughout the South, he very much doubted it. It would be a war of attrition, something these Americans had never seen. The campaign waged by George Washington in the revolution against the stronger British army might provide a useful lesson to the Confederacy. If they were smart enough to realize it.

Warren stood reading a letter he had just received from Stuart's headquarters. The dispatch rider had found them just south of Morgantown.

He turned to Pickering, who sat with his back against a tree, sipping a cup of coffee.

"It seems we are to contact Miss Tyler again. I'm sure Stuart didn't know how far we are from Fairfax Courthouse or he would have sent someone else."

Three days of hard riding would be required to reach the rendezvous point, but it was exactly in the opposite direction that Warren needed to move.

"I could go, retrieve the letter, deliver it to Stuart and meet you in seven or eight days," Pickering offered.

Warren thought about the offer. Certainly Pickering knew the area and had made one meeting already. If he took one of Hawkins's experienced men with him, the trip should be easy. Pickering had come a long way from the young coronet of the 13th Dragoons. He had gained the maturity and experience of many men much older in addition to the strength of youth. Why not?

Corporal Lester Richey had been riding with Hawkins for eight years. The twenty-five year old seemed to belong in a saddle. Lean and wiry like Hawkins, the only difference was that Richey was only five feet and six inches tall. But wearing leather britches, a grey tunic and a wide brimmed hat, he looked every inch the cavalryman.

Their route east had skirted the most active areas of Union patrols, but still followed a direct route to reach the bridge by noon of the day designated. Twice they had to ride out of their way to avoid enemy cavalry, but with Richey's knowledge of the terrain, they lost little time.

Arriving with an hour to spare, the two men dismounted and let their mounts water and graze on the northern bank of the creek.

"Where do you call home?" Pickering asked.

"I come from North Carolina, but I left home a long time ago,"

The Englishman thought of his own story, off to the army before he even knew what it was all about.

"Pretty country," Pickering offered.

Before Richey could answer, they heard a horse coming fast in their direction. Mounting, they moved toward the road and saw Charlotte Tyler galloping up to and across the bridge. They spurred toward her and saw the riders coming fast behind her, riders wearing Union cavalry blue.

"Charlotte, ride, girl, ride!" Pickering yelled as he spurred his horse up to the near edge of the bridge. He drew his Colt and called to Richey.

"Shoot the horses."

Both men began a steady fire at the approaching enemy riders, two horses swerving immediately as the bullets found their mark.

Charlotte had ridden a half-mile down the road, reining to a stop to see what was happening behind her. The two Confederates were finding some cover from the bridge as they continued to fire at the Yankee soldiers.

Pickering pulled his second revolver and waited to see what the Federals were going to do. Three horses lay on the road, crying in pain, while the troopers had taken cover on the side of the road.

"You reload," he called to Richey, who only carried one revolver. "If we have to make a run for it, do you know where to go?"

In between loading his pistol, Richey said, "'bout two miles down this road there's a trail leads south. Hard to see from the road."

Pickering looked back and saw Charlotte by the road,

"You get going and take her to the trail. I'll hold them for five minutes then follow."

Richey slipped the revolver into its holster and said, "Don't tarry, captain, them boys don't look none too friendly."

Quickly wedging his first revolver against the saddle horn, Pickering used his right hand and reloaded the pistol. Glancing up between each round loaded, Pickering watched the enemy soldiers, who must have been deciding what to do next. He finished loading the pistol and fired one round at the Federals to let them know he was still there.

That must be five minutes, he thought as he fired two more rounds at the Federals and spurred south down the road.

Several minutes later, he rounded a turn to see Corporal Richey off to the right side of the road, partially hidden by thick brush.

"Let's get moving," Richey called and pulled his horse's head left and into the forest.

Quickly entering a thick stand of trees, the two men moved fifty yards before they slowed.

"They behind you?" Richey asked?

"Not the last time I looked, but they surely will be soon. Where's the girl?"

"Just up here. Least that's where I left her."

Charlotte sat on her horse, patting the creature's neck to calm them both down. Her mind raced with the enormity of what had happened. Why were the Union troops following her and why did they chase her when she picked up her pace? Did they know something or were they just out to harass the locals?

She looked up as the two men arrived.

"Are you all right?" Pickering asked.

A shaft of sunlight pierced the trees and flashed across Charlotte's face showing the relief in her eyes.

"Yes," she said, nodding her head.

"We best be movin' south," Richey said, taking the lead.

"Why were they after you?" Pickering asked as they followed Richey.

"I don't know," she replied, her voice betraying her fear.

Pickering brought up the rear and wondered where this would lead. He must get the information south to Stuart, but what about the girl?

Four hours later the three riders stopped to water and rest their horses at a small creek. Richey had doubled back two hours prior and had seen no evidence of Union troops.

"Here is the letter," Charlotte said, handing the pale yellow envelope to Pickering.

He smiled and said, "Perhaps you should take it to the general. It might be too dangerous for you to go home."

"I don't know what to do. I'm expected home and my family will be terribly worried. But why were those Yankees after me? Why?"

Pickering said, "We'll get word to your family, Miss Tyler. Right now we'll escort you to headquarters. Someone there will know what to do."

By late afternoon, they were well clear of enemy patrols and within an hour, they had located a good place to camp for the night.

James was surprised that once Charlotte had understood they had to travel south, she acted as if it was the most natural thing in the world to be heading to places unknown with two relative strangers. He found her intriguing.

"Fire?" James asked.

Corporal Richey thought for a moment then nodded.

"We'll keep it low."

The horses were unsaddled and secured to a tie line between two trees. Richey unpacked his saddlebags, producing a pot with a bag of coffee. He busied himself getting a small fire started.

"Can you help me gather firewood?" James asked.

Charlotte nodded and followed him into a nearby clearing.

"I'm sorry for all this," he said, finding some dry wood at the edge of the open area.

She picked up several pieces, inspecting them like someone who truly knows firewood.

"If it weren't for my family, it would be quite the adventure."

"Do you like to travel?"

Charlotte laughed.

"I don't know. I've never been farther than Baltimore, and that was only twice."

"You haven't been to your capitol?"

"Father said that it was 'a place of evil populated by every denizen known to man'."

James laughed.

"Sounds like Constantinople."

"You've been there?"

She turned to look at him as though he was a truly foreign creature.

"Going and coming from Russia," he said, his voice reflecting his experience in the Crimea.

"You were wounded there?" Her eyes moved to his left arm.

He nodded and turned to return to the camp.

"I'm sorry," she said.

"Thank you. I learned a great deal in Russia, about many things."

"I'm glad you're here," she said, reaching out and touching his arm.

Pickering found himself at a loss for anything to say. But he knew that this young woman was someone he very much wanted to know better.

Later that night, after Richey had turned in, they talked while sitting next to the small fire. She told him about her family and growing up in Northern Virginia.

James learned that she loved horses, reading and the changing of seasons. It was comforting to talk with her. He'd never felt comfortable with most women and had resigned himself to a life of bachelorhood.

"You're risking a great deal to do what you do," he said after a pause in their conversation.

"I guess I knew the risk, but it never really seemed real until today," Charlotte said quietly, lowering her head as if praying.

He felt a surge of emotion. He would protect this young woman, regardless of the consequences.

Chapter Twenty-One

"First I'll have the truth, then I'll hang you."

On arrival at the headquarters of the Army of Northern Virginia, Captain Pickering found out that the fate of one young woman did not rise to the level of attention he felt was warranted. In addition, the absence of Stuart left him with little influence amongst the staff officers. Use of the "King's English" did little to help his efforts to find some resolution to Charlotte's dilemma. He looked for Colonel Cable, but found the man was in Richmond.

"James, I will simply have to return home," Charlotte said after two days of fruitless conversations with several different staff officers.

"If we took you north, is there someone you trust that could find out what is really happening?"

She thought for a moment.

"My cousin Tom Pyle lives in Burke. I know he would help me."

"Then we'll ride in the morning. If nothing else, we can get word to your family that you are alive and well."

Surprising both of them, she leaned forward and kissed James on the cheek.

"Thank you," she said quickly stepping back. "I hope you don't think me too forward, but without you, my situation would be unbearable."

He smiled at her and said, "I am happy to be of service."

"Will you be in trouble with Colonel Warren?"

"I'll tell him what happened. He'll understand." He thought for a moment then said, "Charlotte, it seems to me that prudence would dictate we come up with a cover story which would protect you in the event things do not turn out as well as we would like."

"I don't understand what you're saying," she said.

"Does anybody in Fairfax Courthouse know what you've been doing for the Confederacy?"

"No, Robert and I talked about it and decided that only the two of us should know."

Pickering asked, "No friends? Your parents? No one else knows?"

She shook her head, "No one."

"Then our story will be that you were afraid the union cavalry would harm you and you simply ran out of fear."

The assumption of command of the Army of the Potomac by Major General George B. McClellan sent a wave of hope and energy through a very demoralized army. In no time a level of organization and singularity of purpose took control of the army and Union soldiers began preparations for the next phase of the war. The speed of change was breathtaking compared to how business had been conducted in the army for the last fifty years. The "boy general" was only thirty-four years old, but his drive and ability to organize turned out to be the perfect tonic for a sick army. New units were brought on the rolls as the casualties from Manassas were returned to duty or released from service. An infrastructure that could support a modern war machine came together and more supplies began to arrive in the area surrounding the capital.

Lessons learned from the first months of the war also produced a significant expansion of the intelligence service and an attendant growth in the Provost Marshall's organization. When time came for Lieutenant Colonel Hart to return to active service, a few words from an influential senator resulted in his assignment as the second in command of the military police for the army.

It was good to be out of the hospital, Hart thought as he drank his morning coffee. More than that, he reveled in the knowledge that he would never again have to face the enemy line of battle. His wounds gave his assignment legitimacy and a complete lack of concern for what anyone might think of him. It was going to be a very good war.

"Sir, the patrol you sent out to arrest the Tyler woman was attacked by rebel troops." Lieutenant Paxton Hunt stood in the door of Hart's office, a telegraph message in his hand.

"Damnation,"

Southern sympathizers were known to be helping the Confederate forces to position their defenses. Trying to gain knowledge of that network was part of the job of the provost along with the intelligence service. A negro slave had tipped them to the rather curious actions of a Miss Charlotte Tyler, who was known to have family in the Confederate Army. She had been seen on a number of occasions riding well south of her home and alone. The informant had ridden to the nearest provost detachment when he had seen her leaving on another of her solitary rides. Now it appeared their suspicions had been confirmed.

Hunt went on to read the report from the detachment.

"So the question is where our young spy is now, Hunt."

"Yes, sir, I agree."

Paxton Hunt was an unusual young man. Although well educated, he had chosen to join the New York Police Department, rising to detective in only four years. Now the challenge of internal security made him a very useful tool for Hart, who planned to use Hunt's experience to bust open the seditious northern spy networks. That success would pave the road for Hart when the war was over. Knowledge is power and leverage is a great multiplier when people have something to hide. He saw himself building a labyrinth of informants and people whom he could blackmail as needed, to expand his power. But for now, he had to rely on the incompetent fools that were assigned to his command. That is where Lieutenant Paxton Hunt came into the picture. A longtime family friend of the venerable senator from New York, Hunt had already be doing Madison's dirty work before the war began. Paxton Hunt was cut from the same cloth as Brett Hart, and they both understood who controlled their futures.

"Why don't you take charge of this investigation?"

Hunt nodded.

"I'm sure that with a few threats of hanging, we can get some of those rebellious bastards to talk. Know what I mean?"

"Indeed I do," he said, grinning.

Three days of cautious riding brought James and Charlotte to a heavily wooded area south of Burke. He had sent Corporal Richey on from headquarters to find Warren and explain the delay. Now as the sun was setting, the two of them waited to make the final three-mile ride to Tom Pyle's farm. Charlotte had known Pyle her entire life, the two cousins growing up only ten miles apart. He was ten years older and now worked the Pyle farm, which he had to take over when his father died in a fall. He was sympathetic to the southern cause, but his responsibility for the farm had kept him from volunteering for the army.

A partial moon made their ride comfortable and both were relieved that they had encountered no one in the hour it took to cover the distance from the woods.

Tom Pyle looked very surprised when he saw Charlotte standing on his porch.

"My God, girl. The whole town's in a fury over you. Come inside, quickly."

"Tom, I have a friend with me," she said quietly, "A Confederate officer."

"Dear Lord, it just gets better. Well, get him in here."

In the next twenty minutes, Charlotte told Tom that she had been terrified when the Union troopers had galloped toward her and she simply fled. The two Confederate soldiers had begun shooting after she was well past. When one of the southern soldiers had found her, she went with him out of fright.

Tom listened, his expression saying nothing.

"Charlotte, your family was beside themselves with fear. And two Federals came around asking questions. They said that you were under an arrest warrant."

Pickering could see the fear in her eyes. Her cousin seemed very concerned that she was in danger.

"You can't go home. Not now. Maybe not until the war's over." Pyle said. "Maybe you should go back south?"

Pickering knew she wanted to see her parents, but he now agreed with her cousin. He could send her south to Belvoir to stay with Emily.

"I must see my parents," she said, "I just have to."

"I can leave you here and come back in two or three days. If you are agreeable, you could travel to Colonel Warren's plantation in North Carolina. We have several people there who will take good care of you until things sort themselves out."

Charlotte looked at her cousin, her question obvious.

"All right. You'll stay here and I'll get word to Charles and your mother. They can decide what they want to do. Captain, you would be safer waiting here rather than making trips through Union patrols."

"Please stay, James."

The logic was sound, Pickering thought, and spending more time with Charlotte appealed to him greatly.

"Why Mr. Pyle, do come in. I'll let them know you are here."

The middle aged black man opened the Tyler's front door wide to allow Pyle to enter.

"Tom, what brings you to town?" Charles Tyler asked, coming around the hallway corner.

"Henry, please tell Mrs. Tyler that we have company," he said to the servant. "And have Lizzie bring us a pitcher of tea."

"Yes, sir," the man replied and quietly stepped out.

Tyler led his nephew into the parlor and bid him take a seat.

"I have news of Charlotte," Pyle said, adding quickly, "And she is just fine."

Belinda Tyler, a lovely, tall woman entered just in time to hear Pyle's last comment.

"My Charlotte. Is she all right, Tom?"

Pyle nodded and proceeded to relate the events of last night. He told them of Charlotte's encounter with Union troops. Neither Charles nor Belinda said a word as the story unfolded.

"She's hiding at the farm and the young officer that found her is also there."

"My, God," Belinda said, raising her hand to her cheek as Henry Baker, the Tyler's man servant came around the corner, a tray with a pitcher of tea and three glasses.

The three of them, said nothing as the man set the tray on the table and asked, "Is there anything else, ma'am?"

"No, leave us," Charles said, his words abrupt, but he was clearly preoccupied with the problem of Charlotte.

"What shall we do, Charles?" Belinda asked.

"We must arrange for her to travel south. Perhaps to your cousin Amanda's in Raleigh."

Pyle related the offer of Captain Pickering, who had elaborated the details to Pyle late last night.

"On the whole, the young man's plan seemed very sound. She is innocent, but I don't trust the Federals. Better she stays clear of here until we can decide what to do," Pyle said.

"Let me think about it, Tom."

"I want to see her. I must," Belinda said.

Her husband nodded, "Of course, dear."

"The sooner she can head south, the better. Too many Union troops around here, to say nothing of the sympathizers," Pyle said. "Can you come tonight?"

It had been a long afternoon for Charlotte and James. Pyle had cautioned them to stay inside the house and they both felt trapped.

Pickering knew he should be anxious to return to Warren's side, but the more time he spent with Charlotte, the more he was drawn to her. Mature beyond her years, he saw a woman who had made decisions that most women would never even consider. Now it seemed that she was reluctant to escape to the safety of North Carolina and cease her efforts to help the Confederacy.

"Richard Warren taught me that making smart decisions will always prove beneficial over time. I think you have to consider that if you stay here you'll be discovered and arrested. Your value was when no one knew what you were doing. Now you no longer have that advantage."

"But to just sit around doing nothing while the war goes on," Charlotte said, her voice subdued.

"Kimberly's at Belvoir. She's a nurse. You could learn how to help care for wounded. There are never enough nurses, I learned that in Russia."

Charlotte raised her face to James.

"You're right, of course. Thank you for everything you've done for me."

Frustrated at their slow progress through the countryside, Paxton Hunt consoled himself with the thought that, if this Henry fellow was right, he could have the southern spy in handcuffs this very night. That would show that pompous ass Hart that Paxton Hunt knew damn well what he was doing. Too many times the older man had talked to him as if he were a wet nosed recruit.

"How much farther?" he asked the man riding next to him.

"Less than a mile, sir," Henry answered. He felt some remorse that he was betraying the Tyler family, but the one hundred dollar reward that he had been offered by Hunt was all he needed to make a start up north. Henry wanted away from Virginia and everything bad that had happened to him since he had been sold as a small boy in Richmond. Now he would leave that behind forever.

Ten Union soldiers, led by an overweight sergeant followed the two lead horsemen. The weather was good for this time of year and despite the cool temperatures, there had been little wind and no rain. But left up to them, none of the young troopers would have wanted to be out of their billets and chasing a Confederate spy across Prince William County in the middle of the night.

The column continued across a wide field, paralleling a wooden fence that fronted a dirt road.

"There's the road to the Pyle farm. They'll be there," Henry said, keeping his voice down, although they were still well out of sight of the farm itself.

Thirty minutes later Hunt saw the lights from several windows on the first floor of a neat two story house. Smoke was visible in the moonlight coming from a tall brick chimney at the far side of the house. He stopped the column and ordered the soldiers to dismount. His challenge now was to ensure that no one could escape from the farm.

Pickering had said little since the arrival of Charlotte's parents. It had been uncomfortable to watch her father's anger alongside her mother's fear and concern. Thank goodness both of them understood that their daughter could not stay in the area.

Now he had decided to push for Charlotte to travel to North Carolina, where he knew she would be welcomed and looked after.

"Charlotte, we must get you to Amanda's. And as quickly as we can."

The realities of the changes in her life were beginning to dawn on Charlotte. But just as she had made the decision to spy for the Confederacy on her own, she had already made up her mind.

"I know I have to leave, father. But I'm going to North Carolina with James."

Charles Tyler turned, his face questioning the Englishman.

"Exactly what is going on here?"

"Charlotte?" her mother asked.

Pickering started to insert himself in the conversation, but caught himself. He had to let her work this out in her own way.

"I'm a grown woman, father. The decision is up to me."

Her father's jaws tightened.

Perhaps this wasn't going to be as easy as he had imagined, Pickering thought.

Corporal Lester Richey chewed slowly on the dried beef, allowing his saliva to soften the tough salty morsel. Sheltering in a small grove of trees, he checked the farmhouse again and pulled his blanket tighter around his shoulders. He had shadowed his captain and the lady since they left headquarters, ignoring Pickering's orders to return to the detachment. He was following Sergeant Hawkins's orders that he watch out for Pickering until they got back safely to Warren's command. The sergeant had told him that the colonel agreed with Hawkins.

Trying to decide if he had to go bad enough to drop his drawers in the chill night air, Richey stopped and looked again at the farmhouse.

"Shit."

He could see several men leading horses and setting up a perimeter around the house. There was no doubt they were Union troopers, he could see their uniforms in the moonlight. The only chance the captain would have would be to alert him that something was wrong. Richey pulled his pistol and fired two shots, which echoed across the open field toward the farmhouse.

Turning towards the door, Pickering knew something was very wrong. He moved to the window and quickly scanned the area, seeing nothing.

"What the hell?" Pyle asked as he joined the Englishman at the window,

"Charles?" Belinda Tyler questioned, her confusion obvious.

Glass shattered as shots cracked in the night.

"Get down!" Pickering yelled as he lunged across the room and pulled Charlotte to the floor.

Pyle turned toward the rest as a bullet slammed into his back, throwing him forward, blood spattering across the room.

"God damned chowder heads," Hunt yelled across the open yard, "Stop firing, damn it! Cease your firing!"

Several more shots rang out, then silence returned to the shattered night.

Hunt took a moment to survey the house, seeing no change except for two shattered windows.

"Sergeant, have your men close in on the house, but no shooting, understood?"

The big man acknowledged the order and hurried off.

Ten minutes later he returned and reported.

"House is surrounded, sir."

The time had given Hunt an opportunity to survey the farmhouse more carefully. There was an outhouse twenty yards in back of the house and a large barn perhaps forty yards past that. If the woman was in the house, there was no way out.

"In the house, you're surrounded by Federal troops. Come out now with your hands in the air, or we'll burn the house to the ground."

Hunt's breath frosted in the night air as he delivered his ultimatum. Take these people into custody and get the hell back to Burke, he thought to himself. A stiff brandy and warm bed would cap the night nicely.

"I told you they were here, didn't I, captain?" Henry said. "I'll get my reward, won't I?"

"Shut up, Baker, or I'll shoot you myself and keep the money."

Corporal Richey watched the Union officer shove a pistol into the chest of a middle-aged negro, who stepped back quickly.

"No, sir. No, sir."

Belinda Tyler sat on the floor next to her brother, her face blank, the shock having set in after seeing Pyle make two futile efforts to rise then dying as his heart stopped. Blood covered the floor, soaking into Belinda's dress but she was oblivious. Her husband knelt under a window, searching for their assailants. He turned to Pickering.

"Can you get her out of here, son?"

The young man's mind raced, how many enemy troops were outside? Could they reach the barn and retrieve their horses?

He looked at Charlotte, her eyes wide in the candlelight, but looking to him for help.

"I'll try."

"Sergeant, get your best three rifle shots, and begin firing on the house. I want them to aim high, understand? I don't want anyone in the house killed, but I want them to give up."

The fat sergeant saluted and said, "Yes, sir. On your command?"

"Commence fire when ready, sergeant. And watch what they're doing, God damn it."

"Yes, sir."

Pickering looked out the only window at the rear of the house toward the barn. The moonlight that bathed the yard was not going to make an escape easy, but his uniform was grey and her coat dark brown. They might just be able to stay close to the ground and reach the barn. As long as there was no one waiting at the barn, they could saddle the horses and make a run for it. If someone were in the barn, he would have to use his sword. Any shots would give them away.

"Stay low and follow me. Going slow will help us blend in, so don't worry if I stop, just do what I do."

Charlotte nodded.

The window had two panes, set in a sturdy wood frame. Removing a wooden peg lock, he raised the lower window, feeling the cold air surge into the house.

"Ready?"

Nodding her head, she touched his arm and quietly said, "Yes."

He climbed out the window as shots broke the stillness of the night.

"Here," he said, helping her out the window.

Pausing to scan the yard, Pickering said, "Let's go."

A steady fusillade kept up as the two made their way across the yard, using several bushes for cover.

The barn had a wide door on the front, but James had already decided to use the smaller door on the north side. Despite the continued fire, he sensed that no one was firing at them and began to think they might actually get away.

Partially open, the side door was unlatched, the wooden lever lock vertical on the barn's side. Pickering slowly pushed the door open trying to see inside the darkened structure.

The smell of fresh manure greeted him, but the inside was quiet. He tried to remember if he had seen a lantern when they had originally stabled the horse, but that had been during daylight. Now the inside of the barn was black as the bottom of a well at midnight.

"Charlotte, hold the door open," he whispered. Perhaps the moonlight would provide enough light to saddle the horses.

Reaching down to find saddle blankets, he heard a muffled cry from Charlotte.

"In the barn," came the shout from outside. "We got the woman, so come out with your hands up or we'll put a bullet in her head."

Watching from fifty yards away, Corporal Richey watched Pickering emerge from the barn, his hands held above his head.

"Damn it to hell," Richey muttered.

Pickering's humiliation was complete the next day when two soldiers opened his cell at the Burke Jail.

"On your feet," the older man said.

The second man produced a set of steel handcuffs.

"Shit, how the hell am I supposed to use handcuffs when this son of a bitch only has one hand?"

"Lemme see."

Fastening one cuff around Pickering's right wrist, he slid the second cuff through the metal of his prosthetic and clicked it.

"There you go, Harry. Easy. Let's go, reb."

The officer from the previous night sat in the room where the two guards delivered their prisoner. Both men remained in the room, standing against the wall after seating Pickering in a flat-backed chair facing the officer. The ride to Burke had taken almost two hours but there had been no communication between the two.

Now the man took a pen in hand and asked, "Name?"

"James Pickering."

On hearing the Englishman's accent, Paxton Hunt looked up from his paper.

"I was going to ask your unit, but I think it would be good to know your nationality."

"British."

"Well I'll be damned. That certainly makes things more interesting. Although, you were captured in uniform, so I expect you will be considered a prisoner of war."

Those words struck Pickering like a blow. For the second time, he thought, remembering the horrible blur of Sevastopol.

"Not like that little doxy, though. She's a spy, full out, no question about it. And the way this war is going, we'll hang women spies before the year's out. Maybe she'll be the first one."

Say nothing, Pickering thought. Don't let him see your concern. Act like this happens every day.

"I have your name as James Pickering," Paxton Hunt said, reading from a sheet of paper in front of him.

"Rank?"

"Captain."

Hunt made the annotation.

"What unit?"

"Virginia cavalry," Pickering answered, still hearing the man's comments about hanging women spies.

"Really. One of Jeb Stuart's boys."

Pickering didn't answer. He thought of Charlotte hanging from a scaffold like he had seen at Newmarket.

The man stood and turned to one of the guards.

"Keep him here, I'll be back."

Twenty minutes later Pickering heard steps in the corridor and turned to see a face that slammed him back in time, to those terrible days in Russia.

"I'll be damned," Hart said as he recognized the prisoner. He sat down opposite Pickering and looked him over.

"Traded your red coat for rebel gray, I see. What a story that must be."

Paxton Hunt sat down beside the colonel.

"Caught behind the lines, a foreign national assisting a woman, known to be an enemy spy. I do believe we have a serious problem here, Coronet Pickering. Oh, excuse me. Captain Pickering."

Hart paused then said," Cat got your tongue, Pickering?"

"That woman is no spy. She ran from a patrol of your thugs who looked like they were intent on doing her harm. I just happened to find her."

Standing up, Hart stepped around the table and hit Pickering hard across the face.

"You're not a very good liar, Pickering. And before I'm done with you, I'll have the truth. Then I'll hang you and that traitorous bitch."

Chapter Twenty-Two

"She is free to go..."

A natural horseman with a strong mount, Corporal Richey had been able to find Warren's troop in six days. Hard riding and using a network of friends from before the war, he was able to shrink the wide expanse of territory that would have challenged any other man to find the cavalry unit.

Jumping down from the saddle, Richey saw Warren standing with Hawkins in front of a cook fire.

"The captain's been taken by the federals. The woman, too," he said, without saluting or greeting either man.

"When and where?"

"Six days ago, a farm just south of Fairfax Courthouse."

Richey passed on what he'd seen that night while Warren and Hawkins listened without interruption.

Richard Warren knew that he must try to find out more and perhaps mount a rescue. But the area was unfamiliar to him and he knew nothing of Union procedures. Pickering might already be in one of the northern prisons, difficult to find and impossible to help.

"You know that area?" he asked Hawkins.

The tall man nodded seriously.

"Spent some time there. Know some folks I can trust."

Warren considered what might await them. Could he risk these men to save Pickering? He looked at Hawkins. Over the last six months, he'd come to respect the quiet Virginian and he decided to do something he would have never considered in the 13th.

"I've known Captain Pickering for a long time, sergeant. If there is any chance to get him back, I have to try."

Hawkins nodded and said, "I'd do the same."

"I'd like your help, but this calls for risks that I can't ask the men to take."

"You let me be the judge of that. These boys like Pickering and nothing they'd enjoy more than to snatch him back from the federals."

Pickering sat on filthy straw looking up at the small opening on the opposite wall of the wooden shed he had occupied for the last ten days. His mouth was dry and he needed water. While his captors had brought him a bowl of some type of soup on several occasions, there had been little to drink since he'd been chained to the wall. Three times he'd been beaten by two big Union soldiers, but he'd not seen Hart since their first meeting.

Remembering the Russian holding cage from Sevastopol, Pickering wondered where the stone walls and iron bars he assumed would make up his prison were. Blindfolded in the back of a wagon, he knew that he had not travelled far from the Burke Jail. The absence of noise outside the shed told him that he was being held somewhere in isolation. Was this part of Hart's plan to lock him away, telling no one of the captured

Englishman? Did the American intend to punish him for what happened in Russia? And what had happened to Charlotte?

Two guards had attached iron manacles around Pickering's ankles and then connected both to a large bolt secured in one of the beams supporting the roof. He huddled under a wool blanket, shivering at times, but glad his uniform was good quality wool. Perhaps the terrible ordeal in Russia had hardened him more than he knew.

But unlike in Russia, here he was completely alone. No one knew where he was, certainly not Warren. He remembered Michael Scully, how the Irishman had cared for him through Balaclava and losing his hand. But now, Scully was fighting to recover from his own terrible wounds. Pickering knew it was up to him. Then he remembered one afternoon he and Scully had spent at sea, working on opening locks without using keys.

He raised the blanket and looked at the manacles on his ankles. He carefully removed his prosthetic and opened the hidden panel. He pulled out the small metal lever then replaced his hook. Then he began to work on the padlock that connected the chain to his manacles.

God damn all lawyers and judges, Hart thought as he stormed out of the courtroom at the Federal Court for Eastern Virginia. Only two days ago he thought the court proceeding were simply part of the procedure for transferring the Tyler woman to Washington, D.C. What he had not known at the time was that the Honorable Henry Trumbull would look into the case prior to allowing the transfer. The glaring truth that came to light was that there was not a shred of evidence other than the inference of something clandestine by a Negro servant of the

Tylers. God damn Paxton Hunt, he thought, damn him to hell for not having something in the way of evidence.

The words of that pompous judge still ran through his mind.

"I see no evidence whatsoever that would justify keeping this young woman in custody. We are still a nation of laws, colonel. She is free to go."

He reached his horse and violently grabbed the reigns, climbing into the saddle and sinking his spurs into the animal. The Englishman would most certainly never see a courtroom, he told himself. That son of a bitch would pay a price. He would keep his afternoon appointment then pick up some guards and visit the prisoner. It may make no difference in this war, he thought, but I will get my revenge for Russia. He spurred his horse once more, reveling in the thought.

Pickering had examined the door leading out of the shed and a sliding metal bar was all he could see. Gently working on the door, it appeared to be solidly locked and sturdy as well. The small window had two wooden shutters, which were open, but the dimension would never allow Pickering to climb through without a great deal of cutting, something his small blade would not accomplish.

Sitting with a blanket covering his feet, now free of the manacles, Pickering waited for his guards. There had never been more than two, although he hadn't been able to see if there were more men outside. He would have to listen, and then make a decision. He recalled that neither men had ever carried a sidearm, but the private had a musket with him during each visit.

The sounds of approaching horses could be heard through the small opening. A voice came from outside, but he was unable to understand what was said. Was it one guard talking to another or perhaps a single rider talking to his horse?

Pickering shivered involuntarily. He knew that time had come for him to act.

The noise of metallic keys against a lock came from the outside of the door, followed by the rasp of the metal bolt being withdrawn.

"Wake up, you son of a bitch."

His heart pounding in his chest, Pickering sat with his back against the far wall his right leg under his left leg, which was planted solidly on the ground. As the door swung open he waited two seconds then flung himself forward throwing the blanket up and over the first guard's head, slamming the man backwards into the private who was about to step into the shed.

A muffled cry came from under the blanket as the first guard stumbled and fell sideways against the doorjamb. Pickering jerked his knee up violently, catching the first guard's head with a solid blow. Pushing the blanket-covered guard to the side, Pickering stepped through the door, reaching the slim private who was trying to get to his feet, having rolled over onto his hands and knees.

Without pausing, Pickering kicked the man hard in the side, knowing he'd broken some of the private's ribs. The enemy soldier collapsed on the ground with a cry of pain. He pulled his knees up to his chest and covered his head, ignoring the musket that lay on the ground only inches away.

Looking around quickly, Pickering saw he was alone with the two soldiers, their two horses tethered to a second larger cabin across a dirt yard. He grabbed the musket, pulling the private's bayonet from the scabbard and clicking it on the weapon. Turning around, he reached the doorway and saw the first guard struggling to untangle himself from the blanket. For one moment he was prepared to ram the long blade into the man, but the reversed his hold on the musket and brought the butt down hard on the man's head.

The sun was just beginning to set, as Pickering emerged from a thick stand of trees a mile south of where he'd been held. Two hours prior, he had tied up both guards, taken their boots and tied them together, back to back. Now it was time for him to figure out where he was and how to make his way south. Having seen the sunset, he knew the general direction south, but there were federal troops in the area that would likely shoot him on sight. Travelling by night, he hoped to recognize something familiar that would allow him to pinpoint his position and a route back to his own lines. He thought for a moment that he should try to help Charlotte, but realized he had no chance to doing anything other than getting recaptured. If he could find Warren, then they might be able to try to rescue her. But that didn't relieve his feeling of guilt. Charlotte had been captured while under his care.

Pickering pulled the horse up short. He thought about what had happened to him and to Charlotte. Only one man was to blame for her imprisonment and it wasn't him. The bastard from Russia who had returned to plague him again would pay for what he had done to her. Pickering knew that Warren would be fine without him. Scully would always be there to watch over him. Pickering pulled the reins around toward Burke.

While his troopers formed a watchful perimeter around the Tyler house, Warren, Hawkins and Richey knocked on the front door, guns drawn.

The door opened and a negro in a coat and tie jumped back, with a cry of fright.

"Where are the Tylers?"

"Please don't shoot. Please."

Warren pushed past the man who was shoved against the wall by Richey.

"What's this... My God!" Charles Tyler exclaimed as he stood up from his chair, to see two armed men burst into his parlor.

"Sir, my name is Warren. We mean you no harm. I'm searching for one of my men who was with your daughter."

"Pickering? Captain Pickering?"

"I suspect we don't have much time, sir. Please tell me what you know."

Richey pushed the manservant into the parlor.

"Colonel, this was one of the men that were outside that farm when they took the captain."

Henry Baker's eyes flashed a look of terror and he tried to wrest free of Richey, who slammed his pistol into the side of Baker's head, dropping him to the floor.

"Father?"

They all looked to the parlor entrance where Charlotte stood, her hand over her mouth, eyes wide open.

It took ten minutes for Warren, Tyler and Charlotte to cover events of the last two weeks.

"So Thomas could still be at the Burke Jail?"

"Unless they've taken him north," Charles said.

Warren knew that it was a slim chance, but he had to try.

"Can you draw us a map of the jail, outside and in?" Warren asked.

Charlotte and her father both nodded.

Pickering knew the jail had to be within two miles, based on the wagon ride to the shed. That trip, under guard, to the Burke jail was burned into his mind. But until he saw something familiar, he was simply guessing where to go. Fifteen minutes later, he saw the wooden bridge, which they had crossed that night. He knew where he was and a feeling of calm came over him. Charlotte was certainly lost to him forever. For that reason, he had nothing to fear and that made him a very dangerous man.

Under the cover of darkness, Warren and his troops made the four-mile trip to the Burke Jail in an hour and a half. Charles Tyler had insisted that he accompany them and provide directions. The lack of a moon gave the Confederates more cover, but the journey was that much harder on the darkened roads. The occasional light could be seen from houses and farms they passed, but the late hour meant few people would be out in the brisk wind that brought the hint of a hard winter to come.

"There it is," Tyler said. He had approached the one story structure from the south, using trees as a natural cover.

"Sergeant," Warren whispered behind him.

Hawkins said nothing, but with a horseman's expertise he moved up to Warren's side with barely a sound.

"Send two men to check around back and make sure there are no posted men guarding the jail."

"Right," Hawkins replied, and pulled the head of his horse around, heading back toward the troopers.

Ten minutes later, the two men returned to report that there were no sentries in evidence around the periphery of the jail.

Several lighted windows in the front cast a thin light onto the street, and Warren knew what he had to do.

He selected five of his best men and went over the plan. Surprise and speed would give them an advantage. But not knowing what they might be facing was a risk he had to take. Warren suspected that at night, the guards would be the only people in the jail. At least that was his hope.

Sergeant Hawkins returned, nodding to Warren.

"Let's go," he said quietly, pulling his pistol from the holster.

The five men and Hawkins followed Warren across the open area and quietly moved up on the raised wooden sidewalk that ran across the front of the jail. Warren moved to the main entrance and tested the doorknob. It turned easily. Tyler had told him that once in the door, a waist-high wooden partition ran across the room, with several desks on the far side. The entrance to the cell area was on the far wall. The unknown was how many guards would be waiting for them?

Taking a deep breath, he turned the knob and flung the door open, stepping inside, raising his pistol at the same time.

Two men sat at desks, one man's head resting on his hands, asleep. Warren aimed his pistol directly at the other man and said, "Not a sound."

The rest of the Confederates spread out across the room, pistols at the ready.

"How many other guards are there?" Warren asked.

The man shook his head quickly.

"Just us. Me and Bill."

349

The other man now sat with his hands in the air, blinking away the sleep.

"We want one prisoner. Captain Pickering," Warren said, as moved past the partition and up to the first man's desk.

"The reb? He ain't here," the man said, his voice cracking from fear.

"No, honest. They took him away a week, maybe ten days ago."

Warren's fear had been realized. Thomas had been taken north.

"Where did they take him?"

The man shook his head, "Don't know, Colonel Hart was in charge."

Pausing, Warren turned to Hawkins.

"Pull in the lookouts, we ride."

The lanky sergeant nodded and went out the open door.

"Hart? You said a Colonel Hart was in charge?"

Nodding the man said, "Provost. From the capital."

"His first name?"

"Don't know," the man answered, his face fearful.

"Describe him to me," Warren demanded, telling himself it couldn't be him. But as the man talked, he knew that somehow that bastard Hart had surfaced again. And he had Thomas for the second time in a second war.

"Lock these two in one of the cells," he ordered.

"Lookee who I found."

Warren turned to see his sergeant walk through the door followed by Pickering.

Something seemed wrong to him as Hart approached the jail. Then he realized, the door was open, the light flooding out over the wooden porch into the dirt street. And there were several men at the edge of that light. He looked hard as he quietly reined his horse to a stop. Even in the poor light he knew they were Confederate troops. Fear gripped him, alone against how many of them? Discretion was indeed the better part of valor he thought as he slowly pulled his horse around to make his escape.

The click of a pistol cocking sounded like a thunderclap in the quiet night.

"If you move, you Yankee son of a bitch, I'll blow your guts out," Corporal Richey said with a note of fury in his voice.

Warren, Pickering and Hawkins heard Richey calling from outside the jail.

The sight that greeted them was an impeccably attired lieutenant colonel standing ramrod stiff with a short Confederate standing behind him with a pistol pointed at his back. With hands raised over his head, the man emerged into the light, the fury evident on his face.

"My, it appears this night has been more profitable that I would have ever imagined," Warren said, stepping down into the dirt street and walking to Hart.

"Corporal Richey, well done."

"Spies all, slinking around in the night," Hart spat out, his eyes hard. "My patrols will catch you Warren, then I'll settle accounts."

"To the contrary, Hart. You'll never bother me again. You have my word on that. Sergeant Hawkins, we will take this federal south with us. Make sure he doesn't escape or give our position away to any Union patrols."

Twenty minutes later the soldiers rode out quietly. In the middle of the column Hart rode slung over his saddle with a large rag stuffed in his mouth and his hands and feet tied together under his horse's belly. Several other good Virginian horse trader's knots ensured he was unable to move in any way.

Warren estimated it would take the patrol three days to reach Stuart. He suspected that Lieutenant Colonel Hart would be mighty uncomfortable by then.

Hart was more than uncomfortable by the morning of the second day. Complaining of not being able to breathe, he pleaded to be cut loose.

Chapter Twenty-Three

"Lord, the Navy's in town. Lock up the women."

Warren mounted Alexander and pulled the stallion's head around to begin his journey south to Belvoir. He and Thomas were taking two weeks of leave from the Army of Northern Virginia. Warren was travelling south in order to send more information to the Foreign Office, while Thomas was fulfilling his promise to Charlotte. Three hours would put them in Richmond and onto a train for the rest of the journey. He had thought about stabling Alexander in Richmond and decided against it. The train would carry both of them and their mounts south.

Jefferson Davis would not be pleased at the picture Warren would be sending back to Sir Hugh Nicholson. The longer Warren spent with the Confederate forces, the more he became convinced that the north, even with mediocre leaders in the field, would prevail. But more to the point, Warren had watched how the institution of slavery had begun to unravel, and that would prove ultimately fatal to the Confederacy. His personal distaste for slavery had only intensified as he had seen its effects up close.

While he continued to wear the uniform of the South, his belief in anything other than the heart of their soldiers, had died.

But there was one last task prior to leaving. They would stop by the field hospital at Murphy's Crossroads. Louis Thomassy continued his volunteer efforts as a civilian, but for all intents he now served the Confederacy as he had done for the United States and Russia. For Louis, taking care of soldiers had always called to him. Nowhere in the world of medicine could you provide ministrations to a group of men who had no control over their fate or lives. The daily struggle to help these men survive the violence and gore of the modern battlefield consumed him. Warren had been a regular visitor to the hospital and now he would use all of his influence to have Louis accompany them south. It had been over five months since the doctor had last seen Kimberly and Warren knew that be enough to drag him away from the sick and wounded Confederate soldiers.

Michael Scully took a deep breath, enjoying the first hints of spring in the air. Finishing his daily morning walk, he was pleased that his stamina had returned. His recovery had been slow and frustrating. Now, eight months after being wounded, he was finally regaining the full use of his arm. While there would be pain at times, he knew he was ready to return to the field. Richard Warren had been encouraging and told him to enjoy his time off. In the spring they would be busy again.

The winter had been comfortable on the plantation and Scully had enjoyed the ministrations of Kimberly, who had become Roger Hanson's assistant at the clinic. She seemed happy to be of help and he knew that she and Emily Whitehead had become close friends.

The arrival of Charlotte Tyler just before Christmas had resulted in a trio of industrious women who seemed to energize each other. Whether nursing, teaching or taking care of Belvoir, Scully learned to smile, nod and stay out of their way. He was happy for Pickering, as he watched the young couple's romance blossom.

The highlights for all of them were the visits of Warren and Pickering. With the Army of the Potomac now under the command of McClellan, in winter quarters, the activity on the contested border was minimal. General Johnston was now in command of the Confederate forces, which was only slightly larger than the army fielded at Manassas. The expectation was for a major attack by the Union in the spring, but until then, both the north and the south spent most of the winter trying to stay warm.

One incident during late February had shaken the plantation to its very roots. Tolly had disappeared one night and after two days of searching, his terribly beaten body was discovered off the side of the main road to Greenville. Frank Sanderson had tried to figure out what had happened, but nothing was obvious. The county sheriff, Elijah Tombs, had laughed at Sanderson when he rode into Greenville and reported the death, saying he "could care less about a dead nigger."

The war had increased the tension between the whites and slaves, and Sanderson decided that Tolly had just been in the wrong place at the wrong time, the victim of angry white men.

Scully heard riders coming up the drive. He walked from the trees to see Jim Kennedy and two men riding up the driveway. Scully had been expecting the arrival of the *Sonia B*, which had carried letters from Warren to England along with the last of the tobacco crop from last year.

"Lord, the navy's in town. Lock up the women."

Kennedy laughed and jumped down from the saddle.

"As if there are any women left with you hanging about," Kennedy said, grasping Scully's right shoulder.

"One or two, truth be known. Good to see you, Captain Kennedy."

"Aye, you do bring a spot of home on this Godforsaken continent."

The two men walked up the driveway, catching up on the last four months. The passage to England had been tough. Several North Atlantic storms drove the ship south before they could beat north up the coast of France. But the return trip had been uneventful until the end, when they had to outrun a Union warship. The Union blockade of the Confederacy's coastline was slowly tightening, making the import of anything expensive and unreliable.

"When do you expect Richard?" Kennedy asked.

"Hard to say. Big move expected by the Federals coming in the spring, so he's been spending most of his time with the army."

Climbing the steps to the main house, the sound of horses made them turn and watch as a dozen men reined to a stop.

A heavyset man, wearing a dingy brown coat, black trousers and boots looked at Scully and said, "My name is Tombs, sheriff for the county. I'm looking for the Whitehead woman."

Scully took a deep breath, the man's hostile attitude already goading his Irish temper.

"And why, pray tell, would you be wantin' to talk with Mrs. Whitehead?"

Tombs got down from his horse, handing the reins to the man next to him. He walked to the stairs and up to Scully.

"Is she here?" the sheriff asked.

Scully could tell that Sheriff Tombs was used to pushing his authority around, but he also realized that keeping his temper under control was likely a smart thing to do until he figured out what was happening.

Kennedy said nothing but stood his ground next to Scully.

"I believe she is. Wait here."

Moving in front of the doorway, Kennedy crossed his arms on his chest and stared back at the sheriff, his face expressionless.

In a minute Emily appeared at the door.

"Sheriff, I understand you were asking to see me."

Tombs pulled a folded paper from the inside pocket of his coat.

"Emily Whitehead, I have a warrant for your arrest signed by Judge Rutherford."

"Arrest!" Emily exclaimed, "What did I do?"

"Providing aid and assistance to fugitive slaves."

"That's not true," she said, her voice urgent.

"That's not up to me. Judge Rutherford ordered that you be removed to the jail in Greenville to await trial."

Scully noted that the men accompanying Tombs were all armed and looked like they were ready for a fight. Fighting his instinct, he put his hand on Emily's arm.

"Sheriff, we'll ride with Mrs. Whitehead and find out what's happening here." Liam Sullivan and Frank Sanderson had appeared around the edge of the house, both men carrying shotguns.

357

"Suit yourself, Irishman."

Roger Hanson arrived in Greenville two hours after the others had watched Emily being taken into the Sheriff's Office. He had been delivering a baby when Liam Sullivan arrived and had only left when the baby was stable and comfortable. But the young doctor who arrived in town was far from stable himself. They found Scully and the others at a local inn, discussing what they should do.

"It has to be Bloodsworth behind this," Hanson added after he heard what had happened. "He and Haney have the sheriff in their hip pocket. Always have. This is his chance to get even and don't think the son of a whore won't do it."

"Is Emily in danger while she's held in that jail?" Scully asked, his stomach turning.

"I don't think so," Hanson said, "But we need to make sure they don't spirit her off. If that happens, I do fear for her safety."

Michael Scully stood up in anger and frustration. The brutal use of the police to do someone's dirty business reminded him too much of Ireland.

"Captain Kennedy, I want you to stay ashore and watch over things. Liam, you help out and get ready to do some fighting, and you know what I mean."

Sullivan nodded. He was ready to do whatever had to be done.

"Mr. Sanderson, I need you and the doctor to stay on top of what's happening here. You know these people and the land. We can't be caught unawares."

The lanky woodsman nodded.

"I'll send a telegram to Colonel Cable," Scully continued. "If anyone can get word to Richard, it's him. And, Jim, you need to be ready to sail on short notice."

Kennedy said, "*Sonia B.* will be ready."

The cobwebs that hung from the ceiling did not even enter Emily's thoughts, nor did the sour smell that permeated the small room where she had been held since her arrival at the jail. Her mind kept going over what had happened and she kept asking herself, how had she been found out? No one outside of Belvoir had known of her sheltering three escaped slaves earlier in the year. They had only been at Belvoir for two days, she thought, how did anyone discover what she had done? Were those three men caught and beaten? Perhaps they had given her up to the authorities. The sheriff had to tell her, but so far she had been left alone in the locked room. She shivered, not from the cool, but from what the future might bring.

Elijah Tombs did not like Lawrence Bloodsworth. But without the man's money and influence, Tombs would still be a poor farmer, barely making a living off six acres of some of the worst land in the county. So he did what Bloodsworth wanted and accepted his "retainer" at the end of each month. He normally dealt with Stephen Haney and seldom ever visited Rose Springs, which was the way Bloodsworth wanted it. But today was different and both men knew it.

"You have the Whitehead woman locked up?"

"She's at the jail," Tombs answered.

Bloodsworth's eyes narrowed.

"That's not what I asked. Is she locked up?"

The sheriff gritted his teeth.

359

"I put her in the storage room. Wouldn't be proper to put her in the cells. But she's locked up and I've got three deputies watching her."

"Is there a problem?"

Tombs shifted his hat from one hand to the other.

"A group of men from Belvoir followed us into town." He paused then said, "Frank Sanderson's with 'em."

"God damn it."

"And that Irishman."

Bloodsworth remembered his encounters with Scully. Warren's man was dangerous, he knew it then and now the stakes were higher.

"What are you going to do?"

Tombs shrugged.

"Just watch 'em. They ain't done nothing against the law."

"That man Scully is almost as crazy as Warren. Keep a close eye on him and throw him in jail if he does anything wrong. The judge will back us up."

Judge William Rutherford ruled the county with an iron hand. It was something that people accepted, even though they knew the old man bent most rules to suit himself and his cronies. It was just the way of things.

"I'll go see the judge," Bloodsworth said.

It is strange, Warren thought as they rode up the main drive to the big house. Despite being so far from his native England, the charms of this plantation made him think of Albermarle and his love of the land. His years in the army had almost made him forget how being on good land renewed him in a way nothing else could. Perhaps someday he would spend all of his time as a gentleman farmer. But now the future seemed like something that was hanging over his head, not beckoning him forward. This damned war would tear this country apart and change the lives of everyone. But he would prevail. This would prevail. This land would be part of his future and legacy.

"Would that all of our journeys be so pleasant," Thomas said, pulling Warren from his thoughts.

Next to them, Louis rode with his eyes focused on their destination.

The house looked inviting, the awakening of spring decorating the grounds with the beginnings of summer beauty. But Warren was almost oblivious of the changes. It was Emily that he wanted to see. It had been too long since his last visit.

As they dismounted, the front door opened to reveal Phillip, who always seemed to know when anyone arrived at Belvoir. But rather than his normal smile, the older man moved quickly to the steps, his face betraying concern and worry. Behind him in the door, Kimberly stood, her arms folded in front of her. Warren knew immediately that something was dreadfully wrong. And where was Emily? His heart turned cold.

Standing aside for Louis and Kimberly to embrace, Warren turned to Phillip.

"What's wrong? Where is Emily?"

It was if time was standing still and Phillip first, and then Kimberly told him of the events of the day before. Warren needed all of his self-control to allow them both to tell their stories before he began asking questions.

"She's in Greenville, then?"

"We think so, but we've had no word from Michael since then they rode off yesterday."

"Where's Hanson?"

They both shook their heads.

"He never came home. Mrs. Smithfield had gone into labor and he left first thing for their farm. I know Michael sent Liam to find him." Kimberly said.

"Captain Kennedy was here, the *Sonia B.* had just anchored," Phillip added. "He rode off with Mr. Michael and the other men."

"Frank Sanderson?"

Phillip continued, "He was with them too."

Charlotte Tyler came out the front door, walking to James and embracing him.

"Phillip, please have the horses seen to. We'll leave within the hour."

Judge William Rutherford was a small man, in his 60's and totally bald. A grey mustache and goatee highlighted a face that was leathery and heavily lined from age. Hanson had told Warren that the man was corrupt and dangerous. The judge's history had been one of abuse of the law, while protecting a group of the wealthiest men in the county. Upon entering the judge's office Warren sensed he had already made an enemy.

"I am Richard Warren, owner of Belvoir," he said, stopping five feet from the judge's desk.

The man's eyes looked dull, but his manner suggested that he was using his vacant expression to hide his real emotions.

"Warren, yes I've heard of you. What might I do for you?"

"I'm here on behalf of Emily Whitehead."

Rutherford said nothing for a moment then motioned to a chair.

"That is a very gallant thing for you to do, but I'm not sure what that has to do with me. The woman has been charged with aiding escaped slaves and will stand trial."

The aloof manner of the judge infuriated Warren, but he kept his emotions masked.

"I will be providing counsel for her and also post her bail."

Rutherford searched through the papers on his desk and momentarily read one page then replaced it back in the stack.

"No bail."

Again Warren fought his inclination to attack the man, but said with measured calm, "May I ask why?"

"Sheriff Tombs feels that she might run north. Can't take that chance."

"Then I would like to see the charges and also see Mrs. Whitehead."

"Well now, Mr. Warren. If you were a practicing attorney, representing the woman, you would be privy to those charges. And if you were blood kin, you likely would be able to see her. But since none of those things seem to be the case, you seem to be out of luck. Now, if there's nothing else, I'm busy."

Warren stepped up to the desk, his face a mask, hiding his fury.

"Do not take me for one of your locals, Judge Rutherford. I will not stand back while you and your cronies try to use the law for your own purposes."

Warren turned and walked out the door, leaving it wide open.

The judge had been about to lash back at Warren when he had seen the look in his eyes. William Rutherford found himself feeling uneasy. Mr. Bloodsworth would need to take care of this problem and quickly.

It was very late in the afternoon when Warren finally found Scully at McDonough's Hotel on 3rd Street, which was down from the jail, on the opposite side.

Scully sat next to Frank Sanderson, who was smoking a pipe. The sweet smell of the tobacco reminded Warren of his father's library at Albermarle.

Louis remained standing as Scully related events as he had seen them unfold. They had kept the jail under constant watch, but all they had seen was the occasional coming or going of the deputies.

"Then Emily is still in jail?" Warren asked.

"Two of us have been watching both front and back. Doc Hanson and Liam are down there now."

"That judge won't allow me to see her. She must be beside herself. I just want her to know we're here."

"Perhaps if Mrs. Whiteside's personal physician was to demand a visit to ensure her medication is remaining effective," Louis said. "I believe I might be able to intimidate any layman with a medical explanation why it is imperative that I see her."

Scully grinned and said, "The doctor must have some Irish blood in him."

The Doctor might have encountered resistance from the sheriff, but Deputy Ira Hooper was truly frightened following a deep medical explanation of Mrs. Whiteside's condition. The intimation from the doctor was that the deputies could be at risk from contracting a particularly virulent malaria if the woman did not get her medication and became contagious. Ira had seen his mother die of the fever and he wanted no part of that terrible experience ever again.

Emily's look of fear changed instantly when she saw Louis at the door. Deputy Hooper had unlocked the room then scurried back to the front of the jail. She stood and began to say something, but Louis put his finger to his lips. Motioning her to stay where she was, he stepped quietly back into the corridor and moved down to a side door that appeared to lead to the rear of the jail. Quickly checking the lock, he saw that it was a metal slide, reinforced but not locked! It must be used by the jailers to take trash out, and someone forgot to lock it, or they were just lazy.

Louis tried to think. Could he spirit Emily away? He knew that Liam Sullivan was watching the rear of the jail, would he see them and help them in their escape attempt? Or was this a terrible mistake that would put Emily in more trouble? He could tell that Richard felt the cards were stacked against them by the sheriff and the judge. But would that justify taking things into their own hands and escaping from the jail?

Afraid that an attempt would be made to move Emily, the men watching the front and back of the jail kept a saddled horse ready to follow her if needed. Liam Sullivan had been keeping his watch for over two hours, seeing nothing of note during that time. He was able to see the complete backside of the jail and knew that no one could slip away without being seen.

A movement in the deepening shadows brought Sullivan to a tense alert. He could make out two people moving along the jail wall toward where he was crouched. Hesitating, he was shocked to realize it was Emily and the doctor.

Rapidly moving across the alley, he grabbed the doctor's arm.

"Follow me," he said quickly and the three moved past the lookout point to where Sullivan's horse stood.

"How did you get out?"

"That's not important now, they don't know she's gone. We have to get her as far away from here as possible."

Sullivan knew immediately what to do.

"The ship. I'll take her to the ship."

Louis nodded, "You best be starting. Take the pike toward Washington, but stay out of sight. Sun's almost down, so it shouldn't be hard. I'll gather up the rest and we'll follow as fast as we can."

Less than twenty minutes later, Richard left to follow Liam, with the others slipping out quietly at five-minute intervals.

Chapter Twenty-Four

"It will be our adventure..."

"**Y**our orders, Richard?"

Warren stood on the quarterdeck of the *Sonia B.* after a night of travelling to the anchored ship. The women were all safely below in their cabins, resting. Sanderson and Liam were ashore with the horses, watching for any sign of the authorities.

"Jim, I want Emily at sea and away from any trouble. For now I think all the women should stay aboard until I can figure out what's happening ashore. The doctor as well, he's the only one directly connected with her escape from the jail."

Kennedy nodded.

"Weather looks good," the captain offered. "The only challenge might be the Union blockaders, but we can outrun them. What are you going to do?"

"Try to clear her name and clean up this mess."

"Won't they try to arrest you? It seems pretty clear you were running things."

Warren knew that the judge might very well try something after their encounter. But he had a plan.

"Are you ready to go to sea, my dear?"

Emily sat on the bed in her cabin on the second deck. She looked tired but relaxed, her legs folded under her and a shawl around her shoulders.

She smiled and said, "It will be our adventure."

"I'll be staying ashore. I'm going to try and clear up this trouble."

Emily's expression changed, concern showing in her eyes.

"But what can you possibly do? The judge is a wicked man who can't be trusted. Who knows what he might try."

"Let me worry about that. I intend on travelling to Richmond to see President Davis. I have every reason to believe he will intercede on your behalf."

"I will hate being away from you, but if you think it's the right thing."

He took her in his arms.

"You always said you wanted to sail the oceans."

With that reality now here, Emily wasn't quite so sure anymore.

"Richard, you wanted to see me?"

Roger Hanson entered the main aft cabin, which Warren was using while aboard. He sat at a large desk, a sheaf of papers spread across in front of him.

"Come in, doctor. We have some business to transact."

Hanson looked confused, but sat down, removing his hat and placing it on the floor.

"What business is that?"

"Your purchase of Belvoir of course."

"I… I'm not sure what you are talking about."

Warren grinned.

"Haven't you always wanted to own a plantation?"

The doctor laughed.

"Well, yes, I guess I have."

"Roger," Warren continued, his voice turning serious, "I don't know what is going to happen ashore. I will have much more flexibility if someone else was to be the legal owner of Belvoir."

"So the judge can't take legal action against you through Belvoir."

"Exactly. I had a deed of sale prepared for this possibility. Now I believe it's time to execute it."

"But I can't pay you anything," Hanson said.

"The contract is a sale on condition. It will pass the law as a viable sale. It says that you will take a loan on the Bank of England, to be paid over time from the profits of Belvoir, with no specified end date for the contract."

"You're serious. This isn't just a charade for the law?"

"Roger, you know how to run a tobacco plantation. The truth is that I love this country, but England is my home and someday I will return there. In the meantime, you'll take care of Belvoir because it is yours. We'll be business partners and I'll provide the ships to send your tobacco to where it can fetch the best price. We'll both make money and you will eventually own Belvoir outright."

The frigate sailed on the afternoon tide, not long after Warren, Scully, Hanson and Pickering rowed ashore to join Sullivan and Sanderson.

As the men adjusted their saddles and packed their saddlebags, Warren laid out the plan.

"Liam, I want you and Frank to stay at Belvoir to help the new owner take care of his plantation."

"What?" Sanderson asked as if he had not understood.

"Doctor Hanson is now the owner of Belvoir. He'll be filing the papers in Greenville then returning to Belvoir. The three of us will be going to Richmond to try and sort out this problem with Emily. I don't know what the sheriff might have planned, but be careful and stay within the law unless it becomes a matter of life or death. Then do what you must to protect each other and the workers."

"When will you be back?" Sullivan asked.

"Hard to say, but I hope to be gone no more than ten days. In any case, the ship will be back in nine days."

Three days of hard riding put the men at the outskirts of Richmond. They all wore the Confederate uniform and no one had bothered them during the ride. Warren wondered what was happening at Belvoir, but he knew that Hanson, Sullivan and Sanderson would deal with it. He only hoped that the telegram he had the doctor send from Greenville had found David Cable.

Besides clearing Emily's name, Warren's visit to Richmond had a dual purpose. It was midday when he and Scully approached Libby Prison, located in an old tobacco warehouse. Two guards, carrying muskets, stood at each side of a double door leading into the building. They both came to attention, but did not salute.

Inside a corridor to the right lead past several doorways, the second on labeled "Provost."

"I'm Colonel Warren, is the Provost here?"

A heavyset sergeant looked up from a ledger book.

"Just a minute, sir."

Warren surveyed the room, which was newly constructed. Despite the building's new role, the smell of tobacco was very much in evidence. Scully sat down in a chair against the far wall as the sergeant returned.

"You can go in, colonel."

Warren saw a crutch leaning on the wall behind a lanky colonel who did not rise to greet him.

"Welcome to Libby Prison, colonel. My name is Tibbets, I'm the provost here. Please sit down and tell me what I can do for you."

"Colonel, I was leading a small contingent of Stuart's cavalry last November near Fairfax Courthouse and we captured a Union officer. I'm trying to confirm he is being held here in Richmond."

"What's his name?"

"Hart, Lieutenant Colonel Brett Hart."

Tibbets frowned momentarily.

"Name sounds familiar, just a minute."

Warren saw that Tibbets was sitting on a swiveling chair and confirmed that he was missing his left leg below the knee as the colonel turned to a ledger book on the credenza behind him. He opened it and flipped through several pages.

"Here it is... Yes, indeed, your Yankee is being held in area five. Of course, we do lose prisoners here on a regular basis, but as of a month ago, he was alive and kicking."

Warren had always wondered what had kept him from simply shooting Hart that night. But the chance to gain some intelligence had kept his pistol in its holster. Now he was going to remedy that.

371

"Is it possible to see the prisoner?"

Tibbets smiled slightly.

"You may most certainly see him. I'll get my sergeant to take you to one of our day wardens.

Warren's stomach recoiled at the smell as they walked through the prison toward Area Five. Human sweat, urine, and sewage permeated the place. The few traces of tobacco scent were welcome relief from the evidence of human rot. Several wooden doors with small barred windows were unlocked at they crossed the lower floor, arriving at a larger door, with a black "Five" painted on the bolted door.

"You can wait there, sir," the warden said, pointing to a plain wood table under an air vent. Warren thought back to Belvoir and remembered how important airflow was for tobacco during the drying phase. Perhaps it was needed when storing it also.

Another guard unlocked the door, allowing the warden access.

"Would be easier if the bastard has already died," Scully said.

"Right you are, Michael, but I'm hoping for a more appropriate ending for him."

Hart stepped into the corridor, his arm securely held by the warden. Wearing only a shirt and trousers, he looked dirty, tired and without hope. But his face instantly changed from weary boredom to anger and hate when he saw Warren sitting at the table.

The warden felt Hart move toward Warren and restrained him hard.

"You son of a bitch," Hart hissed. "Come here to gloat I expect, well go ahead, you asshole."

Warren stood up and advanced to the prisoner.

"I am here to confirm you are alive, Hart. I have plans for you," he said.

"Return him to his cell, if you will, warden."

With that, Warren walked past the man and down the corridor.

"It's damned good to see you, Richard."

Dave Cable had found them at the Spotswood Hotel. The three men were sitting in the men's lounge, enjoying an afternoon drink.

"You're looking well," Warren said, shaking his friend's hand.

"I'll be better after a drink," he said. "Then you can tell me why you needed me."

Cable sat quietly as Warren related the event surrounding Emily.

"I am sure we can do something about her situation," Cable said.

"That was my original plan when I started. But I've decided I can't take any chances with her. I'm sure the President could intercede, but there is a level of corruption in that county that goes very deep. Emily will return to England with me in the very near future."

"England?"

"It's time for me to see Nicholson in person if I am to make a case for the Confederacy. I would like to offer my services to President Davis to carry any letters he might want delivered to the Foreign Office."

Cable nodded.

"I also have another request of the President."

Frowning slightly, Cable asked, "I'm listening."

"There's a Union officer in Libby Prison. We captured him near Fairfax Courthouse in November."

Looking curious, Cable said, "Go on."

"We crossed paths with him in the Crimea when he was working for the Russians."

"Interesting story."

"He shot a British prisoner in Sevastopol while trying to get information out of me."

Cable said nothing.

"That man was one of mine. I want to take the Union officer back to England to face trial."

"You're asking a lot, my friend."

"Jefferson Davis is an honorable man. He was also a soldier. I would like to think this would be an easy thing. It would certainly be looked upon with favor by the Foreign Office."

Cable smiled.

"You once told Jefferson Davis that you weren't a politician. I think you underestimated yourself."

"Will you help me?"

"Of course I will, Richard. This man sounds like the kind of soldier that the world doesn't need."

Three days later, four men rode south from Atlanta. One of those men was handcuffed and gagged.

Chapter Twenty-Five

"Thank God we found you..."

Warren made the decision to go directly to the Pungo River in hope that the *Sonia B.* would be anchored and waiting. He wanted Hart in chains, aboard the frigate and at sea as soon as possible. The trip had been uneventful, although having a prisoner along proved to be a challenge. Once in the saddle with his hands cuffed behind him he was little trouble. But at night, while camped, the extra effort to ensure that Hart couldn't escape kept a level of tension that proved unpleasant.

Now they were only a mile or so from the river and Warren felt himself begin to relax. Soon they would be on board and headed for the open sea. He would see Emily and tell her of his decision to sail to England. The truth was that he had seen enough of this war to offer an opinion to Nicholson. He also carried a letter from Jefferson Davis to Her Majesty's Government.

Warren remembered the haggard look on the president's face at the final meeting. On the surface, Davis had been very positive on the southern prospects, citing the quality of his generals and the troops they commanded.

"They are as fine a group of commanders as this country has ever seen," he said, "Lee, Jackson, Hood, Longstreet, they will lead our troops to victory."

"Sir, I agree that your generals are superb, and I would add that the men I fought beside are as good as any in the world. But you must have more than good generals and soldiers to win wars, Mr. President. My country is no different. In battle, I'd always want a Scotsman by my side, or an Irishman. But you also need money and steel. That's why neither Scotland nor Ireland stand independent now. I'm afraid I see history repeating itself on this continent. But I will carry you letter and tell the foreign office my opinion."

"And that would be?"

"Sir, I don't think the south can subjugate the north. But a skillful defensive war such as Washington waged might allow a stalemate and return to a stable peace."

"So you don't see Robert Lee as my Cromwell?"

Warren smiled.

Now he stood ready to carry the letter from Davis to Nicholson. He would also give the Foreign Office his own opinion. Once he had done that, the hell with all of them.

"There she be," Scully said as they crested a low ridge. At anchor no more than a half a mile offshore, the *Sonia B.* rode at anchor, her sails furled and men busy on deck.

Pickering had pulled his brass spyglass from its case and looked over the ship.

"There's damage on the port side. It looks as if part of the bulwark has been torn away." He could see several men with saws working on the area.

Warren knew the Union blockade was tightening, perhaps that explained the damage. And if so, what would be waiting for them when they cleared the coast?

"That's not all," Pickering continued, the glass still up to his eye, but now aimed at the shore. "A group of riders on the beach, maybe ten men. They're dismounting. What in God's name?"

"What's that?" Scully asked.

"A team pulling an artillery piece. They're not wearing uniforms, but it looks like they're setting up to fire on the *Sonia B.*"

Pickering offered the glass to Warren.

Warren saw that the horses had been unhitched from the caisson and men were pulling the artillery piece around, its muzzle now facing the ship.

"Richard!"

They turned to see Sullivan and Sanderson riding up the far side of the crest.

"Thank God we found you," Sullivan called as he reined to a halt and jumped to the ground.

Sanderson joined him, the labored breathing of their horses telling the story of a hard-pressed ride.

"What happened?"

Liam took a deep breath and began his report.

"The doctor was attacked three nights ago. Some of the workers found him and brought him to the big house. He was unconscious, but Phillip nursed him and he came to early this morning. That bastard Tombs did it. Worse than that, they beat him into admitting the ship was returning."

"The ship is helpless," Warren said, "Her guns won't bear on the beach from where she's anchored."

"Look," Pickering said, pointing at the *Sonia B.*

A sail was being unfurled on the mizzen mast.

"He's trying to swing her at anchor to get the guns to bear," Warren said. "We need to give him some time."

He turned to Scully.

"Michael, I believe we have one more charge into the guns in front of us."

Scully laughed, "By God we've done it before!"

Warren grabbed Sanderson by the arm.

"Take charge of the prisoner, Mr. Sanderson. Kill him if he tries to escape. Mount up, gentlemen."

Quickly the four former dragoons swung into the saddle.

Warren drew his pistol and pulled Alexander's head around, facing down the slope and spurred the big stallion toward the beach.

A sharp crack echoed across the water, making Jim Kennedy jump as the first shell screamed past his ship, throwing a waterspout into the air, thirty yards left and long from the ship.

"They're using shot, not shell," the gunner Samuel Hogg yelled up at the quarterdeck.

Kennedy watched the mizzen mainsail fill and felt the deck cant just slightly.

"Come on, swing your stern, smartly now," Kennedy willed the ship to move. "Mr. Hogg, be ready with the first port carronade to bear."

"Aye, sir."

Kennedy lifted his glass to watch the artillery piece being reloaded. Damn, he thought, give me two more minutes. As the ship's stern began to move. Then he saw motion up the beach to the north. Putting the glass back to his eye, he realized it was four men at a full gallop coming down the beach toward the artillery piece. It could only be Richard, he thought. Thank the Good Lord.

"Mr. Hogg, be ready but hold your fire."

Warren guided Alexander down the beach, just up from the waterline, the horse able to hold a full gallop on the hard sand. Warren glanced left to see Scully next to him, leaning forward in the saddle. The wild thrill of a mounted attack began to capture Warren, who leveled his pistol and began a steady fire at the men manning the cannon. He knew that his men would follow his lead and empty their pistols. But they would all have holstered the firearms and have drawn their sabers by the time they hit the cannon. A saber attack on undisciplined men would wreak havoc and that was what Warren intended. His anger over Emily was only part of the fury that gripped him. He remembered Tolly's brutal death and knew that these men deserved to die.

Fifty yards to go, Warren and his men were sabers down, preparing for the impact, when the entire area around the artillery piece exploded as hundreds of steel balls shredded the cannon's crew. The carronades had been brought to bear and with horrific results. While the cannon had been their objective, there remained a group of men off to one side, who began firing at the four. Turning Alexander slightly, Warren saw his target. Sheriff Tombs stood in front of their horses, firing his pistol. Some of the other men were trying to mount the spooked animals and two were running up the beach toward high water.

It was as if Tombs knew he was Warren's target. He methodically fired his pistol at the Englishman, his focus total.

Two more shots and the fat man ran out of ammunition, throwing the gun on the sand and turning to run.

With cold precision, Warren slowed Alexander slightly, guiding him alongside Tombs, whose hat flew off just as Warren slashed down viciously, almost severing his neck completely.

The other three were slashing left and right at the remaining men who now had broken and were running for their lives.

"Enough!" Warren yelled and the four men ceased their attack, all breathing heavily and settling their horses down.

Pivoting Alexander around to check for adversaries, Warren felt the rage beginning to subside, but he knew that he had enjoyed it.

He saw Emily leaning down from the main deck as the ship's jolly boat bumped against the side. She was smiling and waved quickly.

Quickly climbing up to the entry port, he took her in his arms.

"You're all right," he whispered, smelling her hair.

"We're fine, Richard," she said moving back slightly. "Thanks to Captain Kennedy."

The captain stood quietly to one side and Warren extended his hand.

"Thank you for the timely artillery fire, my friend."

Kennedy grinned, "I never thought I'd see a real cavalry charge."

Warren returned the smile. "I'm glad we were able to help. Now, how soon can we sail?"

"On the tide would be easier, but that's not for two hours or so."

Warren nodded. "I asked Sanderson to find one of the local boats to ferry Alexander and Henry out. I'll not leave them behind. And I have a prisoner coming out in the next boat. Handcuffed and gagged. Leave him that way until he's chained in the brig. And you'll recognize him."

"I'll get a sling ready for the horses.'"

"Now tell me what happened to the ship."

The captain related that they had sighted a sail early yesterday morning, about twenty miles off shore. The stranger had turned out to be a United States warship, about the same size as the *Sonia B.* The Yankee frigate was positioned perfectly to intercept the ship as she tried to cross the outer banks. But Kennedy had the wind and drove at the enemy ship, forcing her captain to wear ship. At the last moment, Kennedy had tacked away from the Yankee and made for a passage through the bank that he knew she could make. Their opponent had fired a desperate broadside, several of the shots hitting the *Sonia B.* but no casualties. Apparently not comfortable with the dangers to navigation, the Union captain had veered away and failed to pursue.

"So he might be waiting off the coast?"

"It's possible, but he has no idea when we're coming out. If we're underway within the next two hours, we'll have enough light to negotiate the channel and clear in to the open ocean as the sun is setting. He'd have to be very lucky to be in the right place at the right time."

Not looking forward to an encounter with the Union Navy, Warren knew he wanted to be away from this place and the events of the last hour.

"I agree, Jim. Let's head for home."

Emily looked at him, her face asking a question.

Warren gently took Emily's arm and walked her to the port rail.

"I intend to sail for England," he said. "You can't stay here. It's not safe and may not be for a very long time."

She knew he was right, but her life now seemed to be totally out of her control. But she also felt that if she were with Richard Warren, it would be possible to face whatever the future held.

"I know, but it's quite frightening."

He took her in his arms.

"Not when Scully is along, my dear."

Emily laughed and looked up at him.

"But it's you I love."

"Sail, fine on the starboard bow!" came the cry from the mainmast lookout.

"We've the sun behind us," Kennedy said as he walked to the lee rail. "I'll go aloft and see if I recognize the bugger."

Leonard Shaw said, "Do you want me to do it, captain?"

Kennedy laughed as he grasped the ratlines and pulled himself up on the starboard rail.

"No, but thanks for offering Mr. Leonard. Want to see this one for myself." He slung his long glass over his shoulder and began to climb.

Richard Warren came on deck amidships and walked aft, climbing the quarterdeck ladder.

"Good afternoon Mr. Shaw, I'm looking for the captain.

Shaw pointed aloft and said, "The lookout spotted a sail. Captain Kennedy is going up to take a look with his long glass."

"Does he think it's the same ship that chased you?"

"Don't know, sir. But he was intent on seeing for himself."

The ocean is so damned big, Warren thought, why can't we just lose ourselves in it until we reach England?

Kennedy's chest heaved as he caught his breath from the long climb. But his attention was on the darkening sea and his fear was being realized. There, on a closing starboard tack was the American warship that had attacked them earlier. The son of a bitch had the wind and they would be at his mercy.

Warren felt the deck shift as the ship moved into deeper water, the movements deeper as the hull cut into the sea. The wind had turned cold and he felt himself shiver. Was his discomfort at being at sea contributing? He always felt unsure of himself on the water. On a field of battle or crossing terrain, he seemed to be one with the land. But that feeling had never occurred aboard a ship, any ship, including the trusty *Sonia B,*

He looked up as Kennedy slid down a line from the mainmast truck, landing on the deck with just a slight thud.

"It's the same ship," he said, stepping away from the line.

"Are you sure?" Warren asked, hoping the decreasing light of day may have misled the captain.

Kennedy smiled, "Once someone has fired on you, it's hard to forget, Richard."

Scully came on deck followed by Doctor Thomassy. The two joined Warren.

"What's happening?" Scully asked.

"A Union warship."

The captain moved to the wheel and ordered, "Left three points Mr. Shaw."

Kennedy knew his ship was fast and her bottom was clean. He could only hope that months on blockade duty had taken its toll on their pursuer. Now was a time to run, not fight. He turned to look at the setting sun, hoping that darkness would help their flight.

He turned to the three men, "Once she sees that we are trying to run, they'll come about and try to sail down on us. If she can close before the sun sets, they'll be able to take us under fire."

"What will happen then?" Warren asked.

"The unknowns of a sea fight, Richard. Distance, wind and the accuracy of the gunners... I suspect she will fire warning shots telling us to heave to. When we don't, she will likely open fire."

Mr. Shaw lowered his glass and reported, "She's turning."

They walked to the rail, although there was nothing to see other than a darkening horizon.

Warren felt the frustration of having no control over what was about to happen.

Samuel Hogg came up the deck, his objective clearly the captain. Unlike warships, the *Sonia B.* was run on a very informal basis. Kennedy liked to have his senior warrants and specialists advising him at all times.

"Looks like we may be trading shots with that Yankee out there, Mr. Hogg."

"Aye, seems as much to me." The old gunner said. "Sun'll be down in an hour, but likely we'll be firing by then"

Kennedy nodded, "Her captain seems to know what he's about."

Hogg nodded.

"But he's a damned American. I should think a French surprise would catch him unawares."

The reality of what the gunner was saying hit Kennedy like a blow. With the sun setting, all they needed to do was slow the enemy ship down long enough to slip away into the night. And using the French technique of loading with chain or bar shot and aiming for an enemy's rigging might be just the thing.

"You insisted we bring chain shot aboard, Mr. Hogg," Kennedy said. "And I thought it was a waste of time."

"Simply preparing for all eventualities, captain."

Warren had listened to the exchange and looked questioningly at Kennedy.

"If we have to fire, we shoot for their rigging. Then run like the banshees of hell."

Firing on an American warship. Nicholson will not appreciate this no matter the reason, Warren thought. But if it comes to that...

"Chain shot on the starboard guns, if you please," Kennedy called to Hogg, who had headed back forward. "Run out when ready."

"Aye, captain."

Across the waves, now almost indistinct in the gloom, the white sails of the approaching warship told the story of a captain on a parallel course, falling down on them. Now Kennedy knew it would come to something.

"Hanratty, go below and escort all of the women below to the orlop."

The mate nodded to Kennedy and went down the starboard hatch ladder. Below the waterline, their passengers would be safe from harm if gunfire were exchanged. They also had a doctor aboard in the event of injuries. The captain knew that any damage or wounds would be critical with an entire ocean between them and England. They could put back to America if seaworthiness was a concern, but that would mean running the blockade twice more. Events were beginning to crowd together in Kennedy's mind. Just sail the ship, he told himself. Everything else will work itself out.

Warren found Emily with Kimberly and the mate sent down to take them below.

"Richard?"

"A Union ship is closing us," he said, putting his hand on her arm. "The captain wants you farther below in case it comes to a fight. You need to find Charlotte and follow Mr. Hanratty below."

"Have you seen Louis?" Kimberly asked, her eyes showing concern.

"He's on deck, but he'll be coming below. Now hurry."

Charlotte Tyler sat on the hard bench, leaning against James, who was reading a book.

Looking up from the page, he asked, "You've been quiet, is everything all right?"

"I am just trying to take everything as it occurs. Leaving Virginia was quite something, but pales in comparison to a voyage across the Atlantic Ocean."

Pickering laughed.

"You'll adjust readily, trust me."

She took his hand, locking her fingers in his.

"There you are," Emily said from the wardroom door. "The captain wants us on the deck below."

"What?" Pickering asked.

"There's a Yankee warship. He's afraid there could be gunfire."

"I'm going on deck," he said. "Charlotte, go with Emily."

386

Pickering came on deck as the sound of single cannon shot reverberated across the dark water.

Moments later a water plume from the impact of the ball erupted fifty yards in front of the bow. The message had clearly been sent by the warship: heave to and prepare to be boarded.

Kennedy estimated twenty minutes until total darkness. But the American was in position to fire now, and with a broad side of what looked like twelve-pound cannons, the *Sonia B.* would be savaged. But he had a plan.

"Get the way off her, Mr. Shaw."

"You're stopping?" Warren shouted, confusion obvious in his voice.

"They'd destroy us at this range, Richard. We only have one chance. Mr. Hogg, maximum elevation on the starboard guns, if you please. And be quick about it, before our friends across the water can see what we're doing."

Kennedy paused, watching the American frigate close his ship.

"What I propose is a violation of every rule of the sea, but I see no other way if you don't want a deck full of Yankee sailors."

"What are you saying?"

"Chain shot into their rigging, and make a run. With darkness almost on us, we have a chance."

Warren thought of the potential of being taken prisoner by the Union. His role in the Confederate Army would be more than embarrassing to London. The *Sonia B.* was a fast ship and the crew was good. Perhaps it could be done.

"Do it, Jim. And God be with us."

Orders flashed across the deck as Kennedy could see a boat being lowered from the warship. He knew that if the Yankee captain realized what was happening, he would open fire. But if they could cripple his rigging, the surprise of the attack might provide just the chaos to disrupt his gun crews, who were all stationed on the main deck underneath the heavy sails and spars.

Leonard Shaw ran up the small ladder to the quarterdeck.

"Everything's ready, captain."

"Very well, Mr. Shaw. We'll wait until their boat is halfway. Then hands aloft and make sail."

"Aye, captain."

Shaw turned away and paused.

"Captain, should I lower the flag?"

Looking toward the stern, Kennedy saw the red ensign waving defiantly.

"No, Mr. Shaw. It might give us some excuse if we pull this off."

Kennedy turned to the Warren, Pickering, Scully and the doctor.

"It's likely to be tough on deck if the Yankee fires on us. You might want to go below, there's nothing you can do here."

Warren looked at his companions.

"We'll stay out of the way, captain."

Kennedy knew that arguing would be pointless with Warren.

"Doctor, I insist you go below, we can't have you injured."

Louis knew Kennedy was right, but he had always wanted to see a battle at sea.

"As you wish, captain."

Captain Joseph Chambliss of the U.S.S. Small watched his boat making its way across the two-cable distance between the two ships. He wished there was another hour of daylight, but he would deal with this blockade runner in any case.

"Mr. Sims, I do believe we've captured a Blackwaller."

The young midshipmen moved closer to his captain.

"Sir?"

"British-built merchant ship, but almost a perfect frigate hull. She will make a fine addition to our navy and one more on the blockade."

What Chambliss didn't say was that on auction, he was likely to make a fine profit for himself as well as the rest of the crew. Now he must get a prize crew ready to sail her to Norfolk. He pondered who should command the prize. His second officer had the experience, but he hated to lose him, even for the several weeks a prize turnover would likely take. But Ensign Thomas could be sent if the senior master's mate accompanied him and there was no weather on the horizon. Damn, Chambliss thought, never enough qualified sea going officers. As he was lost in thought, he heard the officer of the deck's exclamation.

"What's going on over there?"

Chambliss turned to see the yards on the blockade runner manned and sails beginning to fill. The bastard was running.

"Port guns standby to fire," Chambliss roared, his gun crews scrambling back to their guns.

The near darkness was ripped apart by brilliant gun flashes rippling along the side of the other ship. Almost instantly the night was shattered by the sounds of chain shot slicing through the air above the captain's head. He knew he'd been fooled and looked up to see lines parting, blocks falling and rips appearing in the sails.

"Fire, God damn it! Fire!" he yelled amidst the crashing of rigging onto the deck. But he knew it was too late.

Sonia B.'s bow fell off with the wind as she began to make way in the almost dark sea.

"Bring her three points larboard, Mr. Shaw. We'll run with the wind and show her our stern.

Kennedy knew he was taking a chance. A shot into their stern would strike the most unprotected part of the ship. But he would also be giving the American the smallest target in the now deepening darkness.

A cannon flash from the frigate illuminated the water, the shot screaming up the starboard side and into the darkness.

Gripping the rail so hard his hands hurt, Jim Kennedy willed the darkness to deepen and the distance to open. Once they could get away, the Yankee could not find them in the moonless night and certainly couldn't match speeds. Just a moment more.

Two more brilliant reports came from the almost invisible frigate and Kennedy felt the ship stagger as a ball ripped into the stern below the quarterdeck.

"She answers, captain," the helmsman called, letting Kennedy know the steering gear was undamaged."

"Mr. Shaw, go below and check the damage."

"Aye, sir."

Nothing below the waterline, Kennedy prayed, nothing to hazard the hull.

In ten minutes the ship was sailing in total darkness, with no evidence of their pursuer. The boatswain mates had been checking the deck to make sure no lights were visible. Darkness was the friend tonight.

As he swept the horizon with his glass, Kennedy realized the first mate was next to him.

"Sweet Jesus, captain. It's the doctor... My God."

"What?"

"He must have been in the main passageway. The ball came in through the big cabin and ripped straight through the ship. He's hurt awful bad. I left Taylor with him."

"Go find Mr. Warren," he said.

"I heard, Jim," Warren said quietly from the darkness. "Michael, James, come with me."

As they descended the ladder, Warren kept telling himself this couldn't happen, not now.

Two lanterns provided enough light for the three of them to see Louis reclining against the starboard bulkhead, a blanket from the big cabin behind his back.

Warren knelt down next to the doctor, seeing blood pooling on the wooden deck. Louis's eyes were closed, his face grimacing with the pain.

Taylor, one of the boatswain mates held one of the lanterns closer for Warren to see the wound.

"Christ," Warren said and wished he hadn't. The doctor's left leg was pulp below the knee.

Scully pushed his way next to Louis, pulling off his belt.

"I'm afraid the doctor is now a patient," Louis said, his eyes now open.

"Louis, what should we do?"

"Get my wife." He gasped as the Irishman cinched the leather belt tight to stem the flow of blood.

Several minutes later, the men moved away from Louis to allow his wife to kneel down next to him.

"Louis," she said, her eyes fixed on his.

"I'm sorry," he said.

She shook her head slowly, putting her hand gently on his cheek.

"My dear husband, only you would have said that."

"Michael tells me that my foot has to come off," he said, his voice now hoarse.

Kimberly looked down, focusing on his injury.

Her eyes returned to his and she nodded.

"He's right," she said softly.

"Can you do it?"

She paused and nodded again.

"Michael and I can do it."

Louis smiled and his body relaxed.

The *Sonia B.* did not normally carry a doctor, but there was a full chest of medical supplies and equipment maintained by the first mate. Now that chest had been carried into the big cabin. Scully placed different instruments and bandages on the captain's desk as Warren and Pickering secured the doctor on the makeshift operating table. A carrying stretcher had been placed on several large sheets of wood, supported by empty wooden casks.

Curtains covered the large gallery of windows at the stern, primarily to hide the light from the eight lanterns, which now hung from the overhead.

Emily followed Kimberly as she made her way into the cabin, the arms of her dress rolled up above her elbows. Her face betrayed her fear at what she was about to do. Moving to her husband's side, she put her hand on his shoulder, but said nothing.

"Time," Louis said. Whether it was a question or comment, no one could tell. The effort by Scully had been successful. For the last hour, the Irishman had been administering laudanum as he had done for Pickering in Sevastopol.

Kimberly had seen operations such as this many times, assisting many different doctors. But now she felt totally unable to make the first move.

"We must ensure that the bleeding has been arrested, Michael." Her voice was steady.

Scully remembered watching Louis do exactly that on Pickering and now released the tourniquet to identify where the bleeding must be stopped.

It was if taking the first step was all that Kimberly needed.

"Please hand me the needle and thread."

Over the next twenty minutes, she closed off all of the sources of bleeding, asking for more needles or the cauterizing iron, but never taking her eyes from the work.

"I will need the saw," she said.

In less than a minute it was done.

Pickering entered the ship's wardroom to find Charlotte sitting at the long mess table. Her eyes showed concern and fear.

"They told me it went fine," he said sitting down next to her.

She took his hand.

"I have been saying a prayer for him."

"With Scully taking care of him, he'll do well."

Charlotte turned to face him.

"Why do you say that?"

He smiled and said, "He took care of me in Russia, the doctor saved my life, but Michael kept me alive."

"There's such a strong bond between the three of you. I suppose that's what war does to men. And I guess it even does some good."

He lifted her hand and gently kissed it.

"Without this war I would have never met you."

Charlotte leaned over and kissed his cheek.

The wooden door to the ship's brig swung open, the lights of two lanterns playing off the metal strips running across it for strength. James Hurley, the ship's boatswain mate, held one of the lanterns and now lowered it to illuminate the small space inside. Sitting against the far bulkhead, Brett Hart's eyes were closed, the result of two days of darkness following being hoisted aboard the *Sonia B.* Slowly his eyes opened, but he face remained expressionless.

"Get him out of there," Kennedy ordered.

Hurley pulled Hart to his feet and out the open doorway. The prisoner swayed on his feet, turning to look at the captain.

"You bastard, you're all in on this," he spat out.

Kennedy smiled at Hart.

"Mr. Warren told me to be sure you were looked after well. There's a British court and I suspect a hangman's rope waiting for you on the other side of the Atlantic."

Hart struggled to break free, his anger boiling over, but Hurley pulled his arms behind him.

"Easy, yank. It'll be an easier trip without two broken arms."

Hart stopped struggling, knowing it was a lost battle.

"Mr. Hurley here will be your personal jailer. I'd recommend that you do what he tells you, he had a very bad temper."

"Go to hell," Hart muttered and his arms were instantly pulled hard behind him by Hurley, prompted a cry of pain.

"It's about three weeks to England, you'll learn," Kennedy said. "Now, Mr. Hurley, take our prisoner on deck for a salt water scrub down, he's starting to stink."

Chapter Twenty-Six

"I don't know if I'm ready for this."

"England," Emily said, the coast now visible in the distance.

"The south coast, to be sure," Richard replied, "Tomorrow we'll be in Portsmouth."

She pulled the heavy cloak closer, the wind still icy in early April.

"What will happen?" she asked, moving closer to him as he put his arm around her.

He laughed.

"Why, we'll go to London, of course. Then we'll be married."

For a moment he thought she didn't hear what he had said. The subject had never come up between them, even during their talks about the future. The discussions had always been about the plantation or his distant business interests.

"Don't play games, Richard."

He turned her to face him and said, "I'm not playing a game. I love you and you love me. We should be married, it's that simple."

"How can it be that simple? You're a member of British nobility, I'm a school teacher from North Carolina."

"Do you love me?"

"Yes, you know I do."

"Do you want to marry me?"

"More than anything else in this world," she said softly, almost as if it was her secret.

"Then it's settled. And once we get to London we shall get you a ring to show the world."

That night there was a fine dinner to celebrate the news of Richard and Emily's wedding. Present at the table was Louis, who had been getting around more each day on a set of crutches from the ship's carpenter. The captain brought out some of his finest red wine from France and toasted the future. While the happiness of Richard and Emily was most evident to all attendees, it was also not lost on anyone that James Pickering and Charlotte Tyler were totally taken with each other.

By 10 o'clock the ship was anchored off Gosport, with small boats already clustering around its sides. With remarkable speed, the news of *Sonia B.'s* arrival had travelled around the harbor, and in short order a large cutter used by the Warren Shipping Company Ltd was also on its way to the ship. Aboard the cutter was Mr. Lawrence Brotherton, the senior company manager in Portsmouth. Richard Warren had always possessed full confidence in Brotherton's ability to make decisions and handle the many details of running a maritime cargo company, but the older man was also notorious for his ability to get seasick within his first minute on the water, even in a calm harbor. Which is why his presence on the cutter was puzzling to Warren as he peered over the side.

"That's something you don't see often," Scully said, leaning over the rail next to Warren.

While Brotherton's complexion was a bit pasty, he climbed through the entry port in a most nautical manner, removing his hat, and momentarily bowing his head to Warren.

"Your grace, I have terrible news."

Warren knew immediately by Brotherton's use of 'your grace'.

"My father," he said, it was not a question.

Brotherton nodded.

"I'm sorry, sir. He passed on the 17th. He had been unwell for some time."

Warren knew that his life had just changed forever.

He felt Scully's hand on his shoulder and turned to his friend.

"I don't know if I'm ready for this."

"You are."

Emily and Kimberly stepped up on deck from the midship's ladder, looking around and spotting Warren and Scully, they made their way across the busy deck.

The look on Warren's face told Emily that something had happened.

"It's my father," he said. "He died two weeks ago."

She put her hand on his arm.

"Richard, I'm so sorry."

He said quietly, "I was looking forward to the two of you meeting. You would have liked each other."

"What happens now?" she asked.

"We go to London as planned," he replied. "Mr. Brotherton, we'll need two coaches, one for London and two for Albermarle. I'll leave as soon as you can arrange it. The coach for

Albermarle must be comfortable, Doctor Thomassy is recovering from surgery and I want the journey to be as easy on him as possible. Michael, I need you to take the group to Albermarle. James will come with Emily and myself to London."

Scully nodded, but said nothing. He would prefer to stay with Warren, but understood Richard wanted his friend taking care of the group.

Late the next afternoon, Warren met with Sir Hugh Nicholson. A note had been waiting at Claridge House when the coach arrived from Portsmouth. All he wanted to do was present Jefferson Davis' letter to Nicholson, pass on his thoughts and settle the problem of Hart. At least he and Emily had been able to see some of the city in the morning while Pickering handled some of the details of Warren's return to England.

"Your grace, please accept my deepest condolences on the loss of your father. He will be sorely missed in the highest levels of this government I assure you."

"Thank you, Sir Hugh, I was fortunate to have been able to spend a good deal of time with him after I left the army."

"Do you have any interest in participating in government?"

"For the time being, I will focus on the transition. I will also be getting married."

Nicholson looked momentarily surprised, but smoothly said, "That is wonderful news, my congratulations. Who is the lucky woman?"

"She's an American from North Carolina, actually."

"Oh, I see," he said, his tone suggesting that he did not see a member of the British aristocracy marrying an American from North Carolina.

Sensing Nicholson's mood, Warren said, "I have a letter for the Prime Minister from President Davis of the Confederacy."

He removed a large envelope, sealed with wax from his case and placed it on Nicholson's desk.

"I thank you for your letters over the last year. They have helped me understand the situation in America."

"Will we ally with the south?"

'Truthfully I don't know, however it is appearing less likely. It appears the south must succumb to the wealth, manpower and industrial capability of the north. Do you agree?"

"The Confederates have a strong will and talented army. But if the will to fight remains strong in the north, I don't see how the south could ever prevail. At best, I see a stalemate."

For the next two hours, the men discussed all aspects of the American conflict and only when the sun was almost down did they have a glass of brandy to formally end Warren's task for the Foreign Office.

"I have one final favor to ask of you," Warren said, standing up to stretch his back.

"If I can help, it would be my pleasure."

"This might have diplomatic repercussions, but, by God, it's the right thing to do."

Nicholson looked surprised but said nothing.

Over the next few minutes, Warren related the story of Hart to Sir Hugh. From Russia to America, he laid out the whole story.

"Hart is in the brig on my ship in Portsmouth harbor. He belongs in a prison cell awaiting trial for murder."

Nicholson sipped his brandy and gathered his thoughts.

"You certainly don't come up with small problems, your grace."

"Then we shall just not talk about the exchange of fire with the American warship."

"While I might not like what I hear, I do believe I need to hear it."

Finally, twenty minutes later, Nicholson was totally briefed on the events of the last month, including the skirmish on the beach.

"I am confident we can ensure there is as little attention on these events as possible. It simply wouldn't be convenient for you or the Foreign Office. And the north realizes they don't want to alienate us any further – post war relations and all that."

"Thank you, Sir Hugh."

One final top off of the glasses and Nicholson asked, "So tell me, after the Crimea, was this finally the right war for you?"

Warren shook his head. "Quite the opposite. It showed me that all wars are the same. Regardless of the larger events, men die, mistakes are made and in the end we have more wars. I've come to believe that is simply the way of things, the lot of the soldier. I now accept that."

Sir Hugh Nicholson looked at the Duke of Southwick. Twenty years younger, but now more wise in the way of a world that would continue to threaten England in the uncertain future of the 19ᵗʰ Century.

"You have a bleak picture of the world, sir."

"On the contrary, Sir Hugh, I'm optimistic that if one understands the basic truth of matters, then perhaps progress can be made."

This one might surprise us all, Nicholson thought and lifted his glass to Warren.

Thirteen months following the return of the *Sonia B.* to Portsmouth, Mr. Brett Hart, an American mercenary soldier formerly in service to the Tsar, was hanged at Newgate Prison, London. Contrary to normal procedure, which was to conduct executions on a public gallows outside the prison, Hart was hung on a temporary scaffold constructed in the prison courtyard. There was only a small group of attendees. Richard Warren, the Duke of Southwick was present.

Epilogue

Despite the early hour, it was pleasant on the parade ground of Albermarle Barracks. The regiment was forming for inspection prior to early secure for the Easter weekend. While many regiments did not observe a period of holiday for the observance of Easter, the 22nd Royal Dragoons allowed the troops a period of two and a half days away from duties.

A picnic had traditionally been held on Saturday afternoon with sporting contests for those interested. Later that evening, a dinner and dance was held for officers and non-commissioned officers. Sunday morning, church services were held, and while not mandatory, attendance was highly encouraged.

The four squadrons of the regiment formed a line across the parade ground facing north. Each trooper stood at attention at the left shoulder of his mount, the saddles dressed in a precise line for each rank.

To one side, the headquarters company stood at attention in two ranks, which faced across the field and directly at the squadron commanding officers who stood next to their mounts ten paces in front of the first rank of their men. Behind the squadron commander, a guidon with the appropriate letter flew in the light wind.

From behind the main stables, four mounted cavalry officers trotted easily to a point thirty paces in from of the commanding officers and took their place.

"Regiment, report," came the cry from the adjutant, who sat on a brown mare just behind the regimental commander.

In order, the squadron commanders reported present for duty.

James Pickering responded to the reports, "Very Well."

He then raised his hand in a salute.

"Sir, the regiment is formed for inspection."

Colonel Richard Warren returned the salute. "Thank you, Major Pickering." He turned to his right. "Sergeant Major, shall we?"

Sergeant Major Michael Scully said, "Aye, sir."

The inspection was a formality, but Richard Warren enjoyed walking the ranks and talking with the men of the 22nd. They were his men and this regiment was his regiment. He was the founding colonel and had provided the majority of initial funding. Under his leadership and that of a larger than life Irish regimental sergeant major, the 22nd had already established themselves and one of the best light cavalry regiments in the army. Three members of the regiment were Crimea veterans of the 13th Light Dragoons.

Captain Richard Lennard saluted Warren, turning his horse to proceed to the first rank. Preceding the captain was his senior sergeant, Tom Prescott.

As the sergeant turned at the end of the first rank, in accordance with inspection procedures, his eyes met those of

Warren, who remembered the skinny trooper who had almost dies of dysentery in Russia and survived the charge. Now there were wrinkles on Prescott's wind reddened face, but his pride in A Squadron was obvious.

Following trooping the ranks, Warren turned to Lennard and Prescott.

"Quite correct, gentlemen. The men look superb this morning. Please pass on my compliments."

Both men saluted, but only Prescott saw the look from Warren, which he knew so well. The edges of his lips curved up slightly, in recognition of the camaraderie.

"It will be a fine weekend, I do believe, Michael," Warren said as he walked into the regimental commander's office, throwing his gloves on his desk.

Scully followed him in and said, "Indeed it will be, colonel."

About the Author

John Schork graduated from the U.S. Naval Academy in 1972 and went on to spend 26 years in Naval Aviation. During his career, he accumulated 4,000 flight hours and over 1,000 carrier arrested landings. Operating primarily in the Pacific theater, he took part in Operations Frequent Wind, Praying Mantis and Southern Watch among others.

As the last Executive Officer of the USS Midway (CV-41), he took part in Desert Storm and the evacuation of US personnel from the Philippines following the eruption of Mt. Pinatubo. He commanded an A-6 Intruder Squadron, VA-95 and Naval Air Station Whidbey Island. His final tour was as the Chief of Staff of the Kitty Hawk Battle Group.

He lives with his wife Carole in Sammamish, Washington.

www.ingramcontent.com/pod-product-compliance
Lightning Source LLC
Chambersburg PA
CBHW021125260626
47169CB00005B/1452